The Devil Drinks Coffee

Angela Corbett writing as

Destiny Ford

The Devil Drinks Coffee

Angela Corbett writing as

Destiny Ford

The Devil Drinks Coffee

Cover design by Kat Tallon

ISBN 978-0-9892836-0-1

Published in the United States of America by Midnight Sands Publishing, Utah

Printed in the United States of America

Dedication

For my mom, a constant source of inspiration . . . in so many ways!

Chapter One

If it wasn't for the damn pig . . .

I shook my head as I looked out the window at mirror-like waves rising off the road. It was one hundred and two degrees —the hottest day of the year so far—and I was roasting.

Branson Falls, Utah, has a total of two stoplights. Since catching jaywalkers and light runners is one of the only things for Branson cops to do, Officer Bob had been hiding out between The Snow Cone Hut and Movie Mayhem like a turtle in a Crown Victoria shell. I didn't see him until after I zoomed through a mostly yellow light on the way to cover my next big story: the birth of a bright purple pig.

It had taken Bob a mile to catch up, and me another mile to realize Bob had purposely turned his lights and siren on—I was surprised he knew where the buttons were located. I finally pulled over in front of the Branson convenience store, also known as the den of iniquity that sells beer, condoms, and coffee.

Like me, my Jeep Grand Cherokee doesn't handle heat waves well, so I'd turned the engine off when Officer Bob stopped me. But I could see him relaxing in his idling, air-conditioned squad car, and I was getting angrier by the minute. There sat Bob, comfortable as could be, while the hair on my arms started to singe and the back of my legs glued themselves to my sticky leather seat. I pulled my shoulder length, wavy brown hair up off my neck and swore. I was hot, cranky, and late for an important appointment with a pig. It was time to get proactive.

I got out of my Jeep as a jacked-up black Ford truck with tinted windows roared past me at breakneck-speed and careened down the road. I scowled at the truck, angry that I'd been pulled over when, clearly, the truck driver needed a speeding ticket. Officer Bob seemed unconcerned, however, so I went back to my original plan. I pulled my v-neck sky blue shirt down, and crossed my arms under my chest, propping my boobs up. I'm 5'8", with an average build, but if college taught me one thing, it was how to use boob manipulation. With the girls at their perkiest, I walked up to Officer Bob's door and pasted on my most charming smile before bending down to look at Bob. His round cheeks and gradually receding hairline made him seem older than he was. He was taking great effort to ignore me so I knocked on his window to the tune of shave-and-a-haircut.

Unable to overlook me any longer, Bob pressed the automatic window button. As the glass rolled down, a merciful wave of cool air hit me from inside his car. "I could arrest you for gettin' out of your car, you know." He said it like he thought he was a cartoon cop. I half expected him to flash his badge and tell me to "respect his authoritah."

"Arrest me for what?"

"Standin' there. You're threatenin' me. I could Taser you."

"I'm threatening you?" I held my palms out to show him I wasn't holding anything. "With what?"

"It doesn't matter what you're usin'," he said, trying to pull his eyes away from my chest. "I just have to feel like you're a threat." He started fiddling with a black leather pouch on his belt, which he seemed to be having a problem opening because he had to detour around his stomach to get the pouch unlatched.

I put my hands on the window seal and leaned into the squad car. "Bobby Burns," I said, my blue eyes flashing with a warning glare, "if you even think about using a stun gun on me, you'll be the star of a front page news story about police misconduct."

Bobby pointed at me with a pudgy finger. "That's another threat."

"No, it's a promise. I'm the editor of the Tribune, Bobby. You probably shouldn't get on my bad side." I couldn't tell if the sweat on his upper lip was the result of fear, or the heat seeping into his squad car now that the window was down. I decided to appeal to his sense of nostalgia. "Look, Bobby. We grew up together. You're a nice guy. I only moved back to Branson a few weeks ago and I'm late for a story. I need to get to the Crandall farm before their pig turns back to a normal color. What do I have to do to get out of here without a ticket?" Since the manager at McDonald's makes more money than me, I really couldn't afford a ticket and was willing to listen to any alternatives.

Bobby pulled his aviator sunglasses down slightly, looking at me over the top of the frame. "Are you tryin' to bribe me?"

"No! I'm trying to do my job."

"Too bad. Bribin' might've worked."

At that moment, a static voice crackled from Bobby's police radio, "All units needed immediately at Emerald Lake.

A body—" Bobby reached over faster than any turtle should be able to move and turned the radio volume down.

He glanced at me while he fastened his seat belt. "Looks like it's your lucky day, Kate. I gotta go."

I looked from Officer Bob to the radio, tightening my hands on his open window. "What's going on, Bobby?"

He shook his head. "Can't tell ya, just thank your stars ya didn't get a ticket."

With that, he hit the button to roll up the window. I stepped back as he shifted the car into gear and his tires squealed as he sped away.

I wasn't about to let him leave without me though. I'd heard enough to know there was a body at Emerald Lake, and I was going to find out why. The pig would have to wait. I jumped in my Jeep and followed Officer Bob.

Emerald Lake is usually a popular recreation spot for Branson residents, but today, police cars, ambulances, and the coroner's car were scattered across the park.

A body had been pulled from the lake and was now lying on the ground covered by a stark white sheet. Water slowly seeped through the colorless fabric. I moved in closer, trying to get a better look before police erected a tent to shield the scene from onlookers. Officer Bob stepped in front of me putting his hand up, palm out, to stop me before I could get around the police tape.

"Hey, Bobby. Long time no see," I said. "If you're here, who's on light duty?"

"Dagnabbit, Kate! You weren't supposed to follow me."

"Yeah. Bad timing that you were pulling me over when you

got that call. Want to tell me what happened and let me take a look around?" I held up my camera trying to appeal to his sense of importance. "I'll quote you in the paper and take your photo."

He shook his head. "Can't do it. We're conductin' a serious investigation."

"Bobby," I said, trying to reason with him. "This is probably the biggest news story in Branson history! I need to know what happened and I need to get some photos."

"You can get photos after the body's taken away."

"I wasn't going to take photos of the body! Geez, what kind of person do you think I am?"

Bobby wrinkled his nose. "You're part of the liberal media. Can't be trusted."

I rolled my eyes. "I'm a reporter for the *Branson Tribune*, Bobby. I don't have an agenda. Come on, there has to be something I can do to get past the police tape."

"Sorry, Kate," he said, rubbing his thumb over his badge like he was trying to shine it. "Can't do it."

We each held our ground, glaring at each other in some sort of staring standoff until I heard a deep voice say, "That's fine, officer, she's with me."

Bobby glanced behind me and seemed to wither before my eyes. I turned around to see a tall, broad shouldered man with sandy brown hair, tan skin, and hard green eyes stroll up next to me. Bobby took an immediate step back, clearly intimidated.

I was a little unsettled myself, but mostly confused. "I am?"

He cocked his head, giving me a half smile. "You are," he confirmed.

He flashed some sort of badge at Bobby. Bobby clenched his jaw and then relented. "All right, you can go." He pointed at me. "But if I get in trouble for this from the chief, you're gonna owe me a favor."

I nodded as I passed through the barrier, smiling at the back of the man who could easily be a model—or the leader of a Black Ops team. The guy was dressed in gray cargo pants, black combat boots, and a dark blue tee shirt, which he filled out nicely. I could see the bottom half of a black tattoo on his bicep and kept mentally reminding myself to breathe as I caught up with him.

"I'm sorry," I said, "but, I'm not sure who you are."

He stopped, turned, and looked at me in a way that demanded all of my attention. "I'm Ryker Hawkins. People call me Hawke."

The name didn't ring a bell—and he was definitely someone I would have remembered. "I'm Kate Saxee," I said, holding out my hand. He shook it firmly at first, but then softened his grip, letting his hand linger.

"I know," he said.

I stared at him, wondering what else he knew. He gently slid his hand out of mine.

"And why did you decide to help me get into the crime scene, Mr. Hawkins?"

The corners of his mouth twitched. "It's just Hawke," he said. "And I helped you because I think we both have skills that could be mutually beneficial to each other." His gaze slid up and down my body as he said it.

I narrowed my eyes. It didn't seem like he was talking about work skills at all. "Professional skills, right?"

He glanced down and gave me a smile that could only be described as naughty. I folded my arms across my chest. It was obvious he was well-aware of my assets and I wouldn't need them for any manipulation. "What do you do?"

"Today I'm a P.I.," he answered.

"You're a private investigator?" I asked. "And what do you mean by "today"?"

His lips lifted in a slow smile. "I can be anything you want me to be," he said as his eyes darkened and my mouth fell open, "but these days I do a lot of contract work."

I picked my jaw up. "Contract work like you own a business, right? Not contract work like you kill people?"

He didn't answer, but leaned into me and smiled again instead. Hawke was only inches away and he smelled like a combination of salt, soap, and the beach. I closed my eyes as I took in the sexy scent that had overpowered all of my common sense. When I opened them again, he was watching me with an amused expression. It was obvious he'd noticed me trying to inhale him so it seemed like I should say something. "You smell really good," I murmured weakly.

"It's called Swagger."

I lifted my brow. "I bet it is."

He looked past me before settling his gaze on my face again. "You want to find out whose body is under that sheet or what?"

"Yes!"

"Stay here for a minute. I'll be back."

I'm not in the habit of letting people tell me what to do, but Hawke seemed to have more connections than me, and I didn't want to get kicked out of the crime scene.

Hawke talked to a few cops and the guy in the coroner's shirt, and disappeared behind the tent for a few minutes before coming back. "The coroner is going to take the body soon. Once they're gone, you can get photos."

"Thanks," I said. "Whose body is it?"

"Can I trust you not to release the name or harass the family?"

"What a silly question."

He gave me a level stare. "Is that a yes, or no?"

"Yes, you can tell me."

"It's a teenage girl. Her name was Chelsea Bradford."

Chapter Two

I gasped as soon as I heard the name. The Bradfords lived in the same neighborhood as my parents. They moved in after I left for college, but I'd seen them around town when I was home during school breaks. Chelsea's mom was a housewife and her dad owned a few successful businesses.

"Did you know her?" Hawke asked.

I shook my head. "Not personally. They live near my parents though."

He nodded like that wasn't a surprise. "The coroner thinks Chelsea's been dead for about ten hours," he said. "The police will most likely rule her death an accidental drowning, but I think there's more to the story. I think someone might have wanted to hurt Chelsea."

I studied his face for a moment. "Why would you think that?"

He caught my gaze and held it. "Call it a hunch."

"A hunch?" I widened my eyes. "You expect me to just trust the *hunch* of some life-size G.I. Joe figurine?"

He grinned. "I'm trusting a woman who seems to think she's Lois Lane, so yeah."

Since Lois and I were both damn good reporters, I wasn't insulted by the reference. "Seriously, you've got to give me more than "call it a hunch." What do you know that I don't?"

His eyes narrowed slightly. I could tell he was trying to decide exactly how much he wanted to say. "There are things that don't add up."

"Like what?"

"Well, since her time of death puts her here at two in the morning, I'd like to know what a seventeen-year-old girl was doing at Emerald Lake in the middle of the night. I'm also curious why her parents didn't know she was here." He paused, glancing around the park before settling his eyes back on me and deciding to continue. "Also—and this is just between you and me—when I saw her body—"

"You saw the body?" I interrupted. The police had put up a tent to shield the scene from onlookers since I'd arrived. "How did that happen?"

"I'm kind of—"

"Intimidating?" I offered.

"I was going to say persuasive."

I tilted my head to the right in agreement.

"Some of her wounds look like they were defensive. That means she wasn't out here alone, and her death wasn't accidental."

I watched Hawke steadily as I thought about his concerns. The defensive wounds were disturbing. And the possibility of a murder in Branson Falls? People here rarely die of anything except old age and boredom. A murdered teenage girl would be even more shocking. Not to mention that if news about a potential murderer on the loose got out, pandemonium would strike and people would barricade themselves in their basements. "That seems like a lot of evidence. So why are the police ruling it an accidental drowning?"

"That's what I'd like to find out."

Hawke seemed to know what he was talking about. Everything he mentioned definitely warranted further research. "Okay," I conceded. "You have some good points."

He looked around at the scene. The crowd of Branson residents was getting bigger as news spread that a body had been found. "I can help you investigate this story."

I was surprised and a little bewildered at the offer. "How?"

"I have resources that give me access to information."

"Then why not just investigate by yourself? What do you need me for?"

"You have resources I don't," he said, looking me over again, his eyes lingering on my curves. I should have been offended, but I was actually a little flattered. I'd never had a guy like Hawke pay attention to me before. "You're also well-known and respected in Branson Falls. In a small town like this, respect and personal history is important."

I snorted. "I don't know about the respected part, but I'm definitely well-known. I haven't been to church in years." I looked at him and he looked back. It occurred to me he probably hadn't been to church—any church—ever, which made him even more of a reprobate than me. "What's in this for you?"

"I told you, I do contract work. My clients are private but suffice it to say, you and I both have an interest in this particular case."

"I'd like to know what your interest is."

"And I'm not going to tell you. My offer's on the table—you can take it or leave it."

I took him in with my eyes from head to toe and decided

to agree to the partnership because I thought two heads would be better than one—and because I didn't want to pass up the chance to ogle his ass or smell his 'swagger.' I put my hand out and he met it with his. "It's a deal."

We exchanged contact information before Hawke left to speak with more of the police officers. I walked around talking to officers, taking notes, and getting photos.

I had just finished trying to get more information out of Bobby—it didn't work—when Hawke walked over to me. "The funeral should happen sometime in the next week. I'll stop by your office so we can figure out our next step."

I nodded. "I'll see you then." I watched Hawke walk to a sexy dark blue 1967 GT Shelby Mustang with two thick white racing stripes running up the hood, over the roof, and down the trunk. He fired up the loudest engine I'd ever heard, and the only thing interesting enough to turn the heads of Branson residents away from the scene of Chelsea Bradford's death. As he threw the Mustang into gear and sped out of the park, I had the fleeting thought that contract work must pay a lot more than the salary of a small town newspaper editor.

Branson Falls sits in a sheltered valley in eastern Utah, surrounded by the picturesque Rocky Mountains. Summers are sweltering, winters are freezing, and much to the chagrin of every Branson kid, school doesn't get canceled unless a storm drops at least two feet of snow. The county fair is the social event of the year, high school sports teams are celebrated with a fervor usually reserved for Olympians, and town events are announced on hand-painted paper signs that hang between two street lights over the middle of Main

Street. With less than five-thousand residents, it's a place where everyone knows everyone, and gossip is the only form of entertainment. Most people own police scanners to keep on top of current events, so today, a good chunk of Branson residents were standing behind the police tape at Emerald Lake.

As I surveyed the crowd, I saw people I'd known growing up. The mayor spoke to a group, some of whom I recognized from City Council meetings. The bowery by the lake was decorated in red, white and blue. It looked like there'd been a political event going on when Chelsea's body was found. Interesting.

As I studied the people around the mayor, my eyes caught on the profile of a man wearing a white polo shirt. He turned to shake hands with someone and recognition set in as I tried not to fall over. Dylan Drake. Lawyer turned district representative for the Utah House of Representatives, most eligible bachelor in Branson—if not Utah—and my teenage crush. He looked my way with eyes so blue they'd make the ocean jealous and I caught my breath before I dropped straight to the ground, pretending I'd lost something.

Drake is five years older than me and the biggest womanizer in the state—which is saying something since Utah was built by polygamists. Like every other girl who'd set eyes on him, I'd fallen in lust with Dylan Drake. Unlike every other girl, he'd never really known I existed, and most of the experiences I'd had with him had been in my mind. He knew the cheerleaders though. If the rumors were true—and I was pretty sure they were—he'd acknowledged the hell out of every cheerleader he ever met. And I was no cheerleader.

Hiding on the ground in plain sight isn't very inconspicuous and I was bound to start attracting attention soon; I just didn't want it to be from Drake. I wasn't sure I was ready to talk to him yet, considering our complete lack of history and all. Luckily I have reflexes like a fox and my evasive hide-like-a-child maneuver seemed to be working.

After a minute, I stood slowly, doing a quick Drake-check, then put my notebook in my purse while I looked for my keys as I walked to my Jeep. I still needed to visit the Crandall's pig before I could get started on the stories about Chelsea's death. My key search and rescue mission took longer than expected —which is probably the reason I didn't notice the nest of vipers I'd walked into until I was surrounded.

The Ladies. The most feared group of women in town.

They have houses they can't afford, spend their time gossiping and judging everyone they meet, and have no jobs to speak of except to stay the trophy wives their husbands married. They're Branson's version of *The Real Housewives* and many of them spent high school ridiculing everything from my hair to my clothes size. I try to avoid The Ladies as often as possible, though it's not easy when they're slowly circling me.

I couldn't leave without acknowledging them, so I plastered a fake smile on my lips and placed my left leg to the side while pointing my toe to create the illusion that I was lean. I'd learned that gem of information from watching the Miss America Pageant my entire life.

I did a quick scan of the women, immediately recognizing two I'd gone to high school with: Jackie Wall, the ringleader of The Ladies, and her sidekick, Amber Kane. Jackie was only three years older than me and had somehow climbed to the top of The Lady ladder fast. I theorized that it had to do with Jackie knowing an incriminating piece of gossip some of the other Ladies didn't want to slip.

I greeted Amber first. "Hi," I said with a toothy smile. I noticed her makeup was so heavily applied it looked like it came from a theater supply store. Her blonde hair was frizzy from over-processing, and her long acrylic nails were painted blood red, reminding me of talons fresh off a kill. "It's been a while."

Amber responded with a twist of her lips that was more scowl than smile. "Kate." I watched her for a few seconds wondering if she was going to say more, but it became clear she was done talking to me. I must not meet her Lady standards.

I turned my attention to Jackie instead. As far as style was concerned, she and Amber could be twins. "Hello, Jackie," I said. I nodded toward the others like I was acknowledging mob members. "Ladies." Some of the women in the group nodded in return.

Jackie greeted me with a short, "Kate." She gave a rehearsed smile and asked, "When will we be seein' you in church?"

Ninety percent of Branson Falls residents are Mormons. This means the majority of people in town are right-wing Republicans who, according to the edicts of their church, aren't allowed to swear, smoke, gamble, consume alcohol, drink coffee, watch R-rated movies, or have premarital sex. Of course, just because their religion gives them these rules, it doesn't mean they always follow them. And there are usually a few people—like high school football team heroes named Drake—who have their blatant sinning overlooked.

Having no vices seemed pretty boring to me and though I'd once been a member of the Mormon Church, I'd left the religion in college, along with my virginity. "I'm not Mormon anymore," I answered.

The Ladies gave a collective gasp as Jackie pursed her lips. "Oh," she said, sticking her nose so high in the air that I had a front row seat to her sinuses. "Well, it's only a matter of time until you come back to the fold." She paused and waited for me to respond, but I knew there was no arguing with people like Jackie. When I didn't answer, Jackie tilted her head toward the police officers still working by the lake. "Do you know what happened?"

Hawke had said the police were ruling Chelsea's death an accidental drowning. I didn't see any harm in telling Jackie that much. "They think it's a drowning."

Jackie's eyes widened as murmurs started to rumble through the rest of the group. "Tragic," she said with a shake of her head. "Do they know who it was?"

She should have known better than to ask. "The police aren't releasing the name until they notify family members."

She nodded, slightly curving her mouth. "Surely *you* know though."

I smiled back. "You can read about it in the *Tribune*."

Jackie thinned her eyes, unhappy she didn't get the information she wanted. "We'll do that." She glanced at Amber, exchanging some sort of silent communication before turning back to me. "So," she said, her lips forming a mixture of a smile and a sneer, "you've been gone for what, seven years now? What brought you back to Branson, Kate?" Her voice was full of faux concern meant to be cutting. "We thought you might actually try to make somethin' of yourself, but last we heard, you were *living* with some guy." She said "living" like she meant sinning . . . which, in the eyes of most Branson residents, was the same thing.

My stomach twisted as I exhaled slowly. I could tell this conversation would be about as pleasant as a bikini wax. "We broke up," I answered, trying to keep my face blank and give as little information as possible. The pang of regret that hit me wasn't because of my failed relationship. Instead, it was disappointment that my life hadn't gone as I'd planned. I was supposed to be traveling the world as a famous journalist. Now I was back in the town I'd spent the first eighteen years of my life trying to get away from because it was the one place I thought I could regroup. There was something comforting about home; even though my life plan had detoured, it felt right to be back in Branson.

Jackie's voice pulled me out of my past. "Well, no wonder your relationship didn't work out. You can't expect the Lord to bless a sinful union." I found this amusing since Jackie was recently divorced. In Branson, divorce is sandwiched between murder and premarital sex on the sin scale. Apparently Jackie didn't notice my smirk because she kept talking, "It will take time, but I'm sure someday you'll find someone willin' to overlook your . . . indiscretions, and give you another chance."

There were a lot of reasons my relationship hadn't worked out; near the top of the list was that my ex-boyfriend had wanted a *Stepford Wife* instead of a woman with a mind of her own. When he realized I was lacking in the "docile and submissive" department and had instead been gifted with an abundance of "sassy," we'd come to a mutual agreement that things weren't going to work out. I bit my tongue in a valiant effort to keep myself from telling Jackie exactly what I thought. As I tried to compose a profanity-free response in my head, I felt a hand caress my lower back. Not just touch, caress. A hush fell over The Ladies and I heard a low, strong male voice say, "Hello, Ladies. Good to see you all."

"H-h-hello," Jackie stammered out in a breathy voice.

I turned my head slowly and came face-to-face with Dylan

Drake. It's a good thing I had so many Ladies flanking me or I might have collapsed straight to the ground like a female Gumby—and this time, the floor drop routine wouldn't have been on purpose.

He met my eyes as blood rushed to my cheeks, and then he looked back at Jackie and The Ladies. "If you don't mind, I need to talk to Katie."

I stared in dumbfounded silence. Until that moment, I'd wondered if Drake had mistaken me for someone else. I wasn't sure how he knew me; like I said, I was *not* a cheerleader.

Jackie's gaze tracked over Drake's arm to where it disappeared behind my back. She gave me a swift scowl before flashing Drake a wide smile. "Of course, Dylan. I'm sure you need to discuss this incident and how to handle it in the paper." She put her arm out, gesturing to the lake and police cars. "Kate hasn't lived here for so long that she's practically an outsider. She could definitely benefit from someone with your experience."

"Oh," Drake said, flashing me a sly smile, "I don't doubt it." He turned back to Jackie. "I'll do my best to help her out. Have a good day, Ladies." He steered me away, his hand still on my back as we walked.

Chapter Three

Before today, the last time I saw Drake I was an awkward eighteen-year-old and he was home from college for Christmas break. I'd sat in the corner of the Chinese restaurant with my friends, giggling and blushing, simultaneously desperate for and terrified of him giving me any attention. Now I was awkward and twenty-five, but my Wonderbra gave me confidence that my eighteen-year-old self would have killed for.

In the seven years since I'd seen him, Drake had only expanded his charm. And he was hot. Hotter than I remembered. He had a sexiness to him that only comes with experience—which he'd probably been getting since age twelve. The thick and wavy dark brown hair, strong jaw, and hard body didn't hurt either.

Seeing him up close gave me the overwhelming urge to rip his shirt off, but every available woman in the state—and probably some unavailable ones too—had personal experience with his charm and I was determined not to be added to that list. I took a deep breath and with it inhaled the stormy scent of Drake's cologne—then fought not to close my eyes and breathe it in again. I gathered my composure and locked eyes with him. There were hundreds of questions running through my head, but I asked the most obvious. "What did you need to talk to me about?"

He grinned. "Nothing, really. I was just rescuing you from The Ladies."

I thinned my eyes. It had felt like I was surrounded by a pack of wild animals; apparently it had looked that way too. "Did I seem like I needed saving?"

Drake stopped and put his hands in his pockets as the corner of his mouth twitched. His eyes sparkled while he watched me, clearly entertained. "I saw you fall earlier and thought you might be having some sort of fit. Spending time with The Ladies would just exacerbate the problem so I decided I'd better intervene."

Damn. He'd seen me trying to evade him. Luckily, I'd played the part of "chorus member" in my high school production of *The Music Man*, and my awesome acting skills were about to be called into action. "Fall?" I pushed my bottom lip out and furrowed my brow like I was trying to figure out what he was talking about. "Oh!" My eyes widened. "You mean when I dropped my pen."

His lips curved in a half smile like he knew exactly why I'd dropped to the ground, but instead of pushing it, he changed the subject. "I saw your byline in the paper. I guess that means you're back in town for good. And you're a reporter now?"

"Editor, actually." I held out my hand, since we'd never been formally introduced. "I'm Kate Saxee. And you're a politician."

He took my hand as he flashed his trademark smile, the reason he was so good at politics—and women. "I know who you are," he said. "Politicians and journalists don't always get along, but for you, I would make an exception."

I reclaimed my hand, cocking my head to the side. "You mean because journalists tell the truth about what lying scumbags politicians are?"

He lifted his lips in a polite smile. "Tell me what you really think, Katie."

I loathe the name Katie. "It's Kate," I said, the annoyance making my legs less rubbery than they would have normally been in this situation.

He rocked back on his heels, smiling again. "We should catch up." He paused like he was gauging my reaction. "You know, since we'll probably be working together at some point." I nodded slowly, suspicious. Catch up? My entire history with Drake consisted of him patting me on the head after football games like I was a golden retriever. He must be remembering another girl. "I'll stop by the *Tribune* this week, so we can . . . talk."

I watched him steadily. This entire encounter had seemed a lot like flirting, and now he was setting up appointments that sounded like dates. Unfortunately, I wasn't sixteen anymore and no amount of lust could overrule the voice in my head telling me not to get involved with a player like Drake. I was trying to come up with a reply when a voice started belting out "Forever in Blue Jeans." I looked around, trying to figure out who would be singing at an accident scene, and then realized the voice was coming from my purse and my fancy new smart phone. That's right, I'm a Neil Diamond fan, and it took me a long time to admit it.

Drake cocked an eyebrow. "Interesting ringtone. Is that who I think it is?" I fumbled in my purse for the phone so I could silence it. Somehow, the speaker just kept getting louder, which made Drake even more intrigued. "I'm pretty sure the last time I heard that song was during a campaign visit at the nursing home."

I shook my head as I finally found the phone and pointed it at him. "You should respect Neil. Bad things happen to people who don't."

"Yeah," he agreed. "I've heard it's pretty tough to outrun senior citizens in sequined shirts."

I glared at him as I answered the phone. "Hey, Spence," I said. "Hold on for a second." I put my hand over the speaker and looked at Drake. "As much as I'd like to stay here and continue our witty banter, I have work to do."

He nodded, still smiling about the song. "It was good to talk to you, *Katie*," he said just to aggravate me. "I'm sure we'll be seeing a lot of each other."

I looked over my shoulder as I walked away. "My name is Kate."

I put the phone back up to my ear so I could continue the conversation with my boss, Spence Jacobs. "Sorry," I said as I got in my Jeep. "Things have been hectic here." I leaned my head against the back of the seat to rest my neck.

"I'm sure," he said in a smooth voice. "What did you find out?"

I exhaled a deep breath as I rubbed my palm across my forehead. "The body was a teenage girl. I didn't know her, but I've heard of her parents."

There was a moment of silence from Spence's end of the phone. "You have her name?" he asked, his tone skeptical—and worried. "How did you get that?"

An image of Hawke's tight shirt and bad-boy smile flashed in my head. "I had help," I answered, not wanting to explain. "Her name was Chelsea Bradford. That will make it easier to get started on the stories about her tonight."

Spence blew out a breath loud enough I could hear it through the phone. "I already know one thing about her," he said.

"What?" I asked, pulling out of the parking lot.

"Chelsea Bradford hasn't been in Branson Falls for months."

I decided to make a quick stop at the convenience store. Given how the afternoon was progressing, I was going to need a coffee the size of Montana before the day was over.

I pressed the button, watching the liquid stream from the machine as the smell of French vanilla wafted in the air. When the cup was full, I put the lid on, took a sip and closed my eyes, enjoying a few seconds of peace. When I opened them, I was greeted by a five-foot tall, judgmental beast disguised as an elderly woman named Mrs. Olsen.

"What's that?" she asked in scratchy voice as she pointed at my coffee with a steady finger—quite an accomplishment given her age.

Growing up in Branson had taught me that if you were going to sin, deflection was your first option, followed by denial; if that didn't work, outright lying was your best defense. I smiled sweetly, the bitter aftertaste of coffee still strong on my tongue as I answered, "Hello, Mrs. Olsen! I haven't seen you since before I left for college."

"What's in your cup?" she asked again. Apparently she'd

taken it upon herself to police Branson's coffee supply. "Because I know a good girl like you wouldn't be drinking *coffee*." She said it like the name alone could cause Armageddon.

I put a hand to my chest feigning shock. "Of course not!" I said. "It's just a cup of hot chocolate to get me through the rest of the day."

She squinted, regarding me with doubt. I must have passed her inspection though because after a minute she said, "You better be careful. Sinners never prosper. Just look at the dead sinner at the lake."

My mouth fell open, stunned at Mrs. Olsen's ability to pass judgment on the dead when she didn't even know who the person was. "How do you know the person was a sinner?"

She gave me a look like she thought *I* was crazy. "They're dead, aren't they?"

I thought about pointing out that everyone dies, and she might be on her way there soon too, but there was really no point in arguing with such ridiculous logic.

"The devil drinks coffee," she said, "and nobody likes the devil." She narrowed an eye like she was contemplating whether I'd been recruited to Team Devil. When she came to a conclusion, she added, "I'll be watchin' you." She stepped to the side, allowing me to pay for my drink. I'd need it. I had a purple pig and a possible murder to investigate.

Chapter Four

I spent the next morning scattering clothes around my blue and gray IKEA decorated bedroom looking for something to wear. I eventually decided on a pair of black dress pants, a light pink camisole, and a black suit jacket. I needed to interview people about Chelsea today. I thought the outfit might elicit more information than my standard uniform of shorts and a tee shirt.

I padded across the hardwood floors in my lemon-yellow kitchen and pulled out some bread. I made some toast, topped it with peanut butter and honey, and ate the food while leaning against the sink. I gulped down a glass of milk before grabbing my stuff and locking the door on my way out.

As I pulled out of the detached garage, I surveyed my new house with satisfaction. Cream colored siding blended with royal blue trim around the windows. The front yard was adorned with boxwood shrubs, smoke bushes, and a rainbow of petunias. The house is about two-thousand square feet. When the landlady had told me it would only be five-hundred dollars a month to rent, my jaw dropped. Thanks to small town low rent prices, I hadn't had to move back in with my parents.

It was ten o'clock when I pulled into a crumbled asphalt parking spot behind the red brick strip mall that houses *The Branson Tribune*. I opened the back door and walked inside carrying my "hot chocolate" thermos full of homemade, heavily creamed coffee with chocolate flavoring.

The *Tribune* office is decorated, if you can even call it that, with sage and lime green speckled high-traffic carpet and second-hand chipped desks. The area has an open layout with only two actual rooms. One room serves as the private office for the *Tribune* publisher, Spence. The other is the newspaper archive room, tucked into the back, east corner of the building.

I have my own desk in a corner of the main room directly across from Spence's office door. From my desk, I can see the front counter where a few high school students work as part-time office assistants. There are three more desks scattered around the office for other reporters to use. I put my bag in my bottom drawer and turned my computer on. I could see another "hot chocolate" thermos on Spence's desk, so I knew he'd already been in the office and had probably stepped out to get breakfast.

The night before I'd worked on a couple of stories about Chelsea: a news story about her death, and I'd started outlining a feature story about her life. I sent a quick email with the drafts for Spence to look over. I snapped my memory stick into the computer and downloaded all the photos I'd taken at the lake and the Crandall farm. I was sorting through the photos when our volunteer archivist, Ella James, walked in.

"Hey there, cutie," she said with a smile. Ella is a petite

seventy-five-year-old with bluish-white hair and amber eyes. Ella's husband, Jay, died of a stroke ten years ago. Ella started volunteering at the paper as a way to get out of the house. As the archivist, she spends her time filing old newspapers by the issue date. The archive allows *Tribune* staff to easily access the old issues and look up past story information. Most newspapers have archives online, but the *Tribune* isn't quite that advanced. Ella doesn't have a set schedule and I usually only see her a few times a week.

She put her "hot chocolate" thermos down on a desk as I eyed it suspiciously. I was beginning to think the "hot chocolate" thermos was just a cover and everyone really had coffee in there. I could probably investigate and blow the coffee-masquerading-as-hot-chocolate story wide open.

"Hi, Ella," I said. "How are you today?"

"Still kickin'," she answered. "Horrible news about Chelsea Bradford. I'm just sick over it."

My mouth fell open. News in Branson travels fast, but I didn't think Chelsea's name had been released—apparently it had. "How did you know the name of the girl who died?"

"The Ladies called me."

I leaned back in my chair, shaking my head. "I always forget you're one of The Ladies. You're so much nicer than the rest of them."

"Oh, we get better with age. And they let me in by default because I came from family money and Jay was a doctor. If it wasn't for that, I would've been kicked out a long time ago because I don't follow their rules. I'm always tellin' 'em what a bunch of crazy, entitled women they all are. Guess they don't like hearin' about their faults." She leaned against one of the desks and took a sip of her "hot chocolate." "The older Ladies are mellower though. Mostly, I just hang around them to hear the town gossip."

I snickered. "I like you more every time I talk to you."

"Stick with me, sweetie," she said as she did a little dance that involved moving her hips more than I was comfortable with. "I know everything that goes on in this town."

Ella went back to the archive room as Spence walked into the office. He was wearing his standard jeans-and-a-polo-shirt uniform and carrying a box of doughnuts from the local bakery, Frosted Paradise. Every time I looked at him, I couldn't help thinking that Daniel Sunjata had stepped straight out of my *Rescue Me* fireman fantasies to act as the publisher of *The Branson Tribune*. With Spence's dark skin, square jaw, dimples, and basketball player build, he and Daniel could be twins.

Spence is twenty-nine. He moved to Branson and took over as the *Tribune* publisher a few years ago. He's young, but opportunities to buy into successful print newspaper businesses are rare. The only people embracing technology in Branson are under the age of thirty, so the *Tribune* is still profitable. Small town weekly newspapers are organized differently than large daily papers. Everyone wears a lot of hats, and even though I'm the editor and Spence is the publisher, we often work together on stories and ideas. Plus, one of us is always on-call in case any breaking news happens.

Spence set the pastry box on the table next to the mini-fridge. "If you have a doughnut in there with chocolate frosting and nuts, you'll be my hero for at least a day," I told him. He opened the pink box, tilting it so I could see a glazed doughnut with rich dark chocolate frosting on top and peanuts that had been chopped so fine, some of them had turned to dust. It was pastry perfection and one of my main motivations for moving back to Branson.

"Well then," he said, "let me bring you a doughnut. I don't want to miss my chance to be Superman."

He handed me the doughnut with a napkin. I smiled as I took a bite of the delicious glazed bread. "So," I said, licking chocolate and glaze from my fingers, "where do you keep your unitard, cape, and cute red underpants?"

The corner of Spence's mouth twitched. "Wouldn't you like to know."

Spence and I had been engaging in mild flirtation since he offered me the editor job. Unfortunately for me and my Daniel Sunjata fantasies, the banter didn't seem to be going anywhere . . . though I couldn't exactly put my finger on why.

People in Branson constantly called Spence a menace to society for being older than twenty-five, still single, and one of the few non-Mormons in town. I'd heard The Ladies had tried to convert him and marry him off on many occasions, but he wasn't interested in religion or matrimonial bliss. I was just glad to know I had something in common with at least one person in town.

I let my eyes dance playfully as I looked him up and down. "I'm awaiting the reveal with bated breath." I took another bite of my doughnut. "I emailed you drafts of two articles about Chelsea. Were you able to find out anything about why she left Branson?"

Spence's eyebrows knit together. "Not much."

I took a drink from my thermos to wash down the frosted heaven I'd just eaten. Ella poked her head out of the archive room. "Chelsea left Branson five months ago."

Spence and I both turned to stare at Ella as she sauntered

out. She grabbed a plastic cup and poured a glass of water from the water cooler.

"Did you know her?" Spence asked Ella.

"Yeah, what else do you know about this?" I wondered.

Ella took a drink before answering, "Her parents yanked her out of school and kept tellin' people she was visitin' friends and travelin', but she was gone a long time. If she was just visitin' friends, that was one heck of a visit."

"Huh, that's strange," I said.

"That's what I thought," Ella said, taking a doughnut and walking back into the archive room.

I leaned back in my chair, doodling on a piece of paper as I thought about Hawke's suspicions that Chelsea didn't actually drown. That, combined with the fact that she'd been away and then had suddenly shown up dead in Emerald Lake, made my reporter senses tingle. Maybe Hawke was right and there really was more to this story.

Spence and I spent the rest of the morning working together. This was a huge story for Branson and would be in the paper for weeks. We started outlining story angles to figure out which articles would need to be written first. Feature stories about Chelsea with interviews from her friends; the news story and follow-ups; an editorial about the tragic loss of someone so young. We had a few correspondents who helped cover stories for the various newspaper sections (Features, News, Sports). We assigned a few of the stories to them, but I would be covering the news related articles. To do that, I needed to interview Chelsea's parents, but I wanted to give them time to grieve before having to deal with a reporter.

Just because I wasn't talking to Chelsea's family though, didn't mean I couldn't talk to people who had known her. At Chelsea's age, school would have been the most important part of her life. Teachers often know more about what's going on in a student's life than their own parents. I thought Chelsea's former teachers might have some insight into why she'd left town.

The school is open during the summer to accommodate people taking summer school classes. I decided that would be a good place to start my investigation. I grabbed my purse and took off for Branson Falls High School.

As I wound through the halls of my alma mater, I was hit with the familiar smell of lemon-scented cleaner and new paint—part of the maintenance that was done on the school every summer to get the building ready for a new year and new students.

A cute girl with curly strawberry blonde hair and a heart-shaped face sat behind the front desk of the main office.

"Hi," I said with a disarming smile. "I was wondering if I could talk to someone on the faculty about a former student. Her name was Chelsea Bradford."

The girl's eyes got wide for a second before she glanced down at her desk. I wondered if she'd heard about Chelsea's death. "We can't give information about students to anyone but their family members."

"You can't even tell me when she left?"

Her light lashes blinked several times in quick succession, and she held her bottom lip with her front teeth. She seemed upset, but answered in a quiet voice, "We're not supposed to."

She must have known Chelsea. I didn't want to cause her more distress. "Is there anyone I can talk to about it?"

"Kate Saxee?" I heard a voice ask. I turned around to find

my old high school counselor, Martha Chester. Her blonde hair was highlighted and she wore it wrapped in a chignon at the back of her neck. She was around six feet tall. Before I started at Branson Falls High, she had coached the girls basketball team. She still *looked* like she could run circles around the kids she taught. She gave me a hug and smiled.

"How are you, Mrs. Chester?" No matter how old I got, I would never be able to shake the habit of calling people older than me Mr. and Mrs.

"You're not in high school anymore. You can call me Martha."

"Thanks, Mrs. Ch—I mean, Martha."

"What are you doing at the school? Is there a story you're working on?"

"Actually, there is. I'm looking for some information about a former student—Chelsea Bradford."

Martha gave me a look that indicated I shouldn't say more. "Her parents pulled her out of school so she could travel. It was a great opportunity for her," she paused. "You know, you're one of the only alumni of Branson High to go to Gretna University," she said. "I'd love to hear more about your experience there so I can tell other students what to expect from a small liberal arts college."

I took the hint to stay quiet about Chelsea. "Sure, any time."

"Why don't we go to my office and talk? We can set up a time for you to talk to some of the seniors about the college and what it's like to be a newspaper editor."

"That sounds great," I said, following Martha to the counseling center.

Once we were safely inside her office, Martha shut the door and pressed her lips together. "I'm sorry for the brush off in the main office, but I didn't want anyone to hear this," she said. "I really shouldn't talk about it, but given what happened to her—" Martha broke off and took a deep breath. Clearly, she'd also heard about Chelsea's death. Word spreads fast in a small town.

I sat in a chair across from her desk. "I understand if you can't give me details. I was just hoping you could tell me a little about why she left." I took a notebook and pen from my purse.

Martha sat, absently picking at non-existent lint on her pants. After what seemed like an hour, she looked at me. "I'm telling you this as a neighbor. This is just local gossip among friends. Do you understand?"

I nodded. "I won't use your name and I always keep my sources confidential." Truly, I was happy to have a story in Branson worthy of a confidential source.

"Chelsea was a senior and only four months away from graduating when her parents suddenly pulled her out of school. They said she had the opportunity to travel with friends and that she'd get her GED instead."

"Why would her parents do that?" I asked, shaking my head. "Wouldn't they want her to have a high school diploma?"

Martha raised her shoulders in an, I-give-up gesture. "It's not the first crazy thing I've seen parents in this town do when it comes to their kids, and it won't be the last."

"Were you Chelsea's counselor?"

Martha nodded.

"Did you talk to her before she left?"

Martha nodded again.

"Do you know the real reason her parents pulled her out of school right before graduation?"

Martha looked out the window for several moments. "Chelsea was one of the popular girls. She was on the dance team, the yearbook staff, and had boys trailing after her like she was the only girl on earth. The weird thing was that she never really seemed interested in those boys. I heard rumors that she'd been dating someone though."

I wrinkled my brow. "Who?"

"The rumors going around indicated he was the son of some sort of politician."

"Do you know the name of the politician or his son?"

Martha shook her head. "Like I said, it was just a rumor. I never found out a name. Chelsea was pretty private when it came to her personal life."

I tapped my pen against the arm of the wood chair I was sitting in. "I just don't understand why her parents would take her out of school?"

"I wish they would have given me a better explanation. I tried to find out more, but they wouldn't go into detail."

"Do you think her parents would talk to me if I asked them about it?"

Martha shrugged. "They might, but it doesn't mean they'll tell you the truth."

"Why would they lie?"

"The whole situation was fishy. I don't know the reason they pulled Chelsea out of school, but I don't think it was just to travel. You know how important perceptions are in this town. People will do almost anything to maintain their status."

I nodded as I put my notebook and pen back in my bag. Since Branson was founded in 1873, townspeople had been judged by four things: the size of their home; how much money they made; how expensive their clothes were; and most importantly, if they were Mormon and went to church every week. It didn't matter if they actually followed the teachings of the church, what mattered was that it looked like they did. I zipped my bag shut. "Thanks for your help Mrs. Ches—Martha," I smiled in apology. "I know you shouldn't have spoken with me, but I appreciate the information."

"I shouldn't have," she agreed, "but I've been worried about Chelsea for months. I'd like to know what happened, and why her life ended in such a heartbreaking way."

I nodded, stood up, and opened the door. "Please let me know if you find out anything," Martha said.

"I will."

I got into my Jeep and started it, letting the air conditioning blow the trickles of sweat away from my hairline while I stared absently out the window. I kept thinking about my conversation with Martha, and the politician's son who Chelsea had supposedly been dating. Why had Chelsea kept their relationship a secret? I shoved my SUV into gear and added "find out more about Chelsea's relationship" to my research list.

Chapter Five

Immediately after I got to my desk at the *Tribune,* I started to take my fitted jacket off, grateful for the cool air circulating in the building. The heat outside had left a dry, dusty taste in my mouth. The extra layer of cotton was making it worse. As I stripped the jacket from my arms, I noticed Spence leaning on the doorway to his office.

"Are you supplementing your income with exotic dancing?" he asked.

I didn't think yanking my jacket off like it was full of angry bees was very erotic, but to each his own. "Have you seen my paycheck? It was that or a job in fast food. Stripping seemed more exciting." I put my jacket over the back of the chair and smoothed out my camisole. I grabbed a glass from my desk and filled it at the water cooler. I heard the front door open as I took a long, cold drink.

"I hope you're willing to travel," Spence said. "I'm not sure you'll get much business around here."

"Lookin' good," a deep, familiar voice said.

"I take that back," Spence said. "It looks like your first client just walked in."

I glanced up and saw Drake standing at the front counter. He was dressed in a short sleeve dark blue shirt with a collar and was wearing a watch with a face as big as an orange. When Drake's not in a suit, he looks like the men's department of Macy's exploded on him. Not that it's a bad thing; it would just be nice if he took the time to buy something that wasn't already preselected for him from a catalog—or by an ex-girlfriend.

I ignored Drake and nodded in Spence's direction. "I think Drake's flirting with you, Spence."

"I'm out of his league," Spence deadpanned.

Drake ignored Spence's comment and looked straight at me instead. "Have you eaten yet, Katie?"

My eyes widened in shock. I had already decided Drake and I weren't compatible in any capacity—apparently he hadn't received the message. "Did you come here to ask me to lunch?"

"Maybe," he answered. "I told you I'd stop by to catch up. I was hoping we could start . . . a friendship."

I shook my head. "I'm sorry. You're a Republican. We can't be friends."

His lips curved into that charming smile of his. "If you base your friendships on political parties, you must not have many buddies in Branson—or Utah for that matter," he said. "Besides, I'm so moderate that I'm practically independent."

I tilted my head as the corners of my mouth slid up. "So, you're saying you play the Republican card because it's the only way to get elected around here, but you're really a closet liberal?" I raised my eyebrows. "Can I quote you on that?"

"No," he answered with a mischievous smile. "You can't."

We stared at each other for a minute without saying a word. As I watched him, I remembered Martha's comment that Chelsea had been dating a politician's son. "Hey," I said, trying to sound casual, "you don't happen to have a kid, do you?"

He narrowed his eyes like I'd lost my mind. "Not that I know of. Why?"

I shrugged. "Just asking. With your reputation, you never know." Drake let the statement slide as I quickly moved on to another question. "How well do you know Brian and Julia Bradford?"

Drake tapped a pen on the counter. "Well enough. Brian Bradford's an entrepreneur and his wife, Julia, is one of The Ladies. They had three kids but as you know, their oldest daughter, Chelsea, just died."

"Have you heard anything about her death?"

Drake wrinkled his brow. "No more than you, I'm sure. The police ruled it an accidental drowning. That's all I know."

I widened my eyes and looked at Spence. "There's already an official cause of death?"

Spence nodded. "I got confirmation from the chief of police about an hour ago."

I was stunned. "They didn't even take a day to investigate it!"

Drake's eyes tracked from Spence to me. "Was there something that needed investigating?"

I didn't want word to get out that I was looking into Chelsea's death until I knew more, and had enough information to decide if she was really murdered. I ignored Drake's question and asked him one instead. "What were you doing at the lake yesterday?"

"I was speaking with a few other politicians. It was a meet-and-greet event. You should have gotten a news release about it."

I vaguely remembered seeing something like that. Drake's name wasn't listed on it though. I definitely would have noticed. "Were you there when Chelsea's body was found?"

"I was. Some kids noticed something floating in the water. A few people went to check it out. When they realized it was a body, they called the police."

"Did anyone touch the body before the police got there?"

"Not that I know of. It seemed pretty apparent the person was dead."

"Hmm," I said. "All right. Thanks."

He leaned his arms on the counter, studying me. "I get the feeling there's something you're not telling me."

I smiled instead of answering.

He watched me for a few seconds more. "I have meetings at the capitol during the next week, so I'll be in and out of town. If you decide you need help with anything" —he pulled a business card from his wallet and wrote something on the back of it— "that's my personal cell phone." He pointed to the writing. "Not many people know that number."

I laughed out loud. "Uh huh, and by not many, you mean only every available girl in the state and probably some unavailable ones too."

"You're too young to be so cynical, Katie."

"Years of dealing with men like you has made me that way."

Drake gave me another slow stare. "I'll have to do something to remedy that," he said, and walked out the door.

I noticed that Spence had been leaning against the wall watching the exchange between me and Drake like an overprotective brother. Now he glared at the door Drake had exited and pushed off from the wall. "You're just making it more fun for him."

"What are you talking about?"

"Drake loves the game and you're playing it with him." Spence shook his head. "I bet he hasn't had this kind of resistance from a woman in years, maybe never."

I laughed. "He reminds me of my ex. I learned my lesson the first time. I resist because I'm not interested."

Spence watched me with an assessing expression. "Then you're the first." He turned and walked back into his office.

My mind wandered back to my final encounter with my ex. I'd come home early from a freelance job in New York to find him trying to recreate scenes from a popular erotic novel. Our relationship had been full of problems, but watching my significant other spank my perky naked neighbor was the last straw. He'd wanted a quiet partner who would accept his indiscretions. I wasn't that woman. He moved out, and a few months later, Spence had called offering me the *Tribune* editor job. There are things about Branson I don't like, but the familiarity of the place I grew up and people in town who care about me was too appealing to turn down.

A bing from my email inbox pulled me from my thoughts. It was information about Chelsea's funeral. I couldn't believe the police had already given an official cause of death. No interviewing people, no investigating. If Hawke could see possible defensive wounds after only looking at Chelsea's body for a few minutes, why didn't the police and coroner? Or was there another reason they'd ruled the death an accident so quickly?

Were Hawke and I the only people in town who thought Chelsea's death might have been murder? And even more disconcerting, was a murderer walking around Branson, looking for another victim?

Hawke said he'd stop by the office later this week, but

since it seemed we were the only people investigating Chelsea's death, we didn't have that kind of time. I picked up my phone and called Hawke.

My phone call with Hawke yesterday had been short, but it did the job. When I walked into work this morning, I found Hawke sitting at my desk, his legs stretched out in front of an office chair that was much too small for his body. He was wearing a black muscle shirt with tan cargo pants and matching leather boots that looked like they could cause serious damage in a shit-kicking contest. "Hey," I said, putting my purse down on my desk. "What are you doing here?"

"The autopsy will be done today," he said. "I wanted to let you know."

I pushed my eyebrows together. "Isn't it strange for an autopsy to be done so fast?"

"In bigger cities it takes weeks, but this is a small town so the coroner can get to it quickly. The fact that Chelsea belonged to a prominent family doesn't hurt either."

"Her death was ruled accidental," I said, taking a sip of my coffee. "Why are they doing an autopsy?"

Hawked paused. "It was probably the coroner's call."

"Do you think we'll be able to get a copy of the coroner's report?"

"We can try," Hawke said.

I called the coroner's office. After a lengthy conversation that went nowhere and some begging, I hung up the phone. "They said Chelsea's autopsy is going to be sealed. Only her family will have access to the records. Most of the autopsy is done, but the official report won't be finished until the coroner gets some blood work back next week."

Hawke stood up.

"Where are you going?" I asked.

"To make sure we get a look at the coroner's report when it's finished."

I stared at him blankly. I'd been on the phone for at least thirty minutes trying to do the same thing with no results. I wasn't sure why Hawke thought his outcome would be any different. "So you think you can just stroll in there and take the report?"

He gave the hint of a smile. "When I want something, Kitty Kate, I usually get it."

He walked out the door. I stared after him, wondering when he'd be back and what I'd done to make him think I was cat-like. Oddly enough, the nickname didn't bother me nearly as much as when Drake called me Katie.

Spence came out of his office, sat on the side of my desk, and folded his arms across his chest as he gave me a disapproving look. "Kitty Kate?"

I could feel the blood seeping into my cheeks. "I guess it's just his thing."

"His *thing*?"

"Maybe he likes to give people nicknames?"

Spence gave me a look that said I should know better. "Uh huh."

I tried to change the subject. "It'll be great if Hawke can get the autopsy report."

Spence closed his eyes, nodded, and opened them again. He seemed to be analyzing me. "I get the feeling," he said, "that you're the type of girl who's attracted to men she should probably stay away from."

I leaned back in my chair, returning his gaze. "Well, you're right about that," I said. "I'm attracted to more fictional characters than I care to admit. And I should stay away from them because real men can't compete."

Spence put his hands on the side of my desk, a slow smile forming on his lips.

I gave him a curious look as I flipped on my computer. I needed to work on the articles about Chelsea. "What's the smile for?"

He pushed up off my desk and stood. "Nothing. I just think you're probably right."

Chapter Six

I'd been revising Chelsea's feature article for an hour when a static voice came over the scanner. "All fire and emergency units respond to George Davidson's. His corn field is on fire."

I didn't wait to hear the rest of the information. Spence was out of the office. No one else could cover the story. I rushed to my SUV and sped down Main Street, passing Branson's four fast food restaurants, two gyms, furniture store, and the town library. I hoped Officer Bob wasn't hiding out between buildings again. Since he wasn't, it only took me ten minutes to get to the Davidson's farm. As I approached the scene, the scent of smoke filled the air as ashes rained down with water from the fire hoses. It looked like every ambulance, police car, and fire truck in the county had answered the call.

I pulled onto the side of the road, grabbed my camera and notebook, and approached an officer I didn't recognize—I hadn't been back long enough to know who everyone was. I flashed him my press identification. He didn't seem impressed. "I'm Kate Saxee, editor of *The Branson Tribune*. Can you tell me what happened here?"

"There was a fire."

Hmm, you don't say. "Can you give me any details about the fire? Do you know how it started?"

"The incendiary device was a truck."

"What started the truck on fire?"

The officer was about to answer when I heard someone call, "Kate! Kate, I'm so glad you're here!" My mouth gaped as I turned toward the voice. "I could have died! I could've been burned up in that dang truck." I hit the palm of my hand against my forehead. "I'm calling the manufacturer as soon as I get home. No engine should get hot enough to shoot sparks just from giving it a little gas."

I shook my head as I walked over to the ambulance where she was being treated for minor burns. I should've known she'd be involved in something like this. Sophie Saxee was the queen of calamity. "Exactly how much gas did you give it, Mom?"

"Enough to try and get out of the mud I was stuck in."

I did a visual check of my own to make sure she was all right. The pink and white floral print dress she wore accented her curves and fell just below her knees while her chocolate colored hair spiraled in soft curls to her shoulders. Her clothes and hair had survived the fire far better than her truck.

The paramedics were attempting to treat her, though they were in physical danger given how fast her arms were moving while she spoke.

"Why were you stuck in the mud?" I asked.

"Oh, it was silly," she said, waving a hand. "I missed the turn for the Davidson's house and drove into their field instead. They'd just watered and I don't have four-wheel drive in reverse so I decided it would be better to just drive the perimeter of the field instead of trying to back out. I almost made it too! That one extra muddy spot by the gate got me though. But I can always get unstuck using four-wheel drive, so I gassed it. I was making progress until I started to smell something burning. I got out of the truck to open the hood. The engine was on fire! Can you believe that? Since when do car companies make engines that explode? And it wasn't a little fire either. Sparks were jumping all over the place. I got my jacket from the truck and tried to put out the flames, but that just made the sparks jump further. Before I knew it, the Davidson's fence was on fire. It's a good thing they'd just watered their corn field or they would have had popcorn."

"Why were you using your jacket?" I asked in complete disbelief. "Last time you started a vehicle on fire Dad got fire extinguishers for every car you drive!"

"I couldn't find it," she said sheepishly. I narrowed my eyes at her; Mom wasn't very good at lying. "Okay, okay," she said, putting her hands up, "maybe I didn't look too hard. Those extinguishers are confusing. I was trying to think fast and get the fire out."

I pinched the bridge of my nose with my thumb and forefinger and closed my eyes. "Are the burns on your arm serious?"

One of the paramedics—a tall woman named Annie with short, jet black hair—answered for her. "We'll put some cream on the burns and wrap her arm. The burns should heal in the next few weeks."

"Wonderful!" My mom clapped. "Kate, when you're done taking photos, can you give me a ride home? The police are towing the truck. Oh, and let me pose for a few of the pictures. The neighbors always like proof that I'm alive after an adventure like this. Do you think this will be one of those times your dad laughs when I tell him what happened, or will he shake his head and go work on the Mustang?" My dad recently bought a silver 1966 Mustang to restore as stress relief. Considering the frequency of my mom's bad luck, he was getting quite a bit done.

While my mom was being tended to at the ambulance, I talked to the fire chief and the Davidsons. The fire chief had no explanation for what had happened. He said he'd never seen an engine catch fire and spread so quickly before. My mom's truck was a charred black frame. The Davidson's fence didn't fare much better. After I got all the quotes, pictures, and notes I needed, I found my mom waiting patiently by my Jeep.

She smiled like her truck bursting into flames was an everyday occurrence. She'd grown immune to the chaos she caused, but I'd been away so long I'd forgotten about it. "Thanks for the ride," she said as we got in the Jeep and drove away from the remains of the fence and her truck. "This means I get to go truck shopping soon!"

That's my mom, always looking on the bright side.

My parents live on the west side of Branson in the same area as most of The Ladies. My dad, Damon, is an electrical engineer. My mom is a housewife involved in more charities than Angelina Jolie. At one point, The Ladies tried to recruit my mom but have steered clear since they found out about her knack for attracting trouble wherever she goes. I couldn't complain, though. If it wasn't for my mom, Branson Falls would be even less exciting.

We pulled into the driveway of their three-thousand-square-foot gray brick home. The grass was emerald green with the yard accented by plants all in a shade of red. Blood red petunias, hot pink weigela bushes, and crimson roses surrounded their front yard waterfall made from Redrock my dad got on a trip to southern Utah. The stunning colors almost made me stop wishing for the winter cold and snow. Despite the summer heat, Mom's flowers were flourishing. It's a good thing her bad luck doesn't extend to her plants.

The garage door was open, my dad's legs sticking out from under the Mustang. He was six feet tall and resembled a tank: strong and capable of anything. I was surprised he fit under the car. The fact that he was already working on the Mustang meant he must have heard about the fire and the dead truck from the police scanner he'd bought several years ago to keep track of his wife. My mom saw him too and grabbed her purse, which she'd managed to save before the truck was completely engulfed in flames.

"You better come with me," Mom said. "This is a Mustang situation."

I nodded as we got out of the car, and followed her into the garage.

My mom walked up to the edge of the Mustang. She looked down through the engine compartment, trying to see my dad through all the parts under the hood.

Mom had a wide variety of emotions to pull from depending on the level of chaos she'd caused. For fire, she generally chose timid. "Hi, honey," she said. When she didn't get a response she continued, "Now I'm sure you probably heard about this on the scanner, but I just want you to know that I'm fine, and it wasn't my fault. I didn't get hurt much, and everything is okay." The only sound that came from under the hood was the noise of a ratchet-wrench. "Well, not everything exactly, we need to go truck shopping again soon, but until then, the insurance company should give us a rental."

This time there was a disbelieving grunt from the garage floor. We stood there for a minute waiting to see if the grunt would be followed by anything substantial. When it wasn't, Mom decided on another tactic. "Anyway, Kate got to cover the story, isn't that exciting! And since she was already at the scene, I didn't have to bother you to come pick me up."

Mom waited again. Finally my dad rolled out from under the car, wrench in hand. He pointed the wrench in my direction. "I'm glad you didn't get your mother's disaster genes." He turned to my mom, looking her over, his eyes softening as they lingered on her bandages. "I did hear about it on the scanner. I was just hoping it wasn't you. Wishful thinking. I'm glad you're not seriously hurt. Not your fault..." He snorted and shook his head. "You get to explain this to the insurance company."

And with that, he slid back under the car.

Mom smiled, knowing the argument was over. "Come on inside," she said to me.

I followed her in and sat at the cedar dining table while my mom went into the kitchen. She'd recently convinced my dad to do a home renovation—a direct result of the kitchen fire that started after she put a piece of thick bread in the toaster and the toaster exploded. It's still a matter of contention whether the toaster incident was an accident, or something Mom did on purpose to get the three-inch thick black granite countertops, stainless steel appliances, and Brazilian cherry cabinets with matching hardwood floors.

She opened the refrigerator and pulled out a large glass pan. From this distance, it looked like it contained a lot of potatoes, butter, and cheese. I recognized it as "funeral potatoes," a popular Utah dish topped with everything from cornflakes to bread crumbs, and given to families dealing with a death. My mom, who liked to be on the cutting edge of culinary crafts, used crushed Cheetos for her topping. The unexpected bright orange garnish made the potatoes look nuclear. "I need to take this casserole to the Bradfords," she explained. "Julia shouldn't worry about cooking right now."

I didn't know the Bradfords, but apparently my parents did. "Are you friends with them?"

"Of course we are! They just live around the corner." I'd lived in an apartment during all four years of college, and for another three years after that. I couldn't remember the name of even one of my old neighbors, let alone claim them as friends. But, small towns are different. My mom paused as she snapped a lid on the dish. "What happened to Chelsea is just awful."

"Did you know her?" I asked, curious.

"I'd see her once in a while. She always had friends over and they'd have parties a lot. Cathy Young down the street said she thought Brian and Julia should be stricter with Chelsea though. Cathy used to stay up late watching out the window to find out when Chelsea was coming home—a lot of times it was after *midnight*." She said 'midnight' like it was a naughty word. I snickered. She looked up and pointed at me. "Don't you laugh, young lady. You know the devil comes out after twelve A.M."

My mom's reaction surprised me since she'd been so trusting when I was a teenager. "You didn't think that when I was Chelsea's age."

"Oh, I thought it all right, but you wanted out of Branson Falls so bad that your dad and I knew you wouldn't do anything stupid to jeopardize your chances of leaving."

Huh. Good to know. At least my parents had trusted me; that's more than I could say for a lot of the parents in Branson. "So you think Chelsea was doing something stupid?"

She shrugged. "I don't know what she was up to, but people talk. A lot of the boys in town were interested in her, but that doesn't mean she did anything wrong." This was the second time I'd heard someone mention Chelsea and boys. I needed to find out who she'd been dating. My mom continued, "She had a lot going for her, so her death has been a shock. What a horrible accident."

"Yes," I agreed with my mom, "it was horrible." Covering a death is always difficult for a reporter. I wanted to ask the Bradfords about Chelsea, but didn't want to be insensitive either. I looked at the casserole dish and thought it might be a good way to make a connection with the Bradford family. "Can I take this to the Bradfords for you?"

My mom smiled. "Sure, honey," she said, handing me the pan. "That would be nice."

I took the potatoes out the garage door, past my dad who was still under his Mustang, and walked around the corner to the Bradford's house. It was one of the few homes in town that actually looked like a mansion. It was red brick, and at least four levels with large turrets, a veranda that wrapped to a two-story deck at the back of the house, and sweeping views of the eastern mountains. The landscape was a rainbow of colors, though the various roses in red, pink, and orange took attention away from almost everything else.

I stood on the front porch and rang the doorbell. I was greeted by the sound of a tenacious dog that, when the door opened, was much smaller than his bark had prepared me for.

"What a cute puppy!" I bent down, rubbing the brown and black Yorkshire terrier behind the ears. He jumped with excitement, returning the ear rubbing favor by licking my hands. Apparently the dog's job was only to notify of, not stop, potential intruders.

I glanced up. Mrs. Bradford had perfectly coiffed shoulder-length blonde hair with caramel highlights. She wore white pearl earrings with a matching necklace over a baby blue cashmere shirt and cardigan. Her pressed gray pants complemented her gray and black high-heels. She smiled at me, playing the part of a good host. "His name is Cuddles. If I'm not mistaken, you're Kate Saxee?"

I nodded, standing up. "I am. My parents live around the corner. My mom asked me to bring this over and tell you our family is very sorry for your loss."

"Thank you," she said, taking the dish. She glanced down at the potatoes, her brow wrinkling for half a second.

"They're Cheetos," I said, feeling the need to explain why my mom's funeral potatoes were neon. "My dad swears it's the best potato topping ever."

Mrs. Bradford smiled. "My husband likes me to use crushed potato chips, so I'm sure he'll like this." She held open the door. "Won't you come in?"

I furrowed my brow. For someone who had just lost a daughter, she didn't seem too affected. I wondered where the grieving mother was . . . though I guess everyone deals with death differently. "Are you sure?" I asked. "I don't want to interrupt you or your time with your family."

She gave a pleasant smile. "You're not interrupting." She opened the door wide, gesturing with her hand. "Please, come in."

"Thank you, Mrs. Bradford."

"Call me Julia."

I followed Julia to her sitting room. The walls were canary

yellow with cream accents, and her furniture looked antique. Her *Book of Mormon* and *Bible* were sitting on a side table. The scriptures, combined with a gold framed picture of a Mormon temple, let me know the Bradford's were devout Mormons. I sat on an Italian, brown leather couch so plush and soft I didn't know if I'd be able to get out of it without the Jaws of Life to extricate me.

"Would you like something to eat or drink?" Julia asked, still standing.

"No," I smiled, "but thank you for asking."

Julia sat across from me in a chair and crossed her legs. With how far I'd sunken into the couch, I couldn't cross anything.

"You're the editor of the *Tribune* now, correct?" Julia asked with another practiced smile.

I nodded. "I know this isn't a good time, but when things settle down, I'd like to talk to you more about Chelsea. We're working on some stories for the paper. It would be nice to have input from her family members."

"I'm happy to answer your questions now," she said.

To be honest, I was a little stunned. Her daughter's body was found two days ago. I wasn't sure why she'd want to talk to me now. "Are you sure? I can't imagine how difficult things must be for you. I can come back another time."

Julia shook her head slightly, giving me a tight lipped smile. "Talking makes it easier to deal with."

I wasn't going to judge her way of grieving, and I did want to ask her some questions, so I decided to take the opportunity. "I heard she moved away five months ago. Is that right?"

Julia gave me a slight nod. "She had a wonderful opportunity to live with some family friends and travel. She wanted to go so badly that we just couldn't say no to her."

I tilted my head. "Despite the fact that it was her senior year of high school? Couldn't she have finished school and gone on the trip later?"

Julia gave me an assessing gaze before answering, "No. The plans were time sensitive and we didn't want to deprive her of such an amazing experience. Opportunities to travel the world don't come along very often."

"Even though it meant she wouldn't get her high school diploma?"

Julia gave me a smile that clearly indicated my questions were rude. "You're only young once. We thought she should have the experience while she still could."

I nodded in understanding. "What were her plans after the trip?"

Julia thought for a moment. "She was supposed to come back here and get her GED. After that, she was going to start college."

"So she came back from her trip early?"

Julia held her hands tightly in her lap. "Kate—may I call you Kate?"

"Of course," I answered.

"I was hoping that in talking to you it would help stem the gossip about Chelsea's death. However, I'm not sure where exactly your questions are going. Chelsea was out of town, then came home and had an accident that caused her death. It's as simple as that."

I smiled to reassure her. "I'm sorry, Julia. I didn't mean to upset you."

Julia stood, her shoulders square and tense. "I appreciate that," she said. "Perhaps it was a bad time for me to discuss this. Please tell your parents thank you for the casserole."

I nodded, using both hands to push myself out of the grip

of the couch, and followed Julia. "Thank you for taking the time to talk to me."

Julia walked me to the door. As I stepped onto the porch, I turned. "If you'd like to talk some other time, you can reach me at the *Tribune*."

Julia's mouth formed a strained smile. "I'll keep that in mind."

"Thank you," I said again, and Julia Bradford shut the door.

Chapter Seven

I went back to the office after picking up my Jeep from my parents' house. I sighed as I walked into the cool *Tribune* office. Between the heat from the fire and the wrath of Julia Bradford, the air conditioning was a welcome relief. Spence's voice came out of his office. "I heard about the fire on the radio, thanks for covering it. What's the story?"

"The story," I said, taking my bag off my shoulder and setting it on my desk, "was my mom."

Spence leaned back in his chair. He put his hands behind his head as his mouth broke into a huge grin. "What did she do this time?"

I walked across the room to Spence's office. "She got her truck stuck in the Davidson's field, and burned up the engine and the Davidson's fence trying to get out of the mud."

Spence's laugh started low and got louder.

"Yeah, I know, she's a hoot," I said. "Anyway, I took a lot of notes so you or one of the *Tribune* correspondents can write the article."

Spence waved me off. "No, I want you to write the story."

This went against everything I'd learned in my media

ethics class. "I can't. She's a relative. How will I prove I'm being objective?"

"Kate, if we didn't have your mom, we probably wouldn't have a paper. She's the subject of most news around here—at least the crazy stuff. Being away couldn't have made you forget what a Catasophie she is."

I raised an eyebrow. "Catasophie?"

"That's our nickname for her because wherever Sophie Saxee goes, a catastrophe follows."

"Oh, she'll love to hear that," I said.

He ran a hand through his short brown hair. "Don't tell her. She'll probably come in to cuss us out and end up burning the office down."

I nodded my head as I leaned against the door to Spence's office. Spence was probably joking, but with my mom even the most absurd things can become reality at any moment. "I had to take my mom home after the fire and ended up having an interesting discussion with Julia Bradford."

Spence's eyebrows shot into his hairline. "How did that happen?"

"I took them a casserole from my parents. She invited me in to talk about Chelsea. It was strange."

"What do you mean?"

A crease formed between my eyes as I thought about all the things that had seemed off. "Usually when someone dies, especially someone so young, the house is full of family and friends and the grief is almost palpable. The Bradford's house wasn't like that. Julia seemed to be the only one home, and she was acting like nothing had happened—though she did get upset when my questions were more detailed than she expected."

Spence sat up, resting his elbows on his desk. "That's odd. I think there's a lot about Chelsea's death we don't know yet. I'll see if I can find out more about the Bradfords."

I nodded in agreement and started to walk to my desk.

"Kate, wait."

I turned around.

"I don't want to tell you what to do," he paused like he wasn't sure if he should keep talking, and then decided to press on, "but have you committed to working with Hawke on this story?"

"Yeah. He got me into the crime scene, and today he's convincing the coroner to give him the autopsy report. He's been really helpful so far."

Spence picked up a file from his desk and started thumbing through it. "Be careful. Hawke isn't some easy-going naïve guy who grew up in Branson Falls."

I wrinkled my brow, not sure where this conversation was heading. "Neither are you," I pointed out.

Spence gave me an annoyed look. "But I'm an open book. If there's anything you want to know about me, you just have to ask. Hawke is different. The rumors I've heard indicate he's been everything from a Navy Seal to a drug lord. I think the only reason he's not in prison is because of the information he has about important people. That, and he has a reputation for taking care of things other people won't—he's not afraid of anything." Spence took a deep breath, chewing on his lip. "The bottom line is that he's dangerous and only cares about getting what he wants."

Hawke, dangerous? Well, it wasn't hard to figure out where those rumors got started. I'd only known him a couple of days and already pegged him as mysterious, intimidating, and scary—when he wanted to be. Hearing the laundry list of Hawke's potential former jobs intrigued me even more. For some reason the knowledge that Hawke was fearless and multi-talented only made him sexier. I suddenly had the urge to envision him in the role of some of my favorite fictional crushes. I sighed a little as I daydreamed. Spence cleared his throat, bringing me back to reality.

"Sorry about that," I said. "I didn't hear you. What were you saying?"

Spence rolled his eyes—clearly my thoughts were written across my face. "I said to be careful about trusting him."

"Sure, no problem." I crossed my arms over my chest. "So why do you think he's dangerous?"

"Drake said as much when Hawke moved to Branson a couple of years ago."

"You got your information from Drake?" I asked incredulously. "What makes him an expert on Hawke?"

Spence tapped a pen on his notebook. "Ask Drake yourself. I'm sure he'd be more than willing to talk to you about it."

"Thanks, but the less I have to deal with Drake, the better."

"It's up to you, but I'd suggest doing some homework on Hawke before making him your new best friend. He hasn't lived in the area long and people rarely see him. I've heard he has houses in other cities too—not just the U.S., but around the world. He seems to travel a lot, and hasn't really participated in town events or tried to get to know people. He keeps to himself. He's so covert about his presence that most people don't even realize he lives here."

"He has a pretty fancy car for someone trying to stay on the down-low."

Spence shrugged. "I'm just telling you what I've heard. Don't let him convince you to do anything you're not comfortable with."

The idea of letting Hawke convince me to do those things

was actually pretty appealing. "I'll do my best," I said, sitting down at my desk and opening my email.

Spence nodded once like we'd reached some sort of agreement and stood up, grabbing his wallet from his desk. I did a double-take. I'd never noticed before, but the dark brown and red linear check design with brown leather trim almost looked like the latest Burberry. He wasn't a woman, so I had a hard time believing he'd spent three-hundred dollars on a wallet. Maybe he got it on sale, or just didn't realize it was designer. Spence interrupted my thoughts, "I don't know about you, but I'm starving. I'm going to grab us some dinner."

The thing I like most about my friendship with Spence is that it just feels comfortable. And truthfully, it's nice to have a comrade who isn't already married with babies. I'm pretty sure I'm missing the mom gene because I don't find potty training and bed times remotely interesting. The fact that I'm twenty-five and unmarried is scandalous—around Branson I'm considered an old maid. I leaned back, shifting my eyes away from the computer screen. "That sounds really good."

Spence walked out of his office throwing his keys in the air and catching them. "One grilled cheese and an Oreo shake to dip your fries in, coming up."

I smiled. Between working on stories, editing, and doing the paper layout each week, Spence and I often ate our meals in the office. I had a specific order for each restaurant and my order never changed. "You know me so well."

Spence grinned. "I'll be back."

I was working on my mom's exploding truck story when I heard the bell on the front door ring. I looked up and saw Ella making her way to the archive room.

"Ella, what are you doing here so late?"

"I forgot my dang glasses again," she said, slapping her hand on the top of a desk.

"How have you been getting around without them?" I asked, slightly worried.

"Well they're just little reading glasses, it's not like I need them to walk," she said as she bumped into a chair.

I steadied her, pushing the chair out of the way. "You sure about that?"

"Course I am! They're in the back room. I'll be gone in a jiffy so you can get home."

"Oh, don't worry about it. I'm working and Spence will be back soon with dinner."

Ella stopped and turned. "Did you say Spence? You're havin' dinner with him?"

"Yeah. We're working late so he left to get some food for us."

Ella's mouth morphed into a sly little smile. "Maybe you're just the thing he needs to get all the women around here to stop callin' him a menace to society."

I shook my head as I rearranged some papers on my desk. "I'm pretty sure Spence and I share the same opinion on relationships. I think we're both happy to just have a friend who isn't hell-bent on getting hitched."

Ella stared at me with an assessing expression. "We'll see," she called in a sing-song voice as she walked away to retrieve her glasses.

I hit save on the Mom-torches-truck article as Ella came back into the room. "Did you park out front?" I asked.

"Yep," she answered.

"I'll walk you out," I offered. I followed her, and was about to ask where her car was parked when I saw it: a cherry red Lexus convertible sitting on the sidewalk in the newly installed disabled access curb. "Ella!" I cried. "Why is your car on the sidewalk?"

She shrugged and kept walking. "I needed to park but there weren't any open spots. This was plenty big enough."

"This," I gestured toward the lowered area of curb with both arms, "is for disabled people to get on the sidewalk."

"I didn't see any of 'em. I looked. I knew I wouldn't be here long and figured if anyone needed to get on the sidewalk, they could either wait, or go to the end of the block."

I closed my eyes, sighing. "I think you're missing the point of the curbing."

"No harm, no foul," she said, opening her door.

"You're lucky Officer Bob didn't see this," I said, pointing to her car.

She waved my comment off. "Even if he did, he wouldn't have bothered me about it. I make him key lime pies to get out of tickets."

Geez! Was the whole town bribing the Branson Falls police force? I could add that to the list of stories I needed to investigate. And since I was already thinking of investigations . . . "Ella, do you know Chelsea Bradford's parents well?"

Ella folded her arms on top of the Lexus' soft roof. "I know a fair bit. Her mom's one of The Ladies."

I nodded. "I've been doing some research about Chelsea. You said her parents took her out of school so she could travel, but the timing seems strange. She left Branson right before she was supposed to graduate from high school."

"Yep, that's what I've heard."

"And until her body was found, no one had seen her since she left."

"I think I'm the one who told you that," Ella answered.

"Did you know she was dating a guy? He's supposed to be some politician's son."

"Heard that too."

I stared at her as I heaved an exasperated sigh. "Is there anything else you've heard that I should know?"

Ella tilted her head, thinking. "I'd try to find out who the boy is if I were you. I don't know much about politicians, but I can tell you someone who does. Dylan Drake. And from what I've heard, you two are practically dating."

My mouth dropped. "What? Who told you that?"

"The Ladies were all talkin' about Dylan whisperin' in your ear at Emerald Lake. None too happy about it, either. They don't want one of the most eligible bachelors in the state to go off the market. Some of them aren't married right now. You're messin' with their husband huntin' plans."

"We are *not* dating! In fact, before two days ago, I'm pretty sure he didn't even know who I was."

"That's not true," Ella said. "Before you got back to town Drake came in to the office to place an ad and was askin' Spence about the new editor. Spence mentioned your name and Drake recognized you."

I shook my head in disbelief. "That's impossible. He must have mistaken me for a cheerleader. Anyway, it doesn't matter. We're not dating. Not at all. Let The Ladies know."

Ella nodded. "If you say so." She took her arms off the car. "But Dylan Drake is your best bet for findin' out who Chelsea Bradford's boyfriend is."

I wrinkled my nose. I really didn't want to ask Drake for

help. "Do you think any of The Ladies would talk to me . . . other than you, I mean?"

Ella shrugged as she got in her car. She poked her head out of the window. "You can try, but don't expect to get much information. Most of The Ladies keep things quiet, and they're good at protectin' their own."

"Was that Ella?" Spence asked a few minutes later, as he walked in and put our food on the treat table by the water cooler.

I grabbed some napkins and took the food out of the bag. "Yeah. She forgot her glasses."

Spence shook his head, smiling. "She was probably trying to get information about you for The Ladies."

I looked up at him. "What are you talking about?"

"You're the new girl in town. And you have a couple of pretty eligible bachelors who can't seem to leave you alone. Next to your mom, you're the most interesting thing to happen around here."

I rolled my eyes as I sat. "Speaking of that, Ella seems to think I might be the girl who takes you off the "menace to society" list."

Now Spence was the one to stop and stare. "What?"

I popped a fry in my mouth. "You know, because you're over twenty-five and still not married. In Utah, and especially Branson, that makes you dangerous."

Spence snorted. "Not to women," he mumbled. Then he froze, realizing he'd spoken out loud. I understood how he felt because I occasionally had the same problem with words that didn't stay in my head.

A realization suddenly hit me. "Oh my gosh! Spence, are you gay?"

He pursed his lips tightly, looking at everything but me.

"So that's why our flirtation never got anywhere!" His expression said he wasn't excited about this conversation. At all. "Good Lord! Why would you choose to live in a place like Branson? People here still believe they can shock the gay out of someone! Why aren't you in Salt Lake at least?"

Deciding I wasn't just going to let this go, he finally met my eyes. "I wanted to be a newspaper publisher, Kate. It's not every day a person gets a chance to buy a paper people still actually read."

Okay, I could see that, but still. "I assume no one else knows?"

"Not anyone here."

And for good reason. People would stop buying the paper if they found out. Well, first they'd try to "fix" him. When that didn't work, he'd probably be harassed and run out of town. "So, you're going to keep this secret for the rest of your life?"

"For the immediate future at least." He took a deep breath. "I'm hoping people will become more open-minded."

I didn't want to discourage him, but I get harassed for drinking coffee. Sodomy is far higher on the Branson sin list than hot drinks.

"Does it bother you?" he asked me.

I stared at him, shocked. "No way! I don't care about that. I don't think it's right to judge anyone, and I'm a huge supporter of equal rights." I smiled. "I'd be a bigger supporter if I got a bigger paycheck."

He laughed, the lines of tension around his eyes and mouth falling away.

"Hey, I'm just happy to have a gay friend to consult with

again. I miss that. And in case you haven't noticed, between the Ladies and Drake and Hawke, I need all the help I can get."

"Well," he said thoughtfully, "you know my feelings on Hawke. But," he paused and grinned. "As far as sex goes, I don't think you could go wrong with either one of them."

I gave him a light punch to the shoulder. "It's really too bad you're not in the running. I have a thing for Daniel Sunjata."

He smiled. "I think it's helped having you here. You and I have good chemistry. People see that and don't wonder as much about why I'm not in a relationship."

I totally understood that line of reasoning. "Well, we'll keep up the charade for as long as we can."

He stared at me. "You don't mind?"

I shrugged. "No. I'm not in a relationship. It's not hurting me, and it helps you."

Spence seemed stunned at first, but smiled as he replied, "You're definitely a catch, Kate Saxee. If I weren't gay, I'd be fighting for you too."

I smiled and leaned back in my chair, enjoying the rest of my milkshake, and the company.

Later that night I was watching reruns of *The Office* while I checked my email. When I finished deleting the latest chain letter from my mom, the thought crossed my mind that maybe I should take Spence's advice and try to find out more about Hawke—especially since it seemed like he knew so much about me.

I typed "Ryker Hawkins" into Google. After wading through some websites that had nothing to do with Hawke, I came across his name in a photo. He was dressed in a completely black suit, wearing black sunglasses, and looked like a member of the Secret Service. He was surrounded by four other men who seemed just as intimidating as him. According to the photo caption, Hawke was shaking hands with the ambassador of Spain. An article accompanied the photo on the left side of the screen. I read through it and found out Hawke had spoiled an assassination attempt on the ambassador. The man was thanking Hawke in the photo. My first thought was, *Holy hell! Who is Hawke?*

I found a few more stories about him: Hawke receiving an award for civic service, Hawke volunteering for the Special Olympics, Hawke reading to patients at a children's hospital. Everything I saw made my opinion of Hawke shoot higher. I couldn't figure out what Spence—and apparently Drake—had against him, but decided it didn't matter. I didn't need Google to tell me Hawke was one of the few good men still left in the world. I'd be happy to be his partner anytime he wanted me to.

Chapter Eight

Chelsea's funeral was scheduled for three days after her body was found. I wasn't sure why the Bradfords were pushing to have everything done so quickly, but in a small town it's not unheard of. The viewing was held before the funeral at the Gregory Mortuary, a white brick building in the middle of town.

The inside of the mortuary is decorated in earth tones; caramel colored paint matches carpet on the floor in shades of brown and white. I stood in a corner taking in the light, sweet scent of flowers from the arrangements scattered throughout the viewing room. I watched as people moved through a long line past Chelsea's pink and black coffin and paid their respects to her family. The high school students in line were clearly shaken by Chelsea's death. As soon as the teenagers finished speaking with Chelsea's family they moved toward the back wall of the mortuary where they stood in a circle consoling each other.

I noticed the girl from the high school office standing in the group of teenagers. She had streaks of mascara running down her cheeks. Her hair was pulled up in a French twist, highlighting the makeup that had streamed off her face with her tears. She was being comforted by a tall boy with auburn hair who had his back to me. He held the girl from the office tightly with his arm around her back as she cried into his shoulder. Another blonde girl held her hand, trying to console her. The office girl's reaction was typical of someone going through heartbreaking grief. She must have been close to Chelsea. I thought back to a couple of days ago when I'd been asking her about Chelsea's school records. No wonder the girl had seemed quiet. She was still getting over the shock.

I turned my attention to the Bradfords, watching who they talked with. So far, it was a typical viewing. No suspicious behavior to speak of.

Once viewing hours were over, Chelsea's body was moved to the Mormon Church around the corner for the funeral service. I followed the crowd, slowly walking to the church. Martha Chester was there, as well as other people I knew. I nodded to them in acknowledgment and they nodded back, respecting the somber tone. I felt a strange connection to this girl I'd never known, but still, I didn't feel like I had a right to be at the final celebration of her life. I found a seat in the chapel, on the back pew.

There wasn't a dry eye in the room. Several young girls were sobbing uncontrollably. The Ladies were there to support Julia Bradford and several men in expensive suits kept patting Brian Bradford on the back, offering condolences. As the service was about to start, I felt a hand on my shoulder and a large body slide in next to mine. Hawke was wearing a charcoal suit with a cut so tailored and fabric so rich it was clearly from a designer. His tie had an alternating pattern of black, green, and silver that brought out the color of his eyes. He looked mouthwatering. I took a moment to discreetly check my chin for drool. He leaned toward me whispering, "We need to talk to those kids."

I stared at him, completely shocked at his lack of emotion for the girl who had died so young. "Seriously, that's the first thing you think of?" I hissed.

He gave me a look. "We're not here to grieve. We're here to find out what happened. You're a reporter; you're not supposed to have scruples."

"Nice stereotype."

He shrugged. "Prove me wrong."

I shook my head. "Where did you come from anyway? I haven't seen you all day."

"I've been here . . . watching, just like you." He scanned the crowd in front of us with the precision of a sniper. I wondered if maybe that was one of the jobs in his repertoire. "I particularly liked the view when you dropped your purse."

I gasped and punched him in the shoulder. A few people sitting in the pew in front of us turned around to glare. "Sorry," I whispered to them. I noticed the corners of Hawke's mouth twitch a little.

I leaned in so my mouth was right next to his ear. "Did you learn anything from your sneaky spying?"

He didn't look at me as he answered, "Aside from the fact that you don't have visible panty lines?"

I considered punching him again. "I don't want to hear any more about my ass…or my underwear. I want to know about the story."

"I'm still spying," he said, his eyes resting on the group of teenagers all sitting together six benches in front of us. "I'll let you know if someone hits me over the head and says they killed her."

The service started with a prayer and some words from

members of Chelsea's extended family. There was a musical number, a reading from *The Book of Mormon,* a eulogy, and then the microphone was opened up for members of the audience to share their memories of Chelsea. I was surprised by this since Mormon funerals are usually pretty structured and only people who have been asked by the family are allowed to speak. As people got up and told stories of the girl they had known, I couldn't help but feel like I knew her too.

At first, only friends of Chelsea's parents spoke, but after a while, kids from the group of teenagers got out of their seats. One boy spoke about Chelsea and a group of friends toilet papering the yard of one of their favorite teachers. A girl smiled as she recalled how much Chelsea had loved being on the dance team. Another girl mentioned Chelsea's acting skills and amazing voice.

Hawke and I both listened intently to the things the teenagers were saying. I had a feeling if we were going to get a break in the story, the information would come from one of these kids. Teenagers who, like all other kids their age, probably knew Chelsea better than her parents did.

The girl with the strawberry blonde hair from the high school office stood up, her legs visibly shaking as she walked to the podium with the microphone. The tears formed pools in her eyes, threatening to overflow any second. I didn't know how she was going to make it through her comments. She held a paper in her hands as she adjusted the microphone. She looked at the paper for several seconds before she cleared her throat and started to talk. "Chelsea was a good friend of mine. She was always happy no matter how bad the things in her life seemed to be." She paused, looking down at the Bradford family in the front row with a hard expression. Hawke and I both noticed and glanced at each other. This information was a lead we needed to follow.

"Chelsea kept to herself about a lot of things. She didn't want to burden other people with her problems. Now I wonder if that was a mistake." The girl looked specifically at Brian and Julia Bradford. I glanced around the room, but other people didn't seem to notice the deliberate words, pauses, and stares. To everyone else, the girl's words were just a way to deal with the pain, but Hawke and I saw them as an accusation.

"Emerald Lake was Chelsea's favorite place in Branson Falls. I know she was happy she got to spend her last time on earth there." A tear slid down the girl's cheek. She looked up toward the ceiling as she whispered, "I'll miss you." A few more people stood up to give their remarks before the Bradfords' Mormon bishop concluded the service telling everyone the burial would only be open to family members.

Hawke and I watched as people slowly started to file out of the chapel. When most people had left, we stood and followed the group of mourners. Some people stayed in the foyer, talking, others scattered to their cars. Hawke walked me to my Jeep as a shock-heavy black truck with tinted windows almost ran us over. The truck driver spun out of the parking lot, obviously eager to leave. Something about the truck was familiar. As I tried to remember what it was, Hawke broke me from my thoughts, saying, "That girl knows something."

I nodded in agreement. "I'll talk to her. I met her before when I was asking around about Chelsea's disappearance."

"Are you going to talk to her today?"

I shook my head. "No. She's pretty shaken up. She works in the main office at the high school. I'll stop by tomorrow and offer to take her to lunch. I'll see what I can find out."

"Let me know."

"I will," I said. "What are you going to do?"

He grinned, twisting his key ring around his finger in a circle. "Use my resources."

"Do those resources have anything to do with the police?" I asked. I'd told him about the police ruling on Chelsea's death quickly.

Hawke gave me a level stare. "I'm pretty sure we're on our own with this investigation."

I wrinkled my brow. "Why do you think that?"

"Chelsea's case is closed as far as the police are concerned."

Damn. I was hoping Hawke would be able to use his resources to get them to re-open the case. I knew people too, though. Maybe I could help the police department change their minds. "I could talk to them about it," I offered.

Hawke's smile seemed to indicate I was extremely naïve. "If you want to give it a try, Kitty Kate, go ahead. Just don't be disappointed when I'm right. I'll see you tomorrow."

As I drove back to the *Tribune* office, I hit some traffic. This was odd, because I live in Branson Falls. The only time there's "traffic" is when cows are being moved from one field to another. I didn't see any livestock, so something else was going on.

The commotion seemed to be centered around the crumbling ruins of the old sheet metal plant. The plant was on the industrial side of town and blocked off by a fence. For years, people had used it to write welcome home signs for Mormon missionaries coming back from their two-year church service missions. The signs were Branson's version of graffiti, but acceptable because they were church related. The plant was the only place in town that ever got vandalized, and people only did it after first asking for permission from the former plant owner.

Being a good reporter, I decided I better pull over to find out what all the fuss was about. When I got out, I saw the side of the building had been painted with huge, bright red letters.

She had it coming.

People were mumbling their theories about the note, and everyone had an opinion about who the note referred to. My first thought was that the note referenced Chelsea; but as I listened to the people around me who weren't suspicious of her death, I realized the note was so ambiguous, it could be any female in town. Even me. The thought gave me pause.

As I eavesdropped on various conversations, most of the speculation seemed to refer to someone cheating on someone else. Other people were incensed that the welcome home sign for soon-to-return missionary, Andrew Davies, had been covered up. However, I did hear a few whispers that maybe the note was about Chelsea. There was even a suggestion that she might not have drowned. I was glad Hawke and I weren't the only ones on that thought path.

I grabbed my camera from my bag, snapping a few photos as I continued to listen to the gossip. "When did the note appear?" a woman asked.

"Don't know," another woman answered. "Paint looks fresh though."

I looked closer, noticing the paint brush streaks gleaming in the sunlight. The person who wrote it had used an actual paint brush with a high glossy finish. The note hadn't been there long. I assumed it was painted last night. I doubted the person who wrote the note had gotten permission for their graffiti, and they would have wanted the cover of darkness to do it. I was surprised I didn't hear about the sign at the funeral, but then again, the sheet metal plant wasn't something people passed every day unless they were trying to get to the freeway. I'd only come this way because the stoplight I needed to go through despised me and I didn't want to wait five minutes for it to take a Pamprin.

The gossip would spread now that people had seen the sign though. I listened to the chatter for a few more minutes while I walked around the area, and then went back to my Jeep. As I drove away, I wondered if the message meant the police would take Chelsea's death more seriously.

The next day I went to the high school during lunch. I hoped the offer of free food would entice Chelsea's friend from the funeral to chat with me. The front desk in the office was empty. I was worried the girl hadn't come into work today. I decided to sit in the chair across from the desk and wait. I was flipping through my notes when the girl with strawberry blonde hair came down the office hallway. She gave a nervous smile when she saw me. "Oh, hi," she said, recognizing me from my previous visit. "Is there something else you need?"

I looked around, trying to find a paper or tag with her name on it. "I'm sorry, last time I was here I didn't get your name."

"I'm Piper Adams."

"Piper," I smiled widely. "I was hoping I could talk to you."

Her expression quickly changed from surprised to confused. "I . . . I'm not sure why you would want to talk to me."

I gave her a reassuring glance. "I saw you yesterday at the funeral," I said. "I know you were a friend of Chelsea's. I thought you might be able to help me learn more about her."

Her nose scrunched up and I could tell she was uncomfortable. "I'm just doing a story about Chelsea for the newspaper," I said. "It would be nice to get the perspective of a friend who knew her well." Piper looked at me like she didn't know what to say. "Why don't I take you to lunch? If you feel like talking while we eat, that's great, if not," I shrugged, "you get a free lunch."

Her defenses seemed to go down a little. "Okay, I guess." That's another thing I like about Branson Falls, everyone is so trusting.

I smiled again. "Can you leave now?"

She looked around and nodded. "I just need to tell the other office assistant I'll be gone. Hold on."

Piper disappeared down the hall for a minute before coming back with her purse. "How about *Sticks and Pie*? We can get a few breadsticks and some slices of pizza to go, and eat at the library park?"

Piper nodded in agreement and we left to get our lunch.

We sat across from each other, arranging our food and drinks on the picnic table. I opened my take-out box, the scent of garlic and fresh bread floating through the air. There's nothing on earth like the *Sticks and Pie* breadsticks, twisted with layers of garlic flavoring, butter, dough, and gooey mozzarella cheese. Add in some ranch dressing dipping sauce and it's a heart attack waiting to happen—but it's worth it.

"You and Chelsea must have been good friends," I said between bites of cheese and zesty tomato sauce.

She kept her head down as she ate instead of answering. Huh. I didn't think it would be this difficult to get her to talk to me, but then again, she didn't really know me.

"Piper, you know I'm the editor of *The Branson Tribune,* right?"

It took a minute for her to answer. "Yeah, I know."

I stared at her across the table, willing her to look up at me. "If I tell you something, do you think you can keep it just between the two of us?"

Piper looked up at me. I could tell she was surprised I was willing to trust her. I hoped it would make her trust me back. "I won't tell anyone," she said, nodding her head.

"The police ruled Chelsea's death an accidental drowning, but I don't think it was. There are some things that seem suspicious. If you know anything about what was going on with Chelsea before she disappeared, the information could help me figure out what happened to her."

Piper shifted uncomfortably on the splintered wood picnic table and didn't say anything. I decided to continue eating and wait until she was ready to talk. After two breadsticks and the rest of my pizza slice, Piper said, "I'm afraid people would find out I told."

I shook my head to reassure her. "You don't have to worry about that at all. If a source—like you—doesn't want to be revealed, a reporter can keep that person a secret."

Piper twisted a napkin into submission before she responded. "Do you promise?"

"I promise. I know you were Chelsea's friend. If it turns out someone was responsible for her death, I know you wouldn't want them to get away with her murder."

She looked down at the table for a long pause before meeting my eyes. “Chelsea was like a sister to me.”

I gave a sympathetic look. “I know, Piper. I’m so sorry she’s gone.”

“She was going through a lot before she left. She wasn’t getting along with her parents, and she was upset they were making her leave school.”

I shook my head, confused. Everything I’d heard so far indicated Chelsea had wanted to leave and travel. “Chelsea didn’t want to travel with her friends?”

Piper shook her head slowly, staring at me. “I don’t think she was traveling.”

I bit the corner of my lip as I tried to understand. “Then why did her parents take her out of school?”

She locked eyes with me, holding the stare. “Because Chelsea was pregnant.”

Chapter Nine

My jaw dropped. I couldn't help it. Looking back on the clues, Chelsea's sudden disappearance from Branson made perfect sense if she'd been pregnant. Her parents probably didn't want to deal with the scandal of a teen pregnancy and had tried to keep it a secret. Maybe they should have tried teaching her about birth control instead.

Everyone knows Utah's sex education system is not very educational. Even when I'd gone to high school, Utah had claimed one of the highest teen pregnancy rates in the nation. Parents wanted the freedom to tell their kids about sex instead of letting a teacher do it. I respected that, but the problem was a lot of parents refused to educate their kids about sex at all. At least with a class at school, they'd get more accurate information than a Google search. I had a fleeting thought that I should talk to Drake about it. I was pretty sure he agreed with me on sex education since he'd given it to so many girls on his own.

Piper's revelation added a whole new layer to Chelsea's story. Piper watched me pick my chin up off the table. "How do you know?"

Piper shrugged. "She was my best friend. We told each other everything."

"When did you find out she was pregnant?"

"Last November. She was about six weeks along when she took a test."

"Who else knew about the pregnancy?"

"I don't think anyone at school knew. Her parents didn't even know she told me. They didn't want anyone to find out about it. Everyone in Branson is so religious and they were worried about what Chelsea's pregnancy would do to their family name and how it would hurt the reputations of her younger brother and sister."

The thought of how much reputations mattered in Branson Falls made me want to roll my eyes. I fought the urge and asked, "How were they going to keep it a secret?"

"They let her stay in school until she started gaining enough weight to show. She stayed really small through the pregnancy, so her parents didn't have to pull her out of school until she was five months along."

"Then what happened? Did she really go away somewhere?"

Piper lifted her shoulders. "I don't know. They told everyone she was traveling with friends, but maybe she didn't go anywhere at all? Her parents could have been keeping her locked in her bedroom for all I know." Piper took another sip of her drink. "I tried to email Chelsea but the emails came back as undeliverable, like her account had been closed. I talked to Mrs. Bradford a few times and asked for an address to reach Chelsea. Mrs. Bradford said Chelsea's travel schedule was flexible so she couldn't give me an address, but told me I could give the letters to her and she would get them to Chelsea. I thought it was weird because if she could get letters to Chelsea, why not just give me the same address to send stuff to?"

"Yeah, that's strange." I tapped my fingernails on the table top, a nervous habit I always fall back into when I'm thinking. Chelsea's parents were looking more and more suspicious. "Is there anything else?"

Piper wiped her hands on a napkin. "Not that I can think of."

"What about her boyfriend? Do you know who got her pregnant?"

Piper looked away as she answered, "She dated a lot of guys. I'm not sure who it was. I tried to get her to tell me about the father of the baby, but she wouldn't. She was pretty protective of the information."

I took Piper's hand. "Thank you so much for telling me this. Now that I know about the pregnancy, it gives me a new round of leads to investigate. I'm going to find out what happened to Chelsea, I promise." I squeezed her hand as I lifted my lips in a soft smile to reassure her.

She gave me a tight smile in return. I could see the pain still lingering in her eyes. "I need to get back to the office."

"Okay," I said. We gathered our trash and put it in the garbage can. I drove Piper back to the school and walked her to the front door.

"Here's my number." I handed her a business card. "Call me anytime if you need to talk. And please let me know if you remember anything else."

"Thanks." She took the card and swiveled around to walk into the building. She stopped and looked over her shoulder. "No one will find out that I told you, right?"

I nodded. "No one will ever know."

I walked back to my SUV, thinking instead of paying attention to anything else, so it was no surprise that I almost peed my pants when I opened the Jeep door and Hawke was sitting in my passenger seat. "Hey there, Kitty Kate. How's your day going?"

I put my profanity training to good use before I took a few deep breaths, trying to get my heart rate back to normal. "Where did you come from? You're like a stalker!"

"Thank you," he smiled.

"It wasn't a compliment! You almost gave me a heart attack!"

"I just thought I'd save some time."

"Because crouching like a panther in the passenger seat of my car saves so much more time than just leaning against the door." I folded my arms across my chest. "How did you get in anyway?"

He cocked his head and the corner of his mouth hitched. "Not much can stop me when I want something. I told you that the other day."

I refused to acknowledge the insinuation. "Fine, what do you want? Other than to sit in my Jeep?"

"I want to know what you found out from the girl."

"The *girl's* name is Piper."

"Fine, what did you find out from Piper?"

"A lot." I paused, remembering my promise to Piper. "But she doesn't want anyone to know she gave me information. So the fact that she's my source stays between you and me."

Hawke smiled slowly. "I'm pretty good at keeping secrets."

I stared at him for a few long seconds. I had no doubt about that. I was sure enigmatic Hawke had a castle full of skeletons, not a closet. Knowing he'd keep Piper's name confidential I said, "You're not going to believe this—" at that moment, my cell phone started to ring. Since I was already holding it, I was able to answer the phone before Hawke figured out Neil Diamond was coming from the speaker. I held up my index finger letting Hawke know I'd be a minute.

"Hey, what's going on?" I asked.

"I need you to get to the bank right away," Spence said.

"I'm kind of in the middle of something."

"Trust me, if the scanner is any indication, you'll want to see this for yourself."

Heaven help me. "What did my mom do this time?"

"Your mom's not involved—at least, I don't think she is." He paused. "Actually, it sounds like something that would happen to her so you better go check."

"Okay, I'm about two minutes away."

"Please tell me you have your camera?"

"Of course I do."

"Good. I want lots of photos."

I hung up the phone. "Bad news. Our conversation will have to wait. Something's going on at the bank and I have to leave right now."

Instead of getting out of my Jeep, Hawke buckled his seatbelt. "I'll come along."

I stared at him for a couple of seconds. "Okay," I said, and started the Jeep.

Even though it was only a mile away, I sped through side streets to get to the bank as fast as I could.

"So, what did you learn from Piper?" Hawke asked.

"I don't have time to go into the whole story now."

We careened around a corner. Hawke braced himself against the door. "Since you're probably going to kill us before we get to the bank, you at least owe me the highlights of your conversation."

I couldn't turn to glare at him because I was trying to watch the road and not hit any children, pedestrians, or animals, so I glared out the windshield instead. As we came to the bank, a fire truck, ambulance, and two police cars blocked the street. I pulled into the closest parking spot I could find, grabbed my camera from the back seat and opened the door. Right before I got out I said, "Chelsea was pregnant."

I could tell Hawke was surprised at the news about Chelsea, but nothing compared to the look on his face as we surveyed the situation in front of us.

The bank had just installed a new revolving door. There had even been an article about it in the *Tribune*. The door was big news in Branson because no other store in the town, or even the county, had one. Revolving doors were for fancy offices in big cities. The doors can be tricky for people not used to the constant, circular movement. As we stood back in stunned silence, I decided maybe the bank should have offered a class on 'how to use a revolving door'. I couldn't look away.

I imagined that in Hawke's vast life experience, he'd seen pretty much everything. But it seemed nothing could compare to the image of Mrs. Olsen bent over, her shoulders, torso, butt, arms, and legs hanging out of the town's only revolving door. Her head was stuck between the revolving part of the door and the stationary plate glass that the door passed as it turned. And she wasn't handling the situation with grace. In an effort to get the attention of everyone in the world, her arms were waving around her stomach so fast that it looked like she was trying desperately to swim. I thought if she moved much faster, her arms could act as a propeller and she might be able to take off.

I held back my laughter since collapsing to the ground in a fit of giggles wouldn't be very professional, but I couldn't wipe the huge smile off my face as I lifted my camera and started clicking away. No wonder Spence wanted a lot of pictures. I could imagine him rolling on the floor listening to this debacle on the scanner.

On a scale of embarrassment, this topped every incident my mom had ever been involved in. She'd be glad to know she wasn't the only one with bad luck. Though I imagined this situation was a result of insufficient revolving door experience, whereas my mom's catastrophes were usually just horrible coincidences.

People from all over town were standing on the sidewalks and more were arriving by the minute, coming by foot, bike, and car. If they didn't get Mrs. Olsen's head unstuck soon, people from other towns would start showing up too. I watched a police officer near Mrs. Olsen trying to calm her down. Officer Bob was talking to a group of firemen. "I have to talk to the police," I said to Hawke as I got another memory stick from my bag and slid it into my camera. "Are you going to hang around?"

Hawke smiled. "I wouldn't miss this for the world."

I walked up to the firemen and Officer Bob, all of whom were doing their best not to laugh at the circumstance. "Hey boys," I said. "Any of you want to comment on what happened here?"

"Kate," Bob said. "I figured it was only a matter of time before you showed up."

"Get used to it, Bobby," I smiled. "How in the hell did Mrs. Olsen get her head lodged in the revolving door?"

The two firemen were holding back laughter. Bob said, "We're not exactly sure. Until we get her out of there, she can't tell us what happened."

"She's been yelling since we got here," one of the firemen said. "She's trying to tell us something."

"There were eyewitness reports, though," Bob said. "Near as we can tell, Mrs. Olsen had been lookin' for somethin' in her purse when she started to walk into the bank. With her head down in her purse she was bent over slightly at the waist when the door came by and captured her head, pinnin' it between the rotatin' door and the permanent glass."

I had to try really, really hard not to laugh at the image. Judging by their red faces and sparkle in their eyes, the firemen and Bob looked like they were trying twice as hard as me. When I regained my composure I asked, "So why don't you just push the door open?"

One of the firemen answered, "There's a fail-safe switch and we cut the electricity to the door. The EMT's are looking her over first to make sure it's safe to move her and she isn't hurt. Once they finish up, we'll push the door counter-clockwise and get her out." There was an amused smile as he said it.

I pointed my notebook at them. "You're all taking your time on this because you think it's funny!"

None of them denied it. "Admit it, you do too," Bob said. "Mrs. Olsen is one of the meanest women I know. It's kinda nice to see her in this mess."

I couldn't disagree. Her reputation of constantly judging everyone in town put The Ladies to shame. Now would be a good time for me to get some coffee since the coffee patrol was currently lodged in a door. "I'm going to get photos and talk to some of the people in the crowd."

Officer Bob swept his hand out in front of him. "Go ahead."

I got some great photos from the back, and by back, I mean Mrs. Olsen's backside. I went around to the entrance on the other side of the building to get some photos of her face, which was bright red and looked like it might explode. I also got some good action shots with her arms waving.

I talked to the eyewitnesses and got crowd reactions ranging from amusement to concern that it could happen again. Once the EMT's were finished checking Mrs. Olsen, the firemen went up to the door and pushed it about six inches to the left. Mrs. Olsen's scarlet head popped out like the door had just given birth to a very angry old lady.

I got photos of that too.

I put my camera back in my bag and was on my way to meet Hawke at my Jeep when I saw Bob standing alone next to his police cruiser. It seemed like the perfect time to ask him about Chelsea's death and the police investigation.

He stared at me as I walked up to him. "Do you need another quote for your story or somethin'?"

"No," I said. "Actually, I wanted to ask you about Chelsea Bradford's death."

He gave me a wary look. "What about it?"

I knew they'd ruled her death an accident, but thought I'd feign ignorance to fish for information. "I was wondering how your investigation is going and if there's any information you'd like to share?"

He took a piece of gum from his pocket. "There ain't no investigation," he said as he unwrapped the tutti-fruity flavored gum.

"What do you mean there's no investigation?" I asked. Hawke had said the police wouldn't be any help, but I hadn't believed him.

"Her death was ruled an accident. The investigation is done."

"What about the sign on the sheet metal plant? *She had it coming*. It seemed menacing. It could have been about Chelsea."

Bobby rolled his eyes. "Bunch a ninny's speculatin' on things and causin' me problems," Bobby said. "We got some calls about it, but they didn't last long, and Andrew Davies' welcome home sign was back up by the end of the night. The sign could of been referrin' to any female in town. People just wanna jump on the freshest piece a gossip they can get."

"Are you telling me that no one's talking about the message anymore?"

He flicked a bug from his arm. "You're the reporter. You heard anyone talkin' about it?"

He had me there. Maybe Ella would know something though. She had a better pulse on the gossip circles than I did. "So you're not worried there's a possible murderer running around Branson at all?"

"Nope."

I put my hands on my hips and stared at him. Apparently he wasn't concerned with all the evidence pointing to foul play. "Chelsea went missing before she died."

Bobby shook his head. "We talked to her parents. She wasn't missin', she was visitin' friends. Brian and Julia Bradford didn't know she'd come home."

I looked at him with wide eyes. "Don't you think it's odd her parents didn't know she was back in town?"

Bobby sighed. "Most of the things teenagers do are strange. Heck, I'm terrified of the weird crap my kids will come up with once they're that age." He rubbed his forehead like he had an itch and continued, "We talked to the family Chelsea was travelin' with. They said she'd started gettin' homesick. One morning a few weeks ago they woke up and she was gone. Said she took all her stuff with her."

Hmm. Either Chelsea really had left Branson, or the family Bobby had talked to was covering for the Bradfords. "So did you find her stuff at the lake?"

"What stuff?" Bobby asked.

I closed my eyes. Sometimes talking to Bobby was like talking to a four-year-old. "The stuff Chelsea took with her when she left. Obviously she didn't go home, so her belongings should have been with her at the lake."

Bobby wrinkled his brow. "I'm sure it'll turn up eventually. Besides, I doubt the lake was the first place she went."

"That's another thing!" I almost yelled, trying to emphasize my point. "She didn't go home, so where was she staying before she died? And why the lake? Why not go home to her family if she was homesick?"

Bobby thought about it before responding, "The Bradfords said part of the reason they let her leave school to travel was because they were tryin' to get her away from some boy she was datin'." Bobby chewed his gum loudly, glancing around like a member of the royal guard on patrol. "So I figure Chelsea bein' homesick had more to do with missin' her boyfriend than it had to do with missin' her family. If I were a bettin' man, I'd say the boyfriend was who she stayed with. As for Emerald Lake, the Bradfords said it was one of her favorite places in Branson."

"Did the Bradfords tell you who she was dating before she left?"

"Nope. Said it wasn't important. And since her death was an accident, it don't really matter."

"She went missing and now she's dead!" I said. "It seems like the boyfriend might be a clue."

Bobby rolled his eyes. "Ah, Kate. You know how teenage girls are."

I folded my arms under my chest. I couldn't wait to hear this. "No, Bobby, how are they?"

"Difficult! All those hormones and anger issues. I'd have probably sent my kid away too!"

I took a moment to feel bad for Bobby's kids. "Did you at least get the crime scene unit out to the lake before you closed Chelsea's case?"

Bobby burst out laughing. "Crime scene unit?" He laughed some more. "Cripes, Kate! This is Branson Falls, not Salt Lake City. We don't have a crime scene unit."

Sometimes I forget small towns don't have anywhere close to the same resources as large cities. During my college internship, I'd worked the crime beat for a daily newspaper. It was a completely different experience than this. The city cops seemed to have a lot more rules to follow. "Did the police department search for evidence?"

He hooked his thumbs over his belt, pushing his chest out as he gave me a look indicating he held me in the same esteem as a cockroach. "We followed normal investigation procedures. Chelsea's death was an accident, there's nothin' more to investigate."

I stared at him while I bit my tongue until I could come up

with a response that didn't involve a four-letter word. "I think there's more to the story than an accidental drowning," I said. "And I'm not the only one."

Bobby arched an eyebrow but didn't respond.

"I'm going to find out what really happened, with your help or without it," I said, like I was issuing a dare.

He studied me with an assessing eye. "If you wanna waste your time and chase Chelsea Bradford's ghost, be my guest," he said, motioning with his arm like I had free reign.

My jaw gaped in disbelief. "Are you saying I have permission from the Branson Police Department to investigate Chelsea's death on my own?"

He laughed. "It's a free country—for now at least. I figure you can do whatever you want. Like I said, you're wastin' your time."

I wrapped the camera strap through my arm, over my shoulder, and across my chest. "We'll see, Bobby."

I walked back over to where Hawke was standing. "What were you and the good officer talking about?" he asked.

"Chelsea."

"Did he have any interesting information for you?"

I stared at Hawke, annoyed that he'd been right. "Not really."

"Did he tell you they aren't investigating her death?"

I tightened my lips for a few seconds and met his eyes. "Yeah, he did. So I guess you and I will have to work twice as hard to figure out what happened."

Hawke hooked an arm over the door of the Jeep, giving me a wide grin. "I can't wait."

Chapter Ten

I walked into the *Tribune* office with Hawke following behind me. Spence saw me and grinned. "Was it as good as it sounded on the scanner?"

"Better. One of the funniest things I've ever seen."

Ella came out of the back room. "What was funny?"

"Mrs. Olsen got her head stuck in the new revolving door at the bank."

Ella hooted a laugh. "That woman has always been dumber than dirt and meaner than a rabid dog. Karma. That's what that's called."

"I hope you got pictures," Spence said.

"I don't think I've ever taken more pictures for a story in my life."

"The pictures won't compare to seeing it in person though," Hawke said.

Ella stood back with her hands on her hips and looked Hawke up and down, noticing him standing there for the first time—though how she could have missed him in the first place, I'm not sure. "Who's this strapping young man?"

"Ryker Hawkins," I said. "Hawke, this is our volunteer archivist, Ella James."

Hawke held his hand out. "It's a pleasure to meet you, Ella."

Ella met his hand with a firm shake. "Nice to meet ya," Ella said. "If you're a new reporter, I'll be puttin' in more volunteer hours."

Hawke laughed.

"He's helping me investigate Chelsea Bradford's death."

"Huh," Ella looked him over a second time. "I bet you could find a better use for him than that."

Hawke grinned, I blushed, and Spence scowled. Apparently Spence still wasn't happy about me working with Hawke.

"Hey, Ella," I said. "Have you heard anything about the graffiti on the sheet metal plant that showed up on the day of Chelsea's funeral?"

Ella scrunched up her nose. "Just that everyone thinks it was strange. The nerve of someone bein' so vindictive and secretive. If you're gonna write a sign like that, at least give some names. Person who did it must've been unhinged."

"Any idea who did it, or what the sign was about?"

"Nope. Could've been about anyone."

Yeah, yeah. I'd heard that already, and thought it too. I still couldn't shake the feeling it had something to do with Chelsea. "You hear anything about this, Hawke?"

He shook his head. "I'm looking into it, but nothing so far."

I sighed. "I think you and I are the only ones who truly think Chelsea didn't just trip into the lake and forget how to swim."

He tilted his head in acknowledgment. "Speaking of Chelsea," he said. "I'd like more details about her being pregnant."

I glared, and seriously considered slugging Hawke. He wasn't a very good secret keeper. He'd just announced Chelsea's pregnancy to the whole office—which consisted of Ella and Spence, but still.

Spence's mouth dropped at the news. I expected the same reaction from Ella, but her response was non-descript. I pushed my brows together. "You don't seem very surprised, Ella."

She shrugged. "I'm not. It ain't the first time a girl's disappeared for a while and then come back to Branson. It happened to girls when I was in high school, it happened with Chelsea, and it'll happen again."

I gave her an astonished look. She stared back, unapologetic. I closed my eyes, sighing. "Ella, remember when I asked if you had any other information I should know about? Girls who disappear because they're pregnant is one of those things."

She raised one shoulder while she tilted her head the side. "I figured you'd know. You went to high school here. It probably happened to girls you were in school with."

Ella's statement caught me off-guard and I thought back to my years in high school. There were a few girls who left to spend a year as foreign exchange students. Now I wondered if they'd been visiting a maternity ward instead of another country.

"What else did you find out?" Hawke asked.

In an effort to keep the rest of our conversation private, I pulled Hawke into the archive room and shut the door. I relayed the basics of my conversation with Piper. When I was done, I looked at Hawke. "If Chelsea was pregnant, where's the baby?"

Hawke looked at me. "Another mystery to solve."

"Maybe the person who killed Chelsea has the kid," I suggested.

"It's a definite possibility." I thought it was strange he just accepted the news about Chelsea's pregnancy. If I'd been him, I would have had a hundred questions. It almost seemed like Hawke wasn't that surprised, but he was a hard guy to read.

"So," I said, still trying to gauge his reaction, "I think the next step is to find out who got Chelsea pregnant and get some proof."

"That's not going to be easy."

"Did you know Chelsea was dating the son of a politician?" I asked.

"Yeah," he said. "Do you know which one?"

I narrowed my eyes at him. "Wait, did you say 'yeah'?" I asked. "You already knew about that?" So maybe he did know Chelsea had been pregnant! Clearly he was keeping secrets.

"Obviously you knew about the mystery boyfriend too."

"Of course I did! I'm a good reporter," I said, trying to ignore the suspicious way Hawke was looking at me. "There was a rumor going around after she left that she'd been in love with some boy whose dad was important in the state political arena."

Hawke narrowed his eyes, sliding his tongue over the inside of his cheek. "You just forgot to tell me you knew about all that, huh?"

"Yeah, I did. And apparently you forgot to tell me you knew about it too!"

He pinched his nose in the same way I pinch mine every time I hear about another one of my mom's disasters. "We need to have a discussion about sharing information."

"Well go ahead and share then."

"If you want to find out who the politician is, I imagine

that's where your—" he looked at my chest— "assets could come in handy."

"Stop staring at my boobs!" I warned. "And how is my chest going to help?" He raised an eyebrow; I took offense. "I'm *not* doing anything unethical."

He shook his head. "You're the weirdest reporter I've ever met. You won't have to do anything you're not comfortable with. I just think you should go to the state capitol and snoop around a bit. An unassuming, attractive girl like you will be able to do that a lot easier than someone like me will."

"Because you're a giant?"

"People tell me I'm intimidating."

"Imagine that," I said. "The legislature isn't even in session until winter. I doubt I'll learn much."

"The session isn't going on, but they hold committee meetings throughout the year. You should be able to get into the building and ask some questions." He took a piece of paper from a notepad on the archive room desk. In handwriting that looked so structured it was almost architectural, he wrote some names down and handed the list to me. "These are the names of Utah politicians the Bradfords were friends with before they moved to Branson Falls. You should concentrate on the five names at the top."

I stared at him, mouth agape. "What other lists do you have that I don't know about?"

Hawke smiled. "I share as much information as I can."

I glared at him, waving the list. "So what am I supposed to do with this?"

"You're going to be an intern. Go to the capitol building. Talk to the politicians on the list, and the people who work for them." He handed me a laminated card with my photo on it. Apparently fake ID's were also one of Hawke's specialties.

"Here's a badge; you'll need to look like a legitimate intern if you want to get into the offices and have people answer questions without thinking you're a national security threat."

"Wait a minute," I said, cutting him off. "Why do you already have the badge made and the list of politicians committed to memory? How long have you been planning this reconnaissance mission for me?"

"Long enough to make a badge and a list."

I scowled at him. His lips lifted in a slow, amused smile before he continued, "When you get to the capitol, ask around, get a feel for people, and try to find out what the latest gossip is."

I lifted my shoulders. "Okay. That sounds easy enough."

Hawke's lips quirked slightly at the corners like he was trying to hold back a smile. "This is your first under-cover investigation, isn't it?"

"Yeah. But it doesn't sound difficult."

The grin he was holding back broke through. "You should go tomorrow if you can." He took his keys from his pocket. "I'll call you." As he walked out the door, he turned his head and over his shoulder said, "Good luck, Kitty Kate."

After Hawke left, I told Spence and Ella the whole story about Mrs. Olsen's head in the revolving door and we laughed for at least fifteen minutes. Spence left to get us dinner. I sat at my desk to write the story about Mrs. Olsen and edit some articles that were in my inbox. As I started sorting through the box, a letter with my name typed across the front fell out. I opened it. A note was written with letters from a magazine—like someone had been taking anonymous threat writing lessons from *Murder She Wrote*. It was short, just six words: *Be careful who you work with.*

I stared at it. What was that supposed to mean? I work with a lot of people, and lately the list had grown. Was it referencing Spence, Hawke, Drake, Ella, the police department . . . the possibilities went on and on. I also couldn't tell if it was a threat, or a warning. Staring at it wasn't helping me decipher its meaning. I folded it up, reaching for my bag when I heard Ella ask, "How'd you meet Hawke?" She was suddenly at my side, sitting on the edge of the desk. She watched me closely as I dropped the letter in my bag.

I laughed a little in surprise. "He helped me get into the crime scene when Chelsea's body was found."

Ella looked wistfully at a painting on the wall, lost in thought for a few seconds. "I've heard about him, but I've never seen him until today. I can die a happy woman. He is one sexy, sexy man."

I laughed again. It was so odd to be talking about this with a woman twenty years older than my grandma. "Speaking of sex," Ella said, "what favors have you been promisin' to get Hawke's help?"

I did my best to act disgusted, though the thought of sexual favors for Hawke made my stomach flutter in a very good way. "I didn't promise anything. He just said he wanted to help me out. He thought I could help him too."

Ella broke out into fits of laughter. "Honey, it's been a long time since I've seen a man naked, or even dated one with real teeth, but even I know Hawke has an ulterior motive. You better make sure you've always got sexy underwear on until he's done *helping* you."

I grimaced, wondering if Ella was right. It would be bad if Hawke wanted something from me. I mean, sexual favors would break some sort of journalism law or code of ethics, right? Though, there are a lot of reporters who cross that line —and they're probably just the sort of people Hawke spends time with.

"I bet he has a lot of tattoos. When he starts taking his clothes off you better look for them. And take notes. Like I said, it's been a long time and I've never slept with someone as good lookin' as Hawke."

That night, I pulled the note out of my bag again. I still wasn't sure what to make of it. I knew a lot of people in my life would have an opinion though, and most would be bordering on frantic. If this had something to do with Chelsea's death, sending me a note just made me more determined to figure out what really happened. I looked at it for a few more minutes before I folded it up and put it on my desk. I decided to treat it as both a threat and a warning. For now, I'd keep my eyes open and keep the information to myself.

Chapter Eleven

I decided I'd fit in at the state capitol building better if I was wearing a pencil skirt and fitted jacket—which forced me to sport some Spanx to give the illusion I have a firm butt and thighs. The skirt also meant that in addition to waking up early to drive to the capitol, I'd had to wake up even earlier to shave my legs. Mornings make me angry.

I clipped the ID badge on the bottom of my shirt as I got out of my Jeep, and locked my car door. I walked into the capitol building and read through the offices listed on a board in the foyer. As I scanned the names, my eyes stopped on Dylan Drake. Huh. I'd forgotten there was a chance I could run into him. Though I doubted he was around anyway—I mean, what were the chances he'd be on one of the committees meeting today?

I brought a file folder to use as a prop and hopefully make me seem less suspicious. The goal was to look more like I was supposed to be in the building and less like I was spying on people and trying to get gossip about sons of representatives and senators who might have knocked a girl up.

Like the federal government, Utah's state government is

comprised of Utah House and Senate members representing districts throughout the state. I decided to start with finding out how the politicians on Hawke's list knew the Bradfords. Honestly, I felt like the whole undercover operation was probably a waste of time. We didn't have any clue about the identity of the guy Chelsea had supposedly been dating. I doubted I'd stumble across the information today. But I'd promised to help Hawke and doing this favor was better than taking my clothes off—well, not better exactly, but more professional. Plus, if my suspicions were right, there was still a murderer on the loose. Since the Branson police force was MIA, I felt responsible for finding out who killed Chelsea, and stopping it from happening again.

As I wandered up and down the halls, I read the name tags on the outside of offices and peeked into open rooms. I found the offices for four of the five senators and representatives Hawke had told me to investigate. I chatted with office assistants and other real interns, but I didn't get much information about the Bradfords. It would have been more helpful to talk to the senators and representatives on the list, but they were all either in committee meetings or out of the office because they didn't have meetings scheduled. I'd been wandering and chatting with people most of the morning and hadn't gotten any relevant information, but there was one senator left on Hawke's list. Senator Tanner's office was empty when I strolled by the first time, and the second. On my third pass, I entered the office.

Like other offices I'd seen today, the space consisted of a main room, with a private office for the senator behind a door to my right. I stood in front of the office assistant's desk, my arms at my sides, while I looked at paintings of landscapes and cowboys and tried to be very inconspicuous. The office had the dusty smell of a place that doesn't get used often. Finally, I decided no one was there so I might as well have a look around to see if I could find a connection to the Bradfords.

I glanced at papers on the desk, just in case I'd become the luckiest person in the world and the Bradfords' name along with a confession for murdering their daughter was there. It wasn't. I eyed the filing cabinets next to the west wall. I tried to open the drawers, but they were locked. I'd all but given up when I saw a rolodex sitting on the desk.

I shifted my eyes around the room making sure I was still alone before flipping through the 'B' names as fast as I could to see if Brian and Julia's names were listed. Baylor, Bird, Boone, Bradford! There were their names, listed in bright red ink. The handy color coding system next to the rolodex indicated that as 'reds' they were friends and campaign donors. Bingo! I was so excited at my lead that I wanted to dance around the room. My celebration was cut short, though, when I heard voices coming from behind the Senator's private office door.

I moved away from the desk as fast as I could. I tried to get out of the room, but it was too late. The door opened. I discreetly covered my ID badge with my left hand as an older gentleman with graying hair and a portly stomach came through the door first, followed by someone else I couldn't see. As the second person stepped out of the first man's shadow, I recognized the charming smile I knew all too well: Drake.

Drake's brow wrinkled as surprise and puzzlement flickered across his face, but he recovered quickly.

"Well, hello there young lady," the man with gray hair said in a jovial voice. "What can I do for ya?"

I tried to come up with a good cover story, I really did. If my brain had been working, I could have fabricated an incredible excuse that even a lie-smelling werewolf would have believed. The problem was I'd just been caught snooping around Senator Tanner's office and Dylan Drake had been one of the people to catch me. My brain wasn't functioning, and I couldn't answer the question. I thought it might be best to just pretend to be deaf.

Drake realized I was in trouble and walked up to me. He put his arm around my shoulder, hugging me to him. "Hey, beautiful! What a great surprise! I didn't think you were coming until later."

I managed to eke out a reply, "I got here early."

"I'll have to thank my staff for telling you where I was," he said, pulling me closer and rubbing his hand up and down my arm. He knew I'd been doing something nefarious. His roaming hands were a dare to stop me. I took a deep breath, smiling as I reached around his back and attempted to pinch the side of his torso—"attempted" being the operative word. There was nothing there to pinch. Drake grinned widely in response before turning his attention back to Tanner. "Senator, I'd like you to meet my girlfriend, Katie."

The senator rocked back on his heels and gave a wide smile. "Looks like you're robbin' the cradle a bit with that one, Drake."

Drake held me tighter. "Just trying to live up to my reputation." Drake was one of the non-rule following Mormons who got by on pure charm and the illusion he was a true believer because he knew what to say and went to church every Sunday. Most men in Utah couldn't get away with a playboy attitude; Drake was the exception. I imagined it was probably because the men he spent time around had wives and kids and were trying to live vicariously through bachelor-Drake.

"She the cutie you're bringin' to the legislature party at the Country Club tonight?" He directed his question at Drake like I wasn't even in the room. I clenched my teeth and fought not to tell Senator Tanner exactly what I thought of the patriarchal nature of politics—especially in Utah.

"Sure is," Drake said. "I wouldn't want anyone else to snag her up."

The senator chuckled. "I'll see you tonight." He turned and walked back into his private office.

With his arm still around me, Drake led me out of Senator Tanner's office. As soon as we were down the hall, I slipped out from under Drake's hold. "What did you just commit me to doing with you?" My voice was low and steady, but ready to jump three octaves at a moment's notice.

He gave me a mischievous look. "It's just a party," he said. "You'll have fun."

I gave him a wary stare. "I'm pretty sure my version of fun and yours are two very different things."

Drake smiled slowly. "If that's the case, we need to expand your definition."

"I'm not going with you." I rifled through my purse looking for my Jeep keys. "I'm sure you'll be able to find a Barbie bimbo who would be more convincing as your date to take my place."

Drake shook his head. "Oh, you're coming with me all right."

I stopped searching for my keys and met his eyes. "No. I'm not."

"Katie, why are you here?"

I stared at him in response.

"Because it was pretty obvious you were snooping around Tanner's office," he said. "In fact, if I hadn't been there to save you, I don't know how you would have gotten out of that situation. You couldn't even talk."

I wanted to stick my tongue out at him. If he hadn't shown up, I would have thought of a fabulous reason for why I'd been in Tanner's office. "I'm good at thinking on my feet. I would have figured something out. You just stole my thunder."

He laughed and leaned against the wall, holding me with his bright blue eyes. The eyes that weren't mesmerizing me. They weren't. "Listen, I know you probably won't tell me what you're looking for, but regardless, if you want information about state House and Senate members, this party will be your best chance to network and talk to people."

Hmm. I hated admitting Drake was right, but I couldn't really argue with his logic. He watched me as the internal debate I was having with myself played out on my face. "Fine," I finally consented, "I'll go with you, but this is a professional decision not a personal one."

He tilted his head, cocking an eyebrow in acknowledgment. "I did you a huge favor, you know. I saved you when you couldn't think of a cover story, and I got you into a party that might help you get the information you want. A party that I didn't have to ask you to."

"You're right," I said as I finally found my keys and put my purse back on my shoulder. "You didn't ask. You dictated." I turned and started to walk away as I heard Drake's voice.

"You owe me now."

I spun around. "I *what*?" My voice jumped four octaves, not three.

"I did you a favor. It's only fair you do me one if I ever need it."

I marched back to him. "That's why you want me to come with you?" I poked him hard in the chest. "So I have to give your lying politician's butt a favor?"

"I didn't say you have to, but you should probably consider it."

"What kind of favor are we talking about?"

He shrugged and grinned. "I don't know yet, but I'm sure I'll come up with something eventually."

If I didn't need to get into the party, I never would have agreed to Drake's terms, but he was right. I wanted the kind of access that being with Drake would give me. I pressed my lips together hard, and finally relented. "You know I think you're an asshat?"

"You're cute when you're mad," he said, pinching my cheek like I was five and he was my great uncle.

I pushed his hand away. As I walked off, I called back to him, "Jerk."

"I'll meet you at the Country Club at six," he said. "And get a nice dress for the party tonight, Katie. Something little and black."

I seethed as I kept walking, and fought the urge to flip him off on my way out the door. The only thing that could make this day worse was dress shopping.

I went to the nearest mall and wandered around the stores buying stuff I really didn't need. I stopped by the food court to get something to eat before the party so I could spend my time at the Country Club getting information instead of starving.

When I finished my greasy sub sandwich that was probably way more calories than it was worth, I went into one of the clothing stores to find something to wear. I'd guessed from Drake's 'little and black' description that it was a cocktail party. But since Utah was the least alcohol friendly state in the nation, I doubted they'd be serving any actual cocktails… and if they were, I wouldn't be allowed to partake or "Dylan Drake's Date Drinks" would surely be the lead story on the evening news. That was disappointing because I'd handle spending an evening with Drake much better if I had copious amounts of alcohol.

The store had plenty of little black things but I deliberately avoided them because of Drake's suggestion—which was unfortunate since black is so slimming. I settled on a short-sleeved dark blue dress that fell a few inches above my knees, made my waist seem smaller than it was, and had a neckline that showed a bit of cleavage. I found some black heels with a peep toe, paid for the clothes—which I planned to invoice the *Tribune* for—and changed in one of the dressing rooms.

I took some bobby pins from my purse and twisted my waves into a messy bun, with a few pieces of hair hanging down around my face. The dress color made my blue eyes bright, and the heels made me almost six feet tall. I didn't look like a prom queen, but I wasn't a zombie either.

I drove into the Country Club parking lot at five-forty-five and pulled into a parking spot. I picked my purse up from the seat, got out of the Jeep, and locked it with the keyless entry pad on my key ring.

I walked into the red and gold decorated lobby. Drake was sitting on a dark brown leather couch, still wearing the same black suit, blue shirt, and silver tie he'd been wearing earlier. He looked sexy as hell. He got up from the couch and came toward me, watching me with a steady stare that was so potent I could feel his eyes moving over my body. "That might just be better than little and black."

I glanced down at my dress. I'd thought it was pretty when I tried it on, but didn't think the sexy factor was through the roof.

He put his arm around my shoulder as he whispered, "I'm glad you decided to show up. It would have been hard to get a bimbo at the last minute." I glared as he took the purse from my hands and gave it to a woman in a white dress shirt and black pants at the coat check counter. "Will you put this with my things, Tera?"

"Of course, Mr. Drake," she said.

I watched her walk away with my purse. "I'm not sure I'm comfortable with a stranger having access to my wallet," I said warily. "My American Express card is in there." I love that card and all the Skymiles it gets me.

Drake gave me a condescending look. "People pay over a hundred thousand dollars to be members here."

My jaw dropped. "A hundred thousand dollars for a stupid club membership?" he nodded. "People are insane!"

"I wouldn't disagree with you, but I'm pretty sure if someone wanted to lift a credit card, it would be black, not gold, Katie."

I took offense. "How do you know my card isn't black?"

He tilted his head. "Is it?" he challenged.

I pursed my lips and narrowed my eyes in response. Drake smiled and put his hand on my back as he guided me through the building and onto a red and yellow stone patio. High-boy tables were scattered between smaller tables with chairs. The tablecloths were as blue as a summer sky, and white floral arrangements were placed in the center of all the tables. The Country Club building was on a hill that overlooked the club golf course. I could smell the fresh scent of soil and newly cut grass. A drink bar was set up on the east side of the patio. A buffet with light appetizers was spread on the south side.

"This is just a cocktail party and only lasts an hour," Drake said, steering me toward the drink bar. "People won't stay long; they're here to make an appearance before they go to dinner. Most of the senators and representatives here are people who live close to the capitol. Hopefully the person you need to talk to is in this group."

Without asking what I wanted, Drake ordered a virgin mojito for both of us. I sipped it and decided that without the rum, I might as well be drinking Sprite. We walked away from the drink bar and Drake said hello to some people, introducing me as his girlfriend again. I gave a rehearsed smile. I felt like I was being a pretty good sport about our fake relationship. I hoped my other fake boyfriend back at the *Tribune* wouldn't mind.

We arrived before Senator Tanner, so when he walked in with his wife, I acknowledged his attendance by squeezing Drake's bicep. It was larger than I expected it to be. Drake looked at me wondering what I wanted. It took me a minute to remember. "I'd like to talk to Tanner," I finally said.

"What for?"

"He knows the Bradfords."

"Why do you want to know more about the Bradfords?" he asked. "You've already written the articles about Chelsea's death. And how do you know that Tanner knows them?"

I hedged a little, not wanting to tell him where exactly I'd gotten the information.

"I can't help you with your story if I don't know some of the details."

I sighed and gave him a summary. "I'm investigating Chelsea Bradford's death. There's a rumor the guy she was dating was the son of a high-level Utah politician. So far, Tanner is one of the connections I've been able to find between Utah politics and the Bradfords."

Drake didn't seem at all surprised. "Like I told you before, the Bradfords lived in Salt Lake City before they moved to Branson Falls. I'm sure they know a lot of people from this area."

"Great, let's talk to Tanner now."

I started to walk away, but Drake gently grabbed my arm and pulled me back. "You didn't tell me how you found out Tanner knows the Bradfords."

I bit my lip. I certainly wasn't going to tell Drake about the list Hawke gave me. "I have my sources. Also, I might have seen their name in the rolodex on the desk in his office."

Drake gave me a measured stare. "You're sneaky," he said with a slight smile. "I'll have to watch out for you."

I nodded. "That's probably a good idea."

We walked arm-in-arm to greet Senator Tanner and his wife. She was thin, with smiling eyes and hair dyed a rich brown.

"Joan!" Drake smiled as he hugged the woman. "You're looking as beautiful as ever." Joan beamed at his compliment.

Drake turned to the senator. "You better watch out or some younger man is going to steal her away."

Senator Tanner smiled. "I won't have to worry about you anymore though, not with a pretty thing like that." He reached his hand toward me. "It's Katie, right?"

"Actually, it's Kate. Drake gets away with calling me Katie though," I said with a genuine smile. I couldn't believe the senator had remembered my name, especially since he'd mostly talked to Drake when I'd met him earlier—though I guess in politics, names are pretty important.

The senator's wife directed her attention at me. "So you're the lucky girl who's taken Drake off the market," she said. "I'm glad; he's been a menace to society for years." She smiled brightly. "I'm Joan."

"Well, I'm happy to help," I said, returning a wide smile. "It's nice to meet you, Joan."

"You too, Kate," she said before focusing on Drake once again. "Thank you for all your help with the hospital fundraiser. It makes such a difference to the kids and we wouldn't raise half the money we do without you."

"It's my pleasure, Joan," Drake said. "The kids and their families mean a lot to me."

I raised an eyebrow. I'd heard of Drake's *philandering*, but not his *philanthropy*. "What fundraiser is this?"

"The annual fundraiser for the children's hospital," said Joan. "We raise money so patients can get medical treatment regardless of whether they can pay for it. I'm the chairman of the committee. Drake is on the board of trustees and has always been our biggest supporter."

I looked at Drake, his face taking on a stoic quality. I quickly surmised he was uncomfortable with the topic of his generosity. He met my eyes. "I didn't know that about you."

Joan patted Drake on the arm, leaning in toward me. "He doesn't like to talk about it much, but he does incredible things for the community."

I gave Drake another assessing gaze. Obviously there were a lot of things I didn't know about him. Maybe I'd judged him too harshly. I was still reconsidering my opinion of Drake when Tanner asked, "Where ya from, Kate? I hope it's my district and I hope you're a voter."

I took a drink of my mojito / Sprite. "Actually, I'm in Drake's district. I grew up in Branson Falls."

"Look at that," Tanner said, punching Drake in the shoulder. "All the women you've gone through and the one you were lookin' for was right in your backyard all along."

"Oh," Drake stared at me for a few seconds, "I've had my eye on Katie for a while."

Tanner and Joan exchanged a glance and smiled as Drake took my hand.

"Has he taken you to church with him yet?" Tanner asked. "Because you know it's serious when he takes you to church." This is true. Going to church with someone you're dating is almost the equivalent of an engagement ring.

I bit back what I wanted to say in favor of an answer that wouldn't blow our cover. "No. We're not rushing things."

"Still," Joan said, her eyes sparkling with interest, "you drove all the way up here for a cocktail party. Church is the next step."

"Actually—" I started to say, but Drake cut me off.

"Not just the party," he answered. "Katie and I have reservations for dinner and a carriage ride downtown after this."

Joan's brow lifted. "That's romantic."

Drake grinned. "I'm hoping it will be."

I squeezed his hand and tried to take a deep breath

through my nose to calm myself down. "That's my Drake," I said with another wide smile as I dug my nails into his palm. "He's always planning something."

Drake leaned in to give me a kiss on my cheek and whispered discreetly in my ear, "You have no idea."

I could feel hot blood rushing to my cheeks and pinched Drake's hand until he moved away. Joan and Senator Tanner were still watching, clearly intrigued.

I needed to figure out how Senator Tanner knew the Bradfords and Drake wasn't helping. "So, Senator, have you and Drake known each other long?"

The senator swallowed a piece of the cucumber sandwich he'd been chewing. "Sure have! I met him when he was first elected, what was it . . ." he paused and looked at Drake for confirmation, "'bout two years ago?" Drake nodded in response. "He was put on the same committee as me and we've been friends ever since."

"It's nice he has such a wonderful mentor," I replied. Tanner gave a wide smile at the compliment. "Have you been to Branson Falls before?"

The senator nodded. "My wife and I have friends there."

"Oh, really?" I asked, feigning surprise. "What are their names? I probably know them."

Tanner looked up. "A family named the Bradfords. They lived here for years before they moved. We've visited them a couple of times. Great family."

"They live near my parents," I said.

Joan nodded. "It's just horrible news about their gorgeous daughter, Chelsea."

I looked solemnly at the ground. "Yes. It was an awful tragedy."

"We heard she drowned," the senator said.

I nodded. "Her body was found in Emerald Lake."

Joan looked away as if she was trying to comprehend the reason for such a heartbreaking death. Tanner shook his head. "I don't know how they're handling it so well. We were gonna go to the funeral but they had it so fast, we didn't even hear about it 'till it was over. It's a shame. Chelsea had so much going for her. She could've gone to any college she wanted. Shawn must be devastated."

"Shawn?" I asked, taking a sip from my drink.

Senator Tanner looked up at me. "Yeah, Chelsea's boyfriend. Shawn Wallace. The governor's son."

Chapter Twelve

I immediately choked on the fake mojito I'd been trying to swallow. Chelsea was dating the son of the governor? That was as high-level as politics in the state went! And if she'd been pregnant, no wonder they wanted to keep it quiet. The governor was up for re-election and what his kids did affected him at the polls. No one wanted a leader who couldn't control his own family—or teach them proper birth control.

Drake leaned over, handing me a napkin and patting my back as I coughed violently. A few people turned to see what the commotion was about. When I could talk again I said, "Sorry. I swallowed wrong."

The senator waved it off. "No big deal. Happens to me all the time."

Joan nodded in agreement as a member of the wait-staff brought me a glass of water. I sipped the icy water slowly so I wouldn't give a repeat performance of my liquid choking fit.

I couldn't believe the information I'd gotten. I needed to tell Hawke right away so he could use his own sources to find out more. I excused myself and stopped by the front desk to retrieve my purse. Once I was safely secured in a bathroom stall, I texted Hawke.

> Chelsea was dating Shawn Wallace, the governor's son! This could mean the Governor is involved in her death! Will call you tomorrow.

I got a text back almost immediately.

> You know, with that dress you could get a man to admit to murder. I'll see you soon, Kitty Kate.

Despite being in the women's bathroom, I looked around, now keenly aware that Hawke was watching me and probably had been all day. I put my phone back in my purse, checked my wallet—my gold card was still there—and took my purse back to the front desk before rejoining Drake who was now standing alone.

"Where did Senator Tanner and Joan go?" I asked.

"They left early. I figured the choking meant you got the information you needed, so I didn't try to stop them. I'm sure they'll be asking me when I'm taking you to church every time I see them now."

I snorted. "Good luck with that since I'm not religious anymore."

Drake's lips quirked up. "I'd heard that about you. It could be a problem when things get serious between us."

I lifted my brow. "That's a pretty arrogant thing to assume."

He locked eyes with me. "It would be a bad idea to underestimate me, Katie. I'm confident because I usually get the results I want."

I stared at him for a couple of seconds, trying to figure out how I fit into his results equation. "It takes two people to agree to a relationship. It would be a bad idea to assume you're calling all the shots." I paused long enough to catch my breath, but not long enough for Drake to reply. "Thanks for your help today."

He put his hands in his pockets, assessing me. "I think that's the first time you've ever thanked me." That wasn't entirely true. When I was younger I'd thanked him over and over again in my head for having such a nice butt, especially during football season. "So, you found out who Chelsea was dating. Now what?"

I wasn't sure how much I could trust Drake, and didn't want to give away more information than I needed to, so I gave an evasive answer. "Now I keep investigating."

I looked around at the small gathering of people and wondered why Drake spent so much time at the capitol. Most state House and Senate members have day jobs at home in their districts, but Drake always seemed to be at the capitol doing something political. "I'm pretty sure you spend a lot more time at the legislature than other state representatives and senators. What's the deal? Do you have a crush on an intern or something?"

He took a drink of his mojito / Sprite. "Several," he answered with a playful smile.

"That's great, Drake. How old are the interns, eighteen? You could be their dad. In fact, you might be!"

His eyes thinned infinitesimally. "No, I couldn't. I'm not that old and you know it." he gave me a knowing smile. "You used to say hi to me after football games."

I blinked, completely stunned. If he'd told me he was the reincarnation of Elvis it would have been easier to believe.

Drake's laugh made me regain my senses though. "You remember that?"

"Of course I do. You were cute Katie."

"Cute Katie?" I repeated the name slowly, trying it out. I didn't think I'd been a blip on Drake's radar when he was in high school. Apparently I had been—complete with a nickname that, considering my level of awkward at the time, I imagined was more condescending than complimentary. "Fantastic."

"And you grew up into sexy Katie Saxee."

I felt my face flush and knew I had just transformed into a tomato. I wish someone would invent a way to stop blushing. It gets me in all sorts of trouble. "Stop calling me Katie."

He locked eyes with me. "No."

"Why not?"

"Because I like pushing your buttons."

We stayed like that for several seconds, caught in a stare-off until another House member patted Drake on the back. Drake introduced me and we talked with several other people, me still posing as his girlfriend. When the topic of sex education came up and I gave my two cents that every high school student in the state should be given a banana and shown how to use a condom, Drake laughed it off, made a comment about what a comedian I was, and pulled me away. I thought I was about to get a talking to by my political overlord / date conspirator.

I decided to cut him off before he could get started. "Sorry. I'm kind of opinionated."

He walked me to the front desk, retrieved my purse, and followed me to the parking lot. "Your outspokenness hasn't gone unnoticed," Drake smiled. "And don't apologize. That was the most fun I've had in months."

I snorted. "I highly doubt that. I've heard you have fun at least once a night, sometimes more."

He bit the inside of his cheek giving him a half smile. "Do you want to find out?"

I took a deep breath. "I don't think I have the stamina."

"You're younger than I am by five years." I stared at him. His "cute Katie" revelation had surprised me, but the fact he knew our age difference left me momentarily stunned. "So you're either making excuses," he said with a cocked eyebrow, "or you're scared."

I met his eyes, and shook my head. "I wasn't talking about physical stamina." Drake looked confused. "I hate games, but game playing is your life. Whether it's women or politics, you love the challenge of winning and the thrill of getting what you want. In fact, all the girls' heads you screwed with in high school were probably the reason you decided to become a politician."

He gave me the most somber look I'd ever seen Drake wear. "I can't change who I am, Katie, but don't believe everything you hear."

I frowned, thinking he knew that piece of information about himself and had probably heard it before. "I'm sorry. I didn't mean to hurt your feelings. I thought you acted that way on purpose."

He took my keys, opened my Jeep door, and gently held my hand as he dropped the keys in my palm. He moved out of my way and stood with his hands in his pockets. "Have a safe trip home. Let me know if you need help with anything else," he said. "I'll be back in Branson in a few days."

We stared at each other for a few seconds. "Thanks, Drake. I really do appreciate it." Finally I got in the Jeep and turned the key. "Have a good night," I said, shutting the door. I backed out of the parking spot and drove away with Drake still standing where I'd left him.

Chapter Thirteen

I woke to the pitter-patter of rain on my windows. I love rainstorms and like them even more during the summer. The cool water is a welcome respite from the sweltering July days. I kicked off my top sheet, the only cover I sleep with during the summer heat, and stretched. I convinced myself to sit up, and then stand. Still groggy, I swayed over to the other side of the room.

I opened my window to take a deep breath of the earthy smell of water hitting dusty sidewalks, and decided to leave the window open while I took a shower. When I got out, I threw on some dark-wash jeans, a purple cotton blouse, and brushed on mineral makeup, mascara, and pink lip gloss. I was almost finished drying my wavy hair when "Forever in Blue Jeans" started playing on my cell phone. I answered. "So, I hear you've dumped me and moved on with Drake," Spence said.

I closed my eyes tight and opened them again, hoping I was just having a nightmare. "Where did you hear that?"

"Where didn't I? It's all over town this morning."

"Of course it is. I hope another piece of gossip comes along soon so people will stop talking about me."

Spence chuckled. "I doubt they'll ever stop talking about you, but I have a story that might take the focus off you for a little while."

"What's going on?"

"A call just came in on the scanner. A car accident was reported on Abbey Lane. I don't have much more information than that. Can you go see what happened?"

"Sure." I grabbed my camera and purse as I slipped on a pair of brown leather sandals. "I'll take care of it."

"Thanks," Spence said. "I'll talk to you later."

The rain had tapered off, but the roads were still wet so I was careful as I drove the eight miles to Abbey Lane. The lane was actually a long stretch of rural road that wound its way through fields and farms with an occasional house here and there. I followed the road until I saw the fire truck and ambulance.

I got out of the car and walked past the emergency vehicles. I stopped when I came to a small, white Chevy Metro with the hood smashed in like a boulder had crashed on top of it. In front of the Metro, I found the thing that had done the damage: a huge black and white cow, dead in the middle of the road. I looked from the cow, to the Metro, and back to the cow. I'd heard of people hitting deer before, at night, when it was dark and the sprightly dumb deer went dancing across the road without a care in the world. I'd never heard of someone hitting a cow, regardless of the time of day. Cows generally stay off the road unless they're being herded there, and they move so slowly it's not difficult to dodge them.

I pulled my eyes away from the scene long enough to get my camera out and start snapping photos. As I got a close up of the windshield, I noticed a set of holes about eighteen inches apart. The holes were both the same size and looked like someone had thrown two fist-sized rocks into the windshield parallel to each other. The holes were both in front of the driver's seat, one near the edge of the windshield and the other by the rearview mirror.

I kept taking photos, surprised I hadn't been stopped by the police yet. Then again, maybe they had finally decided to let me onto accident and crime scenes without a fight . . . or Hawke to intervene. I doubted it though; I wasn't that lucky. I needed to find out what had happened and went in search of someone who could help me. I didn't have to go far—Bobby was leaning against a tow truck.

"I should've known you'd show up," Bobby said. "How's your investigation of Chelsea Bradford goin'?" he asked with a smirk. "You figure out it was just an accident yet?"

I gave him a sweet smile in return. "Wouldn't you like to know?"

He watched me for a minute trying to ascertain whether I had actual information or was just trying to bait him. Deciding on the baiting theory, he waved me off. "Eh, you ain't found nothin'. Like I said, it's a waste a time."

I didn't elaborate on all the information I had found, or how embarrassed he'd be when the real story eventually came out. Instead I gestured to the car and dead cow in front of me. "What in the world happened?"

"The fence at the Brady's farm was down. One of the cows got out and got hit."

"And the cow died?" I asked. "From a crash with a Chevy Metro?" I scratched my head trying to figure out how a Metro could kill something as large as a rabbit, let alone a cow.

"The Metro was goin' pretty fast."

Fast? It had to have been going the speed of light to do that kind of damage. "Was the driver hurt?"

"No, but she's pretty shaken up."

"How fast was the car going?"

"Faster than it should've been for the conditions, that's for sure. You ought to talk to your mom about that. With the wet roads, she didn't have time to slow down."

I started to ask another question before what Bobby had said sank in. "Wait, did you just say 'my mom'?"

"Yeah, didn't you know?"

"Of course I didn't!" I yelled, my eyes darting around the scene. "Where is she?"

Bobby pointed to the ambulance. "It's like her second home."

I rushed over. There was my mom, sitting on a bed inside the ambulance getting some scratches on her face and arms treated. "Mom! Are you okay?"

"Oh, I'm fine." She said with a wave of her hand, wincing as Annie applied a sterilizing solution. "I'm glad you're here though. I don't want to bother your dad at work, so you can give me a ride home."

I looked to Annie and the other paramedics for confirmation that she wasn't more hurt than she seemed. "It's just scratches and bruises," Annie answered. "She'll be all right, as usual."

"How did this happen?" I asked, still watching from the outside of the ambulance.

"See," Mom started to explain, "this is why I like trucks. What in the world do the people at the insurance company think will happen when they give me a car the size of a Tinker Toy to drive around? Did you see the prints on the seat where the cow's muddy hooves came through the windshield? If my head would've been a little to the left or right, I would have been smashed by a cow hoof! The insurance company should have given me a truck with a deer catcher like all the other trucks around here. Then I wouldn't have had this problem. Anyone with a brain can see this wasn't my fault."

There was so much information in her breathless explanation that I could hardly process it. "You crashed the car the insurance company gave you to replace the truck you torched?"

She glared at me. "I didn't "torch" it. It had a defective engine that got too hot. That wasn't my fault either. And I'm going to call the insurance company and complain to them about giving me a proper-sized loaner vehicle."

I shook my head. "And you crashed the Metro because you were driving too fast and couldn't stop for the defenseless cow?"

She gave me an indignant look. "It's not my fault the cow meandered into the road and decided to commit cowicide," she said as Annie bandaged her wounds. "The car was so low to the ground that when I saw the cow, I thought it was a person. My first thought was, 'why is someone standing in the middle of the road in a rainstorm wearing fur pants?' I swerved, but it was only enough to miss a person, not a whole cow! What was I supposed to do? I'm not used to those silly, tiny European cars! I'm not French! I'm used to trucks. A truck would have stopped—or at least barreled on through."

I didn't point out that the Chevy Metro is an American car. "Okay, can we go back to the cow hooves? How did *that* happen?"

I could tell the story was going to be good because she took a deep breath before starting her explanation. "When I hit the cow it came flying at me over the hood like Superman trying to take off and failing. The cow smashed the hood of the car and you know," she nodded her head thoughtfully, "I really think it knew what was happening. I could see the terror in its eyes and it could tell it was about to squash me. Its two front legs were out in front of its body and the legs came through the windshield." That explained the two fist-sized holes I'd seen. "Both legs hit the seat on either side of my head and braced the weight of the rest of the cow. Between that and the windshield, I was saved. But I was pinned in the car by cow legs. The nice firemen were able to move the cow enough to get the legs out of my way. I just got some scratches from the broken glass." She gingerly touched the bandages Annie had finished wrapping.

My mouth had fallen open way back at my mom's conviction that the cow had braced itself to save her life. I was having a hard time getting my jaw back to a normal position. My dad would never believe this—actually, he probably would, and that was the scary part.

"Am I good to go, Annie?" she asked the paramedic.

"Yeah, you know the drill. Go to the hospital if you start feeling funny."

"I will. See you next time!" She waved as she hopped down from the ambulance.

"Thanks for helping her . . . again," I said to Annie.

Annie grinned. "She keeps us in business."

"Come on!" My mom pulled me toward the dead Metro—and cow. "I'll pose for some pictures and call the insurance company on the way back to the house."

I drove in silence, listening to my mom's half of the conversation with the insurance company. At some point in my mom's life, she'd been like the rest of us and had to call the number on the back of the insurance card and wait for someone to help her. But for as long as I could remember, she'd had her own personal insurance representative to contact each time she had another disaster. They even exchanged Christmas cards.

Her representative told her that instead of sending another replacement vehicle, they'd just mail the money for her truck to her. It was a wise financial move on their part. They probably would've ended up replacing every loaner car they gave her while waiting for an investigation to conclude that the truck was, in fact, totaled.

I pulled into my parents' driveway at the same time she got off the phone. "What are you going to tell Dad?"

"Same thing I always tell him. That it wasn't my fault." She opened the car door. "Come in and get some sugar cookies. I made them before the cow tried to kill me."

As we walked in the house, my mom said, "I want to know more about the Crandalls' purple pig. If they don't find out what's wrong, no one will buy the pig when the county fair comes around."

"Actually," I said, "the pig has become pretty popular. The Crandalls told me that since the story came out, people all over the state want to visit. They even decided to name it Wilbur, you know, like in *Charlotte's Web*."

My mom gave me her proud motherly smile, patting me on the back. "Look at you! Your story saved that pig's life."

Personally, I thought Mom was giving me a little too much credit, but I didn't contradict her.

I sat at the table while my mom went into the kitchen. A copy of *The Branson Tribune* was on the table. A picture of Chelsea stared up at me from the front page. I wondered if my parents had talked to the Bradfords at all since Chelsea's death. "Have you heard how the Bradfords are doing?" I asked her.

My mom paused, but didn't look up from her cookie frosting. "I talked to Julia when she brought back my casserole dish."

"Did she seem okay?"

"Julia is always okay. I've never seen her in a situation where she wasn't poised and refined. She did mention that Chelsea's siblings were having a hard time, though."

"I can imagine," I said, nodding. "What about Julia's husband?"

"Brian?" my mom asked, her frosting covered knife poised in the air as she thought about it. "You know, I haven't really seen him. His company is based in Salt Lake, and he works so much that he isn't around Branson a lot."

That seemed strange. "His daughter just died, but he hasn't stayed home to help his family cope with the grief?"

She shrugged. "Everyone deals with death in different ways."

I was skeptical, but decided she was probably right. When people have to deal with a difficult situation, a lot of times they'll immerse themselves in a project for a sense of comfort. Maybe that's what Brian Bradford was doing with his work.

My mom went back to frosting her cookies. I picked the newspaper up, only to find ten different colored flash drives lined up like they were in some sort of portable-file-carrying-device army.

"Mom," I said, holding the newspaper in the air and staring at the drives. "Why do you have ten flash drives?"

"What?" My mom asked in a pleasant tone as she threw a kitchen hand towel over her shoulder. She always had one hanging there, just in case there was a sudden liquid emergency. I watched as she carefully placed frosted cookies on a plate.

I pointed to the flash drives. "Why do you have ten of these?" Maybe my mom was some sort of spy and I didn't know it. I couldn't think of any other reason for needing that many flash drives. And if she was a spy, the naïve Catasophie I knew was a very good cover. No one would ever guess.

"Flash drives?" she asked, turning around to look at where I was pointing. "Is that what they're called?" She took two glasses from the cabinet above her head and poured a glass of milk for each of us. "I always just ask the salespeople for the sticks that move files from one computer to the other."

I shook my head, trying not to bang it against the table. I imagined that salespeople dreaded having to help her find anything. "Why in the world do you have so many?" I asked. "Most people only have one!"

She brought the milk and cookies to the table and sat across from me. "Well, my computer was going slow and having all kinds of problems. Sometimes when it turns on, the screen is just a mess of strange letters and things written in Japanese. The salesperson at the computer store said I could use these drives to move files from my computer to my laptop, so that's what I've been doing."

"That still doesn't answer why you have ten of them," I said, taking a bite of my star-shaped sugar cookie heaped with cherry flavored white frosting and red and blue sprinkles. Mom had a different cookie shape for every holiday. Since Independence Day was in July, she made stars.

"Because the sticks keep filling up, silly! As soon as one's full, I have to get another one. That's why they're all different colors, so I can tell them apart." The logic was so astounding I choked on my cookie. "I had to color some of the sticks with a marker to identify them. They should really make more of a color spectrum selection for those things." When I finished coughing, I took a drink of my milk while I held up a hand to let her know I was okay.

"Mom," I said in a hoarse voice from the angry cookie that had been caught in my throat. "Why don't you just delete the files from your flash drive once you move them from your computer to your laptop?"

"You can delete the files?"

This time I did bang my head on the table and left it there. "Yes, you can delete them," I explained to the carpet, which probably grasped my statement about as well as my mom. "Come on," I said, getting up. "I'll teach you."

I showed her how to save files to the laptop from the drive and then delete the files, though I had no doubt if she tried to delete them on her own, she'd probably end up deleting the files from both the flash drive and the laptop. I advised her to have me over to supervise, or do it for her. The old adage of teaching a man to fish was not always wise when my mom was involved. When we were done I stood up and walked back to the kitchen to retrieve my keys and purse.

"We're roasting hot dogs and marshmallows over the fire pit in the back yard two nights from now. You can bring Dylan if you want." She stopped to level a stare at me and point her finger. "And the next time you start seeing someone, especially someone like Dylan Drake, you better tell me immediately. Do you know how embarrassing it was to have to hear who my daughter is dating from one of The Ladies?"

I put my hands on my hips, completely annoyed. "Who told you I was dating him?"

"I ran into Amber Kane at the grocery store. She said you and Dylan had been out a couple of times so it must be pretty serious." Only in a place like Branson Falls could going out a couple of times equate a serious relationship. And we hadn't even "gone out!" We'd had a couple of exchanges in public places. "I told Amber that surely you would have said something," Mom paused, "but she assured me she was right. She also asked when you're going to start going to church again."

I looked up from digging through my purse for some gum. "First of all, they know I'm not religious anymore. Second, why am I getting picked on about this? They don't harass you and dad about not going to church?"

She lifted her shoulders. "Because our names are still on the church records and we still meet with people from church about once a month."

I narrowed my eyes. The lack of respect for my religious beliefs was getting frustrating. "Whatever," I said, shaking it off. "As for the other rumor, *I* assure you that I am not dating Dylan Drake. We just keep running into each other because of a story I'm working on. It has nothing to do with my dating life, or lack thereof."

"If that's what you say," she said, refolding the towel and throwing it back over her shoulder. Then she did a shifty-eyed gaze around the room—just in case Lady spies had infiltrated the house—and bent down to whisper in my ear. "But you know his reputation. Get some protection—but not from here, you'll have to go out of town where people won't recognize you."

I gasped as my eyes went wide with shock. It's not like I have a problem discussing sex with my parents, but we'd never discussed my sex life, or theirs. I think we all like to pretend that none of us has one.

My mom gave a knowing smile. "Don't look so surprised. You're young, there's nothing wrong with finding out what you like." My eyes bulged even more when she giggled—yes, giggled.

I shook my head as I picked up my plate of cookies, glad to be leaving so I wouldn't have to continue this conversation. I said good-bye to my mom, and wished her good luck explaining the cow to my dad. I suggested 'scared out of her mind' as the emotion she should use when she gave her version of the story to him, and I drove home.

Chapter Fourteen

One of the things I like most about being a reporter is the ability to work from home. After the conversation I'd just had with my mom, I needed some time to recover. When I got to my house, I noticed a familiar car sitting on the street. By the time I pulled into the driveway and walked around to the front yard, Hawke was leaning against the house by my front door, one thumb looped inside the pocket on the front of his jeans. "You have a minute?" he asked.

I nodded and he followed me inside.

"How long have you been waiting for me?" I asked, wondering how he knew I'd be at my house instead of the office.

He looked around the living room at my soft beige suede couches, striped blue rug, and black coffee table. When he'd finished his mental catalog of my room, he turned back to me. "I stopped by the office. Spence said you'd been on a story all morning, and would probably work from home for a while."

I pulled my brows together. It surprised me Spence had given "untrustworthy" Hawke any information. Maybe

Spence just didn't want Hawke hanging around the office all day waiting for me though.

"You did a good job getting the information about Shawn Wallace." He put a photo down on my coffee table as he sat on the couch. "That's an updated picture of Shawn. I thought you might want a copy."

"Thanks," I said, picking up the photo. Shawn had auburn hair that was cut short and he wore it spiky in the front. He was young with fair skin, a soft face, and bright red cheeks, but his body was so lean you could see the veins sticking up in his arms.

"We know Shawn was the father of Chelsea's baby, so it's not a stretch to think he's somehow involved in her disappearance and maybe even her death."

"Yeah, but how can we verify our information?" I asked. "We only know that he was dating Chelsea. We don't actually even have proof Shawn was the father." I looked at the hardwood floor, thinking. "I need to talk to Shawn Wallace."

Hawke shook his head. "You can't get an interview with Shawn."

"Why not?"

"Because since Chelsea's death, his mom's had him locked down like he's in Fort Knox."

"How do you know that?"

Hawke just stared at me like I should know by now that he could find Jimmy Hoffa if he wanted to. Unlike everyone else in the world, it seemed Hawke had unlimited access to almost any information. Unless the information required boobs—then he needed me.

"That's just great," I said, plopping down next to Hawke on the couch. "The most important person I need to talk to is unavailable for comment."

"We'll work around it."

"How?"

"I want to talk to some of the people Chelsea went to school with," Hawke said. "Do you have time to go out tonight?"

I shrugged. "Sure. Where are we going?"

"The bowling alley and arcade," Hawke said, standing up. "It's the only place in town where kids can get away from their parents." I couldn't argue with that; I'd spent a lot of time hanging out there myself as a teenager. "I'll pick you up here at seven-thirty," he said as he walked out the door.

As we pulled into the parking lot of the bowling alley, I saw a group of teenagers loitering outside. The girls were blushing and trying to get the guys to pay attention to them. The boys were trying to act like they didn't care and weren't about to trip over their own low-hanging pants. Hawke parked the Mustang several spots away from all the other cars, turned the engine off, locked the doors, and we walked up to the group of teenagers.

"Heeeyyy!" A kid with messy hair dyed a combination of blue and black pointed at me. "It's the reporter lady!" How he knew this about me, I'll never know. It didn't seem like his synapses were firing fast enough to remember his own name. He switched his gaze to Hawke—who at the moment was dressed all in black—and backed away, a nervous expression on his face. "And the scary dude."

Hawke looked at the kid, and then me. "Is he drunk, or high?"

I shrugged. "Maybe both?"

"Duuuude!" he said, inching a bit closer to Hawke, his mouth hanging open in awe. "Why are you so big? You're like the Green Giant!" I wondered if the kid knew how much he sounded like he'd stepped straight out of *Bill and Ted's Excellent Adventure*.

Hawke watched the kid with a combination of amusement and annoyance. There was no doubt in my mind Hawke knew he could have the kid peeing his pants in sheer terror in about three seconds flat. I gave Hawke a look that said don't try it. "We want information," I said to Hawke. "Doing that won't help us get it."

Hawke cocked his head. "It might."

"We're not playing good cop, bad cop."

"Fine," said Hawke. "We'll try your way first."

"Dudes," the kid said, beginning to laugh. "You're not cops!" The laugh had started slow and didn't stop for at least thirty seconds or more. Finally he looked from Hawke to me. "Information about what, my buddies?" Now all the kids around him had directed their attention toward us.

"I was wondering if any of you knew Chelsea Bradford?" I asked.

"Sure!" he said, swaying a little. "Everybody knew that chick." Great. Keanu had been chosen as the group spokesperson.

"Were any of you friends with her? Or did you hang out together much?"

Keanu looked around the group. No one said anything so he answered, "She liked to come to the bowling alley."

"Was she ever with anyone?"

"Umm . . ." his thinking process took at least a minute. I met Hawke's stare. I could tell he wanted to slap Keanu until he came back to his senses and could talk to us. "Yes!" Keanu yelled so loud and out of the blue that I startled a little. "Sometimes she brought a dude with her."

"A dude meaning a boy?" I asked. I felt like I should clarify since 'dude' didn't seem to be gender specific in Keanu's world.

"Yeah, dude! The dude was a boy!"

"Do any of you remember his name?" I asked, looking toward the other kids in the group, hoping we'd be able to deal with one who wasn't as impaired as Keanu. None of them came forward. I was counting on one of them to have some information. I wanted confirmation that Chelsea had been seen with Shawn Wallace. I also wanted to know more about Chelsea and Shawn's relationship. The adults who knew Chelsea weren't talking, and neither were her friends. But Keanu and his buddies weren't shy, so if they had information, I'd be happy to take it.

"Dudes! I know it!" he said. "I just have to think." Great, we could be here for a week.

Keanu surprised me when he came up with a letter. " "S!" It started with an "S." "

"Shawn?" I hinted.

He pointed at me. "Yessss!" He did a quick little dance and looked at me with glassy eyes. "You're like a reporter lady psychic or somethin'."

I ignored him and asked another question. "Do any of you remember Chelsea and Shawn being together? Like if they were happy or not?"

Keanu turned to Hawke. "Giant dude," he pointed at Hawke and slowly moved his hand to gesture in the general direction of the parking lot. "You have a righteous car."

Amusement was clearly winning out over annoyance, and Hawke was doing his best not to laugh.

"Hey, *dude*," I said. "Focus. Do any of you know if Chelsea and Shawn seemed happy?"

A girl with brown stringy hair, who was decidedly more lucid than the others, spoke up, "Sometimes they were happy and would just goof off playing pool and eating pizza. But it seemed like they fought a lot too."

I turned my attention to the girl who could actually answer questions without the word 'dude' or sixty second conversation pauses. "Do you know what they fought about?"

"Not really. But I know they broke up and got back together a lot." The girl twirled her hair around her finger. "He wasn't from around here. Chelsea was already dating him when she moved to Branson Falls, but they broke up and Chelsea went out with a bunch of guys. She wasn't serious with any of them though. One day Chelsea showed up here with her friends and he was with them all again."

"Did they break up any time after that?" I asked.

"Yeah, a few times. Like I said, they were always breaking up and getting back together."

So their relationship was volatile, but that wasn't a surprise. What teenage relationship wasn't? What adult relationship wasn't for that matter?

"When was the last time you saw the two of them together?"

The girl lifted her eyes like she was doing calculations in her head. "In March, during spring break. Right before Chelsea dropped out of school. They were here with a big group of people."

"People from Branson?"

"Yeah. Popular kids."

I sighed. Probably the same kids that had been at Chelsea's funeral. Ones like Piper, who weren't comfortable talking about Chelsea, or what happened to her. The last thing I needed was angry Branson parents upset with me for interrogating their kids. I was surprised I hadn't gotten a phone call from Piper's parents. She must not have told them she'd talked to me. I didn't think we'd get any other information out of the kids. "Thanks for your help," I said and looked at Hawke. "Do you have any questions?"

"Nope, I think you covered it," Hawke said.

"Thanks for chattin' with us, dudes!" Keanu said, holding up his hand in a peace sign. He had his decades seriously confused.

I nodded to the kids as Hawke and I walked back to his car.

"Apparently the police don't take pot and alcohol too seriously in Branson," Hawke said.

I shrugged. "It seems the cops are pretty easy to bribe."

He started the engine. "You have experience?"

"A little."

"What did you bribe them with?" he asked, turning onto the street.

"I got pulled over, but Officer Bob was called away before any bribe suggestions were exchanged. Ella bribes them with key lime pies to get out of tickets though."

Hawke looked over at me to see if I was serious, and laughed. When he was done, he asked, "What do you think about Chelsea and Shawn's relationship?"

I paused for a few seconds to consider his question. "That they were like every other teenager and had a hard time making a relationship last."

"Do you think their relationship had something to do with her death?"

"I'm not sure. I can't put the pieces together yet. If Shawn was the father of Chelsea's baby, I wouldn't be surprised."

"He was."

"How do you know?"

Again, Hawke looked at me like I was crazy and he knew everything. "You're not the only one investigating, Kate."

"Who's your source?"

He shook his head, smiling slightly. "I can't tell you that. And you can't talk to them either."

I thinned my eyes. "That's really annoying. I can't guarantee the information without talking to the source myself."

"You're just going to have to trust me," he answered. "So where do you want to go from here?" he asked, pulling up in front of my house.

Something had been bothering me ever since Piper told me Chelsea had been pregnant. "If Chelsea had the baby, where is it? I mean, her baby wasn't found at the lake. Did she leave it with someone else? Did she decide to go through with the adoption plan? Did she take the baby with her, and if so, does that mean her murderer now has the kid?" I shuddered at the thought. If someone was crazy enough to kill Chelsea, what would they do to her child?

He shifted in his seat, leaning his shoulder against the door. "I was wondering about that too. I'm looking into it."

"Should I be looking into it too?"

He shook his head. "Not right now. We'll figure this out faster if we both follow different angles and keep each other informed."

I nodded and looked out the window, thinking about what the next move should be. "I want to ask around about the governor." Hawke stared at me and I continued, "He wouldn't have wanted the pregnancy to become public. He might be involved in what happened to Chelsea. In any case, it doesn't hurt to check."

Hawke gave me an emotionless cop-face. I wondered if the expression was something that could be taught. If so, I desperately needed to learn how to do it. "Okay, you work on that," he said. "I'll see what I can find out from my end and call you tomorrow."

Chapter Fifteen

"There's a farmer claiming the Bradford's dog bit him," Spence said, hanging up his phone. "The police and an ambulance are on the scene. Can you go over there?"

I took a sip of my mocha coffee—it had been a two cup kind of morning. I'd planned on going to the Bradford's later today to try and get some more information about Chelsea, so this was a perfect excuse. "Yeah, I need to talk to Julia anyway."

"How's the story going?" Spence asked. "Any new leads?"

"Chelsea used to hang out with Shawn and some of her other friends at the bowling alley. People saw her there and knew the guy she was dating was named Shawn, but no one seemed to know he was the governor's son."

"So Shawn and Chelsea were keeping his identity a secret?"

"It seems like it," I said. "I don't know how many people in Branson knew who he really was. Maybe no one. The governor keeps his family out of the press as much as possible, so it wouldn't be surprising if no one around here recognized him. Plus, other than the bowling alley, he and Chelsea didn't seem to go out in public together much."

"Anything else?"

"Aside from the insane number of drunk and doped kids who hang out at the bowling alley, no."

Spence laughed. "Wasn't it like that when you lived here?"

"Not to this extent," I said, grabbing my keys, purse, and camera.

"Well, maybe you can tackle that story when you finish the Bradford investigation."

"Yeah, I'll put it at the top of my list, right up there with police bribery and "hot chocolate" thermoses."

"Only the devil drinks coffee, you know."

"I've heard. I guess that makes me one of his minions." I flashed Spence a smile as I walked out the door.

Spence hadn't been kidding; there really was an ambulance and police car for a simple dog bite. Julia Bradford was standing about fifteen feet away from the ambulance, her hand pressed against her forehead like she was trying to fend off a headache. She was talking to a police officer and barely acknowledged my presence.

As I looked inside the open emergency vehicle doors, I saw EMT Annie, and David Jones, a retired farmer with stark white hair, sitting on the stretcher inside. He was wearing his daily uniform of overalls—and despite the heat—had on a plaid long sleeve shirt more suitable for a rodeo than an afternoon walk. As I watched Annie tend his wounds, I couldn't stop thinking it was a relief to see someone other than my mom sitting there. "Hi, Annie," I said.

She smiled. "Nice to see you at a scene that doesn't involve your mom, Kate."

"I'm surprised she hasn't come over here yet." I looked in the direction of my parents' house. "She's probably listening on the scanner."

"The police scanner is more entertaining than TV in Branson . . . especially with your mom around."

I laughed. "I can't argue with that." I shifted my attention from Annie to the dog bite victim. "Hi, Mr. Jones." I leaned into the ambulance, putting my hand out for him to shake. "I'm Kate Saxee, with *The Branson Tribune*."

Mr. Jones practically jumped off the stretcher. Annie ducked to avoid being hit by his flailing arms. "Gawl dang! I got the press here!" he yelled. "That's what happens when you get attacked by an angry beast!" He was talking loud enough that Julia Bradford and the police officer stopped speaking until he was done.

"Do you want to tell me what happened?" I asked Mr. Jones.

He gave me a wide-eyed, crazed look. "I got bit by a dang devil dog!" he said. "That's what happened!"

I looked up at the Bradford's house. Their tiny brown and black Yorkie was standing between the curtains on the back of their living room couch, his button nose pressed against the window, tail wagging. Not many people could be afraid of something so cute. "Are you talking about the Bradford's Yorkshire Terrier?"

"Darn straight I am! The little sucker's a vampire dog!" he insisted. "Look at these marks!" Admittedly, the marks were more substantial than I expected, but nothing a little peroxide and a Band-Aid couldn't fix.

"You were scared of a five-pound terrier?" I asked.

"They live up to their names," he said. "Little terrorists, that's what they are," he winced as Annie applied some antibiotic to the bites.

"It's not a terrorist," I tried to explain. "It's a terrier."

"Same thing!" he yelled, pointing to the bites.

"It's smaller than a newborn baby!"

"That don't make a bit a difference. Black widows'll kill ya and they don't weigh no more than a peanut!"

He had me there. The logic of a redneck farmer. "Is there a reason he attacked you?"

This time the officer on the scene stepped in. "Yeah, the reason was that Mr. Jones tried to use the dog as a football."

I inhaled a sharp breath. Nothing makes me angrier than animals being abused. I stared at him until I could calmly ask, "You kicked a defenseless dog?"

"You kiddin' me?" Mr. Jones asked. "Look at these marks," he said, pointing to them again. "You think that dog is defenseless?"

I clenched my teeth. "Why did you kick the dog?"

"It looked like it was gonna attack! I was savin' myself."

"And by 'looked like it was going to attack'," the officer said, "Mr. Jones actually means the dog was running in circles in the front yard, playing with its ball and started barking when Mr. Jones walked by."

I was fighting hard to be objective but the story was just making me angrier. "Did other people see this happen?"

"Yes. The neighbors across the street and Julia Bradford saw the whole thing," the officer answered.

"Can I talk to them?"

"Go ahead." The cop pointed to where Julia was having a hushed discussion with a middle-aged woman in a blouse, fitted pants, and high heels.

I turned back to the ambulance. "Mr. Jones, if I publish a story about you kicking a tiny puppy, you'll probably get a lot of hate mail." In my head I added that the first letter would be from me. Mr. Jones wrinkled his nose, waving his hand like he was telling me to go away. "I'm going to interview a few other people, but you should think pretty hard about whether there's anything else you want me to write in the article."

Mr. Jones didn't say anything, so I left to talk to Julia Bradford and her neighbor. "Hi, Julia," I said as I walked up.

"Kate," she answered. "This is my neighbor, Stacy Reed."

"Hi, Stacy. Can you both give me your versions of what happened?"

They repeated the same story the officer had already told me. I jotted down some notes, took some adorable photos of Cuddles, the terrier, and some much less adorable shots of Mr. Jones.

After the police, ambulance, and neighbors left, I caught Julia Bradford as she was going into her house. "Julia, I was wondering if I could talk to you again?"

She looked at me with an emotionless face. "Of course," she said. "Please, come inside."

"Thank you," I answered as Cuddles twirled and wagged his tail, welcoming me back to his home.

"I'm sorry you had to deal with Mr. Jones." My eyes fell on the perfect family photos hanging on the walls in the hall. "With everything else going on in your life, I'm sure that was the last thing you needed today."

"Thank you for your concern," Julia said, "but I'm fine."

"You handle things well."

"Thank you," she said, sitting on a chair in the living room. I looked at the couch, wondering if it would try to eat me again today. I decided to risk it and sat . . . and sank. "What exactly do you need from me, Kate?"

The last time I'd talked to Julia was two days after Chelsea's body had been found. I didn't want to drag up bad memories for her, but I really needed to know what information the Bradfords had about Chelsea, Shawn, and the pregnancy. "I just have some more questions about Chelsea." Julia's mouth formed a thin line. I knew talking about her dead daughter was the last thing she wanted to do, but the police didn't suspect foul play and someone needed to find out what had really happened. "Was she dating anyone at the time of her death?"

Julia's face retained the blank stare. "She dated a number of boys."

"Do you know of any she was particularly interested in?"

It was clear Julia didn't want to answer my question and deflected it. "Why are you here, Kate? The police ruled Chelsea's death an accident. Our family is struggling to deal with this tragedy and we just want to move on. Can't you respect that?"

I glanced at the floor for a few seconds, feeling guilty for pressing the issue. "I'm sorry, Julia. I don't mean to bring up painful memories. I'm just trying to find out if Chelsea's death was really an accident."

"Why in the world would you think it's not?" Julia asked as her eyes narrowed and anger started to show through the controlled masque she was wearing.

"Because the evidence I have points to the contrary."

She gave me a doubtful look. "What evidence?"

I looked her in the eye so I wouldn't miss her reaction. "The fact that she died under what I believe are suspicious circumstances—and that she was pregnant."

Julia let out a little gasp, covering her mouth before she turned away. After a minute I heard her small voice ask, "How did you find out?"

"I investigated," I answered. "Was her pregnancy the reason you got the autopsy done so quickly and had the funeral service so soon after her death?"

She stood and stared out the large living room window, her calm demeanor replaced by anxiety. She'd been hesitant to answer my questions before, but now I knew Chelsea's secret, I hoped she'd be more willing to confide in me. "We didn't want people in Branson to find out. We didn't want her reputation to be soiled. Once her body was found, we decided the quicker we could get the funeral over with, the sooner people would stop talking about Chelsea's death and there would be less chance that the pregnancy information would leak."

Soiled reputation? Who even says that anymore? "Did you send Chelsea away to have the baby somewhere else?"

Julia nodded absently. "She went to live with friends in another state. I was supposed to fly out and help her through the birth."

"What do you mean you were *supposed* to?"

Tears formed at the corners of Julia's eyes. In a raspy voice she was fighting to control she said, "A few weeks before Chelsea was due, she ran away from our friends' home. She had planned to give the baby up for adoption, but she changed her mind."

"Why do you think she decided not to go through with the adoption?"

"I think she truly loved her baby and just couldn't give it up. Maybe some part of her thought she could start a family of her own and that's why she ran." Julia picked up a tissue, dabbing it under her nose. "We don't even know where she had the baby. Obviously she did though, because she wasn't pregnant when she died."

The tears that had been pricking Julia's eyes overflowed. "We talked to her on the phone a lot while she was gone. She just changed her mind." Julia grabbed another tissue from the cream and gold ceramic tissue holder sitting on the side table next to her. "I tried to convince her it was a bad idea. Brian told her the same thing, but she was determined to keep the baby. She knew how we felt and didn't think we'd agree to help her, so she left a note at our friends' house, and ran away." Julia broke down into sobs. "That was the last time anyone we know of saw her before she died. We never met our grandchild. We still don't know where the baby is, or if it's even alive. If someone really killed Chelsea, they might have hurt the baby too." I stood up and put an arm around Julia, letting her cry into my shoulder until the emotion shaking her body subsided.

"Have you told the police about this?" I asked.

She gave me a disbelieving laugh. "Telling the Branson police about this would be like announcing Chelsea's pregnancy on the ten o'clock news." She shook her head. "No. Brian and I discussed it. We didn't want anyone to know about the pregnancy when Chelsea was alive; we certainly don't want rumors spreading now that she's passed away and can't even defend herself. I know you have no reason to keep it a secret, but I would appreciate as much discretion as possible—for Chelsea's sake."

"I understand," I said. "I'm just trying to find out what happened." I thought of Julia's reasons for not going to the authorities. I could see her point of view; I just didn't think it was smart to keep the information from the police. "I know you're worried about rumors starting, but I think the police could at least help you find Chelsea's baby."

Julia sat back in her chair and took another tissue from the box. "I've had a private investigator looking for Chelsea since she ran away. When Chelsea's body was found, I had the investigator start searching for the baby. Considering what I'm paying him, I have a lot more faith in his investigation methods, as well as his commitment to keep the search private, than I do the Branson Falls Police Department."

I was impressed that she'd gone to those lengths to try and find Chelsea, but I guess most parents would. At least if she wasn't willing to trust the police, she had found someone to help her search for her grandchild. I wondered who the P.I. was. I only knew one: Hawke. Could the Bradfords be the person he was working for? If so, why wouldn't he just tell me that? I kept the questions to myself though. "What about the father of the baby? Have you spoken with him?"

"No," she said. That one short word had a curt crispness to it that indicated the Bradfords were not on good terms with Shawn Wallace—assuming he was the father.

"Can you tell me the name of the boy?"

Her eyes held a combination of anger and sadness. "No. I can't."

"Do you know how the boy felt about the pregnancy at all?"

She shook her head as she tore pieces from the tissue in her lap. "Chelsea only told us that she and the father had agreed to put the baby up for adoption. I'm not sure if he even knew Chelsea was back in the area before she died. We didn't know she'd come back to Branson Falls until her body was found."

So Chelsea hadn't contacted any of her family members. Then who did she have contact with? Was it only Shawn? And why come back to Branson if she didn't think she had the support of her parents? I wondered if I might be able to get more information by seeing how Chelsea lived her life before she left Branson. "Would it be all right if I took a look at Chelsea's room?"

Julia nodded and led me over the hardwood floors of the living room into a long hallway. She stopped at the second door, pushing it open. It was the room of any typical teenage girl. Robert Pattinson posters were pinned to the sage green walls and photos of friends were scattered all over, some hanging in frames, others just taped to the walls. Chelsea's full size bed sat in the middle of the room, a pink comforter spread over the top with decorative pillows leaning against the headboard. A cream colored antique dresser hugged the wall near her closet. Julia stepped back as I moved to get a better look at the photos.

There were pictures of Chelsea in her dance uniforms with other girls on the team. I recognized some of the girls from her funeral. There were photos of Chelsea at dances, though none of the boys in any of the pictures I saw resembled the picture of Shawn Wallace that Hawke had given me. Other photos showed Chelsea with her family at holiday parties, and Chelsea goofing off with her friends. Nothing seemed strange or out of the ordinary. She seemed happy. The one thing I did notice was the pink and black beaded bracelet Chelsea was wearing in all the photos. I wondered what the significance was.

I turned to Julia, who was gazing at Chelsea's bed with such intense longing that I imagined only another mother who had lost a child could even begin to understand it. "Julia,"

I said in a tone so low it was almost a whisper. It took her a few seconds to come out of her trance.

"Yes?"

"I noticed Chelsea is wearing the same pink and black bracelet in all of these photos."

Julia walked over and picked up a photo book. The purple cover with white daises painted in the corners showcased Chelsea at a car wash fundraiser for the cheerleading squad. Chelsea was covered in soap, laughing next to Piper and some other girls, wet cars and trucks behind them. Her bracelet could barely be seen through the suds on her arms. "It was a gift from someone who meant a lot to her. She never took it off. We didn't get it back with her personal belongings though. It must have slipped off while she was in the water."

I nodded, thinking about the friendship bracelets my friends and I had made in elementary school. We had convinced ourselves we would wear them forever—it turns out forever is only as long as it takes for a friend to piss you off. I took another look around the room in case I'd missed something the first time. When I was satisfied there was nothing else to see, I turned back to Julia. "Would it be okay if I borrow the photo book? I think it would help me learn more about Chelsea's life, and find out who her friends were. They might have information we haven't uncovered yet. I promise to return it."

She brushed a hand over the front of the book, almost a caress. "That would be fine. But if you could try and keep Chelsea's pregnancy a secret when you talk with people, I would appreciate it." She lifted the photo book toward me.

I took it, nodding in understanding. "Thank you for all your help, Julia. I really appreciate you answering my questions."

"Of course," she said.

I walked out of the room as Julia closed Chelsea's bedroom door with a reverence usually reserved for religious worship. I followed her to the front door. As I stepped outside, she said, "Kate?" I turned around. "Do you really think Chelsea's death wasn't an accident?"

I looked her straight in the eyes. "I do."

"Then please let me know if you have other questions, or if there's anything I can do to help. If someone did this to Chelsea, I want to know, and I want them brought to justice."

"I feel the same," I said. Julia closed the door and I got in my Jeep. It was only noon. I'd go back to the house to make some mac and cheese for lunch and work from there.

Chapter Sixteen

When I got in my Jeep there was a voicemail from my mom reminding me not to forget the hot dog and marshmallow roast at their house tomorrow. Cookouts in our back yard have been a summer tradition for my family since I was a kid. I'd missed them after I moved away to go to college. I was looking forward to them again now that I was back.

I pulled into my driveway and walked through the back door, into the kitchen. I threw my bags and work down on the table, shoved some frozen mac and cheese in the microwave, and flipped my laptop on. As I waited for my lunch, I took the photo book back out and flipped through it. There were a few more photos of the car wash. Some included Piper, others were with the different girls on the dance team. The photos were interesting, but nothing seemed suspect.

I finished going through the photos just as the microwave beeped. I put the photo book in my office, and sat at the table. I had just started working on stories for the week when my cell phone rang to the tune of "Sweet Caroline," the ringtone that indicates the call is from someone I don't already have in my phone contact list. I bobbed my head and sang along to the song while I debated answering, but when the chorus ended I decided I might as well pick up. "Hello."

"Hi, Katie."

I frowned at the nickname, and the voice. "Drake. What do you need?"

"You recognized my voice." His tone was smug.

"No," I said. "You're the only person in the world who refuses to stop calling me Katie. How did you get this number anyway?"

"It wasn't difficult."

"Oh, right," I said, nodding my head as I spoke, "because you're charming, sexy, Dylan Drake."

"No," he said, "the Patriot Act, actually. But I'd like to hear more about me being sexy."

I narrowed my eyes. "I didn't mean to say that part out loud." I tapped my index finger on the table. "And what do you mean the Patriot Act? Don't tell me you put my name on a terrorist watch list."

"Have you met your mother?" I could hear the disbelief in his tone even over the phone. "You only have to look at the front page of the *Tribune* to realize she's a national security threat. In the wrong hands, she could be used as a weapon of mass destruction!"

"That's my mom, not me."

"You're her daughter. You could have the same disaster tendencies."

I clamped my jaw shut until I could get control and not bite his head off through the phone. "You're not scoring any points here."

He paused. "Maybe I could make it up to you over dinner?"

he suggested. "My committee meetings are done for a couple of weeks, so I'm back in town. I'd like to see you."

This caught me completely off-guard. Why would philandering Drake want to see me? Maybe Spence was right and for Drake this was all just a game I kept playing into. When I didn't answer, Drake said, "Katie, are you there?"

I closed my eyes as I leaned my head back against the chair. "I'm here. I'm just trying to decide how to answer."

" 'Yes' would be the easiest."

"Uh huh. I know how you like things easy."

I heard him sigh on the other end of the phone. "I usually don't have to work this hard to get a woman interested."

"Sorry I'm such a stubborn, independent, liberated pain in your ass."

"I'm picking you up at seven tonight."

"Just because you're here to pick me up doesn't mean I'll be here to go with you."

"From what I've heard, most of the town already thinks we're practically engaged. We might as well go to dinner and make it official."

"That's exactly why we shouldn't go to dinner!" I yelled.

"Okay then, let's go to dinner and discuss your story. I'd like to know more about what's happened since the cocktail party. And you can ask me any questions you want," he said. "You can even wear your press badge so people see we're there on professional instead of personal business."

The press badge wasn't a bad idea, but I didn't think it would help. In a place like Branson, even talking on the phone could force you into a relationship. Truth be told though, I did still have some questions for Drake. "All right," I relented. "Seven."

"What's your address?"

"Ask the Patriot Act," I said, and hung up.

I spent a couple of hours working on my mom's cow crash story for the paper and finished the much shorter dog bite article. Since Mr. Jones had chosen not to give me any other comments, he came across as a bitter and mean old man who kicked tiny defenseless dogs—which was pretty accurate. When I was finished writing and editing, I emailed the articles to Spence.

At exactly seven o'clock I heard a knock. The Patriot Act had apparently come through for him. I grabbed my purse and opened the front door.

Drake was wearing fitted tan dress pants and a gray tee shirt with a charcoal sports jacket. His eyes darkened as he looked me up and down. I followed his eyes and looked down at my clothes. Jeans, a belt, white tee shirt, and sandals. No nonsense. What in the world was he seeing? Finally his eyes met mine and in a husky voice he said, "Hi, Katie."

"Hi." I pushed through the door while Drake stepped out of the way so I could lock the deadbolt. I let the storm door close as Drake motioned for me to go first. I thought about telling him to go ahead, but knew what I said wouldn't make a difference, so I walked down the stairs and sidewalk where I came face-to-face with a bright yellow Hummer that was twice as tall as I was and looked like it could run over my house and eat my Jeep. Technically, Hummers are classified as SUVs, but my Jeep is an SUV. This thing was the love-child of a semi and a Tonka Truck.

"Way to be inconspicuous, Drake," I said, standing back to

look at the massive piece of metal in the driveway. "No one will notice the one hundred thousand dollar school bus in the restaurant parking lot. Why don't we just write up our wedding plans in the next issue of the *Tribune*?"

He grinned. "I'll drop an announcement off at the paper in the morning."

"Since you can't even get my name right, we should probably hold off on that." The tires on the Hummer were as tall as my waist. It was clear Drake had customized the shocks, struts, and springs to make the Hummer even bigger than stock. I took a deep breath, willing myself to get through the night. "Seriously, don't you have another car? Like one that didn't cost six figures and doesn't look like Big Bird?"

"You don't like it?" he asked, putting his hand on the hood as a confused look crossed his face.

"Hate would be putting it nicely. Did you get the memo about global warming? What's this sucker get, two miles to the gallon?"

"No. Twelve."

I shook my head in an effort to convey how twelve miles to the gallon wasn't much better than two. "I thought they had to stop making these things because of new fuel laws?"

"They stopped producing the H1s in 2006, but there were a lot that didn't sell until later. I've had it a couple of years."

I shook my head again, staring. "How the hell am I supposed to get in it? Does it come with a ladder?"

"I'll lift you up. That's how I usually help girls get in."

I snorted a laugh and held up my hand. "Now I see why this thing appeals to you."

Drake unlocked the doors with his keyless entry remote as he followed me around to the passenger side of the truck. I noticed him behind me and turned around, folding my arms across my chest. "What are you doing?"

"I'm going to open the door for you."

"And watch me squirm trying to get into your ginormous truck? Oh no, I can get my own damn door."

He gave me one of his amused looks. "You're hostile tonight."

"Good of you to notice," I said with wide eyes. "Maybe some girls don't like being forced into dates."

He gave me a measured stare. "One of these days I'll figure out what exactly you do like being forced to do."

I turned away and swished my hair as indignantly as I could. I opened the door and practiced my shot-put techniques to get my purse up on the truck floor. I lifted my right leg, practically doing the splits in the air—a gymnastic move that I'm sure I should have had training for—to get my leg on the floorboard. I grabbed the seat with my hand, pulling myself up. I breathed a sigh of relief when my butt successfully connected with the leather chair. Who knew you needed to be an Olympian to get in a Hummer?

Drake watched the whole thing while biting his lip, obviously trying not to laugh. After I got my seatbelt buckled, he shut my door and climbed in on his side. "I've never seen a girl get in by herself before," he said, pulling out of the driveway.

I brushed my hair out of my eyes. "Yes, we Hummer climbing feminists are rare," I looked out the window. "Where are we going anyway?"

"Just the Mexican restaurant. There aren't many places in town to choose from and even less if you take out the ones that serve fast food."

"I know, Drake. I live here, remember?"

He smiled like he was back in high school playing a football game he was determined to win. Spence's observation about Drake treating me like a challenge was making more and more sense.

We pulled into the Mexican restaurant, taking up two parking spaces. Greedy. Getting down from the Hummer only involved a jump and was significantly easier than getting up had been. Drake met me on my side of the truck and I followed him into the restaurant.

The spicy smell of peppers, tomatoes, and onions filled the air. It was a weeknight and not too busy. The hostess put us far away from the few other patrons in a corner booth with high sides. This was a blessing because most people wouldn't be able to see us together in the booth unless they went out of their way. It was a curse because most people would go out of their way and there would be gossip tomorrow about what Drake and Kate were doing in the Mexican restaurant's corner booth. It was almost as bad as being caught making out.

We looked over the menu. I ordered chicken enchiladas with a fruit punch, and Drake got a tostada / burrito platter and a Coke—which is pretty scandalous since most people in Branson believe Coke and coffee are basically the same thing. After the waitress brought chips, salsa, and our drinks, we knew we wouldn't be bothered for a while.

"So, have you learned anything else about Chelsea's death?" Drake asked.

"Not really anything new. We've just had confirmation we're on the right track. We're trying to find out who had motive to kill her."

"I assume you think Shawn Wallace is at the top of your list because Chelsea was pregnant?"

My mouth gaped. "How did you know that?" I leaned in, my voice low. "The Bradfords are trying to keep it a secret!"

"I work at the capitol, Katie. I hear things."

I eyed him carefully, wondering how many people actually knew about the pregnancy. It was being kept pretty hush, hush . . . in Branson at least. "He seems to be a reasonable suspect," I agreed, taking a sip of my fruit punch.

"I don't think so."

"Oh really?" I leaned back against the booth seat and folded my hands in my lap. "Why is that?"

"I know Shawn. I've been to a lot of parties at the governor's mansion and I know his dad. He's not the type of kid who would kill someone." Drake dipped a chip in the salsa. "I think your hunch is wrong," he said, popping the chip into his perfectly curved mouth.

I stared a little too long at his lips and looked away, hoping he hadn't seen me. "First, you know the public Shawn," I said. "You know the Shawn his dad wants him to be. The real Shawn might be a completely different person. Would the Shawn you know get a girl pregnant?"

Drake took another chip. "Mistakes happen," he answered with a shrug.

I eyed him as I wondered how many mistakes Drake had running around in the world, but after a few seconds I forced myself to stop thinking about his possible illegitimate children and focus on the current topic. "Yeah, and maybe Chelsea's death was a mistake. Regardless though, someone is responsible."

"I'm just saying you shouldn't put all your resources into

investigating only Shawn. I'm sure there are other people who could have been involved."

"I'm not putting all my resources into just Shawn."

"Who else then?"

I wasn't sure I wanted to tell him this theory, but forged ahead anyway. "Shawn's dad, Governor Wallace."

Drake dropped the chip he was holding and it cracked like a crystal vase all over the Formica tabletop. "You think the governor had something to do with this?"

"I don't know; hence the investigation."

Drake wiped his hands on his napkin and folded his arms on the table. He leaned into me. "I guarantee the governor wasn't involved."

"How can you guarantee that?"

"Because I *know* him."

I lifted my shoulders and wrinkled my brow. "Again with the knowing them," I said. "I know you, but that doesn't mean I can say you wouldn't do something stupid. In fact, if I had to guess, I'd say you've probably done a lot of stupid things. Knowing someone is not a valid defense."

"It's not just knowing him, Katie. I'm friends with him."

"If you asked me to dinner to try and convince me to stop investigating your 'friend' and his son, that's too bad because it's not going to happen," I said. "The governor had a motive. It's a re-election year. Family and morals—or at least the illusion of them—are more important to voters than anything else in this state. Governor Wallace isn't doing great in the polls anyway. A pregnancy scandal could take him out of the running. If he can't manage his own kids, why would people think he can continue to manage the whole state?"

Drake took a deep breath, exhaled, and placed his hands

palms down on the table. "You have some valid points, but let me share this with you. I'd be surprised if the governor even knew Chelsea was pregnant. He's a busy man and he lets his wife take care of the kids. He knew Chelsea and Shawn were dating, but that was about the extent of it, at least from what I've heard."

I looked at him and blinked. "Wait a minute. You knew about Chelsea and Shawn dating? And you didn't tell me?"

Drake popped another chip in his mouth. "You didn't ask."

I glared at him. "You're such a jerk. You could have told me everything I needed to know without making me go to that dumb Country Club party with you."

"I take advantage of every opportunity I can. And trust me," he grinned, "I wouldn't have wanted to miss seeing you in that blue dress. Besides, you never told me what you were looking for."

I gripped my drink and counted to five; when I still wanted to throw my fruit punch on him, I continued counting. When I reached thirty I looked at Drake and almost had to start over because he seemed so freaking entertained at how mad I was. "I'm going to start a list of things you've done to piss me off. Just to make sure I never forget."

Drake took a swig of his Coke, and tipped his glass to me. "It'll probably be a long list."

"Undoubtedly," I said. "What else do you know about Chelsea, Shawn, and the Wallaces?"

"I've told you pretty much everything."

I gave him a level stare trying to ascertain how much I should trust him. "So, since according to you, the governor isn't really a part of Shawn's life, you're saying I need to investigate the first lady instead?"

Drake rolled his eyes, shaking his head. "I'm saying I think Shawn kept it quiet and so did the Bradfords. That's why

Chelsea disappeared. I think her parents sent her away to have the baby. Traveling was just the cover story. That's how they must have decided to handle it." I didn't tell Drake he was right and Julia Bradford had essentially told me the same thing. "Maybe Shawn's mom knew about the pregnancy, but she's the nicest woman in the world; she would have been completely supportive," he said. "If Shawn didn't want his dad to know, his mom wouldn't have said anything."

The server brought our food, asked if we needed anything else, and left. I spread some sour cream on my enchiladas and picked up my knife and fork. "But why wouldn't Shawn want his dad to know?" I asked as I cut my enchilada and tried to reign in the stringy melted cheese.

"Governor Wallace is a good leader, but he has a temper. I doubt he would have reacted well to the news that Chelsea was pregnant."

"Yet another reason why I'm not going to stop investigating him!"

Drake closed his eyes. "Fine, Katie," he said. "I'm just telling you what I know. Do what you want with the information."

"I appreciate the advice," I said between bites. "I just have to cover all the bases."

"I understand, but know that I think this is the wrong direction. And if word gets out you're investigating the governor for murder"—he paused and looked down at his food before glancing back up at me, his mouth pulled into a worried line—"be careful, Katie."

I widened my eyes. "You think I could be in danger?" I asked, thinking of the magazine letter note I'd gotten at the *Tribune*. Was that something I needed to take more seriously? I'd never been threatened before. I wasn't sure whether to be proud, or concerned.

"I think the governor has loyal friends and you should be selective about who you discuss this with."

I stared at him for a minute. I knew people might be upset about what I uncovered, but I hadn't considered that someone might be mad enough to try and hurt me. "Thanks," I said sincerely. "I'll keep that in mind."

We continued to eat in silence, both consumed by our thoughts. After a while, Drake smiled and said, "Now that we have the professional stuff out of the way, you know we're both going to get hell for weeks about this corner booth?"

I nodded. "Yeah, I know. I already got cussed out by my mom for not telling her we were dating."

He laughed. "Thanks for letting me know."

"Don't thank me, thank The Ladies. They're the ones who informed my mom." I took another drink of fruit punch to stop the salsa and enchilada sauce from giving me third degree throat burns. "Who told you we were dating?"

"Several people." He took a bite of his tostada. "Word gets around pretty quick."

"You're not kidding. I forgot that about living in a small town."

"It didn't help that you were seen with me at the Country Club party and we told everyone you were my girlfriend. News like that isn't kept quiet. The legislature is another version of a small town. Between it and Branson, I have two I have to deal with."

"Two what?" a male voice asked. A body slid into the booth beside me as a muscular arm snaked around my shoulders. "Hey, Kitty Kate." Hawke flashed me a devious grin before he glanced at Drake.

Drake gave Hawke a steely stare that Hawke returned without so much as a blink. The tension between the two of them hung in the air until Drake finally turned his attention back to me. "Kitty Kate?" he asked. Disbelief laced his tone. "And you get mad at me for calling you Katie?"

Hawke leaned back, looking me up and down. "Nah, you're not a Katie. Katie's are sweet and innocent," he said. "Kitty Kate's are sexy."

I wanted to hide somewhere, and considering how hot my face felt, I knew I could easily camouflage my head in the enchilada sauce.

"Hawke," Drake said through tight lips. "It's been a while."

Hawke tilted his head and met Drake's hard expression. "It has."

"I didn't realize you were in town," Drake said. "Usually you don't spend much time here."

Hawke turned to me, giving me a slow stare as he picked up my glass and took a drink of my fruit punch, then put it back down in front of me. "I might be changing that," he answered.

Drake squared his shoulders, sitting up straighter. "Are you sure that's a good idea? You're not the type of man who handles roots well."

"I've heard the same about you," said Hawke.

I could tell Drake was getting sick of whatever game Hawke was playing. "What do you want, Hawke?" Drake asked, the authority clear in his voice. "Kate and I are having dinner."

"I can see that, and," Hawke gestured to our plates, "it looks like you're almost done."

"What's going on?" I asked Hawke, thinking he must have some important news since he went to the trouble to find me. "Did something happen?"

Hawke locked eyes with me. "Nope," he looked away and

took another drink from my glass. "I just heard you and Drake were in the corner booth at the Mexican restaurant and came to check it out for myself." I rolled my eyes. We hadn't been at the restaurant more than an hour and rumors were already starting to spread. Damn Twitter and Facebook! "Considering what I've heard so far, I thought Drake might be proposing."

Hawke slid out of the booth. He looked at Drake, whose shoulders were still tensed. "Good to see you, Drake. I'm sure we'll run into each other again soon."

"I can't wait," Drake said through his teeth.

"Glad I got to see you too, Kitty Kate," he smiled. "I'll call you tomorrow." He winked and walked away.

Drake sat back in his chair taking a few deep breaths until his shoulders relaxed. "How do you know that jackass?"

I took issue with Drake calling Hawke names, but let it slide because I didn't know their history. "We're working on Chelsea's investigation together."

Drake laughed until he realized I was serious. "What's he doing investigating her death? Who hired him?"

"I don't know, but he's been really helpful. He said he thought we could work better as a team. He's been right so far."

"Shit, Katie!" Drake said in a voice loud enough to guarantee everyone in town would be talking about his profanity at breakfast tomorrow morning. "If I'd known you were working with him, I never would have told you anything!"

"Why not?" I asked, suddenly angry.

"Do you know what he does for a living?"

"Not really," I shrugged. "I've heard bits and pieces, but it's not a big deal."

"Not a big deal?" Drake fumed. "He's been everything from a four-star general to a hit-man! You never know what his real motives are and he's a manipulation expert. Be careful," he said, pointing his fork at me. He stayed like that for a few beats before he put his fork on his plate and leaned back in his seat. "If I thought you'd listen to me, I'd tell you to stay far, far away from him, but since I know you won't, I'll just say this: don't trust him."

I'd heard the same thing from Spence, who had gotten all his information from Drake. I wanted to listen, I really did, but Hawke had been nothing but helpful to me. Of all the people I was working with on this story, the truth was I probably trusted Hawke the most, and for some reason, I felt safe with him. Maybe it was the fact that he looked like he could drop-kick a linebacker, but my gut feeling was that he wanted to help me. And he made me feel secure.

"You didn't listen to a word I said, did you?" Drake asked.

I played with a stray string hanging from the hem of my tee shirt. "I listened, but my experience with Hawke has been different than yours, apparently."

Drake stared at me. I saw the realization cross his face like a light bulb turning on. "Are you attracted to him?" he asked incredulously.

I gasped and answered a little too quickly, "What? No!" The flush immediately started to creep up my neck. Honestly though, what a stupid question. Who wouldn't be attracted to Hawke?

Drake's eyebrows shot up. "You've got to be kidding me!" he said, his tone a combination of shock and disgust. "Ryker Hawkins? Over me?"

I couldn't believe he'd just said that. I narrowed my eyes and lowered my voice. "Get over yourself."

He sat there in stunned silence, his mouth still hanging open as I grabbed my purse and got up from the table. I searched through my wallet and threw down twenty bucks I couldn't really afford for dinner.

The only thing he said was, "If you leave like this, the rumors about you storming out of the corner booth will be legendary. People will never stop talking."

"People can go to hell," I said, and walked out the door.

Chapter Seventeen

In my hasty and furious exit I hadn't considered how I'd get home. This wasn't a city where I could call a cab. In fact, there was no public transportation at all. You could rent a horse or a tractor easier than you could rent a car. I had my cell phone, though, so I would do the next best thing: I'd call my parents. Although trying to explain to them why I needed a ride and wasn't still having dinner with Dylan Drake didn't really appeal to me.

I stood at the corner of the restaurant, still seething and fumbling for my cell phone in my purse when I heard a familiar loud engine. I looked up. Hawke's Mustang pulled to a stop in front of me. He leaned over the seat, pushing open the passenger door. "I thought you might need a ride."

I breathed a sigh of relief that I wouldn't have to ride home with my parents or Drake, and got in the car.

"Guess the proposal didn't go as planned," Hawke said.

I scowled. "Dylan Drake is the last person on earth I'd marry."

"Good to know." Hawke didn't ask what had happened with Drake, it was like he just knew. Of course, he probably realized showing up at dinner would antagonize Drake. I didn't doubt that had been Hawke's intention.

We rode in silence at first and as Hawke drove to my house, I could smell the gas and oil feeding the engine—an engine that was older than the Hummer's and still got better gas mileage. I took a deep breath, closed my eyes, leaned my head back, and smiled.

"Women usually only get that look for one reason."

I sighed. "I love classic cars." I slowly ran my hands over the supple, black leather seat. "It's a 1967 Shelby GT 500, right? Does it have the four-twenty-eight Police Interceptor engine?" I asked, turning my head to look at him.

Hawke stared at me, clearly surprised I knew anything about cars.

"It's modified actually. I put in a four-twenty-seven Cobra Jet when it was restored. Her name is Roxy."

"Why Roxy?"

He smiled. "There was a girl—"

I held my palm up to stop him. "I don't think I want to know." He just grinned and seemed lost in thought, no doubt remembering his time with Roxy while I tried to forget.

I let my eyes fall over the black leather dash, silver accenting the black interior, and the horse stamped on the new radio designed to look old. "My dad would love this car."

"Is he the reason you're a Mustang fan?"

I nodded. "He had a cherry red 1965 Fastback with white racing stripes when I was growing up. I loved how loud the engine was. As soon as he turned the key, the engine shook the whole car, just like yours. People would always stop and stare on the street any time we took it for a drive."

"Does he still have it?"

"Yeah, and he just started restoring a 1966 Notchback Mustang." I rolled down the window, breathing in the oil and gas a little more. "It's his new project to deal with my mom."

"Don't your parents get along?"

"Oh, they're really happy, it's just my mom has a knack for regularly being involved in some sort of disaster. They're lucky they can still get car and house insurance. My dad works on the Mustang every time she has another incident; lately he's been getting quite a bit done."

Hawke laughed. "Your mom sounds interesting."

"If you read the *Tribune* very often, I'm sure you've heard of her before."

"What's her name?"

"Sophie Saxee."

Hawke's mouth lifted slightly. "Didn't her car roll into Emerald Lake?"

I gave a reluctant smile. "Yeah. She was helping set up for a party in the bowery next to the lake. She said she put the car in park when she got out, but somehow it slipped into gear and made it to the lake before she noticed it was gone. She heard gurgling and tried to lasso the car with some plastic party ribbon. That obviously didn't work. It sunk, so she called my dad—and the insurance company."

Hawke gave a hearty laugh. "This stuff happens to her often?"

I nodded. "All the time. My dad says getting knocked up is probably the only way I'll get a guy to marry me once he finds out about my mom. He tells me that it's a good thing her bad luck isn't genetic."

Hawke pulled up in front of my house. He turned the car off and followed me to my front door. He held the storm door for me while I unlocked the deadbolt. "Thanks for giving me a ride," I said with a smile.

"No problem."

"So, I'll see you tomorrow?"

"Yeah, I'll call you." He walked down the steps with his hands in his pockets.

"Have a good night," I said.

Right before I walked into my house Hawke turned around. "Hey, Kitty Kate." I stopped and looked at him. "Let me know if you need any help with the 'knocked up' part." He flashed me a confident grin as he walked across the lawn to his car.

I chose to open the door and go in the house instead of trying to respond. An offer like that doesn't come around every day.

Early in the morning, a lovely and rather detailed dream involving Hawke's offer was interrupted by a clattering noise that sounded like it was coming from the kitchen. Since I don't own a cat, or even a cricket, I quickly deduced that someone was in my house. I was already pissed that my dream had been ruined; now someone was trying to rob me too? Glaring, I silently walked to my closet, grabbing a couple of shoes. Other than a fingernail file, shoes were the only weapon I had at my disposal. At least they were heavy with a sharp enough stiletto heel that they could do some damage.

I crept down the hall as the noise grew louder. Something fell to the floor. The burglar wasn't being particularly quiet.

Maybe they didn't think I was home. I tiptoed over the creaky floorboards, sticking as close to the wall as possible. As I came to the kitchen I peeked around the corner. A small dark figure was huddled by my cabinets. My first thought was "Gremlin!", but since they're fictional, I amended my theory to "ghost." It looked too solid to be a specter though.

I reached around the corner and flipped the light switch, holding my shoes in the air heel first, ready to attack. As the light flickered on, Midnight, my neighbor's black cat, looked at me like I'd just interrupted the most important thing in the world, and went back to eating my mom's left-over sugar cookies on the counter. I wrinkled my nose, annoyed. I'd been looking forward to those. I sighed at my lost treat as I shooed Midnight off the counter. I opened the back door to let him out, and stopped in my tracks.

The back door was unlocked.

It hadn't been when I went to sleep.

At least, I didn't think it had. I'd lived in the city long enough to get in the habit of always locking my doors. I couldn't believe I'd left it unsecured. I looked around the house to see if anything was missing. Just in case someone was here, I traded my shoes for kitchen knives.

I slowly crept into the living room. I looked behind my furniture, and checked the front door—it was locked. I went down the hall and searched through the office, guest room, bathrooms, and my bedroom. Everything seemed fine, but I couldn't shake the feeling that someone other than a cat had been in my house in the past twelve hours. A shiver ran up my spine. I looked at my alarm; it was five o'clock. I knew I wouldn't get back to sleep. I grabbed some workout clothes from my dresser and went to the living room, hoping some yoga would help me calm down.

Chapter Eighteen

When I got to work, I didn't even have time to put my purse under my desk before Ella and Spence were standing in front of me like the Swiss Guard. "So, are you gonna tell us what happened last night?" Ella had her arms folded across her chest. She looked like she wouldn't take 'no' for an answer.

"What are you talking about?" I asked, wondering if they knew something about my possible intruder.

"Betsy at the hair salon told Amber Kane that you and Drake were doing all sorts of unmentionable things in the corner booth of the Mexican restaurant last night. Then she said he started yelling like a professional swearer and you stormed out of the restaurant and said something about everyone goin' to hell," Ella summarized.

Of course the parts with swearing would be what everyone remembered. I rolled my eyes. "That's not what happened."

"So what did happen?" Spence asked. "Because I heard a similar version at the bakery, and usually the difference between rumor and fact is how much various stories resemble each other."

I pointed at him. "I can't believe you're buying into this crap too?"

"We're in the news business, Kate. Most stories we write start off as a rumor that's proven true or false based on our investigations. I'm investigating."

"You're investigating my life!" I said, flipping my computer on. "And it's none of your business!"

"The whole town is talking about it," Ella said. "You might as well tell us what really happened so we can get the truth circulating."

I fell into my chair, leaning my head back for a moment before I sat up and looked at them both. "Drake asked me to go to dinner so we could talk more about the Chelsea Bradford story I'm working on. Everything was fine until Hawke showed up."

"Hawke came to the restaurant?" Spence asked, his eyes wide. "While you were with Drake?"

"Yeah," I nodded. "So, Hawke stopped by the table for a couple of minutes. Apparently he and Drake don't get along too well. After Hawke left, Drake got mad that I've been working with Hawke, and I got mad that Drake was telling me what to do and arguing over something so stupid. I paid for my food, and left."

"Did you storm out and tell everyone to go to hell?" Ella asked, her eyes bright with anticipation.

I winced. "I might have said something like that."

"Woo-eee," Ella chortled as she plopped down in a chair across from my desk. "You better hope someone else does something scandalous or people will be talking about this for weeks! I heard about it last night. The news was big enough to start the Lady phone-tree. That's why I'm here so early. I told everyone I'd get to the bottom of the gossip."

"Well, now you know." I looked at her, and then Spence. "You both do."

"I'm surprised Drake lost his cool," Spence said, giving me a measured stare. "That doesn't happen often. Drake's used to playing lawyer and politician and not letting his emotions show. Although, if it was Hawke, I guess that explains things."

"Why? What difference does Hawke make?"

Spence picked a paper clip up off my desk and started to unravel it. "I've heard they have a mutual dislike for each other."

"Well, it's not my problem," I said, pushing my memory stick into the computer. I needed to transfer photos from the cow crash and dog bite stories so I could put them in the newspaper layout.

Spence looked at me. "It is your problem if they're both helping you with the Bradford story."

I looked at him and considered. He was right. "Point taken," I said. "I'll have to do a better job of keeping them away from each other."

Ella stood up. "I'm gonna let everyone know the real story." She went to the back room where I assumed she'd be on her cell phone for the next three hours.

Spence came around and half-sat, half-leaned against my desk in his usual pose, with his feet crossed in front of him. "What's going on with the Bradford story?"

I told him what I'd learned from Julia Bradford and Drake, and my theories about the governor. "I want to talk to some people who know the governor and see if I can learn anything else about him. I'd like to know if Drake's impressions of the governor's family life are accurate."

Spence was working to put the mutilated paper clip back

together. "Governor Wallace has been in politics for a while. You could call a couple of the past district representatives."

"Great idea," I said.

Spence stood up. "Try not to do anything newsworthy today. You're almost as bad as your mom. Catasophie and Kateastrophe." I glared and Spence laughed.

I finished transferring the photos onto my computer and picked the ones I wanted, dropping them in the layout program we use to design the newspaper each week. Thank God for computers. I couldn't imagine trying to do layout by hand again like I'd had to do when I was on the newspaper staff in high school. We had computers in school, but Branson Falls High couldn't afford a luxury like a design program.

I picked up the phone book and thumbed through, looking for the names of the past four Utah state district representatives and senators for Branson Falls—they would be the most likely to know Governor Wallace since they'd worked with him. I spent the rest of the morning calling them and found out Governor Wallace had always had political aspirations. He planned to use his position as governor as a springboard to a position in Washington D.C.

All the people I spoke with confirmed Governor Wallace didn't have a lot to do with raising his family and he mostly let his wife take care of the things concerning their kids. They all also agreed the governor had a temper, which, like Drake said, would be a reason for Shawn and his mother to keep quiet about the pregnancy. I couldn't believe a parent wouldn't know his kid was going to be a dad soon, but I hadn't grown up in that kind of secretive life either. By the time I was finished with the calls, I felt like the interviews were helpful, but didn't really get me any closer to the truth.

I decided to take a break and get lunch at the fast food

place a few blocks away. I walked past the pet shelter, stopping to admire the kittens playing with some yarn. I waved at Michelle James, the shelter owner. She smiled widely and waved back, her curly hair bouncing as she chased a puppy around the room. In addition to managing the shelter, she also juggled eight kids. I wouldn't be able to juggle one. She was a pretty amazing woman.

When I got to the restaurant, I ordered my food and sat at a table. I started looking through my notebook, hoping my notes contained the clues I needed to keep investigating. While I was waiting for my grilled cheese, fries, and Oreo shake, Hawke walked in and sat across from me. I blinked. "How do you always know where I'm at?"

Hawke just smiled.

"Seriously," I narrowed my eyes. "Did you put some sort of tracking device on me?" It would make sense. He was my partner and seemed to consider me—or at least my boobs—an asset. Investigating a murder with the murderer still running around is risky. Drake seemed to think my investigation was downright dangerous. There was also the issue of the note I'd gotten and my unlocked back door. Both of which were unsettling. I wasn't happy about the idea, but I wouldn't put it past Hawke to stick a GPS unit on my car. Maybe it would help keep me safe.

He slung his right arm over the half of the bench seat he wasn't occupying. "It's a small town, Kitty Kate. You're not that difficult to find."

I noticed he didn't answer my question. I leaned in so people eating lunch at the other tables wouldn't be able to hear me as clearly, though I suspected they all had at least one ear turned in our direction for a reason. "Do you have any idea how much trouble you caused last night?"

His lips slid into a sly grin. "If you'd wanted me to cause trouble, you should have said something. I could have caused a lot more."

The girl at the counter called my name as every head in the room swiveled to look at me and Hawke. "I have no doubt about that," I said, and walked to the counter for my food.

I sat back down and offered Hawke half of my sandwich and some fries. He took some of the food and leaned back in his seat with a smile. "Did you really tell everyone to go to hell?"

I shook my head. "I'll never live that down."

"It seems like a lot happened after I left the restaurant and before you got in my car."

"Drake and I don't always agree on things."

Hawke stared at me. "You and I have something in common then."

"How do you and Drake know each other anyway?" I asked, dipping a fry in my shake.

"We work in the same circles sometimes," he said, smothering a fry in a Utah condiment staple: fry sauce, a mixture of mayonnaise and ketchup. "Drake doesn't like my profession, and I think he's a pretentious ass."

"Speaking of your profession, what exactly do you do?"

He ran the tip of his tongue over his top lip. "Anything you want me to." He took a bite of his half of the sandwich. Though his answer was vague, I had a feeling it was honest. "Drake was pretty mad when I decided to move to Branson Falls. I think part of me did it just to tick him off."

"Sounds like something I'd do," I said, putting a spoonful of cold, chocolate cookie shake in my mouth. Hawke watched me lick the spoon clean. When I finished, he locked eyes with me and reached over to gently take the spoon from my hand. He dipped the spoon in the shake, a heaping pile of ice cream weighing down the plastic. He lifted the spoon to his mouth and the tip of his tongue slid over the cold treat in circular motions. He shaped the outside of the ice cream lightly with his teeth and then swallowed, licking his lips. He finished the spoonful off with several long strokes of his tongue, all while keeping his eyes welded to mine.

My mouth fell open and I swallowed. Hard.

I noticed the restaurant had become eerily quiet. I wrenched my eyes away from Hawke's and glanced around the room to see everyone staring. As soon as they noticed me watching them, they all turned back to their food. But it didn't take long for them to get out their cell phones and start texting. I was sure the phone-tree would be busy for the rest of the day.

Hawke also noticed the flying fingers, and gave me his trademark naughty grin before continuing our conversation like he hadn't just had a sexual experience with a spoon. "Were you able to find anything else out this morning?"

I pushed the image of the milkshake and Hawke's tongue to the side of my mind and told him about my conversation with Drake the previous night. I also told him what the other representatives and senators had said regarding Governor Wallace.

"I don't think we should rule the governor out," Hawke said, "but I'm not sure he's the guy we're looking for either."

"What about you?" I asked. "What have your "resources" told you the last couple of days?"

Hawke smiled and moved to get up from the booth. "There are a lot of ears here; walk with me?"

"Sure." We'd finished the food, but I still had part of my

shake. I threw the trash away and took the shake with me as we walked down Main Street.

"I read the autopsy." I stopped walking and stared at him. I really didn't think he'd be able to get it.

"Are you surprised?" he asked.

"To be honest," I lifted a shoulder and cocked my head, "a little."

"You shouldn't doubt me, Kitty Kate; you'll always be disappointed if you do."

Interesting. I guess he really did do all the things he said he would. I filed that information in the front of my mind so I could easily access it the next time he said something overtly sexual. "What did the autopsy say?"

"The coroner listed the death as an accidental drowning."

I nodded, swirling my shake in the cup before taking another bite. "Right, we knew that."

"But, we didn't know Chelsea also had blunt force trauma to her head."

I stopped the spoon mid-way to my mouth and put it back in the cup. "What?"

Hawke took the cup from me, scooping up some ice cream for himself. "The autopsy listed the cause of death as drowning, but I'm friendly with the Coroner and he told me Chelsea had blunt force head trauma as well. However, people higher up in his department told him not to include it in the report."

"Who asked him to leave that information off?"

Hawke lifted a shoulder. "He wouldn't say, but I can think of a few people who wouldn't want anything suspicious showing up on the coroner's report."

I nodded, thinking of a few people myself. "So how did she get the head trauma?" I asked. "And what really killed her, the head trauma, or the drowning?"

We walked a few paces while Hawke thought. "There was water in her lungs so she had to be breathing when she went into the lake, but the head trauma is definitely suspicious." Hawke kept walking and thought some more.

"Did the report say when the head trauma happened? Was it close to Chelsea's time of death?"

Hawke threw the shake cup into a trash can on the street corner and took a drink from the water fountain there. "Yes, it was."

"So we're looking for someone who hit her until she was unconscious and then dragged her into the lake?" I asked.

"Yep, that's what it seems like."

"We have suspects, motives, and even know how Chelsea was killed, but we still aren't sure who did it, or why. We're missing something."

"We just have to keep searching."

We'd walked up Main Street and were now in front of the *Tribune* office where Hawke's Mustang was parked. "I'll call you if I find anything else out," I said.

Hawke hit the button on his keychain that disarmed his car alarm. "I'll do the same."

He got in and drove off.

I turned around to walk into the office and jumped, my heart racing. Ella was standing in the middle of the picture window, watching me like the ghost of a Golden Girl.

I pushed the *Tribune* door open. "Geez, Ella! You scared me to death. Why were you staring at me?"

"I wasn't really starin' at you. I was starin' at Hawke. He's as good lookin' as Clark Gable!" I was pretty sure that was the first, and only time, I would ever hear Hawke compared to a 1930s actor. "I like the sporty, noisy car he drives too. I wish I had one."

I snorted a laugh. "Ella, if you had a car like that, you'd have to spend every spare minute making key lime pies."

She put her index finger to her lips, wrinkling her brow. "It'd be worth it."

I laughed and started to walk back to my desk. Ella followed me. "What were you doing eating lunch with Hawke?"

I just stared at her.

"There's a video message going around of him taking your spoon and eating your milkshake. From the video, it looks like he's more interested in eating you."

Of course some asshat took a video of that. Dammit! And it hadn't been more than thirty minutes since it happened! I was just digging myself a deeper hole.

"I haven't had a man look at me like that in at least twenty years," Ella said with a wistful expression.

"Jay only died ten years ago, Ella," I pointed out as I sat at my desk.

"I know," she said. "If you decide to sleep with Hawke, you better give me all the details."

"Right," I smiled. "So you can pass those details along to The Ladies through your phone-tree?"

Ella looked incensed. "If you say it's off the record, I won't tell a soul. It'll just be you and me who knows, like I'm the reporter and it's locked in a safe."

I laughed. "Okay, Ella. If anything ever happens with my sex life, I'll keep you informed."

She gave me a huge smile back. "I have to live vicariously through someone, you know."

"Glad I can help."

"Speakin' of the phone-tree, you should know everyone's

sayin' your wedding with Drake's off because you're sleeping with that criminal Hawke."

I closed my eyes, pressing my fingers against my forehead as I took a few deep breaths. "Of course they are."

"Don't you worry though, I'll set them straight."

I was about to ask how she was going to do that—Ella's story might end up being worse than the rumors going around—when Spence came out of his office. "Are you and Hawke planning dates every day now?"

"No," I said. "I was just eating lunch and he stopped to talk to me about Chelsea's autopsy."

"Did you learn anything interesting?"

Yes. Lots of interesting things. Hadn't Spence seen the video? But then I realized he was talking about Chelsea. "Yeah. We now know that Chelsea was hit in the head with something that caused blunt force trauma. It happened right before she died."

"So, the hit knocked her unconscious, but the water is what killed her?"

"That's what we're thinking."

Spence pursed his lips. "Hawke sure seems to be able to get a lot of information without a problem."

I grinned. "He's a pretty good friend for a reporter to have."

Spence frowned. "Maybe. Maybe not. Be careful, Kate."

By the time I was finished with the layout and leaned back in my chair to stretch, I looked at the clock and realized it was six-thirty. Within a few minutes, I got a call from my mom.

"Kate? Where are you? You're supposed to be here for

dinner. What are you doing? Did you get called away on a story? You're still coming, right?"

There were way too many questions in that greeting to even attempt to answer, so I focused on the last one. "I lost track of time. I'm still at work, but I'll be right there." I shut my computer down and started to gather my things. "Is there anything you want me to bring?"

"No! Just get here!"

"Okay, okay!" Geez! What was the rush?

"And I heard about the corner booth," she half-whispered, half-hissed into the phone, "and the milkshake! I thought we talked about this." Great, I could only imagine what the story had morphed into by now. Just wait until she watched the video instead of only hearing about it.

"I'll see you soon, Mom."

Spence was walking out at the same time as me. "Thanks for staying late. I know you've been working like crazy on all of these stories." He gave me a genuine smile. "I really appreciate it."

I stared at him with an assessing eye.

He stared back, a nervous expression settling on his face. "Why are you looking at me like that?"

I smiled slowly, nodding my head. Spence would make an excellent corner booth / milkshake question deflector. My mom wouldn't ask questions like that with a guest present. "You're coming with me."

"Where?"

"To my parents' house."

Chapter Nineteen

Spence followed me to the back yard where my dad had the fire going. "Hi, Dad," I said, giving him a kiss on the cheek.

My dad looked from me to Spence as an amused smile flitted across his face. "Hi, honey," he said, putting his hand out in Spence's direction. "Spence, it's good to see you."

"You too, Damon. I don't think I've talked to you since Sophie's car rolled into the lake."

My dad nodded, dropping another log on the fire. "She's a scary woman to be married to." He turned to me. "Kate, your mom's in the house. I think she needs help bringing everything outside."

"Okay."

"I'll help you," Spence offered.

My dad put his hand on Spence's shoulder. "They won't be long," he said, directing Spence to the garage. "And this way I can show you my new project."

Spence followed my dad around the side of the house. I walked over the red and orange flagstone patio and opened the French doors. Hot dog buns, condiments, and chips were on the table. My mom was in the kitchen mixing some Sprite-spiked fruit punch—Utah's version of a mixed drink. "Kate! You're finally here," she said with more enthusiasm than usual.

"What can I help you with, Mom?"

"You can start taking the food out to the patio table."

"Okay." I looked down and noticed four plates and glasses. She must have seen Spence outside with me and added the extra dishes already. "Thanks for getting a dish for Spence."

My mom stopped stirring abruptly and looked up. "Who?"

"Spence," I said, addressing her blank stare. "From the *Tribune*. You know, my boss."

My mom's face fell as she turned a shade of ghostly white. "You asked Spence to come with you to dinner?"

"Yeah. He's in the garage with Dad. We were working late. Neither of us had eaten, so I decided to bring him along. I didn't think it would be a problem."

My mom pursed her lips and I could see the anger building on her face. She clutched the towel hanging over her shoulder, and put her hands on the granite countertop to steady herself. "Kate! What's going on?" she asked in an angry whisper. "First I hear you're dating Dylan and making out and fighting with him in the corner booth of the Mexican restaurant. Then I find out some mysterious guy named Hawke has been seen at your house and there's this . . . this . . . *porno* video with the two of you eating a milkshake. And now you bring Spence to dinner?" Her breath was coming in gasps and I thought she might hyperventilate.

She burns down a field, destroys a truck, kills a cow, and crashes her rental car, yet she's as calm as a yogi. But I spend time with a few guys, and *that's* what she chooses to get upset about?

"Mom, calm down! You're overreacting."

"You're going to get a reputation, Kate! It's one thing to date one man, but dating three? People are going to say you're a . . . a . . . hussy!"

I burst out laughing. The only time I'd ever heard the word 'hussy' was when my mom and dad used to make me watch old western movies with them.

She hit me with her shoulder towel. "This is NOT a laughing matter."

"Mom! Stop!" I put my hands up trying to shield myself from the towel lashing. "I'm not sleeping with any of them."

She stopped and stared at me. "Kate Violet Saxee! Don't you lie to your mother."

I also couldn't remember the last time I'd heard anyone use my full name. I felt like I was five again. "I'm not lying! I think Drake and Hawke both kind of like me—or something —but I'm not sleeping with either of them. I'm not even dating them! As for Spence . . . trust me, I'm not his type. He's my boss. That's all."

"What about The Ladies? They all think you're dating Dylan."

"I told you not to listen to The Ladies, or any rumors for that matter. I told you Drake was helping me with a story. That's it."

Mom suddenly bit her lip, worry lines forming on her forehead and at the corners of her mouth.

"What's wrong?" I asked.

"Nothing," Mom hedged, her eyes growing softer and more concerned.

I narrowed my eyes. I knew that look from her. "What did you do, Mom?"

"Oh," she slapped the towel down on the counter, a gesture that let me know just how bad it was. The towel rarely left her shoulder if she was in the house. "I thought you really were dating Drake, so I invited him to dinner."

I clenched and unclenched my jaw. "You did what?" I asked through my teeth.

"In my defense, you weren't very convincing when you said you weren't dating him. As soon as I mentioned condoms you turned as red as a beet."

I fought to keep myself from screaming. "Because it was the first time you'd ever discussed my sex life with me!"

She looked down at the counter, absently brushing off non-existent crumbs. "Well, he'll be here any minute."

"Great. Just perfect," I said, throwing my hands in the air. "Drake is the last person I want to see right now. We got in a huge fight last night. I don't want to deal with him."

"That's what Mrs. Johns said, but I didn't believe her. What were you fighting about?"

I stalked around the room trying to figure out what to do. "Stupid shit, that's what." I could see my mom's jaw tighten. She was fairly liberal but she hated swearing, which made it difficult to talk to her since I'd become a doctorate level profanity user in college. "He doesn't agree with some of the investigations I'm doing for a story I'm working on. He thinks I'm going in the "wrong direction" and doesn't like the people I'm working with. It's none of his business."

Mom leaned against the counter. "I'm sorry, Kate. I didn't know all of this was going on. I shouldn't have invited him."

I took a few deep breaths to calm down. "It's fine. I'll get through it. It's just an hour or so, right? I can handle it." I was trying to convince myself more than my mom.

She smiled and was about to say something else when the doorbell rang. "I'll get it," she said.

I swore some more and took another plate and glass from the cabinet.

It didn't take long before Drake strutted into the kitchen. "Hello, Katie."

I looked at him as I grabbed some napkins. It was the first time I'd seen him in jeans and a tee shirt since high school. The clothes fit him in all the right places. I took a deep breath, determined not to let my hormones override my anger. "Drake," I said in acknowledgment as I looked past him for my mom. She got me into this mess, she better be here to offer small talk. She wasn't. "Where's my mom?"

Drake folded his arms over his chest. "In the garage talking with your dad—and Spence."

Shit.

"Why is it," Drake asked, coming closer to me, "that whenever I think I'm going to spend some time with you, another guy shows up?"

I backed up to move away from him. "Well, that's not really what happened, is it?" I pointed out. "Spence was already here when you arrived."

"Is there a reason you invited him?"

"Does the reason concern you?"

He put his hands out and looked at me like I was an idiot. "I'm here aren't I? So yeah, it concerns me. I thought I was coming over for a family dinner."

"So did I," I said. "But then you showed up."

"I was invited."

"Not by me."

He moved closer. I moved another step back. "You know,"

he said, pointing at me with an annoyed look on his face. "I saw a video of you today. I knew you wouldn't listen to me when I told you to stay away from Hawke, but practically having sex with him on the tabletop of a family restaurant with kids in the room is bad manners at best."

"That's quite an imagination you have."

"Have you seen the video?"

"I was there; I don't need to see the video to know what happened," I answered, and then took it a step further. "And I can promise you" —I paused, letting the corners of my mouth slide into a sly smile— "I would remember if I'd had sex on the table—especially if the sex was with Hawke."

Drake scowled and a vein near his temple was so enlarged it looked like it was about to burst. "You could see what Hawke wanted just from looking in his eyes, Katie. And I was watching a grainy cell phone video," he shook his head. "The Bradford story is dangerous for you to keep pursuing, and so is Hawke."

My eyes narrowed into slits. "Here's the thing about me, Drake," I said. "And it's probably something you should remember. Write it down if you need to because you might even have to do some research to understand it. I'm not the type of girl who does what she's told, or gives people what they want just because they want it."

"Is that so?" he asked.

I nodded.

"Well, here's something you should remember, so write it down if you need to," he said as he kept walking toward me. I backed up until I ran into the countertop and I was literally in the corner. "Hawke's not the type of man to stop until he gets what he wants." He moved in until our bodies were parallel and we were standing only an inch apart. The tension was running at an all-time high. I was dangerously close to giving in to my hormones. "And neither am I." He put his hands on my waist and moved his head until his lips were inches from mine. "I don't do things halfway. Halfway is bullshit. Halfway and you get hurt."

Up to that moment, I'd been falling under the Dylan Drake sexy-charm-trance. As soon as he quoted a line from *The Cutting Edge,* I lost it. I burst out laughing. "That's your move? Quoting a line from an eighties movie?" I asked, still giggling. "How old *are* you?"

He moved his hands from my waist and took a step back, clearly annoyed the moment had been ruined. I wasn't. Regardless of how fitting it would have been to have my first kiss with my teenage crush in my parents' kitchen a decade later than I'd wanted it to be, I could think of better places for a kiss like that to happen. And I wasn't ready for what a kiss with Drake would mean anyway. Plus, I was still pissed off at him for his comments about Hawke.

"It was made in the nineties," he said, "and obviously you know the movie the line comes from, so you have no leeway to mock."

I pressed my lips together to make myself stop laughing, but I couldn't hide the amusement in my eyes.

"At least you're laughing now and not telling me to get over myself and everyone else to go to hell," he said.

"You're right," I admitted. "Next time you act like a jackass and piss me off—which I'm sure will happen sooner than later—just quote me another movie line." I grabbed the food off the table and nodded in the direction of the plates and glasses. "Can you get those?" I asked, opening the door. Drake picked up the dishes, and followed me to the back yard.

I'd been through a lot of awkward moments in my life—most of my teenage years had been one running tally of embarrassing situations—but nothing compared to dinner with Mom, Dad, Spence, and Drake.

Mom watched me closely, trying to discern whether I'd been telling her the truth earlier, or if I was actually having clandestine relations with both of the men at our weenie roast. We sat at the table making small talk while we ate. Dad asked Spence about the paper, and Mom asked Drake about the legislature. As fake boyfriend number one, Spence wasn't sure how to react, but seemed rather amused by the situation. As fake boyfriend number two however, Drake seemed less than thrilled. Oh, he was polite, but he wasn't sincere about it. And he eyed me suspiciously every time I paid attention to Spence.

We gathered around the fire pit to roast marshmallows and the conversation died down into uncomfortable quiet. Unaccustomed to the silence, my mom perked up. "Kate, why don't you tell us about this story you're working on that seems to have you so—*busy*." She said it like she was trying to find another word for *hussy*.

"I'm investigating Chelsea Bradford's death."

My mom looked up, confusion on her face. "Why? Her death was an accident."

"That's what it was ruled as, but I've found information indicating there might have been foul play."

"Who would have murdered a nice girl like Chelsea?" my mom asked. "And murder? It's absurd! People don't get *murdered* in Branson Falls!"

I thought it was interesting the rumors about Chelsea,

Shawn, and her pregnancy hadn't filtered through the grapevine yet. The Bradfords, and even Piper, really were keeping the information under wraps—a feat I would have thought impossible to accomplish in Branson. "I guess there's a first time for everything," I said.

"No offense, Sophie," Spence said, "but a lot happens in Branson Falls that people would have a hard time believing. If we could print the stuff we can't back up with facts yet, people would be shocked—to say the least."

My mom considered that for a minute before saying, "But Chelsea is from such a good family! Her parents were just devastated when they found out what happened, weren't they, Damon?" she said, bringing my dad into the conversation. My dad knew Chelsea's dad, Brian. They'd been golfing together a few times.

"Yeah," my dad agreed. "It couldn't have happened at a worse time. Brian Bradford has spent the last couple of years trying to get a contract with the state for one of his businesses. He was getting close to closing the deal when Chelsea died and everything was put on hold." My dad poked the fire, moving some of the logs around to redirect the smoke. "I think the deal is probably one of the reasons they had Chelsea's funeral so fast."

I stared at my dad in stunned silence for a few seconds before I asked, "Are you saying they rushed Chelsea's funeral so Brian didn't have to worry about his daughter's death and could work on his business contract again?"

"Well, when you say it like that, it sounds crass," my dad answered.

"It is crass!" I yelled. "What kind of dad acts that way?"

Drake shrugged. "One who's trying to provide for his family."

I turned to him with a suspicious expression. "Did you know about the deal Brian Bradford was working on?"

Drake got up to get a graham cracker and some chocolate for his marshmallow. "I'd heard bits and pieces about it, but it's not a surprise. Brian is an entrepreneur and knows a lot of people at the capitol. It's how his businesses have been so successful. He works hard and gets things done."

I shook my head. "I just can't believe work was more important than the death of his daughter. Most parents would take time off from their job to grieve if their kid had just died, not jump right back into work."

"People deal with death in different ways," my dad said.

"If that's how you ever deal with my death, I'll come back and haunt the hell out of you."

My dad laughed and Spence and Drake both chuckled a little. My mom wrinkled her nose at my swearing. Luckily, "hell" was one of the lowest swears on the "threat to eternal salvation" level.

"At least being a journalist in a place like Branson is pretty safe," my mom said. "It's not like bigger cities where you'd have to carry Mace, or maybe even a gun." Mom looked like she was contemplating me with a nine millimeter and shuddered. She had serious fears about big cities. Every time a murder happened in Salt Lake while I was in college, she'd call to make sure I was still alive. She kept thinking of the city as a larger version of Branson, only with way more gang members, prison escapees, and killers.

I looked over and saw Drake smiling. He was like me. He lived in Branson but considered himself more metropolitan than small town.

As the fire began to die down, I turned to Spence whose eyes were drooping. "Are you ready to go?" I asked.

He startled, shaking his head. "Yeah." He got up from his chair and looked at my parents. "Thanks for dinner. It was really great."

I gave my mom and dad a hug, thanking them for the food.

Drake stood up. "I should go too," he said. "Thank you for your hospitality and the wonderful dinner, Damon and Sophie. I'm glad I finally got to see the beautiful home Katie grew up in." My mom beamed at his compliment. I had to admit Drake sounded much smoother than Spence. The charm came from being a politician, but it just made me more suspicious of him. When a person lies for a living, it's hard to get cynics like myself to trust them.

I walked out to the front of the house with Drake and Spence. Drake's Hummer was parked in front of the driveway. That would start a whole new slew of rumors. I unlocked my Jeep, opening the door. Spence walked around to the other side while Drake paused by me. He seemed like he wanted to say something, but looked past me to Spence and instead just said, "I'll see you soon."

I got in the Jeep and leaned my head back against the seat, shifting my neck until I could see Spence. "I'm sorry about tonight. I didn't know my mom had invited Drake. Instead of asking me what was going on, she listened to the current rumors about Drake and me dating."

"I was wondering about those rumors myself," he said, like he was waiting for a response. When I didn't answer he changed the subject. "Honestly, it wasn't the worst night I've ever had."

I smiled. "What was?"

"That's a longer story than I want to tell right now."

Chapter Twenty

I woke up the next morning to sun streaming through the window. It would be another hot day. I stumbled down the stairs and put bread in the toaster while I poured myself a glass of milk. I spread my special mixture of butter, peanut butter, and honey over the still warm toast. I was watching the morning news while I ate when I heard a knock on my door.

I got up to answer it and my seventy-year-old neighbor, Phyllis, was on the other side wearing a red morning dress. A pink scarf covered the curlers wrapped around her white hair. She was one of the sweetest women in town and she made excellent treats. She'd brought me homemade brownies when I'd moved in, and helped me unpack while we watched *The Bachelorette*. We shared an appreciation for baked goods and hot men. "Good morning, Kate," she said, though the worried lines at the corners of her mouth didn't indicate there was anything good about it.

"Hi, Phyllis. Do you want to come in?"

She slowly shook her head. "Actually, I'd like you to come outside." I looked down at the bright blue soccer shorts and white tank top I'd worn to bed. I decided the outfit wouldn't be too appalling to wear in public. I slipped on my flip flops as I followed Phyllis out the door. When we got to the end of the sidewalk, she paused and glanced up at me. "You might want to prepare yourself, dear."

I wrinkled my brow, growing more concerned by the second. Phyllis moved out of the way as I stepped onto my driveway and froze in stunned silence.

I stared at what had once been my beautiful black Jeep—it now resembled a cream puff. White foam dripped from the hood, roof, and doors. At least two dozen egg yolks and shells made the SUV look like some kind of strange contemporary art. I was pretty sure the foam wasn't cleaning solution either. I walked up and smelled the cool mint scent of shaving cream and started to swear. When I was finished with a verbal tirade that would have impressed the British, I turned and realized Phyllis was still there. "I'm sorry," I said with a wince.

She patted my arm. "It's all right, honey, I said a few of those words myself when I looked out the window while I was waiting for my cof—hot chocolate—to be done and saw your car. Will you be all right?"

I nodded. "I just have to call work and let them know I'll be late. Thanks for telling me. Hopefully I can get it clean before the paint is ruined."

She gave me a genuine smile. "You just call if you need anything." She walked down the driveway and back to her house.

I stared a few minutes longer before I flipped open my cell phone. When Spence answered I asked, "Are you at work?"

"Yeah, where are you?"

"I'm at my house wondering how long the shaving cream

and eggs covering my Jeep have been on it, and if I'll be able to get it clean before the paint is destroyed."

"Damn," Spence breathed the word out in a stunned tone. "Do you know who did it?"

"Would I be standing here talking to you if I did?" I started picking pieces of eggshell off the Jeep and that's when I noticed the note plastered to the window on the driver's side. I peeled it, still dripping in egg yolk, from the window. "Hold on, I just found a note."

I read the note as Spence asked, "What does it say?"

"*Stay away*," I answered with a snort. "And get this, it's written with letters from a magazine." I didn't add that it looked eerily similar to the other note I'd found on my desk at work.

"Apparently someone's trying to send you a message. I'm coming over." I could hear Spence's keys jangling over the phone.

"A message to shave and bake a cake?" I shook my head even though he couldn't see me. "You don't have to come over. I'll just call the police. They can write a report, and I'll start scrubbing."

"Kate," Spence's voice sounded almost worried, "maybe you should stop investigating Chelsea's murder? I don't want you to get hurt."

I balked at the idea. "No way! Other reporters have gone through a lot worse than this to find out the truth." I threw some more eggshells on the ground. "Plus, my car got hurt, not me. Insurance probably covers this kind of thing, right?"

"Eggs and shaving cream? I have no idea. But ask your mom, I'm sure she'd know." Spence's voice had a slight lilt to it that let me know he was smiling. "Are you sure you don't want me to come over?"

"Yeah, I'll be fine. Call me if there are any story emergencies. You might have to pick me up if I can't get the Jeep clean. I'll let you know if I need help." I hung up.

I called the police next. My house is only half a mile from the police station and, like usual, there was nothing else going on so they arrived within two minutes of my call. Officer Bob got out of his car and pulled his pants up, adjusting his belt. He walked a circle around my SUV. When he reached me, he gave a long whistle as his eyes moved from the front to the back of the Jeep. "Who did you piss off?"

"The possibilities are endless," I replied.

I showed the police the egg and shaving cream covered note drying on my lawn. They took some pictures and gave me a case number to call my insurance with before they left. I knew the incident would be mentioned in the *Tribune's* police report. I couldn't wait to find out what rumors started because of it.

I needed to get the Jeep clean as soon as possible so I got the car wash mitt from inside the house and filled a bucket with warm, soapy water. It was sticky, but it was coming off and my paint seemed to be surviving. The vandalism must have happened recently. Luckily, I'd gotten to it before the morning heat baked it into a crusty mess. I'd still have to take it to the detail shop for a serious cleaning and wax job once I got the crap off of it though—that money would have to come out of my grocery budget for the month.

As I went through bucket after bucket of soap, I tried to figure out why someone would choose to ruin my SUV as a threat? They could have just as easily stuck the note to the front door. And regardless of where they put the warning, I wouldn't stop investigating, so the damage was pointless. Though I had to admit, the situation made me uneasy. First I'd gotten the note, and then my house might have been broken into. Now my Jeep was destroyed and another warning note came with the vandalism. Things had been escalating. I couldn't help but wonder how much further they'd go.

I was scrubbing in circles, my chest leaning over the hood of the Jeep as I tried to get a particularly stubborn egg spot out when I heard a deep voice say, "You can do me next."

I looked up, soap bubbles dancing on my face and in my hair. Hawke was standing there looking as hot as ever, and decidedly less wet and bubbly than me. "Hey, what's up?" I asked.

He raised an eyebrow at my comment and grinned. I looked down under the guise of vigorous cleaning, but really it was an attempt to hide the flush creeping into my face.

"You just decided to do an early morning car wash?"

"No, not exactly," I said, still scrubbing. "I'm trying to get my Jeep clean before the paint is ruined. Someone plastered it with shaving cream and eggs last night."

I glanced up. Hawke did not look happy. "Do you think it was just a prank?"

"I did until I saw that note taped to the window." I pointed toward the paper drying on the grass with *'stay away'* written on it.

Hawke walked over to it, read the warning, and frowned. "What are your plans today?"

I shrugged. "After I get the Jeep clean, I'm going to change and do some more investigating on Chelsea's murder."

"I'm coming with you," Hawke stated matter-of-factly. "We'll take my car. And tonight, I'm giving you a self-defense lesson."

I got the hood clean and stepped back, surveying the paint and my handiwork. "You know self-defense?"

Hawke gave me one of his sexy half smiles that implied a lot more than any words could. "I know a lot of things I could teach you, Kitty Kate." I nodded slightly as I opened my eyes wide. I knew exactly what he was talking about, but wasn't sure I was ready for that lesson.

I rinsed the soap off while Hawke watched. When I was satisfied it was clean, I washed out the soap bucket and walked toward the back door. "You're welcome to come inside," I said.

He followed me into the house.

"I'm going to take a shower and change," I said.

"Am I welcome in there, too?"

I didn't answer the question out loud, but my heart started beating faster as I turned away, trying not to bolt down the hall. From behind me, I heard Hawke's voice. "Sure was nice of you to wear a white shirt to clean your Jeep." I looked down and could clearly see through the front of my tank...the one I was wearing without a bra. I hadn't even thought about the color when I started the car wash. At the time I'd just been trying to get the crap off my SUV. Damn it!

I wasn't about to tell that to Hawke though so I settled for, "You're welcome." I threw my wet clothes in the laundry basket and stepped into the bathroom.

I was half-expecting, half-hoping to see Hawke lying naked on my bed when I came out of the shower. He wasn't, and it was disappointing. I threw on some jeans and a black shirt, dried my hair, and pulled it into a half-ponytail. I put on some light pink lipstick, brown eye shadow to emphasize my blue eyes, and mascara.

When I walked into the living room, Hawke was flipping through one of the women's magazines sitting on my table, a read he'd no doubt been drawn to by the cover highlighting one of the articles: "Fifty Sexy Ways to Thrill Him in Bed."

"Learning a lot?" I asked, struggling to latch my watchband to my wrist.

He put the magazine back on the table. "I'm more interested in how much you're learning from these magazines."

I arched an eyebrow, giving him a wicked smile. "Wouldn't you like to find out?"

He stood up and walked toward me. He took the watch from my hand and fastened it gently to my wrist. "Careful, Kitty Kate," he warned, his hands lightly rubbed my pulse point. "I might take advantage of an offer like that." My eyes went wide and Hawke smiled.

"What makes you think I'm the type of girl who does things like that without being married?"

His smile shifted from amused to shrewd. "Because a good girl wouldn't have known what I was doing to her milkshake, but clearly, you understood." My cheeks, and other parts of me, got hotter before he continued, "So, what are we doing today?" he asked, putting the magazine back on the table.

I stared at him, shocked he was still so intent on being my bodyguard. "Honestly, I'm fine. You don't have to waste your whole day with me."

He caught my eye in the way he's so good at; the way that makes me feel like I can't turn away and don't want to. "Spending time with you is never a waste."

I tried to laugh the comment off. "Because of my professional prowess?"

He still held my eyes. "Because of everything you are."

It felt like the house was getting hotter by the second. It

was a good thing I'd had the forethought to wear black. If I was going to spend the whole day with Hawke, I didn't want him to see me sweat. "I need to drop the Jeep off at the car detail shop, and I was thinking we could talk to Julia Bradford again. I was at my parents' house last night and they said Brian Bradford was trying to get a business deal with the state. My dad thought that's why Chelsea's funeral was pushed through so fast. When I spoke to Julia about it though, she said they tried to get it over quickly to minimize the chances of people finding out Chelsea had been pregnant." I picked up my purse. "I'd like to ask her more about her husband. He's never been home when I've stopped by, and the only time I've seen him was at Chelsea's funeral. I get the impression he's a workaholic."

"I think that's a good plan." Hawke stood up, pulling his keys from his pocket.

"I just have to stop by the *Tribune* to pick up the memory stick for my camera. I was running late for dinner at my parents' last night and forgot it."

"It sounds like you had a hectic night."

I looked at him. "Like you wouldn't believe."

Hawke followed me to the car detail shop. When we finally made it to the office, it was almost noon.

"Hey," Spence said when he saw me walk in. "Did you get your SUV," —his voice trailed off for a second as he noticed Hawke following me— "clean?"

"I scrubbed it this morning, and I just took it to the detail shop," I answered, looking around my desk. "The paint should be all right once they wax it."

Hawke sat in my chair as Spence pulled me into his office and away from Hawke. "I thought you said you didn't need any help? I would have come over."

"I didn't need any help. I was fine. The police came and I cleaned the Jeep."

"Then what is he," Spence nodded slightly toward where Hawke sat in my chair, fiddling with his cell phone, "doing here?"

"He just showed up at my house. I didn't invite him, and he didn't help either. He didn't even get there until I was almost finished."

"What did he want?" Spence held up his palm and closed his eyes. "Actually, I can probably guess."

I rolled my eyes at him. "We're still working on Chelsea's case together, Spence. That's why he's here."

"Sure it is." He paused, biting the corner of his lip in contemplation. "I'm worried about you, Kate."

I inclined my head. "Join the club." I walked out of the room to my desk. As I passed by Hawke, I couldn't help but notice the smirk on his face. The *Tribune* office was small. If Hawke had been paying any sort of attention, he'd just heard my entire conversation with Spence. I grabbed my memory stick, camera, and purse. "Are you ready to go?" I asked Hawke.

He nodded, following me out the door. As we walked to Hawke's Mustang he put a hand on my arm to stop me. I turned and he met my eyes with an intense look. "Spence's guess would've been right."

With Hawke's declaration hanging in the air, we drove to the Bradfords' house. I rang the doorbell, the sound overwhelmed by the high-pitched yelps of Cuddles. As soon as Julia opened the door, Cuddles went crazy wagging his tail and jumping up to greet us. He was a good watch-dog until someone opened the door, then the best he'd be able to do is lick them to death.

"Hi, Julia," I said, rubbing Cuddles under his chin. "If you have a couple of minutes, I have a few more questions."

Julia looked from me, to Hawke, and back to me again. "Is your . . . friend coming in too?"

I smiled. "This is Ryker Hawkins. He's helping me with the investigation."

"Oh, I've heard of you." Julia held out her hand and Hawke shook it. "It's nice to finally meet you."

"Nice to meet you too, Mrs. Bradford."

I looked back and forth between the two of them. They showed no sign of recognizing each other or meeting before. Huh. I guess Hawke wasn't the P.I. Julia hired after all.

We went into the bright sitting room I'd become familiar with during the past few weeks. I sat on the couch sinking in again. Hawke sat next to me, though he managed not to be engulfed in cow hide. Being there with a sidekick and trying to solve a crime made me feel like we should have badges and work on a police detective show.

"What can I answer for you?" Julia asked.

I flipped open my notebook. "I was just wondering about your husband, Brian. He hasn't been around when I've stopped by before."

"He's gone most of the time working on things for his company. He stays in Salt Lake a lot."

"I've heard he was trying to get a business deal pushed through with the state when Chelsea died, is that correct?"

"Yes. He's been working on it for over a year and it was finally coming to fruition."

"What's happening with it now?"

Her hands were folded over each other in her lap, her back stick-straight, shoulders tense. She looked a little nervous. "I think it's on hold. Brian hasn't really talked to me about it."

"Why would it be on hold now if he thought it was going to go through?"

She shrugged. "I'm not sure. When Chelsea died, he had to take three days off to help me with funeral arrangements. Maybe taking time off caused the contract to stall."

He only took a few days off though. It didn't seem like that would have affected his contract negotiations. "When I talked to you before, you said you tried to push Chelsea's autopsy and funeral through quickly so people wouldn't find out she'd been pregnant. Was that the only reason, or did Brian's contract have something to do with the speed as well?"

Julia took a deep breath. "Brian and I both felt like we should get the services over as soon as possible and move on. We thought it would draw less attention to why Chelsea had been gone. But Brian also wanted to have it out of the way so he could get back to work."

"He didn't take any additional time off to deal with Chelsea's death?"

Julia tightened her lips, taking several seconds to answer. "Brian is a very stoic man. Making sure he provides for his family is important to him. I think he just mourns differently than other people—and maybe he hasn't even hit that stage of grief yet."

I turned to Hawke who hadn't said anything the entire time we'd been there. Instead he just seemed to be watching Julia and her body language. I could tell having *The Incredible*

Hulk in her living room was making Julia uneasy. "Thank you, Julia," I said. "I appreciate your help." Hawke and I both stood up.

"Are you investigating Brian?" she asked, her tone conveying her confusion.

"Not Brian, exactly," I answered. "We're just trying to explore all connections to figure out who would have a reason to kill Chelsea."

"I see," Julia answered as she walked us to the door, worry lines forming on her forehead. "Please let me know if you need anything else."

"Thank you again," I said. Hawke hung back, saying something to Julia. I wondered why, but chalked it up to him offering her comfort. As we walked back to Hawke's Mustang, I couldn't shake the thought that maybe Brian Bradford really did have something to do with his daughter's death.

Chapter Twenty-One

"She was tense. I'm not sure she was being entirely truthful," Hawke said. He started the car, pulling away from the Bradfords' house.

"Goliath was sitting on her living room couch," I pointed out. "No wonder she was apprehensive."

Hawke grinned. "What did you think of her answers?"

"That she's telling the truth. I don't think she knows much about her husband's businesses. If Brian was involved in Chelsea's murder somehow, Julia doesn't have a clue."

"Why do you say that?"

"Because I've talked to her over and over again. She was devastated by Chelsea's death. You saw her at the funeral. She couldn't stop crying. She still has a difficult time with it. I'm sure she always will," I said. "Plus, she's upset enough that if she had anything to do with the murder, or knew anything about it, she wouldn't be able to hide it. She's clearly a mother grieving the loss of her child. I saw the determination on her face when I told her I thought there was more to the story. She seems to think so too, or she wouldn't have hired a private investigator."

Hawke listened intently to my points before pulling into a sandwich shop. "Come on. It's way past lunch time." I got a BLT and Hawke ordered some sort of Italian sandwich with a lot of sauce. "Let's eat at the park," he said. "Maybe there will be fewer people with camera phones there."

We got back in the car and I looked over at him. "Did you see the video?"

"Yep." He gave a smug smile.

"That video got me in a lot of trouble," I said. "I always seem to get into trouble when you're around."

"In trouble with whom?"

"With my mom, Spence, and Drake."

"Why?" he asked, pulling into a parking space. We got out of the car and walked to the picnic tables.

"It's a long story," I answered.

He gestured at the table and food. "We've got time."

"Well," I said, unwrapping my sandwich. "The video got around pretty fast." Hawke nodded as if he already knew that. "Spence wasn't happy about it. He thinks you're selfish and manipulative by the way." The corners of Hawke's mouth twitched. "And I had to go to dinner at my parents' house last night. I was already late and invited Spence along to stop my mom from asking me questions about the video—and the corner booth at the Mexican restaurant. Spence agreed to come, but when we got to the house, I found out my mom had already invited Drake."

Hawke's mouth turned into a full-on grin.

"My mom confronted me about the video and you being seen at my house. She was also mad that I'd invited Spence even though I was also apparently dating Drake—she has a problem with listening to rumors instead of me. She called me a hussy,"—Hawke started to laugh—"and told me to stop sleeping with and dating so many men because my reputation wouldn't be able to survive in such a small town. When Drake arrived, he got me alone and was pissed about me still spending time with you when he'd warned me to stay away. He tried to charm me into submission, which might have worked if he hadn't started quoting lines from old movies."

"All of that happened from one innocent bite of milkshake?" Hawke asked after he stopped laughing.

I stared at him. "That bite of milkshake was one of the least innocent things I've ever experienced, and you know it."

Hawke smiled. "If I'd known you were sleeping with Spence and Drake, I'd have gotten in line." I picked up a piece of lettuce that had dropped from my sandwich and threw it at him. He held up his hands to shield himself from my sandwich assault.

"I'm not sleeping with anyone."

"I could fix that problem for you."

I stared at him, stunned. "I don't doubt it."

He watched me for a few heartbeats, his eyes steady. "So Drake and Spence both told you not to spend time with me."

I nodded.

"But you're still here. With me."

I lifted a shoulder, tilting my head in a half-shrug. "You haven't given me a reason not to be," I said, taking a bite of food. When I finished it, I continued, "And Drake and Spence haven't given me a solid reason for why I should listen to them. I think they don't actually have one and they're both going off of rumors they've heard from each other. I have first-hand experience with gossip and things being blown way out of proportion, so I try not to listen to it."

Hawke gave me a level stare. "That's one of the reasons I like you. You're stubborn, independent, willing to see all sides, and not afraid of anything. You don't realize how sexy that makes you."

I wasn't sure what to be more surprised at: the fact that Hawke admitted he liked me—which most men seemed to have a problem articulating—or that he thought I was sexy. Both revelations made the heat start creeping up my face. I took a quick drink of my icy fruit punch hoping the cold would stun my blush.

Hawke didn't let it go unnoticed. "Does that make you uncomfortable?"

I gulped down my punch. "Which part?"

He looked at me while he ate. "The part about me liking you, or the part about me thinking you're sexy."

"I wasn't uncomfortable. Just surprised. Most men are hesitant to admit things like that."

He smiled, wiping his hands on his napkin. "In case you haven't noticed, I'm not most men."

I nodded and looked away so he couldn't see my wide eyes or bottom lip—which I was trying not to bite through. "I've gathered that about you."

We ate in silence for a few minutes until Hawke said, "It must have been awkward having Spence and Drake both hanging out at your parents' house."

"Yeah," I agreed. "Not the best time I've ever had."

"How did they react when they realized they were both attending family dinner?"

"Drake was pissed. Spence didn't say anything to me about it. He lets things roll off of him most of the time."

Hawke took a drink. "Don't expect that to continue."

I wrinkled my brow, confused. "What do you mean?"

A disbelieving look crossed Hawke's face. "Kitty Kate, it's obvious Spence is interested in more than just the standard boss / employee relationship. If you can't see that, you're not paying attention."

My mouth gaped for a minute before I quickly picked my jaw up. I hoped it had come across as shock about Spence wanting a relationship instead of shock that Hawke didn't already know Spence was gay. I stared at him and wondered if it was possible Spence's ruse had fooled even Hawke. If so, Spence, and maybe even me, deserved a pat on the back. I didn't imagine much got by Hawke. He was like a modern day Sherlock Holmes. So, if Spence being gay had flown under his radar, congratulations were well deserved.

"Spence and I both have the same opinions about relationships." I shrugged. "It's just harmless flirting." I finished my sandwich and balled my paper wrapper up to throw in the trash. "I don't have time for drama. It's not my problem if they want to act like a couple of teenage boys."

Hawke gave a slow smile. "You are the center of the problem, Kitty Kate."

I stood up, grabbed my trash and Hawke's, and threw it all in the garbage can behind me. "I'm not dealing with it now."

Hawke walked beside me back to the car. "You'll have to soon enough." I frowned at him. He gave me an impatient look. "I'm a man, Kitty Kate, and I'm telling you, this is just the beginning of the relationship issues you're going to have to deal with."

Hawke unlocked the Mustang and we both opened our doors. Hawke stopped, put his arms on the roof of the car, and locked eyes with me. "And Kitty Kate, of all the men in your life . . . I'm the one you should worry about the most."

Hawke was making all sorts of pronouncements today that left me simultaneously excited and uneasy. He pulled up in front of the *Tribune* office. "Do you have stuff to do in the office today?"

"Yeah, I need to finish the editing I didn't get done last night."

"Okay," Hawke said. "I'm going to drop you off. If you need to go anywhere, just call my cell phone."

"Where are you going?"

"I need to do some more checking on things."

"Why is it that we're investigating this story together, but I never know where you are, or who you're getting your information from?"

"Those things aren't important. The only thing that matters is whether the information I give you is accurate or not," he said. "It always is."

I stared at him for a couple of seconds. "I think you know more about this case than you're telling me, and I think it's been that way from the beginning."

Hawke only responded with a mysterious smile.

"What else are you keeping from me?" I asked, a little annoyed.

Hawke sighed. "I told you before; I give you as much information as I can, when I'm able to. I can't tell you who I work for, or where the information comes from. You knew that going in."

"I don't like feeling as if I'm being used," I said, the frustration making my voice lower than usual.

"You shouldn't feel that way. We're partners, just like I told you in the beginning. You give me information I need, and I do the same for you."

"I don't like secrets."

He shrugged. "Is it a deal breaker?"

I stared at him, wondering what kind of deal breaker we were talking about. "What do you mean?"

"My job is secretive by nature and there will always be things I have to keep from you. You need to decide if that's a deal breaker."

"A deal breaker to our partnership?"

He studied me for several heartbeats. "If that's what you want to call it."

I sat in silence, looking at the floor and tried to figure out why my stomach was in knots. Hawke was just a friend helping me with a story, so why did I feel like we were about to define our relationship?

Hawke finally spoke up, "This *partnership* can be whatever you want it to be. You don't have to decide now. I just think it's better for you to know what you're getting into up front. "

"Thanks. I think," I said, opening my door.

"I'll be back to pick you up in a few hours."

"Where are we going?" I asked.

"To your self-defense lesson."

I let my shoulders fall. I'd forgotten about that. I hated being told what to do and hated it even more when I felt like I was being railroaded. "Honestly, I can take care of myself."

"Maybe. But I'd rather know for sure," he said. "I'll see you tonight."

I closed my eyes and nodded my assent, knowing I wouldn't win if I tried to argue. I opened the office door as Hawke's Mustang engine grew quieter the further away it got. I stood there for a minute considering Hawke's deal breaker question. When I realized I didn't have an answer, I went inside.

Chapter Twenty-Two

"What was that?" Ella asked. "You two havin' a lovers' quarrel?" Spence looked up from the counter where he was sorting through papers and gave an almost imperceptible shake of his head. I knew he wasn't happy I'd been spending time with Hawke again.

"What?" I asked.

"You two looked like you were havin' a serious conversation out there." Ella pointed to where Hawke's Mustang had been parked.

"What are you, the friendly neighborhood Branson Falls spy?"

"It's not my fault you were bein' so public about it."

I sighed. "We weren't arguing, so make sure you get that spread around your gossip tree."

"What *were* you doin'?"

"Talking about the Bradford case, and my Jeep."

"Hot-dang," Ella said, clapping her hands. "Spence told me all about that! You've made someone good and mad."

"I seem to have a talent for it."

"Is Hawke fixin' your Jeep for you or somethin'?"

I walked over to my desk, rifling through the box with articles I needed to edit. Sometimes I really wish we had a copy editor—other than me. Even more articles had accumulated since last night. "No, but he seems to think I need self-defense lessons if I'm going to keep pissing people off."

Spence turned around. "That's one thing Hawke and I agree on."

I rolled my eyes. "I think you're both overreacting."

I sat as Ella pulled a chair up, parking it in front of my desk. "What was goin' on at your parents' house last night?"

"I just went to dinner; Spence went with me. Why?"

"Because people saw Drake's Hummer parked in front of the house for a long time. The rumor is Drake was there askin' your dad for his permission to propose," Ella said. "Has he done it yet? Is the ring huge? Can I see it?"

Spence gave a disbelieving laugh and shook his head some more.

I threw my hands in the air. "Are you kidding me?" I yelled. "First of all, Drake and I hardly know each other, so we definitely won't be getting married."

"Knowin' each other doesn't seem to matter," Ella rationalized. "Most people around here meet someone and are married in two months."

"I'm *not* one of those people. I'm one of the women who will have to know a man for years and live with him before I ever commit to spending my entire life with him—and that's a hell of a long way off—if ever."

Ella gasped. "Live with them? Without being married?" She put her hands on her hips and thought about it for a few seconds. "I don't have a problem with it, but you know if you do that, your nickname around town will be Jezebel."

I rolled my eyes. "Second, if a man ever asks my dad for

permission to marry me, I'll turn the idiot down flat. My dad's not the one marrying the guy! My dad doesn't need to give permission, I do!"

Ella looked like I'd shocked the skirt off her. When she recovered she turned her attention to Spence. "Hear that, Spence? This one," she pointed at me, "isn't traditional, so you'd better be prepared for that."

"I'll keep it in mind," Spence mumbled from across the room.

"I don't understand why people are so interested in my love life?"

"'Cause you're cavortin' with the most eligible bachelors in town!" Ella answered.

I rolled my eyes. "Why does everything have to be scandalous around here? People need to understand the difference between work and personal life. I'm just working with Drake on this story." I paused. "And for that matter, why are most of the rumors about me and Drake instead of me and Hawke?"

Ella shrugged. "People know Drake. Hawke's still a mystery. And people are scared of him. There's plenty of speculation about the two of you, but it's kept pretty hush, hush."

"Geez!" I blew out a breath, sinking back into my office chair. "Who starts these rumors?"

"I heard about it from Amber Kane. She told all The Ladies." Ella looked like she was about to say something else, but stopped herself.

I narrowed my eyes at her. "What is it, Ella?"

She closed her lips tight, making a motion like she was zipping them shut.

"I'd rather find out now than later."

Ella struggled for a minute as she tried to decide what to

do, then unzipped her lips. "Amber said some not-so-nice things about you too."

I shrugged. "I'm a journalist. I'm used to it."

"Not this kind of thing. At least, I don't think so."

I stared at her. I wasn't sure I really wanted to know, but came to the conclusion that it was better to find out and fight the trending topic than pretend it didn't exist. "Spit it out."

Ella squirmed in her seat and wouldn't look at me. "Well, she thinks you'd be better at your job if you'd learn to get a clue—I'm not sure what that means," Ella answered. She paused before she continued, "She also said that between Drake, Hawke, and Spence, you're takin' up all the eligible men in town and since you're fat and ugly, you must be havin' hot sex with all of them to keep them from findin' decent wives."

Spence dropped the stapler he was using. His face was almost as red with fury as mine felt. In a dangerously calm voice I said, "Anything else?"

Ella shrank back from my expression. "I don't think I want to tell you."

"Ella," I said, trying not to growl.

Her voice was timid as she answered, "She might have said somethin' about you being the Branson Falls hussy and . . . a whore."

I clenched my teeth and balled my fists as I tried to process the slanderous statement. I wondered what I could do to get Amber back while emphasizing my point that I was not, in fact, a "hussy" or a "whore" and wasn't even dating the guys she had accused me of having sex with. I didn't respect Amber Kane, and I didn't really care what she thought, but the fact that she was spreading complete lies about me and calling me names, which other people were surely taking as gospel, made me furious.

Ella probably would have come over to comfort me, but I was so coldly distraught that she didn't dare. After a few minutes, I realized I'd squeezed the pen I was holding so hard I'd broken it in two. The black ink dripping from my leg to the floor brought me back from my anger coma and the rage became conscious. I stood up, grabbing my purse. "Someone give me their car keys so I can murder Amber Kane."

Spence approached me like he was trying to tame a wild animal. "I think you need to take some deep breaths and try to calm down."

"That's easy for you to say!"

"You're not the only one she was talking about, Kate. My name is in that rumor cluster too."

Yeah, it was, but a rumor about Spence sleeping with me would *help* his situation. I put my purse back on the desk and fell into my chair. "This is the danger of living in a small town. I can't even talk to a couple of guys without being accused of having sex with them." I shook my head.

"It will blow over," Spence said. "As soon as a new piece of gossip comes along, they'll stop talking about you."

"Maybe for a while, but as long as I live here, it won't be over." I couldn't lift my eyes from the ground.

I heard Ella get up out of her chair and say softly, "I'll let The Ladies know they were wrong."

Spence lingered at my desk as Ella left the room. He put his hands on my shoulders and massaged them for a minute before leaning down so our conversation couldn't be overheard, "I wish I could help, but I don't think me coming out would do either of us any favors."

He was right about that. We'd both be out of a job if people in Branson found out Spence was gay.

He touched my arm in a comforting gesture. "It will be okay, Kate. I'll be in my office if you want to talk."

I attempted a half-hearted smile, but don't think I succeeded. Trying to carry on a conversation with anyone at the moment wasn't what I needed. Instead, I took the articles from the box on my desk and lost myself in editing.

Chapter Twenty-Three

Hours later, in the silence of the office, I heard the front door open. "Ready for your lesson, Kitty Kate?" Hawke asked, walking toward me.

My eyes were burning from staring at articles and computer screens all afternoon. My only break had been a trip to get dinner. Even then, my anger at Amber Kane and the gossip around town made it difficult to eat. I couldn't wait to leave the office and get rid of some of my aggression, even if it was just for a self-defense lesson.

"Yeah, let's go." I grabbed my purse, following Hawke to his Mustang. "I need to pick up my Jeep."

Hawke nodded and took me to the car detail shop. I paid for the cleaning and drove my Jeep home, where this time, I locked it safely in my detached garage.

I got in Hawke's car and didn't say anything as we drove to who-the-hell-knows-where. I wasn't sure if we were going to a gym, or a corn field. Maybe Hawke was one of those people who liked to teach in the element. Hawke sensed my mood. "Are you all right?"

I didn't look at him as I answered, "I didn't have a very good day."

Instead of asking any questions he said, "You can take it out on the punching bag." I folded my arms across my chest and stared out the window, a slight smile curving my lips as I thought of beating the hell out of Amber. Hawke could tell I was lost in my thoughts and we stayed in comfortable silence for the rest of the drive.

We were about ten miles outside of town in the middle of some farming areas when we turned onto a blacktopped lane heading toward the mountains. The lane wound down until we came to a large two-story red brick house with white shutters on the windows and a white portico surrounding the entrance to the front door.

"Where are we?" I asked.

Hawke cut the engine. "My house."

I sucked in my breath. I hadn't considered that Hawke would take me to his house. Inviting someone into your personal space is a big deal; at least, it was to me. I was surprised someone as private as him would be comfortable letting me in so fast. I got out, staring at the massive home and meticulous landscaping. In all my years living in Branson Falls, I'd never seen this house, didn't even know it was here. Then again, I'd been gone for seven years. Hawke had probably built it during that time.

I let my gaze wander around the property. The maple trees were strategically planted around the perimeter of the yard to ensure extra privacy. Burning bush shrubs wrapped around the foundation of the entire house like a leafy army, and white petunias were planted below the shrubs. Two large red brick buildings were situated about two hundred yards from where we stood. They looked like they were almost as big as the house.

"What's in there?" I asked, pointing to the buildings.

"One building is my garage."

I snorted. "You must have a lot of cars."

Hawke smiled. "And the other is the gym."

I stared at it, more than a little intimidated. That was one gigantic gym.

"Come on." Hawke motioned for me to follow him into the building on the right. I was seriously hoping he was going to show me his car collection. He wasn't.

I let my gaze wander as he turned on the lights. The gym floor looked like white oak. The walls were painted a dark chocolate color. Four windows, at least eight feet tall, were built into the south wall and another four mirrored those windows on the north. Each window was tinted almost black, allowing you to see out the windows, but not look in from outside.

The building was full of equipment. Every type of strength training and aerobic machine I'd ever seen seemed to be in Hawke's gym. As I followed Hawke through the building, a lot of the machines left me staring at them, trying to figure out exactly how they worked and what they were supposed to do. Most of them reminded me of medieval torture devices—which fit right in with my opinion of exercising.

Hawke stopped in front of a bench press. "I was thinking we could do some target practice, but I realized you probably don't know how to shoot—do you?"

"Psshh," I breathed. "Sure I do." Water guns. I know how to shoot water guns. Unlike most of the kids I'd grown up with, I'd never gone hunting or learned how to shoot a real gun. I'd never even held one. Considering how I felt about Amber Kane at the moment, that was probably a good thing.

Hawke read the look on my face. "Maybe we should start with something less . . . intense."

I followed Hawke across the floor to a set of metal cabinets with a lock on them. "So where's the gun range? In the basement with the dungeon?" I joked.

"Actually, the gun range and dungeon are in the side of the mountain," Hawke answered immediately, missing my flippant tone.

I blinked. "You're kidding, right?"

"Nope."

"First of all, you own the mountain behind your garage?"

He paused. "Parts of it."

I took a few seconds to come to terms with that. "And you're telling me you have a gun range and a dungeon built into the mountain?"

"It's more like a holding facility than a dungeon."

I nodded my head and ran my tongue over my teeth, then in a raised voice said, "Who are you?"

He clicked the corner of his mouth. "You know how the saying goes. I could tell you, but then I'd have to kill you." I stared at him, wondering how literally he took that adage. He opened the cabinet to reveal several shelves stocked with everything from handcuffs to spare cell phones. He handed me a can of Mace from one of the shelves. "I assume you know how this works?"

I snapped the lid off the can, looking at the pressurized sprayer. "Yeah. Like hairspray."

He gave a slight shake of his head as if he was disgusted I'd just compared a disabling device to Aqua Net. "Let's warm up on the punching bag; you look like you could use it."

"What's that supposed to mean?"

Hawke grabbed some black boxing gloves off the punching bag stand. "It means you've had a bad day and need to get rid of some of your aggression." I narrowed my eyes at him. He ignored it. "Have you boxed before?"

"A little." If the imaginary opponents I beat up while suffering through my workout DVDs counted.

Hawke helped me put the gloves on and gave me some tips about how to hold my wrists so I wouldn't injure them. After a few practice punches, Hawke held the bag as I punched the black logo with every ounce of strength I had. As soon as I thought I couldn't punch it any more, I thought of Amber's face, and punched even harder. At that point, I started adding in some kicks as well. Hawke moved out of the way and stood back in silence, letting me abuse the bag. After about twenty minutes, I slowed down and finally slumped over as I took the gloves off, trying to catch my breath.

Hawke walked to a refrigerator in the corner of the room. He came back with a cold bottle of water, unscrewed the cap, and handed it to me. I gulped down the water, inhaling some deep breaths through my nose, and repeated the process until my breathing slowed. Hawke took the water from me and put it on the hardwood floor.

"Have you taken a self-defense class before?" he asked, walking me to a large mat on the floor in the corner of the room.

"In college."

"Good," he said. "Show me."

My eyebrows shot up into my forehead. "Show you what?"

"I'm going to attack you. Defend yourself."

"No way!" I yelled. "I don't want to risk hurting you."

Hawke's eyes flashed with amusement. "Try," he drawled in a taunting tone.

"No."

"Kitty Kate, you need to practice this."

"I won't."

He stood back, put his index finger over his lips, and gave me a measured stare. "Think of it like sex."

I shook my head in confusion. "I've never had sex that required self-defense moves."

His eyes danced as he lifted one corner of his mouth. "Then you've never had good sex."

And it was at that moment, when I was caught completely off-guard, that he chose to attack. Even though the thought of wrestling Hawke appealed to many of my senses, I refused to fight back and just stood there. With Hawke so close, I could smell his Swagger body wash. I inhaled a deep breath with a smile, waiting for him to give up and stop trying to instigate violence against himself. Instead, with his arms still wrapped around me in a vice grip, he said, "I thought Drake would be pulling out all the moves with you. His reputation in bed will go to hell when people find out you're having shitty sex."

In a swift move I brought my arms up, wrapping them around Hawke's so he had to either break his hold on me, or end up with two broken arms. I pushed him away and spun around, kicked his shin, and punched him in the jaw. "I am NOT sleeping with Dylan Drake!"

Hawke rubbed his jaw and walked off the pain in his leg. "So you were just teasing him with the sexy dress you wore when you showed up for the legislature party as his date."

I glared at him. "It wasn't a date," I explained. "It was reconnaissance. I had to wear the dress to fit in with my surroundings."

"Whatever you want to call it, Kitty Kate."

"I've been meaning to ask you about that. When did you show up? And what were you doing there?"

"I was there all day. I was watching to make sure you were okay. We're partners, and you're the only one with boobs; you're valuable to have around."

"My boobs are nothing special. If something happens to them you can purchase another set on State Street for an hourly rate."

"Not like yours."

"I didn't know you were there until you sent me the text about my dress. It would have been nice to know you were surveilling me."

"It was the first time you'd done anything undercover. If you'd known I was there, you would have acted differently."

I thought about that. He was probably right, especially when it came to being around Drake. Despite my better judgment, I was attracted to both of them and wouldn't have wanted Hawke to see me acting like a couple with Drake. Knowing about Hawke's presence too soon could have blown my cover.

"So," Hawke said, still rubbing his shin, "obviously, you remember how to defend yourself." He gave me a few more tips on getting out of situations before an attack happens, and showed me how to defend myself if it did. By the time we were done, it was close to ten o'clock. Hawke gave me another bottle of water to drink and drove me back to my house.

He pulled into my driveway. I was about to get out of the car when Hawke grabbed a paper from the backseat. "You need to see this," he said, turning off the Mustang engine and switching on the interior lights.

I gave him a curious look as I glanced at the paper. It appeared to be some sort of conversation.

Fordguy18: "Tell her that wasn't part of the deal."

Cutiepie94: "You know she doesn't care what you think."

Fordguy18: "She used to care. Just because she's not here right now doesn't change things. We agreed to do this and we're following through with the plan."

Cutiepie94: "Then you'll have to convince her."

Fordguy18: "I'll convince her. One way or another."

I finished reading and looked at Hawke. "What is this?"

He leaned his shoulder against the door, turning so he could talk to me more easily. "It's the text from an instant messaging conversation that took place a week before Chelsea was murdered."

I stared at him. "How did you get it?"

"From my sources," he said without apology. "What do you make of it?"

I laughed as I tilted my head back and shrugged. "I have no idea. I don't know the context. It seems kind of threatening, but I don't know who was talking or who they were talking about."

Hawke's gaze was level as he answered, "I have it on good authority they were discussing Chelsea."

I watched him for a minute wondering who exactly his sources were and how they had a copy of this conversation. Things would be a lot easier if Hawke would just let me in on his part of the investigation. I read the messages again before shaking my head. "It could mean a hundred different things. If it's about Chelsea, it seems like the girl is defending her and the boy is angry. I don't know what the part about the plan means."

Hawke nodded. "That copy is yours."

"Thanks." Hawke would never tell me everything he knew about Chelsea's murder, but the copy of the conversation made me feel like he was at least trying to include me more. "I'll think about it and look it over. Maybe something will click."

Hawke nodded again.

"Thanks for spending the day with me and helping me brush up on defending myself."

"Anytime you want to use the gym, you're welcome to it."

"And the gun range in your mountain?" I teased.

The side of his mouth twitched into the alluring half smile he used so much he should probably patent it. "When you're ready to learn, I'll be happy to teach you *everything* I know."

My stomach fluttered. It felt like our conversation had just shifted from guns to sex. They were both equally scary and either way, I knew Hawke had more experience. The thing that unnerved me was how quickly I'd thought of taking him up on the offer. I guess that answered his earlier question about deal breakers—there weren't any.

I didn't respond to Hawke's suggestive offer and instead just smiled as I got out of the car. I was about to shut the door when Hawke leaned over, reaching across the seat. "Don't forget your can of Mace," he said, holding it out to me.

Hawke waited while I unlocked the front door. Between the Mace and my renewed sense of strength, I walked into my house ready to take on anything—even Amber Kane.

Chapter Twenty-Four

When I got up to make coffee the next day, I realized all I had were some left over grounds and a filter. I found enough quarters and dimes in my change jar for a McDonald's combo meal with coffee. I decided I deserved it for not killing Amber. I got some breakfast and brought it home to enjoy my greasy egg sandwich and hash brown in privacy.

Eating the heart clogging food made me feel guilty, so I decided to go for a run to redeem myself. I put on some soccer shorts and a tank top, grabbed my iPod, tied my running shoes, and took off out the door, my house key secured in a lock box under the porch railing.

I ran down the street, winding my way through neighborhoods. I passed the fair grounds and police department, and jogged by the hospital and high school. A few blocks from my house, I noticed Mrs. Pool happily planting flowers in her front yard. She was seriously committed to be gardening this early. She waved as I passed and I smiled, waving back. When I got home, I unlocked the door and went inside to shower. By the time I was out, it was late morning. I pulled on black capri pants and a sea green tee shirt, and swiped on eye shadow, mascara, and rose pink lipstick. I picked up my bag on the way out the back door. My Jeep was still in the garage where I hoped it had stayed safe from any new vandalism.

I walked out to my garage, but stopped when I saw Hawke's Mustang blocking the driveway. Hawke was leaning against the car wearing a dark red shirt that could barely accommodate his bulging arms. He also had on blue jeans and black combat boots. The boots had gone out of fashion in the nineties, but in Hawke's life, combat boots seemed to be standard—and unlike most people, he looked like he'd been in combat, so he could pull them off.

I started toward Hawke when I realized his car door was open. Hawke was talking to someone sitting inside. I squinted, seeing the unmistakable outline of my dad's broad shoulders and pepper colored hair.

I approached them. "Good morning."

"Morning yourself," Hawke smiled. "I knocked, but you didn't answer."

"I was in the shower."

Hawke's eyes darkened. I knew how he would have responded if my dad hadn't been there. Speaking of my dad, I shouldn't ignore him. "Hi, Dad. When did you get here?"

"Ten or fifteen minutes ago," he said, getting out of the car and giving it a covetous look. "I've been talking to Hawke. Isn't his car great?"

"Yeah, it is. Did he give you a ride in it?"

My dad nodded. "Around the block. The engine just purrs."

"I'd describe it as more of a roar," I said. Hawke smiled again.

"You've been in it?" my dad asked.

"A few times."

"Why didn't you tell me?"

I shrugged. "I guess it slipped my mind. Usually when I'm at your house it's to deal with another one of Mom's Catasophies."

"Catasophie?" my dad asked.

"You haven't heard that before?" He shook his head. "How is that possible? It's the nickname people around town use for Mom."

He laughed, but stopped short, pointing at me. "Don't tell her that. She'll be madder than a wet hen, and you know how she gets when she's mad. That look in her eyes is evil."

I couldn't agree more. When she got that look, worse things than normal happened. "I won't say anything." I glanced from my dad to Hawke. "So, was there something you both needed?"

My dad answered first. "You know the other night when we were talking about the Bradfords?"

"Yeah. Thanks for the information on Brian. It was a big help. I asked Julia some questions about it."

My dad's forehead creased in worry. "When did you talk to her?"

"Yesterday morning, why?"

"Last night your mom and I came home from dinner and saw Brian carrying a bunch of luggage to his Range Rover. At first we thought he was just going on a business trip, but it looked like he was carrying his whole closet outside."

"That's really weird. I wonder what happened."

"I'm not sure, but I can say this: I've never heard Julia Bradford lose her temper, but she was yelling like a banshee at Brian last night. It didn't go on for very long because she noticed some of the neighbors staring, but she wasn't happy."

I shook my head, trying to figure out what might have gone wrong. She didn't seem thrilled when Hawke and I were there yesterday, but she was still trying to make sense of her daughter's death; I wouldn't expect her to be happy. "We just asked her questions about Brian's business and the contract he was working on. I don't know why that would have made her so upset."

"Maybe the questions made her think about it more," Hawke said. "Maybe she realized how mad she was that Brian hadn't been there for her. He was obviously more concerned about his business deal than the death of his daughter."

I tapped my finger against my purse as I thought about Hawke's theory. "I've talked to Julia a few times. It seems like it would take a lot to get her mad enough to yell at someone in front of the whole neighborhood."

"I don't know what happened, but I thought I should tell you," my dad said. "Maybe it will help with your story." He got out of Hawke's Mustang and ran his eyes over it, the longing evident on his face. "If you ever want to sell it, you better call me first." He extended his hand to Hawke. "It was good to meet you."

Hawke smiled. "You too, Damon. Maybe we need to build you one of your own."

My dad beamed as he turned and gave me a hug. "Have a good day, sweetie."

"You too, Dad."

He walked to his car parked in front of my house, waving as he drove away.

"I didn't know you restored this yourself," I said to Hawke. The information made me look at the car with a whole new layer of admiration.

"There's a lot you don't know about me."

"So I've heard."

Hawke nodded. "I have no doubt you've heard all kinds of things."

"I'm a reporter. Getting information is kind of my specialty."

He cocked his head, pushing his chin out. "And what have you found out about me so far?"

"Wouldn't you like to know?" I tried to sound coy even though aside from my Google search, I didn't really know anything. After a few seconds I looked up and saw that he was patiently watching me. "What are you doing here this morning?"

"Checking on you."

I did a little twirl for him. "I'm fine, see."

His eyes darkened as he slowly moved them over my body, and then met my gaze. "I would have seen a lot more if your dad hadn't shown up."

I watched him, my lips curling up slightly. "You're pretty confident."

He gave a single nod of his head.

"What makes you think I'd just let you take me?" I asked.

"What have you done to indicate you wouldn't?"

Huh. He had me there, and he knew it. I wrinkled my nose and his sly smile grew into a seductive one. I knew I needed to change the subject before we really did end up back in the house. That would be bad for many reasons; number one being that I hadn't had sex in so long I didn't know where my diaphragm was and I hadn't been out of town recently to buy condoms. Like my mom had warned, a single girl buying condoms in Branson would be another scandal. It makes me grateful I have final approval for newspaper stories so my relationship activities don't end up plastered all over the pages of the *Tribune*.

Then again, Hawke probably had plenty of protection. I bet if I opened his glove compartment, he'd be stocked like a convenience store on prom night.

"So, uh . . . what are you doing today?" I asked.

"I was planning to spend the day with you." He gave me another look that seemed to say his plans had nothing to do with Chelsea's investigation. "But now I have some things I need to look into."

I nodded, a brief flutter of relief coursing through me. "Okay, I guess I'll see you later?"

He opened his mouth slightly, running his tongue along his teeth. "Uh huh." He didn't move. I was expecting sexy Hawke to get in his sexy car and drive away, but he didn't even twitch. "It's Friday night."

"Yeah," I said slowly, trying to figure out what he was getting at.

"You have plans."

I shook my head, thinking it was a question. "Not that I know of."

"No," he said. "I'm telling you. You have plans."

"Are we going on a stakeout? Or is this your way of asking me out on a date?"

"I'm not asking."

I blinked. "Why do I keep spending time with arrogant idiots who think they can tell me what to do?"

He smiled slowly, watching me from under his brow. "I'm only telling you what you want to do anyway but won't initiate on your own, Kitty Kate."

I stared at him for a minute and unconsciously licked my lips. "What are we doing tonight?" I asked, the butterflies in my stomach fluttering down toward places I hadn't noticed for a while.

Hawke just smiled and got in his car. He didn't break eye contact with me until he had to look for traffic before pulling into the street.

As he drove away, I stood there stunned, completely unable to move. I was pretty sure I'd just agreed to have sex with Hawke, and I was positive it would be the best sex of my life—and the most terrifying.

Aside from thinking it was lucky I'd remembered to shave this morning, the only other thought running through my head was *holy shit*.

When I got to work, Spence wasn't there. One of the part-time employees, a cheerful girl still in high school, was sitting at the front desk, reading. "Hi, Stacy."

"Hi!" she called back with a toothy smile. Her perky attitude is a personality staple for most Branson women. I find it hard to tolerate. Like, don't they ever get PMS or just have a day when they want to rage against the world? Why are they so damn likeable all the time?

I sat at my desk, going through the edits Spence had given me on the cow crash article and the dog bite story. They didn't take long since most of the notes were jokes from Spence about my mom. When I finished the revisions, I opened the layout program and put the articles in. I couldn't help but laugh at the pictures from the cow crash. I even used a diagram to show where the cow had hit and how its hooves had come through the window. I knew my mom would cut the pictures out to put on her fridge. The photos were going to be legendary.

I did the layout for the other articles I had. Between text

and ads, it didn't take long to fill the paper up. I even had articles left over that I'd have to push to next week. It wasn't a big deal; it just usually didn't happen that way. It seemed like we were always scrambling to find stories to fill the pages. During times like that, Spence often joked he should just send me out with a camera to follow my mom around.

Since I was done with the layout and articles I needed to finish, I looked around for something to do. My eyes fell on the Magic Eight Ball sitting on the corner of my desk. I picked it up, asking questions in my head. The first one was, "Will I win the lottery?" That answer was "No." Next, I asked, "Will my mom have a disaster today?" The Eight Ball said, "Signs point to yes." After that I asked, "Will I have sex with Hawke tonight?" The enlightened answer on that one was, "Ask again later."

Terrific. I put the Eight Ball down. I opened up a news website and scanned the headlines, barely paying attention to what I was reading because my mind was still consumed with thoughts of Hawke, his huge house, and his mountainside gun range / dungeon. Then a thought hit me. The Google search I'd done on Hawke was helpful, but a search through a people finding website would give me more information. I really wanted to know if any of the crap Drake and Spence had told me about Hawke was actually true.

I typed in "Ryker Hawkins." After wading through several pages, I found some results that were actually about him. Hawke rescuing a hostage in Pakistan; Hawke consulting on a kidnapping; Hawke saving a kitten from a tree. Geez! Was there anything Hawke couldn't do? I was almost as interested in finding out more about Hawke as I was in finding out what had really happened to Chelsea Bradford. I printed the articles and put them in my bag so I could ask Hawke about them tonight. At dinner. Before sex. Hopefully . . . unless sex was the appetizer. The thought made my stomach cramp with simultaneous excitement and nervousness. To get my mind off of it, I turned my attention back to the search engines.

I was so lost in the information on my computer, I didn't notice when Spence came up behind me. He put a cup down on my desk. The noise startled me so much that I reflexively threw my stress ball at him.

"Dammit, Spence! You're always sneaking up on me. One of these days I'm going to hit you with something that will actually hurt."

"It hasn't happened yet."

"If you keep showing up like some sort of phantom it will!" I picked up the drink he had deposited in front of me. "Is this for me?"

"Yeah. It's a lime rickey."

"My favorite!"

"Are you doing a story on Hawke?" he asked, motioning to my computer screen.

I shook my head. "No, I finished the layout and stories for the week so I was just doing some research to find out if anything people have said about him is true."

"You don't believe what you've heard?"

I took a sip of the cold, sweet, grape and lime flavored drink. "The only people who have told me anything about him are you and Drake. I'm pretty sure you both just got your information from each other."

Spence looked down at me like he couldn't believe what I'd just said. "What have you found so far?"

"That he's a real-life James Bond. He's saved the lives of a bunch of people and I think he was part of the Secret Service.

It looks like he might have been in some crazy-dangerous branch of the military."

"And you got all this information from where?"

"The internet," I answered, like I was saying duh. "I did a Google search for his name right after I met him, but I just did a more detailed search using some of the people finding search engines.

"Did you run his name through the background check service?"

I stared at him. "We're a small town newspaper, Spence. I didn't think we had a background check service."

"We do."

I considered slapping him. "It would have been nice to know about that earlier. I could've used it."

Spence shrugged. "I did searches on the names you told me about: Governor Wallace, Shawn Wallace, Chelsea, Brian and Julia Bradford. I would have told you if I'd found something."

I was annoyed Spence hadn't told me about the background check service, or the fact that he was being a silent partner in my investigation and checking names. "Next time, you either need to tell me you're working on a story with me, or not do it at all."

Spence looked surprised. "I didn't mean to undermine you. I was just trying to help."

I nodded. "I appreciate the thought but I already had Hawke's help, and Drake's too. It would have been nice to know you were also part of the team."

Spence tilted his head. "Speaking of Hawke, you might want to type his name in."

I frowned. "Have you done a background check on him?"

Spence stared at me and gestured toward the computer. "See for yourself."

I opened the background service web site and typed in Hawke's name. It took about a minute to process before the page flickered to life. I saw Hawke's name, a list of aliases, and that was it. Nothing else. "Well, that's not very helpful."

"Exactly," Spence said. I wrinkled my brow as he pointed at the screen. "Usually the service brings up all the public information about a person: mortgages, properties related to the name, past marriages, divorces. It also brings up a lot of stuff that isn't public at all: bank records, phone records, utility bills, credit card statements. You name it, you could probably find it. Hawke doesn't have any of that."

I glanced at Spence, who seemed rather satisfied with himself. "I don't understand. What does this mean?"

"It means he's a ghost. He comes and goes when he wants, he disappears for months at a time doing God only knows what, and occasionally, he comes back to Branson Falls. People rarely saw him in town before you came around."

"I don't have anything to do with him being here."

Spence's eyes narrowed. "Yeah. I think you do."

I rolled my eyes. "He's just helping me on this story, that's all. And I'm helping him too."

Spence folded his arms across his chest. "Did he tell you why he needed your help?"

I leaned back in my chair as I took another sip of my drink. "For his job."

"But he didn't tell you what he does," Spence said, making it a statement, not a question.

"No, but he's getting me accurate information; that's all I care about."

"How do you think he's getting you that accurate information?" Spence asked, his voice terse.

"From his resources."

"The resources he won't tell you about because they're probably illegal." Spence said, his voice rising. "I told you, Kate. He's dangerous."

I let my arms fall to my side, shaking my head. "How do you know that? You said yourself you'd hardly seen him before I moved back. How do you know he's dangerous—or any of the other things you've insinuated about him?"

"Hawke's not the only one with resources."

I scowled at him. "You mean Drake."

Spence shook his head. "Not just Drake. I've heard rumors from other people too. The bottom line is that what I told you before was true. Don't get too attached to Hawke. You never know when he's going to be around, or for how long. You also don't know which team he's actually on. Sometimes he's a good guy, sometimes he's not."

I folded my arms across my chest, mirroring Spence's defensive stance. "And who decides the good and bad?"

"The rules of polite society," Spence answered. "Like I said, the only reason he's not in prison somewhere is because of the connections he has and the secrets he knows. Be careful around him, Kate."

"Hawke would never hurt me. He's gone out of his way to make sure I stay safe."

"It's not necessarily Hawke I'm worried about," Spence said. "It's the people he associates with when he's on the wrong side."

I just looked at him. I wasn't going to keep having this stupid argument about Hawke. Spence held my stare for a minute, before glancing away. I felt like I'd won some sort of small victory for Team Hawke. "Anything new on the Bradford story?" Spence asked over his shoulder as he walked away.

"Not really," I said. "I'll let you know if I come up with something."

He nodded and walked into his office. I picked up my purse and car keys. After a conversation like that, I needed some fresh air.

Chapter Twenty-Five

On my way to the car, I stopped by the *Crimp and Cut* a few stores down from the *Tribune* office. This week was Branson's annual Sidewalk Sale. It's really an excuse for stores to get rid of old Christmas sweaters, hair scrunchies, and other outdated items. Many a child has spent their entire summer allowance on Sidewalk Sale treasures. I might have been one of them.

The sale is one of the busiest retail times of the year. I needed a new hairbrush and some texturing cream. Luckily, they were marked down so I wouldn't have to pawn my Jeep to get them. I found the things I needed, and rummaged through some of the other clearance bins—and by "bins," I mean laundry baskets decorated with glitter to be eye-catching.

"You don't want people to see you holding those, dear."

I turned around and saw my mom and dad's—and the Bradfords'—neighbor, Cathy.

She looked pointedly at my hands. I was holding two bottles of Bed Head hair products. Apparently the insinuation of having bed styled hair was too much for Cathy to take. "I don't think your reputation can handle it."

I smiled sweetly. Cathy and I had never gotten along. When I was in high school, she used to wait at her window for me to get home—just like she'd done with Chelsea. I wasn't sure if she actually cared what was happening to me, or if she just wanted to be the first to know the latest gossip. My gut told me it was the latter. She'd never been invited to join The Ladies. Maybe she thought enough gossip would get her there. I had no doubt my Bed Head purchases were going to be reported immediately. "Cathy, so nice to see you. It's been too long."

She scrutinized me, trying to decide if I was being sincere. I smiled winningly again.

"I heard you're investigating Chelsea Bradford's death."

I picked up another bottle, wondering where she'd heard that. "Did you?"

"Found anything out yet?"

"I'm still investigating."

"Sad story." Cathy shook her head. "But she had it coming. All those late night liaisons." She tsked. "Girls shouldn't be allowed to have boyfriends in high school, let alone date them without other people present."

It wasn't easy, but I refrained from rolling my eyes. The double date rule had been the bane of my high school existence. Most Mormons aren't allowed to date until they're sixteen. At that point, they're only allowed to go on double dates and group dates until they turn eighteen. This meant I couldn't go on a date without an entourage. Mormons generally use the dating policy as a way to discourage sexual curiosity by keeping teens in a group where they can police each other. However, I always found that large groups are great for brainstorming bad ideas and convincing someone to act on them. Considering Chelsea had been raised Mormon and shouldn't be single dating, I was interested in Cathy's information. "She went out with guys on her own?"

"Yep. Lots of times. And the same guy. No wonder she got in trouble."

"How do you know it was the same guy?"

"Always had the same truck. Black and tall with big tires."

Something about that seemed familiar. "Did you ever see the guy?"

She shook her head. "Nope. He never got out of the truck. I could see it bouncing though. Not hard to figure out what was going on in there."

If I'd been Chelsea and knew Cathy was watching across the street, I probably would have bounced around in the truck just to shock her.

Like any good gossip hound, Cathy leaned in close, a conspiratorial look on her face. "Want to know something else? I saw someone sneaking into the Bradfords' house last week. They climbed the back deck and went in through Chelsea's bedroom. Bet you anything it was that same boy."

That was strange. But really, it could have been anyone. "How do you know it wasn't one of Chelsea's siblings?"

"I know what they look like. This one was taller. And this person snuck in at night. They were only there for six minutes, before they snuck back out and ran down the street where I couldn't see them anymore."

"Why would someone sneak into Chelsea's bedroom after she was already dead?"

"Don't know. Maybe she had something they wanted to make sure no one else found."

"That's interesting. I'll look into it. Thanks, Cathy." I made a mental note to ask Julia Bradford about it and find out if anything was missing from Chelsea's room.

She beamed like she'd done something extraordinary. "Anytime. Let me know if you need more help."

I was sure when this was all over and we knew what had happened to Chelsea, Cathy would somehow try to get credit for solving the case.

"And just between you and me, people are saying some nasty things about you lately. You might want to keep your chest in your shirt for a while."

My lips thinned to a line as I bit my tongue. She eyed me closely to make sure I'd gotten her message. When she was sure I had, she turned and walked to another store to peruse their sales.

I decided to get out of there before I said something I shouldn't.

There are a couple of great things about living in a rural farming community. I love being able to go outside in the summer and smell the fresh air that carries whiffs of newly turned soil, flowers, and even the apple pies baking at a neighbor's house down the road. I missed that when I lived in the city—full of exhaust fumes and foul smells.

I love being able to look up at the bright blue sky, and at night, lie on the grass and see millions of stars. In the city, those sights are clouded by pollution and electricity. But my favorite thing about living in a small town is the rural roads. On the long stretches of asphalt, if you see another person at all, it's usually someone on a tractor or four-wheeler. The unpoliced roads are perfect for a leisurely drive when you want to think or for a gas-fueled frenzy when you're pissed off. At the moment, I was burning through my gas like crazy.

I was pissed about Cathy and her reminder that everyone in town still thought I was the Branson whore. Add to that the things Spence had said about Hawke, and I wasn't a happy reporter. Part of the problem stemmed from me being worried Spence might be right. Not about the good guy versus bad guy stuff. I realized the thing I worried most about was having feelings for Hawke and then having him leave. I needed to nip this emotion in the bud. I wanted my relationship with Hawke to be fun, maybe even a friends-with-benefits kind of thing when he was in town. For now, that's what I needed from Hawke. Maybe someday, if our lives ever synced up, we could decide if we wanted more.

After my drive through the countryside, I needed to refuel. I stopped at one of two gas stations in Branson. While I was filling my tank, Julia Bradford pulled into the full service lane. She saw me. While the station attendants went to work filling her car with gas, checking the pressure of her tires, and cleaning the windows, Julia came over to my Jeep.

"Hello, Kate."

"Julia, I was going to call you or stop by today. How are you doing?"

She was wearing large, black sunglasses that covered most of her face, but the glasses couldn't disguise the red blotches on her cheeks or her puffy nose. Since it wasn't cold season, I knew she'd been crying.

"I've been better." I could tell she was trying to keep her tone even.

"I heard that Brian moved out. I'm so sorry."

"Don't be. Talking to you and your . . . friend the other day made me start thinking about things."

I grimaced inside. I was really hoping my visit to her house hadn't been the catalyst for Brian leaving.

"I realized I've been dealing with our family by myself for years. I guess that's what I signed up for—it was kind of an unspoken agreement between Brian and I when we got married. But the fact that he wasn't there for me or our kids when Chelsea died, that he was still so concerned with his business deal, was the straw that broke the camel's back. I guess I didn't see it until you came over to talk to me."

"Julia, I'm so sorry. I didn't mean to cause any problems."

She absently rubbed her hand over her forearm and gave me a smile that wavered a little. She swallowed, steadying her voice. "No. You did me a favor. I don't even recognize Brian anymore. He's not the man I married." She looked down at the keys in her hands. "I need to pay for my gas; I just wanted to say thanks."

I didn't know what the appropriate response for breaking up a marriage was. "Um, sure." Cathy's information about Chelsea was still fresh in my mind. I wanted to ask Julia about it. "Can I ask you another question about Chelsea before you go?"

She nodded.

"I bumped into your neighbor, Cathy. She mentioned she saw someone break into Chelsea's room last week. Did you notice anything strange, missing, or out of place?"

Julie shook her head. "Cathy told me about her suspicions the day after she saw someone going in through Chelsea's room. I checked the room, but everything looked the same as the last time I'd been in there with you. I think it was just Chelsea's sister. She's been having a hard time with the death. She goes in there at least once a day to "talk" to Chelsea for a few minutes. I told Cathy that, but she insisted it was someone else. Between you and me, I think Cathy's eyes aren't what they used to be."

I smiled and nodded. "You're probably right. Thanks for your help, Julia."

She nodded and started to walk away, but turned back to me. "I don't know if this will help you, but even as Brian was getting his things, he still wouldn't admit he was wrong. He just kept saying he had to make sure the governor was protected."

I stared at her. "What did he mean by that?"

She shrugged her shoulders, lifting her arms in an 'I don't know' gesture. "I haven't a clue." She walked over to her car and got her purse before going inside to pay for her gas. As I watched her go, I exhaled a deep breath. I felt like it was probably one of the first times in years Julia Bradford had actually been in control of her life.

Chapter Twenty-Six

After my gas tank was full, I drove home to get a late lunch. I searched through the cabinets and found some old pasta and canned food that had probably been there since before I moved in—undoubtedly part of the previous renters' food storage. Mormons are taught to keep a two month food storage supply on hand. I didn't even have two days. I hoped one of my Mormon neighbors would take pity on me during any natural disasters; otherwise, I'd have to learn to eat dandelions.

I looked through my fridge, it was pretty bare too. I always forgot to make time to go shopping. I was able to scrounge up enough non-moldy bread and cheese to make a grilled cheese sandwich. I wrote a note on my whiteboard to remind myself to get groceries . . . and I wouldn't be getting much since the Jeep's cleaning came out of my grocery money.

I'd almost finished eating my sandwich when I heard the doorbell ring. I usually don't get visitors in the middle of the day; but, I'm usually not home in the middle of the day to know whether people stop by or not. It could be the missionaries. Hmm. I paused, deliberating about whether I was up for an argument.

The doorbell rang again, only this time it was accompanied by a series of loud thumps that came across a lot less friendly than a knock. Usually the missionaries aren't so persistent. I opened the front door and saw the yellow Hummer in front of my house before I saw him. The lighter strands of his hair were highlighted by the sunlight, his blue eyes dark with anger. He pushed past me into my house as I seethed. "Dammit, Drake! You brought the Hummer again! I thought we talked about this. I'm already the subject of five hundred rumors around town. I don't need to add Drake and Kate having a nooner to that list."

"Why didn't you tell me about your Jeep?" He had his hands on his narrow hips and did not look pleased.

I shrugged and scrunched up my nose, completely baffled by Drake's anger. "It was cream puffed. I got it cleaned."

He paced around the living room. "You should have called me."

"For what?" I asked. "So you could take photos?"

"So I could do something about it."

I widened my eyes. "Oh, you mean you wanted to clean the crap off my Jeep for me? Yeah, right." I laughed skeptically. "Seriously. What would you have done?"

He just stared at me. I stared back.

"You know," I said, putting my hands on my hips, mimicking his stance, "you have a real problem with women who can take care of themselves."

"No," he said, pointing at me, "I have a problem with women who aren't careful."

"What's that supposed to mean?"

"What if the person who did that to your SUV had come into your house instead of just destroying your Jeep?"

I paused, thinking about it. "Then *I* would have been cream puffed?" I guessed, holding out my hands like I didn't know. "My Jeep was hardly destroyed. It's not like I asked for this to happen. I'm working on a story that could involve the governor. You even told me it might be dangerous. I'm not going to stop working on the article, so this is just something I have to deal with. I have insurance."

Drake's face was hot with anger. "That's exactly my point! I warned you to be careful and you weren't!"

I rolled my eyes. "I was! I've been on guard ever since I got the first note, and thought someone broke into my house!" I stopped short, realizing that was probably way too much information.

Drake suddenly became very still. Like a volcano on the verge of erupting. "What. Note?"

I sighed and tilted my head down, closing my eyes for a moment. When I was ready, I looked back up at the barely contained fury also known as Drake. "I got a note at the *Tribune* a while ago telling me to be careful about who I worked with."

I could see the veins in his neck pulsing.

"And the break-in?"

I waved my hand in front of my face like it wasn't a big deal. "My back door was just unlocked one morning. I must have forgotten to check it before I went to bed."

The skin across Drake's cheeks and jaw was pulled tight, shadows settling into the hollows of his face. I could almost see the steam coming out of his nose like an angry Drake dragon.

"Geez, Drake. Calm down before you have a stroke. Why

are you so upset about this? We've only been…" I struggled for a word and came up with, "friends for a few weeks. You barely even knew me before I moved back to Branson."

He took a deep breath. "Oh, I knew you."

I rolled my eyes. "Since I wasn't parading around in a cheerleading uniform, I find that hard to believe." I waited for him to elaborate, but he didn't, so I continued, "Listen, you're mad at me for not being careful—why, I'll never understand—but I *have* been careful. Last night I even worked with Hawke to refresh my self-defense skills."

He stopped pacing and stared. "Hawke." He said the name like he was spitting something unpleasant out of his mouth. "You might as well wrestle an alligator. It would be about as safe as spending time with Hawke."

Considering the Hawke lecture I'd already been given from Spence today, I was up for a fight. I folded my arms under my chest. "I don't know what you have against him, but I think Hawke's great. He helped me out a lot last night."

Drake gave me a steely stare, his eyes hitching on my propped up boobs. The corner of his lip curled up. "I just bet he did."

"Give it a rest, Drake."

"You know, Hawke's car is just as recognizable as mine, but you don't care when people see his Mustang parked at your house and talk about it," he said. "And believe me, they talk about it."

Apparently the gossip about Hawke and I had elevated from whisper status. I shrugged. "I don't mind having Roxy in front of my house. She's a hot car—and less of a threat to the environment than your Hummer, I might add."

"Roxy?" Drake's eyebrows shot up.

I nodded. "That's the name of Hawke's Mustang."

Drake stared at me, stunned. "You've got to be kidding me."

"Nope."

He took a minute to process that, and snorted. "Figures," he said. "It still doesn't answer why it's okay for his car to start rumors, but not mine."

Seriously, a pissing contest over a parking spot? Why did it feel like I was having another relationship discussion with someone I wasn't in a relationship with? I shook my head, answering, "Because Hawke doesn't have the reputation you do."

"No, his is worse." Drake stood with his legs shoulder-width apart, clenching and unclenching his jaw. After it looked like he'd made a difficult but conscious decision not to strangle me, he said, "I have a lot going on. I can't be worrying about your butt all the time."

"No one asked you to!" I said, not sure I wanted Drake thinking about my butt in any scenario.

"But I do," he told me. "And since you won't stop doing stupid shit, I'm taking preventative measures."

"Like what?" I asked, half angry, half worried. The fact that he'd used a word definitely *not* on the town-approved imitation swear list made me even more concerned.

He stalked over until he was close enough for me to call it looming. "I'm having video monitoring installed on your house and a tracker put on your car. I'm going to know where you are every minute of the day, Katie."

I was so angry I could feel my blood start to boil. "You can't do that," I said through my teeth.

"Watch me."

"It's illegal."

He moved past me, opened the door, and over his shoulder said, "Patriot Act, sweetheart." The door slammed behind him.

I was pretty sure Drake was spouting idle threats. He was probably just mad about the time I'd been spending with Hawke. Still, his visit unnerved me . . . and pissed me off. I went back into the kitchen and saw the remains of my sandwich. I didn't really feel like finishing it now though. I threw it in the trash, checked the lock on the back door, and went out the front to go back to work.

When I got there, Spence was out of the office. I'd been thinking about what Brian Bradford told Julia while he was moving out. Something about needing to protect the governor. It made no sense. I walked back into the archives to grab the issue with the article I'd written about Chelsea's death a couple of weeks ago. I thought maybe reading it again might help me pick up on some clues I'd missed. I was looking through the piles of papers when Ella's head popped up from behind one of the stacks.

"Hey, Katie."

"Oh no," I said, pointing at her. "Don't you start calling me that too."

"Why not?" Ella asked. "Drake always calls you Katie."

"And I get mad at him every time."

"But it's a cute name!"

"Exactly, it's cute. Like bunnies are cute. It's not very professional."

Ella made a hmmph noise and went back to sorting through the papers. "So, what were you doin' with Drake just now?"

I threw my hands in the air, breathing an exasperated sigh. "Who knows about it this time?"

She shrugged. "Probably everyone. The Ladies have your house under surveillance and they just assigned more patrols to keep tabs on you and the men who stop by. But I know because he came in here lookin' for you."

"He did?"

"Yeah. Spence said you weren't here and they started talkin' too low for me to hear. They went into Spence's office and shut the door."

Spence rarely shut his office door. "That's weird. How long were they talking?"

"Ten, maybe fifteen minutes."

"Huh. I wonder what it was about."

Ella gave me a knowing look. "I'll give you one guess."

I waved my hand like I was brushing her comment away. "Not everything in this town has something to do with me."

"When it comes to those two it probably does."

I shrugged, still wondering what they'd been talking about.

"So," Ella said. "Rumor goin' around is that you went somewhere with Hawke last night."

"I suppose that came from the surveillance as well?"

"Some of the girls saw you get in his car and drive off."

I found the newspaper I was looking for and opened it as I answered, "I went to his house."

Ella's eyes got wide. "What for?"

"For self-defense lessons."

"Why didn't he just meet you at the gym?" she asked.

"Because he has a huge gym at his house."

Ella stared at the wall considering that. "I'm sure most of the things Hawke has are big."

My eyes went wide and I gasped a little.

"What?" she said. "I'm just pointin' it out." She took her glasses off, cleaning them on her shirt. "Did you learn any new moves?"

"A few. It was mostly just Hawke going over the basics I'd learned in my college self-defense course."

"That Hawke sure is handy to have around," Ella said with a wink.

"Yes," I agreed, "he is."

I took the paper back to my desk and read through the article again. Nothing seemed to click. I took out a notebook and started to write in hopes that getting the information on paper would help me figure things out. I knew Chelsea had been pregnant and was pretty sure Shawn Wallace was the father. I didn't know yet whether the governor had anything to do with Chelsea's death, or if he even knew about the pregnancy. Chelsea and Shawn's relationship had been volatile and the relationship between Brian and Julia Bradford was just as bad. Brian was trying to protect the governor, but I wasn't sure why—though I had a feeling it had something to do with the contract he was trying to get for his business. Hawke had said he was going to look into things with the governor a while ago. I needed to ask him about it tonight.

I leaned back in my chair, trying to sort through the connections in my head. I stayed there for a long time until Spence walked in the back door. "Where have you been?" I asked, grateful for the thought reprieve.

He gave me a fake smile. "I had some things to take care of." He walked into his office. Apparently Spence wasn't in a talkative mood.

I took some of the articles for next week's paper from my inbox, sorting through them. From the word count, I had a good idea of how much space they would take up. I opened the layout program to get a head start on the next issue. I used the articles I had already edited first, and then I moved on to editing the rest, fixing the digital copies, and dropping them in the design program. I was working on the last article when my cell rang to the tune of "Play Me," Hawke's Neil Diamond ring tone. I refused to think about my subconscious—or conscious—reasons for choosing that song.

"Hey, Kitty Kate. How's work?"

"Pretty uneventful."

"Are you almost finished?"

I hesitated, unsure whether I really wanted to answer. Saying yes meant I'd be expected to be with Hawke—and that was a little scary. "Yeah," I finally admitted.

"Do you remember where my house is?"

"What, you're not even going to pick me up?"

I could tell he was smiling even over the phone. "Oh, I'll be picking you up, but not at the paper. We need somewhere a little more private for that—unless you want it to be front page news."

I caught my breath. It took several seconds before I remembered I needed air in my lungs to respond. I couldn't come up with anything though, so not breathing was probably okay. Maybe fainting would get me out of Hawke's plans for the night—somehow I doubted it though.

"I'll see you soon?" he asked.

"Yeah. I don't know what we're doing, so what should I wear?"

There was a long pause on the other end of the phone. Finally Hawke answered. "Does it really matter?"

I had absolutely no words. And Hawke knew it. "I'll see you soon, Kitty Kate." I attempted to say good-bye, but it only formed on my lips after Hawke hung up.

Spence had been watching me with interest from his office. He came out when I was off the phone. "Big plans for tonight?"

I stared at him. "I'm going out with Hawke." Considering the conversation I'd had with him about Hawke this morning, I knew Spence wouldn't be happy. He was probably preparing an entire speech in his head but instead of giving it, he just sighed.

"Keep your cell phone close this weekend," he said. "You're on call."

I held up the phone to show Spence I had it. "I haven't forgotten."

"And remember to be at the Pioneer Day celebration tomorrow night. We'll need lots of photos of kids."

"I'll be there." I picked up my purse and walked out the back door, my stomach fluttering with nerves.

Chapter Twenty-Seven

I pulled into Hawke's driveway about an hour later and followed the blacktop until I made it to his house. It wasn't dark yet, but the house was in such a recessed location that there were lights on in a few rooms of the house. Between the setting sun and the light inside, the house almost glowed. I got out of the car, locking the door with my remote.

With Hawke's complete lack of information about clothes, I'd chosen a sky blue halter dress with a big skirt that swished around my knees. I paired it with a cardigan, belt, and strappy sandals—all black—and hooked my cell phone to the belt. My hair had actually cooperated during the day and I still had the loose, chunky waves that made me look like I'd just come from the beach. I'd even taken the time to put on foundation and eyeliner in addition to my grey eye shadow and mascara. I'd decided to go bold on the lip color: bright pink. If I was going to draw attention somewhere, it might as well be my lips.

I followed a flagstone walkway up to the white portico surrounding the front door in place of a porch. The door was heavy maple and oversized. It looked like it was at least nine feet tall and five feet wide. An old fashioned door knocker hung in the middle of the wood panels. Smaller etched glass windows with ivy-like designs were built into the house on either side of the door. I lifted the knocker to let Hawke know I was there.

I heard the sound of feet padding across the floor. The door opened to reveal a rather domesticated Hawke. His three-quarter sleeve v-neck sage and black striped shirt looked like a second skin. He'd pushed the sleeves up above his elbow so I could clearly see his bronzed forearms. His distressed jeans fit him nicely. Instead of the combat boots I was used to, Hawke was wearing socks. I was so surprised at the change in him, I couldn't speak. He smiled, motioning me inside. "Don't let the outfit fool you. I'm still just as scary as the background check services make you think I am."

What the . . .? I blinked. How did he know about that? Hawke laughed. "Come on. Dinner's almost ready."

I followed him into the kitchen. As I started to regain my senses, I noticed the smell of garlic and basil in the air. "Dinner, like you actually cooked this instead of picking up take-out or something?" I put my purse down on one of four bar stools. Hawke motioned me over to a large, round oak table.

The room smelled like Italian heaven on earth. I realized I hadn't eaten anything since my hastily thrown together half-eaten grilled cheese. I knew the meal Hawke was making would be significantly more satisfying.

"I enjoy cooking," Hawke said. "I love taking something from scratch and making it into anything I want it to be. I like the trial and error part too. Some of the best things I've ever made have come from my mistakes."

"So you cook a lot?"

He brought over a cucumber, tomato, and feta cheese salad

that looked like it had been tossed with pepper and olive oil. He put the wood bowl down in front of me on the table and went back to the oven. When he opened it, the unmistakable mouthwatering scent of garlic bread wafted out. "Not as much as I'd like to," he said. "I try to cook when I'm home, but I usually only cook for myself."

The statement made me sad. "That sounds lonely."

He brought the garlic bread to the table, placing it on a hot pad. "I'm used to being alone."

"You have that reputation," I mumbled.

He smiled, leaning against the counter. "Where did you hear that? Because I know it wasn't in the background check you did today."

"How do you know I checked your file? I mean, it could have been anyone."

"I have alerts set up so I know whenever someone runs my name or any of my aliases anywhere."

I stared at him, dumbfounded. "How?"

"I told you Kitty Kate, there's a whole world of things out there you don't know about." He took two wine glasses from a holder hanging under one of the kitchen cabinets. A bottle of red wine was already open on the table so it could breathe. I wondered where he'd gotten it from. Wine is only available at state liquor stores and Branson doesn't have one. That meant Hawke either had the bottle on hand, or he'd driven at least fifty miles to get it.

Hawke pulled a casserole dish out of the oven and brought it to the table with a hot pad and spatula. Once everything was situated, he sat next to me.

"Okay," I said, spreading the black cloth napkin across my lap. "So you have some super sleuths telling you any time your name is searched. That still doesn't explain how you knew it was me doing the searching."

He poured me a glass of wine, the color so dark it was almost black. He handed it to me before pouring one for himself. "I can pinpoint the physical location of a computer as long as I can find the IP address. It's not difficult. I knew the IP address was from a computer at the *Tribune*, so I assumed it was you." He handed me the salad bowl and I put some on my plate. I took a piece of the lasagna he'd made, and a slice of garlic bread. He filled his plate as soon as I was done.

"Great. So, do you want to elaborate on what I found out?"

"I don't know?" he said, picking up his fork and knife. "What did you find?"

"Oh, you know," I said, "nothing! The only information available was a list of your aliases. And why do you even need aliases?"

His lips turned down slightly before he took a sip of wine. "I thought those were taken care of. I'll have to deal with that." He motioned to my plate. "Try it."

I picked up my fork and tasted the lasagna, trying not to scream with pleasure it was so good. There were spices I couldn't even recognize and the tomato sauce was zesty without being overbearing. It was the perfect accompaniment to the meat and smoky cheese. Hawke smiled at my expression. "The trick is to make your own sauce instead of using the kind in a jar from the store."

Hawke makes his own sauce? I stared for a minute, trying to figure him out. If I only wanted a friends-with-benefits relationship with Hawke, he was going to have to stop cooking. Food like this could make a girl fall in love. "This might be the best thing I've ever tasted."

"Good," he said, pleased. "I'll cook you dinner anytime you want me to."

"You might want to reconsider your offer. I'll be over here every night."

He cocked his head, holding my eyes. "I could get used to that."

I looked down at my food so he couldn't see my expression. Hawke didn't seem like the type to settle down, or even be monogamous. I couldn't understand why he kept insinuating he wanted to do that with me—especially since we hadn't known each other long. When I felt like I had control of myself, I asked, "Who do you know with the ability to get all that information removed? It doesn't even list your house or your car!"

"I have more than one house and car," he said. "And you're right; it doesn't list any of my personal information."

"Is there a reason for that?"

He nodded, taking another sip of his wine. "Yes, several."

I crossed my legs, leaning my shoulder against the back of the chair as I watched him closely. He watched me back. "What do you do, Hawke?" I picked up my glass and took a drink. I thought the alcohol might help prepare me for whatever he was going to say next.

He gave me an innocent look and I knew I hadn't needed the wine since he didn't plan on answering my question. I got up from the table, opened my purse and pulled out the articles I'd printed earlier. "What are these?" I slid the articles I'd found across the table and sat back down.

He moved closer to see them. After a few minutes he finally said, "That was another life."

"Then what's this one?"

He pressed his lips together like he was thinking. "My evolution, I guess."

"What were you? Secret Service?"

He nodded. "Sometimes."

"What were you other times?"

"A lot of things. I was whatever I needed to be."

I stared at him. "If you don't want to answer that's fine, just say so. I only want to find out what I'm getting myself into here. Spence seems to think you choose sides and a lot of times you end up on the wrong one."

Hawke smiled. "I guess that depends on your definition of right and wrong."

"He thinks the people you associate with could put me in danger."

At that, Hawke's face changed and he shifted his lower jaw from left to right. He looked me straight in the eye. "A lot of the people I associate with have dangerous skills—just like me. But I would never hurt you or put you in a position where you could get hurt."

"So you work with these people?"

He shook his head. "Not in the traditional sense. We aren't co-workers. We're all independent contractors, but our network of associates allows us to contact one another if we need help from someone with a specific skill. These people are just resources to me and I'm a resource to them. Truthfully, I prefer to work alone. I don't have the patience to work with other people on a continual basis. You're one of the first. You have good instincts and I like how determined you are."

I'm sure the shock was written on my face. "Seriously?"

He smiled. "Seriously."

He picked his fork up again and didn't say anything else. Damn him for being even sexier *because* he's so mysterious.

When we finished our food, I leaned back in my chair, slowly sipping my wine.

"So," Hawke said, crossing his leg toward me, his right ankle resting on his left knee. "I've been wondering why a woman like you with a good freelance career would take a job at *The Branson Tribune*."

I tilted my head, wondering how he knew about my old job. "I guess I'm not the only one doing background checks."

"I don't work with people unless I know everything about them."

I wrinkled my nose. "That seems a little hypocritical."

He answered with a smile that said, "take me or leave me." I thought about leaving for at least three seconds. He seemed to know I wasn't going to though and continued the conversation, "So, why did you come back?"

"Honestly?"

He nodded.

I picked up the bottle of wine. I needed a refill if I was going to have this discussion. "Right after college I needed a change. Freelancing was a good way to get out of the state, and learn new things. I did it for three years, but when Spence gave me the job offer, I was ready to come back. Plus, the appeal of a steady salary and health insurance was too much to pass up."

"And you needed the change because of the relationship you were in?"

Geez! "How in depth are your background checks?"

"I probably know more about you than you do."

"That's great. Care to make it mutual and give me some more information about you?"

He gave me a steady stare. "I could see that happening. Eventually." He took a drink. "So what about the guy?"

"I met him in college. We were pretty serious."

"What went wrong?"

"We had differing opinions on what a relationship should be."

"How long were you with him?"

"Almost three years." I took another sip of my wine. "I left after I caught him cheating on me, but things between us had been strained for a while. We both changed and wanted different things. We didn't agree on anything and I realized he was trying to control me. He wanted a wife who was barefoot, pregnant, and home taking care of the kids. That wasn't how I envisioned my life. I wanted to work, travel, and have adventures with someone I loved. I didn't care if I ever got married. To me, it's just a piece of paper."

Hawke tilted his head, watching me for a few beats. "How did he handle that?"

I laughed. "He didn't. He wanted a 1950s housewife. I couldn't give that to him. Plus he was a pompous, patriarchal jackass."

"So why did you stay with him for as long as you did?"

I looked down at my glass, a small smile playing on my lips. I wondered if I should tell the truth, or lie. I looked up and met Hawke's eyes, deciding on the truth, "Not *everything* about the relationship was bad."

Hawke gave a knowing smile. "The good-sex rationalization."

"What can I say? Fighting is good foreplay."

He lifted his glass. "I'll drink to that."

The conversation lulled for a few minutes until Hawke asked, "Did you talk to anyone about Chelsea today?"

"Yeah. The Bradfords' neighbor is convinced someone broke into Chelsea's room recently. I saw Julia Bradford at the gas station and asked her about it, but she thought the burglar was actually just her other daughter. She did confirm what my dad said about Brian moving out, though. She admitted it was our talk with her that prompted the fight."

"Did she say anything about Brian?"

"Mostly how disappointed she was in him that he was more concerned with work than his family and dead daughter. She did say something strange, though. Brian told her he had to push the funeral through fast to protect the governor. Even Julia didn't understand what Brian meant." I looked at Hawke but his face was unreadable. "That seems like a strange thing to say, don't you think? Like he's covering something up?"

Hawke gave me a measured stare. "It is strange, but I can tell you why he said it."

"You can?" I asked, confused. "How?"

"After I heard your dad's story this morning, I found Brian Bradford. He was staying at the only hotel in Branson, so it's not like it was hard." Huh. I guess I should have done some investigating of Brian myself, but Hawke had and he's my partner, so I decided not to feel guilty about it.

"What did he say?"

"He admitted to bribing the coroner's office to keep the head trauma off the report. He didn't want anyone thinking it was suspicious and investigating Chelsea's death further. He also said he pushed Chelsea's funeral through so fast because he was worried Shawn Wallace was involved in Chelsea's death. Brian owns several technical companies. He's been trying to get the state of Utah to buy his software for years. He didn't want to lose the potential state contract he'd been working on, so to protect the Wallaces, he did everything in his power to make sure no one knew about the pregnancy, or the fact that Chelsea's death probably wasn't an accident. In the end, he didn't even get the contract. The state went with a lower bid."

"Are you kidding? He traded his daughter's justice for a contract he didn't even get!"

Hawke nodded once. "He won't be winning father of the year."

"So, Brian Bradford really thinks the Wallaces are involved in Chelsea's murder?"

Hawke shook his head. "Not the governor, but he indicated Shawn might have had something to do with it. He confirmed Chelsea was dating Shawn, and said he couldn't think of anyone else who would gain anything from her death."

I stared at the table. "So we're back to our original suspect, Shawn."

"That's what it seems."

"And you still can't get us an interview with him?"

He grimaced slightly. "No. I can't."

I'd try to get it myself, but if Hawke didn't have the connections to get us access to Shawn Wallace, I certainly didn't. Not even as the fake girlfriend of Dylan Drake.

"Thanks for talking to Brian and letting me know what he said."

"We're partners. That's what we do."

I stared at him for a minute before deciding to ask him my most burning question—again. "Why are you helping me on this? Who are you working for?"

Hawke gave me a mischievous smile. "Maybe I'm not working for anyone. Maybe I just wanted an excuse to spend time with you."

I leaned back a little, trying not to let the confusion show on my face. "Well, if that's the case, you could have just asked me out."

"Would you have said yes?" His expression indicated he already knew the answer. Truthfully, if I'd met him on the street without getting to know him first, the answer probably would have been no. Hawke is a *little* intimidating. "Plus, this way I got to spend a lot more time with you than I could have on a few dates."

"Well, regardless of who you are or aren't working for, thanks for your help."

He caught my eye, watching me like he was trying to figure something out. He put his glass on the table, then gently took my glass from my hand and set it down next to his. "Come on," he said, standing and pulling me out of the chair. "I'll show you around."

This was a different side of Hawke. His trademark innuendo was still there, but he was opening up to me in a way I hadn't expected. I was surprised at how easily such a guarded person was letting me into his home—and some parts of his life.

As I got up, I realized I hadn't even noticed the inside of the house when I came in. I was too stunned by Hawke's declaration that he knew I'd done a background check on him. Now the colors and décor started to come into focus. The walls were painted a deep merlot, almost the color of the wine we'd just been drinking. The countertops were white marble with streaks of black so flawless, they looked like they'd been painted on. The cabinets were top-of-the-line in a shaker style with an espresso finish. I wasn't sure what kind of wood was on the floor, but it was similar to the color of the cabinets, though the flooring had a slightly redder tint to it.

The refrigerator was oversized and built into the cabinets.

A person would have mistaken it for a large cabinet door unless they knew it was there. There was a cooktop stove on the countertop, and a built-in stainless steel oven on the opposite wall. A matching stainless steel dishwasher sat under the countertop, to the right of the sink.

The hardwood floors continued into the living room and hallway, the walls painted a caramel color with bright white moldings that ran along the middle of the walls. We passed by an office, bedroom, and large bathroom. When we got to the end of the hall, I followed Hawke up a set of stairs. The hardwood floor theme seemed to be throughout the whole house.

"Don't the floors get cold in the winter?" I wondered, thinking about the hardwood in my own living room. I wasn't looking forward to winter. I'd have to wear socks around the house or risk frost-bite.

Hawke shook his head. "There's a heating mat underneath the flooring to keep the wood warm."

I didn't even know they made under-flooring heating mats.

Hawke came to a large set of French doors and opened them, revealing a massive master suite with a huge bed and a bathroom the size of my living room and kitchen combined. I followed Hawke into the master bath, which included a white jetted bathtub so large it could be a hot tub. The tub was surrounded by patterned gray and sage slate extending onto the floor and into the rounded half-moon open air shower. The large shower area and rounded construction made a shower door unnecessary. A round twelve-inch wide shower head hung from the ceiling. There were at least ten more shower heads attached to the tiled walls. I had no trouble envisioning Hawke naked there, rubbing his Swagger body wash all over.

"I've only seen a shower like this once," I told him. "It was on a TV show profiling homes of millionaires."

He looked at me. "Trust me, it's worth every penny." With the corners of his mouth twitching he added, "You should try it sometime." I flushed immediately. I think he'd started to get used to my bouts of embarrassment because he just smiled and turned to walk out of the bath area.

A black leather couch sat in an alcove with books scattered on an ottoman in front of it. An antique wood canopy bed was on one end of the room with a cream and black quilt spread over the bed. Even from a distance, I could tell the quilt had been hand sewn. You don't get stitching that puckers so beautifully from a quilt machine. The canopy was black and see-through. It reminded me of lingerie, which reminded me I was staring at Hawke's bed, which made me think of the things I might be doing in that bed at some point tonight.

Apparently it wasn't going to be soon though, because Hawke had slipped on some shoes and was opening another set of French doors. I followed him outside onto a two-story, redwood deck overlooking his property and part of the valley below us. I followed him down the stairs to the back yard. With so much greenery it was obvious the yard, like the trees in the front, had been landscaped on purpose to ensure privacy.

An outdoor table and lounge chairs rested on a patio made of the same flagstone as the front yard. A six-foot waterfall dropped into a pond next to the patio. It felt like I'd stepped out of Branson and straight into a Disney forest. Hawke took my hand as we walked past the table to a stark white pergola framing a square, brick fire pit. Gorgeous rose bushes surrounded the pergola, the color a deep, vibrant hot pink.

"The roses are beautiful," I said, leaning down to smell their sweet perfume. "I've never seen a color like this before."

"Thank you."

"I know it's a cliché, but roses have always been my favorite." I took another deep breath of their scent. Still bending over, I suddenly felt the tips of Hawke's fingers tracing a line down my spine. When his hands got dangerously close to the place my tattoo would have been if I'd had enough guts in college to get one, I stood up and turned around.

Hawke edged closer to me.

In my opinion, the barometer of sexual experience spans from nun to porn star. I was somewhere in the middle. Not a virgin, but not a professional either. Still, I was sure even the best sex I'd had in college, and after, had not prepared me for Ryker Hawkins. Not at all.

I caught my breath as he pulled me into the pergola, caressing my waist with his hands. He held my eyes as he pushed me up against the wood pole, leaning in until I couldn't move. His corded body connected with mine. I could feel my chest pressing against him like it was pressing against steel. He gently moved the hair off my neck, whispering in my ear, "I've been waiting to do this since the moment I met you."

He bent down, brushing my neck with light kisses. I leaned my head back to give him better access as I sighed. Like magic, my cardigan was off and Hawke's hand was slowly moving inside my halter top. He traced the line of my lacy black bra as his other hand pushed my skirt up. His fingertips swept lightly up my thigh where he found my matching lace panties. He smiled slowly, his hand going over the fabric to the band at the top. He slipped his hand under the seam. I breathed in a rattled breath and heard music. At first I thought Hawke had an outdoor stereo system—or the angels were pleased I was finally getting some action—but when I realized it was "Forever in Blue Jeans," I swore. Hawke's hands stilled as he lifted his head, staring at me. "Is that Neil Diamond?"

"Yeah, it is," I said, wincing. "And I have to answer it."

Hawke stroked the skin on my stomach, his fingers slowly inching down. "You sure about that?"

I had an internal debate with myself about the merits of ignoring Spence's phone call. I groaned. "I'm sure." I untangled myself from his hold, ducked under his arm, away from the pergola pole, and grabbed my phone from my belt.

"Hi, Spence."

"Hey, Kate. I hope I'm not," he paused and seemed to be choosing his words, "interrupting something."

"What do you need?" I asked, clearly annoyed.

"I didn't want to bother you, but there's a story that needs to be covered. Someone stole the Paxton's combine."

I shook my head, wondering if I'd heard him right. "Say that again?"

"You know, the big piece of agricultural equipment that farmers use in their fields? Someone took it."

"Are you kidding me? Who steals a combine?" Hawke cocked an eyebrow listening to my half of the conversation.

"That's not even the whole story. Another call came into the police station that the combine was spotted on the freeway. I guess the thieves decided to take it for a joyride."

"Those things can't go more than what, fifteen miles per hour?"

"They definitely don't go fast enough to get on a freeway."

"Did the police catch the joyrider?"

"No. They found the combine abandoned and still running

next to the Branson freeway exit. I need you to go get the details."

I pressed my fingers against the sides of my nose, closing my eyes. "Yeah, I know. I'll do it."

"Thanks. Sorry if I spoiled your plans for the night," he said, though he didn't sound very sorry at all. He'd probably hijacked the combine himself to interrupt my date with Hawke.

"No problem," I said, feeling deflated.

I ended the call. "I have to go cover this story. I can come back later, or we can do this another time."

"Staying here won't be any fun if you're gone," Hawke smiled. "Can't you get someone else to go?"

"I'm on call this weekend. I have to take it."

"You're the editor. Don't you have people for that?"

"I'm the editor of a small town paper," I said, exaggerating the word 'small.' "That means I have to do everything from photography to layout. I don't have minions and interns like editors at large newspapers. It's not very glamorous."

"I'll come with you," he said, "but if you've got a Neil Diamond CD playing in your Jeep, we'll need to have a serious discussion."

"Listen," I pointed the phone at him to emphasize my point. "It took me a long time to admit I'm a Neil Fan. Don't mock me for it."

Hawke started to laugh. "I'll never let you live it down."

"You know," I said as we walked to the Jeep, "you always seem to be with me when a crazy story happens."

He smiled. "Guess I'm just good luck." I said a silent prayer of thanks that, so far, Hawke had never been present for one of my mom's mishaps.

Chapter Twenty-Eight

It only took us ten minutes to get to the Branson Falls freeway exit. Spence hadn't lied. There was a dark red combine sitting under a freeway exit light. We got out of the Jeep and saw Officer Bob.

"Geez, Bobby! You're on every case I investigate! Don't you ever get a break?" I asked.

"It's a small town. I'm always one of the first people called." He noticed Hawke standing behind me. "What're you doin' here?" he asked.

"Helping," Hawke answered.

Bobby narrowed his eyes to slits like he didn't believe a word Hawke uttered and liked him even less.

I stepped in. "He was working on another story with me when I got a call about the combine." I glanced at Hawke long enough to see the amused smile spread over his lips. I guess you could call what we'd been doing a story—and it certainly would be if anyone ever found out about it. Plus, we *had* talked about Brian and Julia Bradford after dinner, so it wasn't a total lie. I turned my attention back to Bobby. "Speaking of the combine, do you know who took it?"

"Hoodlums! That's who." I recognized the voice and cringed, before turning around to see my mom walking up to us. She stumbled a little when she noticed Hawke standing next to me. "Kate, you didn't tell me you were out with a . . . friend tonight."

I stared at her for a few seconds. "Sorry, Mom. I thought moving out of the house seven years ago meant I didn't need to report my whereabouts anymore." She gave me that motherly glare that isn't really a glare at all but makes you think you'd still get your butt swatted if you were in spanking range.

"Who's your friend?" she asked. "I haven't seen him at church."

I rolled my eyes and made an obvious observation, "Because you rarely go to church."

"Well," she said, watching him closely, "I still would have heard about it if someone like him had shown up there."

Without a doubt. Hawke in church would have been gossip fodder for weeks. As it was, I got the impression Hawke was only the religious type if one of his jobs called for it. I was about to introduce Hawke when he stepped up, putting his hand out. "I'm Ryker Hawkins, Mrs. Saxee. I've been helping Kate with a story she's working on."

My mom looked him up and down. "I've heard about the helping. I've seen it too."

Hawke gave her a wide smile that was so unapologetic it was charming.

"What are you doing here anyway, Mom?" I looked around the area for a car I recognized. It took me about thirty seconds to find my dad's blue Nissan Xterra parked next to some of the cop cars. "How did you get Dad to let you use his SUV?"

She shrugged. "I made him some cookies."

More proof that everyone in Branson Falls can be bribed by treats.

"Did you hear about this on the scanner and decide you don't get into enough trouble on your own?" I asked.

"No!" She gave me an indignant look, putting her hands on her hips. "I was coming home from shopping and saw the combine chugging down the road. It was late, so I thought the combine might be lost."

I interrupted her. "Because combines wandering off on their own is such a big problem. Next thing you know, we'll start seeing John Deere farm equipment on the sides of milk cartons."

Hawke and Bobby both suppressed a laugh. My mom scowled. "It's easy to get lost, Kate. All these fields look the same."

"But the combine wasn't in a field. It was driving down the freeway."

"I know!" she said with wide eyes. "I thought the driver just took a wrong turn and needed help finding their way home."

"How did you help them?"

"I got behind them and I was going to turn the hazard lights on, but I couldn't find them in your dad's SUV. So instead, I just slowed down behind the combine and slammed on my brakes over and over so it would look like the hazards were working. I flashed my headlights too." She made it sound like it was the most logical thing in the world.

This time, Hawke didn't try to hide his laughter. I hit my forehead with the palm of my hand. "You made your SUV look like it was having the mechanical equivalent of a seizure!" I shook my head. "You probably scared the driver of the combine to death. I'm sure they thought you were giving them some sort of gang symbol."

My mom scrunched up her nose. "Now that's just silly. I don't know anything about gang symbols."

"Right. Remind me never to let you go to the city alone again," I said. "What happened after you got behind the combine?"

She thought about it. "Well, a lot of people were passing us, honking their horns." I nodded in complete understanding; I would have been one of those people too. And I would have added a hand gesture as well. "After about five minutes, the combine pulled over. I pulled up behind it and parked the Xterra. I opened the door so I could give the combine directions back to its field, but before I could even get out of the car, two people wearing black jumped from the combine and ran. A truck pulled over and they got inside and sped away. They left the door wide open and the combine running!"

"What kind of truck was it?"

She shook her head, "Just a regular truck like every other truck in town. It was dark and they stopped too far away for me to get any other details."

"Did you see their faces?"

"No. They didn't look at me." She paused and seemed to be working herself into a tizzy. "And of all the nerve, they didn't even say thank you!"

I closed my eyes and counted to five. "You wanted them to thank you for catching them while they were stealing a combine, and then escorting them from the freeway like you were making a citizen's arrest in an SUV that seemed to be having a medical emergency? I can't imagine why they didn't take the time to show their appreciation."

She frowned at me. "Who knows where they'd be if I hadn't shown up."

I thought about it. "Since they were going roughly fifteen miles an hour, they'd probably be about five miles further down the freeway."

Bobby piped up, "We would've caught 'em sooner than that. Your mom's help just sped up the process."

I turned to him. "Do you have any idea who stole it, or is Citizen Inspector Clouseau here," I pointed to my mom, "your only witness?"

Bobby smiled, cracking his knuckles. "We don't know; probably just a couple of kids."

"Who reported it?"

"Who didn't?" Bobby answered. "Every yahoo with a cell phone passin' the combine called it in, but it was too dark for anyone to identify the people inside."

"I called them too," my mom said with a pleased smile. "The Branson Police Department is on my speed dial."

I gave her a disbelieving look and addressed Bobby again. "Do you think you'll be able to figure out who stole it?"

Bobby shrugged. "We'll do an investigation, but I'm sure we won't find anythin'. It's not like we can narrow suspects down to people who know how to drive a combine. That only knocks out kids who haven't learned yet and old folks who've forgotten. There's not enough detail to identify the truck they jumped into either."

Great. This wouldn't be a long story. I took notes about my mom's involvement, and Bobby confirmed all the details Spence had told me on the phone. I also took some photos of the combine, and at her request, some with my mom standing in front of the large machine with her arm in the air like she was some kind of combine model. She was a little disappointed when the Paxtons came by to retrieve their property and her photo shoot had to end. I had the fleeting thought that maybe all of my mom's mishaps were really her attempt to break into the modeling world.

The police left the scene and I gave my mom a hug. "I'm glad you didn't explode anything this time."

"That hardly ever happens," she said with an offended look. "And the rare times it does happen, it's never my fault."

Hawke smiled. "I think you'd be an interesting woman to spend time with."

My mom gave him an appraising look. "I live an exciting life."

I rolled my eyes, and looked at Hawke. "Exciting in a whole different universe from your version of exciting."

"I don't know about that," he said. "I'm rarely a front page newspaper story. Sophie Saxee is famous though."

My mom's face brightened at the thought of being famous, though I don't think Hawke meant it as a compliment. "You can come over and visit any old time you want to," my mom told Hawke.

"Thanks, Mrs. Saxee."

She pointed at me with a smile. "Bring him over next week. I'll make sugar cookies."

Hawke gave her another grin. "Sugar cookies are my favorite."

She smiled again. "You two have a fun night." She gave me another hug as she whispered in my ear, "I'd ask if you went out of town to get some protection, but from the looks of him, I think he could probably supply condoms to the whole county."

I blushed deeply, hoping the dark night concealed it. My mom walked back to the Xterra, about twenty yards away.

Once she was safely on the freeway and not burning anything up, we left the scene of the abandoned joyride.

As we pulled off the freeway, Hawke started chuckling. "What's so funny?" I asked.

He looked out the window as we passed corn fields on the side of the road. "Small towns," he answered. "Stuff like this would never have happened where I grew up."

"Where did you grow up?"

He shifted in his seat. "A city."

"Any city in particular?"

"Nope."

"You're a hard guy to get to know. I don't think I want someone who won't even tell me where he comes from to knock me up," I teased.

He cocked an eyebrow. "We could start with just *practicing* getting you knocked up."

I would have given him a witty response back if I hadn't been in the process of slamming on my brakes and staring at the sheet metal plant. Andrew Davies' welcome home sign had been covered again, this time by a huge red heart.

"That's interesting," Hawke said.

"It's the same color as the *she had it coming* note that was written on the plant the night before Chelsea's funeral."

"Who do you think left it?"

"Probably the same person who wrote the other note," I answered. An uneasy feeling settled in the pit of my stomach. "The question is whether or not it has anything to do with Chelsea."

Chapter Twenty-Nine

Utah celebrates Pioneer Day, the arrival of the first pioneer settlers in the Salt Lake valley, on the twenty-fourth of July. To commemorate the state holiday, Branson Falls always sets off fireworks at one of the city parks. Afterwards, a dance is held for the teenagers in town.

I'd have to go to the celebration to take photos, but I still had a few hours before the fireworks started. I'd spent the afternoon at my parents' house for a barbeque, reconnecting with old friends and extended family members. I hadn't been back in Branson long, and I'd been so focused on my job and the investigation into Chelsea's death that I hadn't had a chance to do much socializing. I spend a lot of time covering crazy stories for work. So, it was nice to have a few hours with friends who didn't get stuck in revolving doors, spread rumors about me, or kick defenseless dogs.

I'd left the barbeque early to get some work done. I called Ella and a few other people about the heart on the sheet metal plant, but so far, no one had any information. I thought I'd take advantage of my free time and deal with the fact that the food fairies hadn't visited my house in a while. I went to the grocery store, attempting to restock.

Branson Falls only has one grocery store, so I wasn't surprised when I ran into the high school counselor, Martha Chester, in the cereal aisle. Getting groceries is kind of a social event in Branson.

"Hi, Martha." I smiled, putting some Cap'n Crunch's Crunch Berries cereal in the shopping cart. I decided to splurge on the cereal since Cap'n Crunch Berries are my favorite, but it takes forever to dig the yellow barrels out and get a bowl of just berries. I used to get the All Berries version when I was in college. It made my life a lot easier, but the Branson grocery store doesn't stock it.

"Kate!" Martha said with a smile. She was alone. I wondered how she'd managed that. My mom could never sneak a grocery store trip in without me. When she wasn't looking, I always put stuff in the cart that she didn't want to buy. She rarely saw my items until they were already through check out.

Martha pushed her cart close to mine, leaning in toward me so our conversation would be as private as the cereal aisle could be. If Tony the Tiger and Toucan Sam could talk, they'd have more gossip than The Ladies. "I've heard you're still trying to figure out what happened to Chelsea Bradford. How's the investigation going?"

"Good," I said. "I have a lot of leads I'm looking into." I furrowed my brow, unsure if I should give her the next bit of information. I forged ahead. "The Bradfords took Chelsea out of school because she was pregnant."

Martha's eyebrows went up a little as she nodded her head a few times. "I was hoping that wasn't the reason, but it's not the first time it's happened."

I gave her a surprised look. "I didn't realize pregnancy was such a problem at Branson Falls High. At least, I don't remember it being an issue when I went there."

"Because most parents treat it just like the Bradfords; they take their daughters out of school."

"Where are the girls sent?"

"Most go to an alternative school in the county, but even going to the school gives girls a bad reputation. You know kids in Branson are taught to be abstinent until marriage. For most people around here, getting pregnant outside of marriage is a visual reminder of what a sinner a girl is—and it's usually a cross the girl has to bear on her own."

I nodded my head, understanding. "It seems silly though. I'm sure the community would have rallied around Chelsea and the Bradfords. Plus, Chelsea had such great friends. People like Piper Adams would have stood by her regardless."

Martha gave me a confused look. "What do you mean?"

"I've talked to Piper about Chelsea a few times. She's loyal to Chelsea even now—but I guess that's what best friends are for."

Martha pushed her chin out, shaking her head. "Piper and Chelsea were friends, but I wouldn't say they were best friends. There was a bit of rivalry between them. Piper has lived in Branson her whole life. She was the most popular girl in school before Chelsea moved in. Everyone loved Chelsea, so naturally, Piper accepted her into their group of friends, but there was always an underlying competition between the two of them."

Now I was confused. "When I spoke with Piper after Chelsea's funeral, it seemed like she and Chelsea were best friends."

Martha shook her head. "That's not how things were when

Chelsea was alive. Death tends to make people recall only positive things about their relationship with the deceased. Maybe that's how Piper wants to remember her history with Chelsea. I was Piper and Chelsea's counselor. The two of them fought a lot. From what little information I got from them, it seemed the arguments had something to do with Piper and Chelsea both liking the same guy."

I was stunned. "That's not the impression I got at all." I thought back to my conversations with Piper. I couldn't remember her exuding anything but care, concern, and a sense of loss for her friend. "You said they both liked the same guy?"

Martha nodded as she bypassed the sugary cereal and grabbed a couple of boxes of bran flakes. Her kids would not be happy. "Yeah, but you remember high school. It's pretty common for girls to like the same boy. One thing I thought was strange though was that they were both pretty careful about keeping his identity a secret. When they talked to me about him, they never mentioned his name."

The gears in my head were shifting into overdrive. Could the boy Martha was talking about actually be Shawn Wallace?

"Did Piper say anything else about her relationship with Chelsea or the mystery guy?"

"She was obsessed with the boy. Chelsea's relationship with him was so off and on that I think Piper kept holding out hope they would break things off completely and Piper would get to be with him for longer than a few weeks at a time."

"So Piper actually dated him?"

"According to her," Martha said. "But it could have been a product of her imagination too. Piper seemed to live in a fantasy world when it came to him."

I absently tapped my fingers on the shopping cart while I

stood there thinking. If Piper and Chelsea were fighting over the same guy, why did Piper make it sound like she and Chelsea were such good friends? Martha took my silence as an indication that the conversation was over. "Have fun tonight watching the fireworks," she said. "And if you're free next week, we should get together for a game of basketball."

I wondered if she'd ever seen me play. I could shoot, but I was much better at H-O-R-S-E than one-on-one. "I have a feeling you'll kick my butt, but it sounds fun. Have a good night." Martha laughed, and walked away to continue shopping. I thought about what Martha had said as I pushed my cart to the next aisle. For the rest of the grocery store trip, I couldn't stop thinking about how Piper, Shawn, and Chelsea were all connected.

I unloaded my purchases from the Jeep and took them in the house. As I put the groceries away, my fridge and cabinets slowly started to look like an actual person lived there.

I poured myself a bowl of Crunch Berries. As I stood over the garbage can picking out the yellow barrels, I kept thinking about what Martha had said. If Piper and Chelsea both liked Shawn, who did Shawn like the most? Was he upset when Chelsea got pregnant? Did he actually want to be with Piper? Julia Bradford had said Chelsea decided to keep the baby. If Shawn wanted to be with Piper, Chelsea keeping the baby would have been a problem—especially if Chelsea wanted them to be a family. Now the question was whether or not it was enough of a problem for Shawn to confront Chelsea about it.

As soon as I thought about the confrontation, the gears in

my mind clicked again. I dropped my bowl full of dry cereal on the counter and rushed to my office in the back room. From the middle of my desk, I grabbed the instant messaging conversation Hawke had given me.

Fordguy18: "Tell her that wasn't part of the deal."

Cutiepie94: "You know she doesn't care what you think."

Fordguy18: "She used to care. Just because she's not here right now doesn't change things. We agreed to do this and we're following through with the plan."

Cutiepie94: "Then you'll have to convince her."

Fordguy18: "I'll convince her. One way or another."

I read through the conversation several times before letting it rest on my legs. I stared blankly at my desk, thinking about the instant messages, and noticed Chelsea's photo book. I reached for it so I could flip through the pictures again.

As I picked it up, I immediately noticed something wrong. The picture on the front of the album was gone. I opened the pages. Random pictures here and there had been taken out, and all of the pictures from the car wash were missing. I closed my eyes, trying to recreate the images in my mind. The images involved a lot of soap and Chelsea with people I didn't recognize. Damn. What was in the photos that someone didn't want me to see? And when had the photos been taken from me?

The realization hit me like a brick as I slumped back in my chair. The night my back door had been unlocked and my neighbor's cat got in, someone actually had been in the house. Only they hadn't taken anything of mine. They'd taken something of Chelsea's. I needed to remember what was in the photos. It was a car wash . . . so maybe, a car? Could it be that simple?

I looked at the instant messaging conversation. One of the usernames was "Fordguy." I thought about it, and remembered a black Ford truck in some of the photos. Could that have been the reason the photos were stolen? Could the truck be used as a means of identification? That was hard to believe in a place like Branson where everyone who wants to get out of their driveway in the winter owns a truck. But I remembered Cathy saying Chelsea was always with a guy in a black truck with big tires. And there was the black truck at Chelsea's funeral that almost ran me over. Not to mention the black truck that sped by me and Officer Bob near Emerald Lake the day Chelsea's body was found. Could they all be the same truck? I needed to find out if Shawn had a black Ford. That would be easy for Hawke to check.

I looked at the instant messages again. The conversation happened a week before Chelsea died. There was a good chance Chelsea was already back in Branson by then, hiding somewhere. The only people who knew about the baby were Chelsea's parents, Piper, and Shawn. If Chelsea wasn't with her family, she might have been staying with, or at least communicating with, Piper. So, what if this conversation was actually Shawn talking to Piper about Chelsea? The plan was to put the baby up for adoption and Chelsea changed her mind. I had a feeling Shawn tried to convince Chelsea to go along with the adoption and somehow the situation went horribly wrong.

I called Hawke immediately, letting him know about my conversation with Martha. I told him my theory that Shawn had tried to convince Chelsea to put the baby up for adoption, but something went awry and Chelsea ended up dead. I also told him about the photos stolen from my house, and the black Ford truck in the pictures. I asked him to find out what kind of vehicle Shawn drove. Hawke said he would look into it immediately, and hung up. I picked up the phone book, found the name of Piper's parents, and called her house.

A high voice answered the phone. "Hello?"

"Hi, I'm looking for Piper, is she there?"

"This is Piper."

"Hi," I said, trying to sound comforting. "This is Kate Saxee from *The Branson Tribune*."

"Oh," Piper said, much less enthusiastic than I'd been. "Hi."

"I was wondering if I could talk to you again. I have a couple of questions."

Silence came from the other end of the phone and then in a quiet voice, Piper said, "I don't think that's a good idea."

That seemed strange. Maybe she didn't want me talking to her with her parents around though. "I could pick you up? We could go to the park again."

"No," she was quick to answer. "The phone is better. I can answer your questions over the phone."

I like being able to see the people I interview. The slight

nuances and body language always gives me a better idea of what they're thinking—or hiding. But if the phone was the only thing Piper was comfortable with, it would have to do. "I think I know who might be involved in Chelsea's death."

"Oh," she said slowly. "Who?"

"A boy she was dating. His name is Shawn Wallace."

There was complete silence on the other end of the phone. Dammit. I'd give anything to see her face right now. Was she mad that I knew? Scared? Upset?

"Do you know him?" I asked, even though I was already sure of the answer.

It took several seconds for Piper to respond. "Yes, I know him." So Piper had lied to me earlier when she said she didn't know the father of Chelsea's baby.

"Do you know if he saw Chelsea often?"

Another pause. "Yeah, he saw her."

"Do you know if he saw her before her death?"

Piper seemed to be choosing her words carefully. "I . . . I don't think so."

"So he never saw his and Chelsea's baby?"

Piper took a moment to answer. "They weren't getting along very well before she died." Piper paused again before surging forward. "Chelsea was making choices Shawn didn't agree with. She wanted to keep the baby, but she and Shawn had planned to put it up for adoption. He didn't want to raise a family so young, and told her that wasn't the plan they agreed on. I think Chelsea came back to Branson to see her friends and find people to help her convince Shawn they should keep the baby."

"So you talked to Chelsea about it?"

"Yes, she needed support."

"Piper, do you think Shawn might have been involved in Chelsea's death?"

The silence coming from the other end of the phone was all the answer I needed. Finally, Piper said, "I . . . I don't know. I can't tell you anything else. I don't want to be hurt too. I have to go. I'm sorry." And with that, she was gone, her voice replaced by the sound of the dial tone.

Chapter Thirty

I called Hawke again but got his voicemail, so I left a message telling him about my conversation with Piper. I quickly cleaned up the cereal mess I'd made, grabbed my things, and left for the park hoping Piper would be there so I could talk to her more.

I milled around taking photos as I looked for Piper. I almost got a shower when some teenagers started throwing water balloons. I moved out of firing range and took some pictures. I talked to some of the people I knew, and got quotes for my article about the Pioneer Day festivities. Most people had spent the day with family and friends, and were ending it with the firework display. As the sun began its descent, the lighted chemical glow necklaces and bracelets—popular Pioneer Day accessories—got brighter. I switched my camera to night mode so I could get photos of the fireworks once they started.

As I surveyed the crowd, I noticed Piper walking across the park about twenty feet in front of me. I yelled her name as she passed under a light wearing a white tee shirt and shorts that didn't even come close to meeting Branson's unwritten conservative dress code. Hearing her name, Piper turned in my direction. As recognition set in, I could see her cheeks lose color under the park light. She lifted her hand in a half wave as a pink and black beaded bracelet slipped down her arm, and she scurried off toward a large group of kids gathered near the park bowery. I watched her sit on one of the picnic tables. I was about to go after her when I felt a hand slap my butt. I expected to see Hawke or Drake, but instead it was Ella.

"Hey!" I said, my butt still stinging.

"That's for gettin' yourself caught up in trouble you shouldn't have," Ella said.

"What are you talking about?"

"I'm just givin' you a warning. Amber Kane is pissed off!"

"What for?" I asked in utter confusion. "If anything, I should be mad at her for spreading rumors about me!"

Ella shook her head. "I just know she's mad and says she's lookin' for you. It'd be best if you stay out of her way tonight."

I rolled my eyes. "I really doubt I could find Amber Kane in this crowd if I wanted to."

"I told you, *she's* lookin' for *you*. Don't be surprised if she finds you."

"Thanks for the heads-up. I'll keep an eye out."

Ella smiled. "How was last night with Hawke?"

I shut my eyes tight, shaking my head as I heaved a huge sigh. "How do you know about that?"

"Know about what?" A male voice asked behind me.

Ella looked up. "Where have you been lately?" I turned around and came face to chest with Drake. I was still pissed at him for the whole surveillance-tracker-Patriot-Act thing, but

I couldn't help noticing the tight fit of his jeans. I told myself it didn't hurt to look at attractive, arrogant men like Drake as long as looking was the only thing I did. I closed my eyes, trying to shake off the sexual frustration I was feeling.

"I've been around, just busy." He turned his attention from Ella to me. "Katie. How are you?"

"I'm fine," I answered.

An awkward lull in conversation followed before Ella said, "I have to get back to my grandkids. Have a good night you two." As she passed me, she leaned in, whispering. "I wouldn't let Amber Kane see you talkin' to him, either."

I nodded my head, noting Ella's warnings. She'd never been wrong in the past, and the information she did know was selectively shared, so I was surprised she was going out of her way to do it now. I must be in serious trouble. "Are you still pissed at me?" Drake asked.

I stared at him. "For which part?" I said. "Barging into my home and telling me you were going to invoke the Patriot Act on my ass? Or for parking your damn Hummer in front of my house again and starting another round of gossip about us?"

He held up a hand. "You don't have to list all the things you're mad at me for. I'm sure that would take all night. I didn't barge into your house to make you mad. I was worried about you, Katie. I still am."

I shook my head, fighting the urge to roll my eyes.

"I have a nice blanket over here. I bet you don't have a place to watch fireworks. Come sit with me?"

I started to say no and he cut me off. "Come on. It's a peace offering."

I looked around and knew I wouldn't find another place to sit. Once the fireworks started, I'd get yelled at for standing. I wanted to find Piper, but I didn't want to make her miss the fireworks, or cause a scene. I thought I'd have a better chance of getting her to talk to me after the show was over. I thought about it for a few more seconds. "I don't know. I've heard Amber Kane is mad at me for some reason. I'd hate for you to be caught in the middle when the fight breaks out."

Drake cocked his head, his lips sliding into a smile. "Do you really care what Amber Kane thinks?"

"No, not really. I'm just warning you there could be a problem if she finds me."

"I appreciate it, but I think I can take care of myself." He paused. "I could take care of you too, if you'd let me." The offer sounded innocent enough until I looked in his eyes and saw the familiar amused flicker.

"When you say things like that, you're lucky I even still talk to you. I don't need someone to take care of me," I said, and added, "in any way."

He laughed. "You're fun to tease. Come on, the fireworks are going to start soon."

"I'll find another place to watch them," I said, starting to walk off. He grabbed my hand, gesturing out over the park that was so crowded it looked like people were sitting on top of each other. "Where, exactly, will you find a place to sit?" I wrinkled my nose knowing he had a point. My parents were all the way over on the other side of the park. I'd get yelled at if I was still trying to reach their blanket when the fireworks started. "Will you sit with me if I apologize?"

I narrowed my eyes. "Maybe."

"All right. I'm sorry for teasing you, and for all the other things I've done—and will do—to make you mad."

He seemed sincere, though being a lawyer and politician basically means he's trained to lie. "Are you ready to sit now?" he asked.

I studied him for a minute. "Yeah, I guess. But you stay on your side of the blanket, and I'll stay on mine."

He grinned. I followed him to a blue and black checkered blanket and sat, leaving a respectable gap between us. I didn't want anyone to get the wrong idea, but the rumors were probably already spreading. Sharing a blanket was almost the equivalent of buying a house together. Oh well. It's not like the rumors could get much worse than they already were. I leaned back as the fireworks started. The noise from the explosions going off shook the ground and pounded against my ears. Luckily it only happened every minute or so. The display had been going on for about five minutes when Drake leaned over to me.

"So, what have you been up to lately?" he asked between firework sets. "Any new leads on the Bradford case, or are you still chasing after the governor?"

"Not the governor," I said, putting my camera up to my face and snapping a photo of a cute kid twirling a sparkler. "The governor's son."

"You still think Shawn had something to do with it?"

Another firework went off and I took some photos. "Yeah." I nodded too in case he couldn't hear my answer.

Branson puts on a good fireworks display, but they don't have the six-figure budget required for a lengthy show. Fifteen minutes is about as long as the display lasts. The next set of fireworks went off one right after the other. I knew the finale was coming soon.

"What makes you think so?" Drake yelled over screams from the crowd. The excitement for the finale was building.

I leaned in close to his ear so he could still hear me when the finale began—which ensured there would be rumors about Drake and me making out during the fireworks too.

"Because Shawn didn't want Chelsea to keep the baby, but she wanted to. I think she came back here to get help and he killed her and tried to make it look like an accident. Her own parents didn't even know where Chelsea had gone. She ran away before she gave birth and they didn't get to see her, or the baby, before she died." Drake looked surprised.

At that moment, a little girl ran by in front of me. She wore about twenty pink glowing bracelets that bounced from her shoulder to her wrist. The image gnawed at me as my brain tried to make a connection to whatever I was missing. Suddenly the finale exploded in the sky in designs of pink, gold, orange, red, green, and purple, like stars forming and trailing to their death—and it all clicked. I remembered the photos in Chelsea's bedroom and the pink and black bracelet Julia Bradford had said was Chelsea's favorite. The same bracelet Chelsea rarely took off, yet it hadn't been on her wrist when her body was found. Like Julia, I'd assumed it had been washed away in the lake, or lost with Chelsea's other missing items. But it wasn't. In fact, I was pretty sure I'd seen the bracelet tonight. Piper was wearing it.

The thoughts kept coming as pieces fell into place. Piper had wanted to date Shawn Wallace and she was jealous of Chelsea! Maybe Shawn had been involved in Chelsea's death, but now I realized Piper was probably a part of it too.

The firework display ended and I jumped up off the ground moving in the direction of where I'd last seen Piper: the bowery. As I wove through the crowd of people, trying not to step on blankets, or children, I heard Drake yell, "Katie! Where are you going?" I waved at him as I searched through the dark. If I wanted to know what really happened to Chelsea, I had to find Piper.

People were getting up from the grass now, making it difficult for me to get through the crowd. I didn't want to lose Piper. I had to talk to her. I swore under my breath and heard a rebuke from my right. Mrs. Simpson glared up at me with all of her five feet—which meant she was just short enough to clearly hear my whispered profanity.

"Katie Saxee! Language like that might've been fine at that liberal lovin' devil college you went to, but it's not okay here."

I wanted to tell her I'd heard much worse from her husband at church basketball games when I was growing up, but I held my tongue. Instead I rolled my eyes and pushed past her, trying to get to the bowery.

I was closer now, only about a hundred yards away when I saw her through the crowd. Piper was talking to a boy—and she didn't look happy.

I could hear Piper and the boy arguing even from where I stood, but I couldn't make out what they were saying. Piper was gesturing fiercely with her hands, Chelsea's pink and black bracelet shifting from Piper's wrist to her forearm as she moved. The boy's legs were spread shoulder-width apart in a defensive stance as he pointed at the bracelet on Piper's wrist and yelled.

I worked my way through the crowd of people who were still moving out of the park, attempting to get back to their cars to go home. I was pushed farther away from the dance and bowery with each step I took, bumping into people and trying not to step on any kids. As I wound through the crowd, my entire vocabulary consisted of "Excuse me," and "I'm sorry."

I made it to a spot next to a tree where no one was trying to trample me. I had a clear view of Piper and the boy, and could see that the arguing was becoming more intense. I was about to press my way into the crowd again to go the thirty feet I needed to reach Piper when I was pulled back by my hair. I'd already been poked, prodded, and almost run over; I couldn't imagine who would have the nerve to pull my hair too. I spun around. Five-foot-four-inch Amber Kane was standing in front of me with a sneer on her face and arms crossed showing off dagger-like fake fingernails painted a patriotic blue and silver. I did not have time for this.

"What the hell is your problem?" I practically screamed at her.

"You are!" she yelled back, sounding like a spoiled teenager. "Just because you sent your boyfriends to come over and threaten me doesn't mean I have to stop sayin' anything. There's a thing called freedom of speech. I can say whatever I want." It was nice to know Amber had attended at least one civics class at Branson Falls High. Apparently she skipped out on the one about slander.

"There's also a thing called defamation of character," I said. "And you can be sued for it."

She gave me a bitchy stare. "That's what your boyfriend, Drake, said. I don't give a crap." Crap was one of Branson's imitation swears. Using a word like shit would get you black-listed. I was already there, so I didn't give a shit.

"Good hell, Amber! Why do you think these guys are all my boyfriends? They aren't!"

"Oh yeah? Someone better tell them that."

"Listen," I said, holding out my hand to count off the men

with my fingers. "Drake is a friend who's been helping me on a story." I put up finger number two. "Hawke is my partner on the same story." Then finger number three. "And Spence is my boss! I don't know why you have your bra in a twist over this, or why you feel the need to spread lies about me. I'm not dating or sleeping with any of them!"

"They sure don't act like it," she huffed.

"What the hell are you talking about?"

"Drake told me if I said anythin' else about you he'd sue me."

I shrugged. "I suppose I could hire him as my attorney."

"Hawke told me if he heard another, cal . . . cumny . . . camaty . . ." I could tell the word was way too big for her to remember, let alone know the definition of.

"Calumny," I said. "It means to lie to hurt someone's reputation."

She waved my explanation off. "It doesn't matter. He said if he heard another bad thing about you, he'd consider me the source and nothin' good would come of it." She paused, giving me a confused look. "I'm not sure exactly what he means by that, but I know it's not nice."

Since we were discussing rude people, Amber's name should be at the top of the list. And if Hawke said something like that, she shouldn't just be scared—she should be terrified. I'd only have to tell him Amber pulled my hair and he'd probably take out her kneecaps . . . or whatever it is he specialized in.

"Then Spence stopped by and said if I ever spread another rumor about you, he'll put the before and after pictures of my nose job on the front page of the *Tribune*!" She was so angry at the thought, tears welled at the corners of her eyes. I didn't feel a bit bad about it as I stared at her in disbelief.

"Of all those threats, your nose job on the front page of the paper is the one you're the most upset about?"

She glared at me with her over-processed hair frizzing in a way that made me think she'd stuck her head in a microwave.

I shook my head. "You are the most spoiled, superficial, brainless woman I've ever met." She gasped at my insults. I needed to get to Piper and I really didn't have time for this, but I wasn't holding back. "First, even with all those threats, you're still here telling me you're going to be a lying bitch and say shit about me." Her mouth formed a shocked 'O' in response to what she undoubtedly considered an aggressive use of profanity. "So all I can figure is that you must be below-average stupid to even talk to me right now. Second, you need to think about those threats and reprioritize which of them you should be the most afraid of. While you're doing that, let me add one of my own. If you keep spreading lies around Branson about me, you won't have to worry about the nose job pictures because by the time I'm done with you, you'll need another one."

She stood in stunned silence for about thirty seconds until she recovered her scowl. "You can't threaten me," she said, darting her head around the park. "I'll tell the police."

"Tell them what? That I warned you to stop slandering me? The things you're saying are lies the cops have heard too. Cops who are my friends. They're not going to sympathize with you, I promise you that. And really, you shouldn't consider it a threat as much as a warning."

She stared at me. I could tell her tiny brain was having a difficult time following my logic. "If you keep this up, it won't end without a fight. You should seriously consider the fact that I'm friends with three of the most powerful men in town, before you unwisely open your mouth again."

Her hands were balled into fists. I knew she wanted to give me her version of a verbal lashing, but now the consequences were running through her head and she didn't dare. Undoubtedly, her rebuke would contain several imitation swears: crap, dang, heck, fiddle-sticks. She was mad enough that I was hoping she'd flip me off so I could take a picture. It would make a great photo for my blackmail file. Instead she growled through her teeth, "This isn't over," and stomped off.

I took a few seconds to calm down. The small crowd that had gathered to watch our fight began to leave. I was sure The Ladies had the phone-tree going already. Rumors about my cat-fight with Amber Kane would soon be running rampant. On the bright side, our altercation had given people time to clear out of the park so the crowd had dissipated a bit.

I could still see kids milling about in the bowery. The music started, the bass pounding the ground as I searched for Piper. I couldn't find her. I waded through the crowd of teenagers dancing so close to each other that you couldn't even fit a tissue between them.

I went up and down the length of the bowery like a lawn-mower cutting grass, looking for Piper and the boy she'd been arguing with, but they were nowhere to be found. I heard voices in the dark playground area behind the bowery. I walked over to see if the two teenagers had decided on a more private location for their disagreement.

Twisted like snakes in various positions on the jungle gym were the kids I'd talked to at the bowling alley. In the middle of them all sat my good friend, Keanu. His blue-black hair was spiked into a mohawk. He was sporting black and white Converse sneakers and skinny jeans that seemed to only be staying on his waist with the aid of a chain he was using as a belt. He held a plastic yellow party cup in one hand. When I was a kid, I thought the large cups meant I was getting older and could drink from adult glasses. In college I'd learned they're called party cups for a reason. Keanu's other hand held a smoldering tube of white paper with an intensely sweet and spicy smell that I'd also become familiar with in college. Hawke and I had been right when we talked to the kids before. They were drunk *and* high.

"Duuuude!" Keanu said, waving at me and almost spilling the contents of his cup. "It's the reporter lady!"

I stepped closer, the kids all greeting me with drooping red eyes. Some smiled like they recognized me, though that seemed unlikely. In their current doped state, I didn't think they'd even recognize Ryan Seacrest. The closer I got, the more they smelled like the grainy scent of cheap beer.

"What's up, my buddy?" Keanu said with a huge grin. "Did you see those explosions in the heavens? They were, like"—he struggled for the word—"excellent!" He stared at the sky as if expecting the fireworks to spontaneously start again.

"Hey," I said, snapping my fingers in front of his face, trying to get his attention. He kept staring at the stars. "Dude!" I said, loudly. That jolted him away from his trance. Apparently, I just need to speak his language. "Do you remember when I was at the bowling alley and asked you about Chelsea Bradford?"

He nodded his head several times, a stupid grin plastered on his face. "You were super nice." He thought about it for a minute and got a worried look on his face. "Where's the giant scary dude?" He started turning his head in every direction. I kind of wished Hawke was there so he could pop out and say, "Boo!"

"He's not with me tonight," I said.

Keanu leaned in toward me. "Is he hunting big things?"

I didn't have time for this. "Listen. Remember we talked about Chelsea and you said she used to come to the bowling alley with her friends? Was a girl named Piper ever with her?"

Keanu nodded again.

"Did you see Piper here tonight?"

His eyes went wide and he nodded his head some more. "She was one angry chick. She should stay away from that Shawn guy. He always makes her mad. He used to make Chelsea mad too."

I stared at him. "What did you say?"

"Piper and Shawn. They don't get along." He was quiet for about ten seconds and then piped up, "Heyyy! That rhymes!" He laughed at his wit and took a chug of his illegal beer to congratulate himself.

"Are you saying Chelsea's boyfriend, Shawn, was here tonight?" I should have realized Piper was talking to Shawn, but it was dark and I couldn't see him well.

"Yeah! With Piper. They were maaaad!"

"What were they fighting about?" I asked, hoping Keanu had retained enough information to tell me anything of use. Frankly, I was impressed he'd been able to tell me this much so far.

He took a drag on his joint and started to giggle. "Shawn said Chelsea was the one he'd wanted to be with, not Piper." He stopped, looking off in space like he was thinking. "Know what? I think Shawn-dude was breakin' up with Piper-chick."

I looked around to see if anyone else could give me information. They were all at least as stoned and drunk as Keanu. "Do you know where they are now?"

"Piper was piiiisssed! Especially when Shawn said he was leaving."

I felt like I was pulling teeth trying to find out what had happened. "Where did he go?"

Keanu shrugged. "Shawn said he was going to Chelsea's favorite place."

I suddenly remembered Chelsea's funeral and Piper telling everyone in her eulogy that Chelsea's favorite place was Emerald Lake. "Thanks!" I yelled to Keanu and his friends. I ran full speed to my car, the camera bouncing on my stomach.

Chapter Thirty-One

I didn't know how long they'd been gone, but I was certain Shawn's destination was Emerald Lake. If Piper hadn't gone with him, I knew she would follow him there. Assuming Keanu was right and Shawn had just declared his love for Chelsea instead of Piper, maybe Piper would be jealous enough to try to hurt Shawn.

Emerald Lake is in a recessed location at the bottom of a hill. Its private setting with built-in sound buffering mountains makes it popular for family parties and church gatherings. Parking at the top of the hill, I switched my headlights off before quietly opening and then shutting the Jeep door. I kept to the side of the road near the trees, following the asphalt down the hill into the park area.

Picnic tables sat under a bowery that had been built across from the restrooms; the lake was just beyond the bowery. At the bottom of the road, a jacked up black Ford truck with tinted windows was parked near the bowery. I'd been right. The black Ford was Shawn's. The passenger-side door was flung open. Light emanated from the ghostly cab. I felt like I'd stumbled onto the aftermath of a horrible argument. My only hope was that it wasn't over yet.

I crouched down as I walked up to the side of the restrooms. I peered around the corner at the bowery, the moon illuminating a gravel road on one side and the lake on the other, but I couldn't see anyone there. I slowly made my way across the road, and that's when I heard it. A female voice crying. Piper.

I ducked down next to the truck, creeping around the back of it to see what was happening on the other side. When Chelsea's body was found, the paramedics had pulled her out of the water and onto the grass next to a large, two ton red and white rock with a plaque on it. Now Piper was standing between the truck and the rock. She was holding a handgun. Shawn Wallace was standing with his back against the rock, terror on his face. From my vantage point, I could see Shawn completely, and had a good view of Piper's profile. Between her sobs, Piper yelled, "We could have been happy! Don't you see that?"

Shawn didn't say a word. I moved slightly so he could see me, but Piper couldn't unless she turned her head. His eyes flitted in my direction for a moment. I saw a flicker of hope before he turned his attention back to Piper so she wouldn't get suspicious.

"You could have been the father of our baby instead of Chelsea's! Why did you want her? She was mean! And she didn't care about you. She even told me so. Every time you two broke up she said horrible things about you." Piper shook her head. "I tried to get her to stop. I tried to make her see how great you were, but she never listened."

With the knowledge that I was there, Shawn seemed to be

regaining some of his control. “Thank you, Piper. Thank you for sticking up for me.”

She looked up, her cheekbone highlighted by the tears staining her face as her lips curved into a smile. “See! I helped you! I got rid of her and now you don’t have to be with her. She’s gone and you can be with someone who really loves you. You can be with me.”

I watched in stunned silence. This was a completely different girl than the Piper I’d talked to a couple of weeks ago. This girl had lost her mind.

“Did you see my messages on the sheet metal plant?” Her eyes were wide, curious. “I wanted people coming to the funeral to know Chelsea deserved to die. And last night I was so excited for you to come see me, for us to finally be together, that I left you a heart. Did you see it?”

Shawn nodded slowly, carefully. “Thank you for the notes and for taking care of Chelsea for me.”

“I didn’t mind.” Piper shifted her weight from one foot to the other like she was dancing. I crouched down lower so she wouldn’t see me if she looked my way. “When you met with her and she told you she was going to keep the baby, you were so upset. After you messaged me about it, I knew Chelsea wouldn’t listen and I had to help you. At first I just wanted to talk to Chelsea, so I called her and told her to come back to Branson Falls. I said she’d be safe here and I could help her raise the baby. But I lied. I just did it to get her back to Branson so I could tell her what a bitch I thought she was to her face. But when she got here, she had your stupid kid with her.”

Shawn’s face froze like someone had slapped him. “Piper, what happened to the baby?”

Piper frowned and didn’t answer his question. She opted

to continue telling her story instead. "We fought about how she'd treated you. She knew you didn't want her baby, Shawn, but she decided to keep it anyway. It was wrong. But if it was our baby, you would have wanted it. I know you would have." Even in the dark I could see her expression and knew she expected Shawn to agree.

"Of course I would have, Piper."

Piper gave Shawn the kind of smile usually reserved for people who are deliriously happy—and maybe Piper was. She jumped up and down in place, unconcerned about the loaded gun in her hands. "I knew it! I knew you loved me best. That's why I had to talk to her. To tell her to leave us alone. I knew we could be happy, but you would never have been happy with Chelsea and that brat."

"It's good you talked to Chelsea, Piper. But if you just asked her to come here and talk, how did she die?"

Piper wrinkled her nose. "We yelled for a long time and started hitting each other. It was raining. She slipped and hit her head on a rock." Piper was making circles in the gravel now with the toe of her foot. "She was bleeding a lot and I knew she was dead. I rolled her body into the lake so it would look like she drowned. It was an accident that she fell and died, but I'm not sorry she's gone because now we finally have a chance!"

Shawn was clearly upset at hearing the details of Chelsea's death. He was having a difficult time keeping the emotion off his face. Piper looked at Shawn for a few seconds, noticing his distress. Her lips fell into a tight line. "Why didn't you see how perfect we were for each other earlier? Why wasn't it me having your baby?"

Shawn came out of his trance. "Piper, you know it was an accident, right? Chelsea didn't get pregnant on purpose."

Her expression suddenly turned fierce. "You're so stupid. Chelsea would have done anything to keep you from me."

Shawn's face shifted into a bloodless and stunned expression. "What do you mean?"

"Didn't you think it was strange that as soon as we started dating, Chelsea suddenly wanted you back? And you fell for it. You went right back to her and within a couple of weeks, Chelsea was pregnant." Piper stared at him as the hard lines of anger became visible around her eyes and lips. "I thought we would finally get to be together. That you would realize you loved me as much as I loved you." Piper scowled. "You didn't though. You didn't care."

"Of course I did!" Shawn said. "I cared about you both!"

I fought the urge to hit my forehead against the truck. Shawn bringing up his feelings for Chelsea was not a good idea at the moment. You don't antagonize the person with the gun.

"That doesn't matter!" Piper yelled. "You didn't treat me the same way you treated Chelsea at all!" She held up her wrist, pointing to Chelsea's bracelet. "You never gave me any jewelry. You didn't care enough about me to even think about it. But Chelsea was different. You loved her. You never felt that way about me." She stopped and I could see her face pale and her arms start to shake as the realization dawned on her. "You still don't!"

Piper was getting more unstable. In an effort to try and calm her down, Shawn put his hands up in a peace offering gesture—it didn't help. "You used me!" Piper yelled. "You used me so you'd have someone to screw until Chelsea came back!" Her eyes narrowed in anger as the awareness kept hitting her harder. "After everything I did for you! Did you know people thought you killed Chelsea? They were asking so many questions about her boyfriend. I made sure no one could find out who you were. I even snuck into Chelsea's bedroom to take all the photos of you and your truck, and when I couldn't find some of them, I broke into a house and stole the pictures from the reporter who had them."

She was shaking, her face red. "I did everything for you, and you didn't care!" she screamed. I knew if the gun was loaded, it wouldn't be long before she emptied it in the direction of Shawn Wallace. She lifted the gun up and took aim, her arms unsteady. "I hate you! I hate you more than I hated Chelsea!" As she said it, Piper cocked the gun.

I rushed Piper right as she fired. I hit her hard as the shot went off and Piper fell to the ground, the gun dropping out of her hand. Stunned, Piper took a fleeting moment to focus on my face before she grabbed me around the waist and started hitting me. We rolled on the gravel, me trying to keep Piper from getting to the gun, and Piper doing a pretty good impression of a UFC fighter. I wasn't sure if Shawn had been hit or not. The only thing I knew was that Piper seemed to have demons in her eyes and they were directed at me.

"You!" she yelled. "Why are you here? Why did you have to start asking questions?" She punched me in the face with her fist. I put my arm up to try and block her from doing it again. You'd think I could take a petite eighteen-year-old down—apparently not.

"If you'd have left things alone, everyone would have just thought it was an accident," she said between punches.

I fought back, trying to move her arms away from my neck where she was holding me down and strangling me at the same time. I moved my eyes, attempting to see where we had rolled to during our fight and if the gun was anywhere close, but I couldn't find it. Piper sat on top of my stomach, still holding my neck as I struggled to breathe. She leaned forward, her eyes on fire. "I didn't kill Chelsea, but I'm going to kill you."

Piper started to grab for something above my head. When she got a hold of it she gripped it tight, bringing it up until the gun was pointed straight at my chest, only inches away.

I stopped fighting her and put my hands up. I gulped in a breath, coughing a few times before I could find the voice to talk again. "Piper, I never wanted to get you in trouble. I was just trying to find out what happened to Chelsea."

"Now you know," she sneered. "I hope it was worth it." She raised her left arm to help steady the gun she was holding with her right hand, and I knew I didn't have much time.

With as much force as I could muster, I lifted my fist, punching Piper in the throat. She wavered momentarily, trying to catch her breath. It was long enough for me to wrench the gun from her hands and throw her off me. She landed with a thud.

I looked around and saw Shawn Wallace slumped down on the ground against the rock. I couldn't tell how badly he'd been hurt. Piper curled into a fetal position on the gravel, sobbing again. I held the gun in both hands, pointing it at Piper while I took some deep breaths. I had no intention of using it, but it helped to know the gun was in my control. As I stood there trying to get over the shock, a voice came from behind me.

"Guess we should have done the target practice after all."

I kept watching Piper, but saw Hawke move next to me out of the corner of my eye. He was carrying a gun that he tucked into the back waistband of his pants before he gently took Piper's gun from my hands and put his arms around my waist, holding me tight. I'm the type of person who can handle intense situations without a lot of drama, but wrestling a bi-polar teenager with a gun was crazier than anything I'd ever done before. I stayed in Hawke's arms and gave myself a minute to stop shaking. Finally, I said, "Teaching me to shoot would be a good idea."

Hawke looked me over. "You're a mess."

"Thanks. I've had a busy night."

Hawke nodded. "Yeah, I heard about Amber Kane."

That made me move my gaze from the sobbing girl on the gravel. "How the hell did you hear about that already? It only happened, what, thirty minutes ago?"

"I told you, Kitty Kate, I know everything about you."

"Is that how you knew I'd gone to Emerald Lake too?"

He nodded.

"You were a little slow," I said. "Next time you think I might be putting myself in mortal danger, maybe you should show up faster."

Hawke grinned, squeezing me. "Noted."

I stayed in his arms for about thirty seconds more before I pulled away and looked at Shawn's body lying in front of the rock. "I need to check on Shawn," I said, walking forward.

"No," Hawke said, pulling me to one of the picnic tables and sitting me down. "You're in shock, let me check on him."

I didn't argue and watched as Hawke moved toward Shawn. I could hear the muffled sounds of their conversation. Shawn started to sit up, leaning against the rock as Hawke looked him over thoroughly, making sure he was okay. When Hawke seemed satisfied Shawn wasn't going to die, he came back to me. I noticed the sound of sirens—and they seemed to be getting louder.

"It looks like the bullet just grazed him," Hawke said. He took notice of my arm, rolling my sleeve up to examine my wound. "Looks like you were grazed too."

I stared at the blood and torn skin like it was a mirage. The adrenaline was still coursing through me and I didn't feel the pain. "I hit Piper as she fired the gun. I must have gotten in the way." I shook my head in disbelief. "I worked freelance for three years in some of the biggest cities in the world and never got shot at."

Hawke smiled slightly and put his hand on the small of my back.

With Hawke's touch grounding me, I glanced at Piper's huddled form. She wasn't restrained and might go nuts again any second, but with Hawke there I wasn't worried anymore. I had one thought as I lifted my eyes to meet his. "The pink and black bracelet Piper is wearing was Chelsea's. Make sure Julia Bradford gets it back," I mumbled as the cop cars and ambulances came to a stop in the park, their lights blazing in swirls of red and blue.

Annie, the paramedic, gently pushed me toward the ambulance. "I need to check your arm," she said. As I climbed in the back of the ambulance, I couldn't help thinking maybe my dad had been wrong. Maybe I did get some of my mom's disaster genes.

I winced as Annie rubbed some disinfectant on my arm.

"The good news is you were just grazed," she said as she inspected my bicep. "I don't think you'll even need stitches." She glanced up at my face. "But you'll want to put some ice on that eye or you'll have a bruise ten shades of black by tomorrow."

I nodded my assent and turned my attention to the back of the ambulance, looking for something to concentrate on that wasn't blood—I don't do well with blood.

The back doors of the ambulance were open. I could see Drake standing near Hawke, talking to some police officers. Hawke stood with a wide stance, arms folded across his chest, a no-nonsense look on his face. He seemed completely at ease, like he'd done this sort of thing a thousand times before. Drake was holding his right elbow with his left hand and had his right hand balled in a fist under his chin. I wasn't sure whether he was giving or getting information, but he looked intense. Spence and Drake had both shown up with the police. I wasn't sure why they had come, or how they knew I was involved, but here they were.

Annie must have noticed where my attention was directed. "Drake's attractive—if you like that tall, dark, and handsome thing—but he's a player. Hawke is smoking hot, but everyone thinks he's some sort of assassin . . . might make it risky to sleep with him. Still, he has that dangerous mystery appeal."

I raised an eyebrow and looked back at her. "So those rumors are still going around? I was hoping someone had been caught buying beer and my love life was old news."

She shook her head, her lips turning up in a smile. "Wishful thinking."

I sighed.

"They both have an excellent ass though. If that was the only criteria, I'd have no advice to give."

I grinned. I thought Annie was Mormon, but she used the actual swear, not the imitation: bum. "Better not let your bishop hear you say that. You'll get called in for a meeting."

She laughed. "It wouldn't be the first time." She applied something that made me wince. "I'm pretty laid back. I even read romance novels."

I widened my eyes, surprised. Annie wasn't from Branson originally, but her husband, Cory, was. They'd moved back here a few years ago. Talking with her reminded me of conversations with my friends in college. I missed those days, and missed having someone to vent to and get advice from.

"Who's your favorite romance novel hero?" I asked.

"I have too many to count," she answered without missing a beat.

I grinned. "I think we're going to be good friends."

Spence appeared around the back of the doors. "Hi," he said with a big smile. He climbed into the ambulance.

I smiled back. "Hi."

He sat on the stretcher next to me. "Are you all right?"

I nodded. "I'll be okay. I'll have a black eye from the fight, but Annie here says I don't even need stitches for my arm." We both glanced at Annie and she smiled in agreement. I turned my attention back to Spence to avoid the blood. "Where did you and Drake come from tonight?"

Spence tightened his lips. "You won't like the answer."

I decided to hazard a glance at the arm Annie was still working on. "Then you better tell me fast while I'm still a little incapacitated."

"We followed you through the tracking device on your Jeep."

"You what?" I yelled. I jerked so much that Annie had to start bandaging my wound all over again.

"Drake said he told you he was going to install it."

I thought back to our argument a couple of days ago. "Yeah, he told me, but I thought it was an empty threat and he was just being an overbearing jerk."

Spence winced. "Guess it wasn't," he said. "He was worried about you. He even talked to me about it. Your job was the reason Drake was concerned. Since I'm your boss—and friend—he thought we should discuss it."

It took a minute to process the information since I was still stuck thinking about the tracking device and Drake. "Wait a minute. He talked to you about this before he did it? That's what the meeting in your office at the *Tribune* was about?"

"Yes."

"Since when are you and Drake buddies?"

"Well, we're both your fake boyfriends," he said, joking. Annie raised an eyebrow at the news, and smiled. "We wouldn't be doing our job if we didn't try to keep you alive."

Right. I wondered how long Spence and I would be able to keep up this flirting charade. My actual love-life was complicated enough.

"I can't believe you collaborated with Drake to track me!"

Spence leaned away from me a little, though it was pointless since he wasn't out of slugging range. "Drake and I both agreed it would be good to know where you were—given the circumstances."

"Dammit, Spence! Why didn't you just tell me you were concerned and ask me if it was okay?"

"Drake did tell you, you just didn't believe him. We didn't elaborate on the plan because we knew you wouldn't see it our way."

I fought the urge to yell at both of them. “Who are you two? My parents?”

“We were worried about you,” Spence said. “Drake saw you running off after you talked to the kids at the park. They told him you’d been asking about Piper and Shawn. He checked the tracking device and found your Jeep at the lake. After what you told him about Shawn during the fireworks, he thought you might need reinforcements and called the cops.”

“Yeah, my hunch was wrong,” I said. “Shawn wasn’t involved in Chelsea’s death.”

“I know, I heard. But if you hadn’t shown up, he’d probably be dead.”

I shrugged, not knowing what to say.

Spence stared at the scuffed white floor of the ambulance for several seconds before he looked up at me. “I’m glad it was just your arm . . . and your eye.” He paused. “It could have been a lot worse.”

“I know,” I agreed. “I think we should talk about giving me hazard pay.”

Spence smiled.

Annie finished wrapping the bandage around my arm. “Change the dressing twice a day.” She handed me some ointment. “Put this on before you re-bandage it. Also, take a few days off and get some rest.”

“Thanks, Annie.”

“No problem,” she said with another cheery smile.

Spence got up, holding my forearm to help me out of the ambulance. Drake noticed me and said something to the officer he was talking to, and then walked in my direction taking long strides. At first he looked upset, but when he stopped in front of me he rocked back on his heels and grinned. "You know, you don't have to get shot to get out of an argument with Amber Kane."

I looked from Drake to Spence. "Yeah, she told me she'd had some visitors warning her not to talk about me anymore."

Drake and Spence looked at each other like they were surprised. They each must have thought they were the only ones to talk to her. I didn't tell them Hawke had also joined the "threaten Amber" party. Drake shifted his attention back to me. "I'm glad you're going to be all right," he said.

"Thanks," I answered. "Have the police talked to Piper yet? Do they know what happened to Chelsea's baby?"

Spence gave me a blank look, but Drake knew the answer. "Piper said she knew about the baby safe haven laws and dropped the little girl off at a hospital out of town. Apparently Julia Bradford already had a private investigator trying to find her missing grandchild. The P.I. is working with the police to find out where the baby was placed."

I shook my head. "The whole story is so screwed up."

"At least Piper had enough sense not to harm the baby," Spence said.

"And what about Shawn? He'll be all right?" I asked. I knew Shawn was being treated in the other ambulance.

"His wound is worse than yours and he'll have to get stitches, but yeah, he'll be fine," Drake said. "You and Shawn both heard Piper admit to everything that happened when she explained it all to Shawn. Piper will probably be charged with attempted murder for what she did to Shawn—and you. Since Chelsea ultimately died because Piper put her in the lake and she drowned, Piper will probably be charged with second degree murder or manslaughter for Chelsea's death. She's eighteen and will be tried as an adult, but I'm sure her lawyer will advise her to take a plea bargain and get the charges down."

I heard the sound of more cars coming down the Emerald Lake road. I figured all the people with scanners in town were finally hearing the news and coming to check out what had happened.

But instead of curious townspeople, a pair of black SUVs with black tinted windows and chrome trim pulled into the parking area. Several men dressed in black suits got out of the cars. I saw Hawke walk up and talk to one of the men. The man opened the door and said something to the passengers of the car before pointing to the ambulance where Shawn Wallace was being treated. Immediately, Tish Wallace, the governor's wife, jumped out of the car and went running to the ambulance.

The door on the other side of the SUV opened and Governor Wallace stepped out of the car. He smiled when he saw Hawke, giving him a handshake that was so solid I could see it from where I stood. Hawke said a few words to the governor. The men in black suits moved back as Hawke and Governor Wallace walked several paces away to talk privately. In that moment, it became clear who had hired Hawke.

I glanced at Spence, who was watching Hawke and the governor with a curious expression, and Drake, who seemed to be clenching his jaw. I still didn't understand the bad blood between him and Hawke.

After a few moments, Spence turned to me. "I think we should get you home. I'll drive you."

I nodded in agreement, glad the night was over and I could get some rest. "Thanks for your help, Drake," I said. He nodded in return. "And we'll discuss the tracker later." He gave me a tight smile as I turned to follow Spence.

As we passed the black SUVs, I looked in Hawke's direction. He glanced up and for a moment, he met my eyes with a steady stare. I knew with that one look he was checking to make sure I was okay. I smiled at him in acknowledgment and Hawke turned his attention back to Governor Wallace.

Chapter Thirty-Two

The day after the shooting I wrote a front page article for the newspaper. For the first time in *Branson Tribune* history, we put out a special issue detailing Chelsea's murder, Piper's involvement, and the post-fireworks events at the lake.

Now, I was relaxing at home, about to pour a bowl of Crunch Berries and start picking out barrels when I heard the doorbell ring. I wandered into the living room to open the door. Spence was on the other side. He handed me a box of doughnuts from the bakery. An orgasm couldn't have made me happier.

I was trying to do what Annie told me and rest, so I hadn't been out of the house for a couple of days, but plenty of people had called, stopped by, and texted—including Drake. He hadn't brought me doughnuts though, and he'd come in his Hummer claiming he'd saved me because of the tracker on my Jeep. Yelling followed. Drake didn't get to stay long. My parents stopped by a few times, and my mom had made me a special batch of don't-you-dare-get-shot-at-again sugar cookies.

I motioned for Spence to come in and he followed me to

the kitchen. I grabbed two plates and poured two glasses of milk.

"You haven't even been the editor for two months and you're already famous," Spence said, sitting at the table.

I laughed as I sat across from him. "Don't you think that's going a little far?"

"Your story was picked up by the Utah media and the *Associated Press*," he said. "You should be proud of that."

"It's not a big deal," I said, grabbing a glazed doughnut covered in chocolate frosting, and nuts. "I had a lot of people helping me figure out what happened; I didn't do it on my own."

"Without your hunch to investigate Chelsea's disappearance and death, no one ever would have known and Shawn Wallace would probably be dead too," he said, taking a bite out of a caramel flavored cake doughnut with cream cheese frosting. "Give yourself some credit."

"So did you come over just to flatter me?"

"No, I wanted to stop by and give you some other information I thought you might be interested in."

"About Chelsea's murder?" I asked, picking up a peanut that had fallen on my plate and popping it in my mouth.

Spence nodded. "Your hunch about Shawn Wallace wasn't completely off. Piper said he had threatened Chelsea when she told him she didn't want to give the baby up for adoption. I doubt he would have done anything to hurt her or the baby; he just didn't want his dad finding out about the pregnancy, or the fact that he was about to be governor grandpa."

"Drake mentioned the governor has a temper," I said.

"But the governor already knew about it, as well as Chelsea running away. He hired Hawke to find Chelsea.

When she died, he told Hawke to investigate and see if Shawn was involved in her death."

When I saw them talking at the lake, I knew Hawke had been working for the governor, I just hadn't figured out the details. I nodded realizing why the governor had wanted Hawke's help. "Governor Wallace wanted to know about Shawn's involvement so he could get his son out of the situation if he was at fault."

Spence shook his head. "No, so he could make sure Shawn was held accountable if he was involved."

I wrinkled my brow trying to make sense of that. Usually the privileged get away with anything they want. I was shocked the governor was going to make Shawn take responsibility for his actions. "That's surprising," I said, raising an eyebrow. "So Hawke knew Shawn was Chelsea's boyfriend all along and didn't tell me."

"He probably didn't want you to figure out Governor Wallace was his client. Plus, he seemed to be using you to help him get information he couldn't get on his own."

"What do you mean?"

"He knew about Shawn, but he didn't have the connections in Branson to find out what happened to Chelsea. You did. So he let you do the digging and gave you information when you needed it, but ultimately he was counting on your investigation to help him figure out if Shawn was involved in her death. He got the name of Julia's private investigator when you both went to speak with her. Hawke was working with the investigator to try and figure out where Chelsea's baby was."

I nodded as I thought about it. I knew Hawke had been using me. The fact was, we'd both been using each other for one thing or another. At least we'd both gotten information out of it.

"And I have some other news for you too," Spence said.

I finished off my doughnut. "What?"

"I know who left you the note made from magazine letters, and egged and creamed your Jeep."

I gasped a little. "Who?"

Spence smiled. "A disgruntled ex-girlfriend."

"What?"

"It was Amber Kane."

"Are you kidding me?" I yelled, slapping my hand on the table. "Now I have another reason to break her stupid nose!"

Spence laughed. "She used to date Drake. After her divorce, she thought she might have a chance with him again —until he became so captivated by you."

"So the note to stay away was telling me to stay away from Drake, not the Bradford story?"

"Yep. She admitted everything when Drake went to talk to her about how she treated you after the fireworks were over. She seems pretty crazy if you ask me."

"It would have helped if she'd been clearer in her note about what I should stay away from." I took a drink of my milk. "All The Ladies are a little nuts—except for Ella."

"I know," Spence said, "but it might not be a bad idea to stay off Amber's radar for a while."

I shrugged. "I doubt it will matter. She hates me. And the feeling is mutual."

Spence got up from the table, grabbing his keys. "Take as much time as you need before you come back to the office, but I miss having you around."

I smiled, following him to the door. "Thanks for coming over."

"Anytime. If you need me, just call."

I nodded, closing the door behind him.

I went to the kitchen and looked over the doughnut selection to find my next victim. I'd been shot. I deserved it. I reached down to get a thickly frosted maple bar when I heard the doorbell again.

Spence must have forgotten something. I went back to the living room and opened the door to find a teenage boy holding a vase the size of a toddler with at least two dozen fuchsia roses blooming beautifully.

"Are you Kate Saxee?"

"Yes."

The vase was so large he had to put it on the ground while he fumbled for his clipboard. "Sign here."

I signed and he put the board down on the porch. He struggled to pick the heavy vase up again. I would have helped him, but I was afraid my arm would protest. As it was, I didn't know how I'd carry them into the house.

"I'm supposed to bring the flowers inside and put them on your table."

"Great!" Problem solved. I motioned him into the house. I moved the doughnuts out of his way and he put the flowers in the center of the table. "Thanks," I said. I gave him a five dollar tip and followed him to the front door. He stopped to pick the clipboard up off the porch before he got in his van and drove away.

I shut the door, taking a deep breath. The flowers had been in the kitchen less than a minute and the house already smelled like it had been transported to the middle of a summer garden. I picked up my maple doughnut and took a bite as I gazed at the beautiful blooms and flawless arrangement. After a few minutes of just appreciating their beauty, I decided to find out who had sent them.

I put my doughnut down, daintily sifting through the petals until I found a white envelope. It wasn't sealed. I lifted the flap and pulled out a piece of cream colored cardstock with a silver foil border. As I read the card, I had to remind myself not to pass out. I set the card on the table, writing side up, and ate the rest of my doughnut with a combination of excitement and terror while I thought about the words on the card. I looked down and read it again.

Shooting lessons, Friday night at five o'clock. And this time, Kitty Kate, I'm getting what I want.

THE END

Start Kate's next adventure in The Devil Wears Tank Tops

THE DEVIL WEARS TANK TOPS - SNEAK PEEK

Chapter One

Some days I love being a reporter, other days I hate it. Then there were days like today.

"Gary Smith's chickens got out again! I'm tellin' ya! We can't just have chickens runnin' around willy-nilly in the middle of the street chasin' kids and cars. They're birds, not dogs!" Norm Crane, Branson's resident rabble-rouser was standing at the podium in front of the Branson Falls City Council, trying to incite chicken-hate furor.

Jessie Green, a Branson Falls City Councilman, pounded his fist on the table. "Dang those chickens!"

Dale Call, another council member, barely looked up over his brown, plastic-rimmed eye glass frames as he raised his hand and said, "Second."

All of the commotion in the room stopped as everyone's heads swiveled simultaneously in Dale Call's direction.

Finally, Councilman Mark Brady spoke up, "Shoot, Dale! That wasn't a motion! You can't dang chickens!"

I sat listening to the ridiculous discussion, and taking notes. City council meetings weren't usually this lively and I could generally browse the celebrity gossip sites on my phone in between discussions about the latest tractors, or whether ATVs should get their own lane on the road. But thanks to the chickens, today's meeting was more animated than usual.

"First, people start tryin' to take our guns away, then men start marryin' men, and now chickens are runnin' citizens off the road. This country is goin' to heck in a handbasket!" Norm threw his hands in the air, exasperated.

I stared at Norm through his outburst, trying to figure out what in the world gun rights and marriage equality had to do with chickens. No one else seemed to be able to make the connection either. "We'll talk to Gary about constructing a better cage," Councilman Brady said.

Norm huffed and crossed his arms over his chest. "Well, I guess that'll have to do. In the meantime, I'll just pray for the second comin.' Nothin' else is gonna stop the madness."

My eyes were huge as I watched the crazy back and forth in utter disbelief. I'd considered skipping the meeting and going home to binge watch TV shows on Netflix. Now, I was happy I'd been there to witness it all in person instead of asking one of the other reporters to cover the meeting.

Suddenly, Councilman Brady remembered me sitting in the back of the room and the blood drained from his face. "You listen here, Kate," he said, pointing at me with a stern look, "that chicken thing? That's off the record."

I smiled dutifully, and nodded my head. *The Branson Tribune* certainly wouldn't want to be the cause of a scandal by reporting that people were upset about chickens crossing roads. Though, I was mighty tempted to ask our graphics guy to make a comic about it for the opinion page. I was also pretty sure everyone in the meeting would get the council's message back to Gary Smith and every other person in town before tomorrow morning, let alone the *Tribune's* next printing in a week.

Brady adjourned the meeting and I gathered my things, smiling at June Tate, a Branson resident who'd been sitting next to me. She'd come to complain about increased traffic by her property. Her house sat next to a highway, so there wasn't much the city council could do. "I'm sorry they couldn't help you," I said to June, noticing her white shirt under a matching lavender skirt and jacket. She looked very put-together in the business attire.

She shrugged. "We bought the house before the highway was there. I guess we should have moved before it got so busy." She was in her sixties and she and her husband had lived in Branson Falls all of their lives. "I just don't know why it's picked up so much during the last six months."

"Well, if it's only happened recently, maybe it will slow down again too," I offered, trying to make her feel better. With the population growing in Branson and neighboring towns, I had a feeling it probably wouldn't be getting better.

June fanned herself as she stood. It was August in Branson, and still hotter than the ninth circle of hell. The city council met in a building that was constructed sometime around the extinction of dinosaurs, and didn't have central air, or even a swamp cooler. "Aren't you dying of heat?" I asked, looking again at her very professional, but stifling layers. "I don't know how you can stand it. The less clothes, the better I say."

"I agree."

The deep voice brought me, and everything south of my navel, right to attention...even though I wasn't particularly happy about it. June looked at him the same way as every other woman on the planet...well, every other woman except me: with complete adoration. "Dylan Drake! I thought I saw you sneak in," June said with a warm smile. June had seen him sneak in and I hadn't? Observant reporter fail.

"What are you doing at the meeting tonight?" June asked.

Drake gave his winning politician's smile, practiced over years of working in the Utah House of Representatives. "Well, when I heard you were going to be here, June, I cancelled all of my other plans."

June waved a hand in front of her face, blushing. "You're such a charmer, Dylan." I did a double take at the use of his first name. Most people—me included—called him Drake because that's what he'd been known as on the football field. June put her hand on his forearm. "If I was thirty years younger, you'd be in trouble." She gathered her things. "I better get home before Paul burns the house down trying to cook dinner." She glanced at me, eyes twinkling. "You two have a nice night."

I wrinkled my nose at that twinkle, and wanted to correct her and say there would be no "two" of us at all, but she was surprisingly spry for a sixty-something year old, and already out the door. I turned my attention back to the man who'd snuck up on me—something he did frequently. His thick, dark hair framed his perfectly sculpted square jaw. Broad shoulders filled out a grey polo shirt and his black slacks draped over his lower body like fabric temptation. I shook myself out of the haze he almost always seemed to create in my head. I blamed it on his serious excess of testosterone. My ovaries just needed a minute to calibrate with the new hormones in the air. Eventually, they'd calm down and get blood back to my brain.

"Hey, Drake," I said, picking up my own things and trying to avoid eye contact. Locking gazes wouldn't help my ovary situation. But once I had my purse, camera, phone, and notebook, there was nothing else to do unless I wanted to start folding up chairs. I took a deep breath and looked up at the six-foot-three extremely attractive giant in front of me.

His smile was slow and deliberate as his eyes trailed over me, taking in my teal ruffled skirt that fell four inches above my knee, and my lacy grey tank top showing a bit of cleavage—none of which met Branson's conservative dress code. I was a rebel. Drake didn't seem to mind the rebelliousness at all—at least, not when it came to my clothes. "Katie," he said, his eyes coming to rest on mine. "Will I see you at the parade this week?"

I stuffed my notebook into my purse and searched for my keys as I answered, "Probably not."

"You're not covering it?"

"No, I am. But I'll be reporting from the parade route, not a float."

Drake's brow lifted. "That's a bad move on Spence's part. He'd get a lot more *Tribune* subscribers with a pretty girl in the front seat."

I fought back a blush. Because as much as I didn't want Drake's flirting to affect me, it did. When I was younger, I'd dreamed about him saying things *exactly* like that to me. Now, I knew his reputation—even if my ovaries hadn't gotten the memo. "I'm making it a goal to not draw attention to myself."

I tried to skirt by him, but he laughed and followed me outside to my car. A move that would undoubtedly start the Ladies'—Branson's version of *The Real Housewives*, with less money, perms, talon-like fingernails, and the ability to ruin a person's reputation in less than an hour flat—gossip phone tree. You know, because they didn't already have enough information to terrorize me with. As a prerequisite to becoming a Lady, you generally had to be perky, pretty, and popular in high school. I was none of the above, and I would never want to be a part of their gossipy group.

Drake gave a hearty laugh. "Good luck with that. Do you know who your mother is?"

"Ha, ha, Drake," I said with my best glare. "I'll also be avoiding you."

His lips slid into a hurt frown. "That's not nice, Katie."

I tried my best not to be nice to Drake. He pushed every single one of my buttons, both good and bad and I had a hard time managing him, and my completely conflicted feelings about him. My strategy so far had been constant offense that bordered on hostility. I'd learned it in elementary school. "I assume you'll be on a float, fake-smiling and waving to people, trying to get votes for something?" Drake was Branson's district representative for the Utah House of Representatives. He was also a lawyer. I despised him on both counts.

He shook his head. "You're confusing me with the Branson Falls pageant royalty."

I smirked. "Am I? Because around here, everyone seems to think you're Branson's version of Prince William."

His mouth widened into a grin. "And you would make the perfect Princess Kate."

My stomach fluttered and my eyes narrowed in anger at my tummy treason. My stomach wasn't supposed to flutter for Drake, regardless of how obsessed I'd once been with him. Drake's five years older than me, but he'd been my teenage crush. Though he claimed to remember me from our youth, I didn't buy it for a second, and he'd never given me any proof to back up his claim.

"Nope," I said, shaking my head. "That would never happen. I couldn't stand to wear the panty hose, and I'm far too opinionated. I'd offend people left and right, and probably start wars." He laughed, and I got in my dark blue Jeep Grand Cherokee. "Night, Drake."

He leaned back on his heels. "I'll see you soon, Katie."

"You know that's not my name," I said.

"You'll always be Katie to me."

I shook my head as I pulled away. I could see him grinning in my rearview mirror all the way to the end of the street.

Acknowledgments

This book would not have happened without so many wonderful people in my life.

Thank you to my incredible cover designer, Kat Tallon, and my amazing book designer, Ali Cross. I'm lucky to work with such talented people. Huge thanks to Dr. Ashley Argyle, my best friend, fabulous editor, and T.E.G. You changed my life when you told me what I should be writing. And thank the goddesses you caught the paws!!! To Dan, who is unbelievably supportive. I'm the luckiest woman in the world to have you by my side. Thank you for the crisis cupcakes . . . again, and for always making me laugh.

To my mom—Wonder Woman. Thank you for fostering my love of mysteries as a kid by letting me stay up way past my bedtime to watch Simon and Simon, and re-runs of Perry Mason. And thank you for letting me embrace your Natastrophe side and make it my own. To my dad, for contributing the Cheetos. Also, to my dad, brother, and sister for calling to report my mom's adventures after she stopped telling me stories because they were all going in my idea file. Thanks to Tash, whose skills are being seriously underused by the revolving door testing industry. And a big thanks to Tammy for the fur pants.

Thank you to my beta readers: Heather, Shelly, Rachelle, Natalie, Autumn, Ashley, and Dan. To Angee, for letting me steal her awesome last name. Michelle Witte for all of the advice. Jennifer Miller for being a great cheerleader! Jean

Booknerd for being a wonderful friend, and for promoting my books like crazy! And to all of my awesome readers who I truly count as friends—thank you for your tweets, Facebook messages, emails, and letters. You have no idea how much they brighten my day, or how much I appreciate you and your support!

Books by
Angela Corbett/Destiny Ford

<u>Kate Saxee Mystery Series</u>

The Devil Drinks Coffee

Devilishly Short #1

The Devil Wears Tank Tops

The Devil Has Tattoos

Devilishly Short #2 (Coming Soon)

<u>Tempting Series</u>

Tempting Sydney

Chasing Brynn

Convincing Courtney (Coming Soon)

<u>A Dude Reads Romance Series</u>

A Dude Reads Romance-Tempting Sydney

A Dude Reads Romance-Chasing Brynn

<u>Hollywood Crush Series</u>

A-List

<u>Fractured Fairy Tale Series</u>

Withering Woods

Scattered Cinders

Emblem of Eternity Trilogy

Eternal Starling

Eternal Echoes

For special sneak peeks, giveaways, and super secret news, join Angela's newsletter!

http://eepurl.com/KhLAn

If you enjoyed reading *The Devil Drinks Coffee,* please help others enjoy this book too by recommending it, and reviewing it on Amazon, Barnes and Noble, Google Play, iBooks, or Goodreads. If you do write a review, please send me a message through my website so I can thank you personally! www.angelacorbett.com

xoxo,
Ang

About the Author

Angela Corbett is a *USA Today* bestselling author, and a graduate of Westminster College where she double majored in communication and sociology and minored in business. She has worked as a journalist, freelance writer, and director of communications and marketing. She lives in Utah with her extremely supportive husband, and their sweet Pug-Zu, S'more. She loves classic cars, traveling, puppies, and can be bribed with handbags, and mochas from The People's Coffee. She's the author of Young Adult, New Adult, and Adult fiction —with lots of kissing. She writes under two names: Angela Corbett, and Destiny Ford.

http://www.angelacorbett.com/

Join my newsletter to get a free book!
http://eepurl.com/KhLAn

facebook.com/AuthorAngelaCorbett
x.com/angcorbett
instagram.com/byangcorbett
tiktok.com/@authorangelacorbett

Made in United States
North Haven, CT
29 April 2024

51904194R00202